**"It's like a part of you is afraid of me," said Brody.**

"Not afraid, just cautious."

"Why do you feel the need to be cautious?"

"You make me feel things I'm not used to. I'm just not sure how to handle them."

He stepped even closer to her, so that Elisa's sweet body heat flowed around him like a blanket of sexuality. "Like what kind of stuff?"

"I don't know. But my mind doesn't know how to make sense of them."

His mouth quirked in a small smile. "There's your problem. You should stop thinking so much and allow yourself to feel."

After waiting for what felt like a lifetime, he gave in to his craving and leaned down. His mouth lowered to hers with a gentleness that contradicted the raging desire he felt for her. She didn't push him away, as he expected her to. Instead, her hand came up to grip his shoulder and her fingers dug into his muscles. Holy sweet mother...

Also by Erin Kern

*Looking for Trouble*
*Here Comes Trouble*

# ALONG CAME TROUBLE

## ERIN KERN

FOREVER

NEW YORK   BOSTON

Copyright © 2013 by Erin Kern
Excerpt from *Looking for Trouble* copyright © 2010 by Erin Kern

Forever
Hachette Book Group
237 Park Avenue
New York, NY 10017

www.HachetteBookGroup.com

Printed in the United States of America

First Edition: November 2013
10  9  8  7  6  5  4  3  2  1

OPM

Forever is an imprint of Grand Central Publishing.
The Forever name and logo are trademarks of Hachette Book Group, Inc.

The Hachette Speakers Bureau provides a wide range of authors for speaking events. To find out more, go to www.hachettespeakersbureau.com or call (866) 376-6591.

The publisher is not responsible for websites (or their content) that are not owned by the publisher.

*This one's for my kids. Specifically their softheartedness for dogs.*

# ACKNOWLEDGMENTS

This book seems like it's been a long time coming. And in a way it has. From start to finish, this one has been a labor of love and especially difficult to get through. And I could not have pulled it off without the help of some very special people. To my husband, who's always ready to toss in his two cents. I know sometimes he thinks I'm not listening. I promise, I am. To my tireless, hardworking agent, Kristyn Keene. Thank you for always answering my mindless questions and for the brainstorming sessions that got the rusty gears in my head spinning.

And to my invaluable peeps at Grand Central Publishing, specifically my editor, Lauren Plude, who probably never sleeps. Thank you, and to editorial director, Amy Pierpont, for seeing something in this book that even I myself didn't see. You put the joy back in my writing during those times when it felt like such a chore. Again, I offer my never-ending thanks for your enthusiasm.

# ALONG CAME TROUBLE

# ONE

DESPITE THE RESTAURANT'S CHAOTIC SPORT-THEMED decor, the waitstaff was efficient, friendly, and brought the entree in a *very* timely manner. However, I can only assume the reason the food was mediocre is due to the fact that it arrived in less than ten minutes. I'd like to be able to say the appearance made up for the bland, overcooked hamburger and French fries with enough seasoning to set my mouth on fire...' "

Brody leaned back against his desk as his assistant manager, Charlene, lifted her eyes up to his. "And?" he prompted.

Her tongue darted out along her bare lower lip before she continued reading. " 'But unfortunately the dish looked just as unsatisfying as it tasted. The hamburger, large enough to feed a small horse, sat on a bun much more suited to a silver dollar. Only about a dozen French fries accompanied the burger, and while most fries tend to please my palate, these weren't worth eating more than one.' " Charlene dropped the magazine down to her lap and sent him a desperate look. He knew the feeling. "Do I have to keep reading this?"

He pinched the bridge of his nose in an attempt to ward off a bitch of a headache. "Yes."

The magazine trembled when her fingers grasped the pages once again. " 'I forced myself to eat as much as I could, hoping to find some redemption, only to get my fifteen ninety-nine worth out of the meal. The only pleasant part was my waitress, who seemed to sense my disdain as she shot me a look of sympathy before carting away my half-eaten meal. The Golden Glove has been a staple of the small town of Trouble, Wyoming, for more than ten years now, but it's hardly worth the price. On the upside, I was able to catch the game from one of the dozen televisions mounted on the walls. Maybe the owner should have taken the money he spent on forty-six-inch LCD televisions and hired a better chef instead.' "

Charlene placed the magazine down with great care on his immaculate desk so as not to add yet another blow to poor Brody's day. "This is the second bad review we've had in six months, Brody."

His assistant manager was four years younger than he and a force to be reckoned with. She also had a tender streak that ran deep, which wasn't something she allowed a lot of people to see. Shortly after his divorce, she'd allowed him to see that side of her when she showed up at his house with a bottle of wine and told him he needed to shave. For one weak moment he indulged himself and broke one of his own cardinal rules by sleeping with her. Almost immediately thereafter, they realized they'd made a huge mistake. Granted, the release had been much needed, but they were far better as friends than lovers. Neither one had mentioned that night since. Both were happy to pretend it had never happened. In addition, they'd mutually agreed that they were better off as friends. Working together, and all that.

"Yeah, no shit." He pushed away from the desk and tried to walk the agitation out of his bones. One bad review was enough to send a restaurant into restaurant hell, but two? He kept reminding himself that these kinds of restaurant reviewers were just freelance writers who couldn't make it as chefs so they spent their time dogging every restaurant they could. But what were the chances of two different reviewers giving his restaurant such a similarly poor report? And, perhaps more important, his two previous chefs possessed more power to bring the restaurant down than a couple of magazine reviews.

When the Golden Glove had opened eleven years ago, the place had had a line wrapped around the building just to get a seat at the bar. Even though he'd known next to nothing about restaurants, his father had placed him in charge. Brody had stepped in and done the best he could, which had been damn good, if he did say so himself. The Golden Glove had thrived under his leadership for several years. Unfortunately, a series of simultaneous events, including losing their chef and RJ, had caused their numbers to dwindle. Despite his efforts, the Golden Glove was on a downward slide in terms of diners and profits.

In fact, the situation was so dire, if they kept up like this, they'd have to close their doors in six months. The thought created a sick feeling in the pit of his stomach, something he'd been dealing with a lot lately. If the Golden Glove went under, not only would all his employees be without jobs, but Brody would lose his meal ticket and his means of taking care of Tyler.

No matter what it took, Brody had to save the restaurant.

"Well, the only good thing is this was written when we had Gary. Now we have Travis."

"That doesn't make me feel better." Brody eased into

his chair and leaned his head back. Travis was their third executive chef this year. The man had come highly recommended by a manager of another restaurant in town. The fact that said restaurant had recently closed its doors sent tremors of uncertainty through Brody. Michael, the man who'd been the Golden Glove's original chef and a freakin' miracle worker, had left them for the greener pastures of being the executive chef of a major five-star hotel in Los Angeles. Now, Brody wasn't going to lie to himself; Michael's departure had rubbed him the wrong way, mostly because the man had been there longer than anyone, and Brody had expected more loyalty. After the sting had worn off, Brody admitted that Michael needed to do what was best for him and his three kids. Then Gary had come strolling in, promising to outshine Michael and put the Golden Glove on the map of great restaurants. After three short months, Brody had shown his incompetent ass the door.

Charlene stood from the chair, grabbed the magazine, and tossed it in the trash can. "That guy doesn't know what he's talking about. He's probably some loser who has nothing better to do with his time."

"He's right though. Gary was a terrible chef. That's why I fired him."

She placed her hands on her narrow hips. "I'm trying to make you feel better here. Tell me it's helping a little."

Brody stared back at her out of stormy gray eyes. "It's not helping."

She plowed fingers through her chin-length black hair. "Okay, here's what we're going to do. We're going to ignore this stupid review, go forward with the photo shoot today, and pray this relaunch will put this place back on its feet. Then we'll show people like that idiot reviewer we're worth coming back to." Her legs ate up the expanse of his office.

"You're awfully confident," Brody muttered.

"Why wouldn't I be? We've completely redecorated, and the place looks way better than it did when it first opened, plus we have a new chef." Then she added, "With a new menu."

"Are you saying you think Travis can turn this place around?" Brody shifted his thick shoulders around to ease some of the tension that had his muscles coiled.

"Don't you think he can?" Charlene's thin brows shot up her forehead.

Brody swiveled back and forth in his chair and ran a hand along the edge of his desk. "I'm not sure yet. To be honest, I'm not all that impressed with him." But if Travis wasn't the savior this place needed, then who was? Although Brody liked the guy, his future in his own restaurant hinged on the young chef's abilities. The thought sent a tremor of alarm through his already weary body.

"He's a hell of a lot better than Gary was."

A snort popped out of him. "My eleven-year-old son can cook better than Gary."

The corners of Charlene's lips turned up in a smile. She inhaled a deep breath and sat back down in the chair. "Look, I know you're still kind of pissed about Michael leaving and you think you won't find anyone as good as him. But you will."

"I hope you're right." He ran a hand through his midnight dark hair. Man, he needed a haircut. "If not, there's a good chance I'll have to sell my house and find another job." Another thought that had the contents of his breakfast churning like acid in his stomach.

She leaned forward in her chair and propped an elbow

on the edge of his desk. "There's no way Martin will fire you." Then she jumped ahead when he opened his mouth to argue. "I think we're taking a step in the right direction today. We've got that photographer coming in to take pictures. And I know Travis is young, but I think he shows a lot of promise."

One of Charlene's best assets was her positive attitude. At times when Brody found himself moping like a moody teenager, Charlene would come in with her Mary Poppins–like persona and pep talk him into straightening his act up. Brody would be the first one to tell anyone he'd been an unbearable hard-ass since his divorce four years ago. Something about separating from Kelly had opened up a side of him even he hadn't known existed. Charlene had never let a moment escape without telling him to get his shit together. Being spoken to like that wasn't something he appreciated, but from Charlene he tolerated it. She didn't put up with his crap anyway, so telling her to stuff it would only be speaking to air.

"Tell me again why we're publishing pictures in the same magazine that just gave us a bad review?" he asked Charlene.

She lifted a finger. "First of all, that reviewer isn't employed by this magazine. Second of all, they're the only ones who agreed to do this spread. We need the good publicity."

At this point Brody wasn't sure the restaurant was capable of generating good publicity. "Are you sure this photographer is any good?"

An exasperated sigh came from Charlene. "What happened to the Brody who never let anything bother him? I miss that guy."

"So do I," he muttered to the ceiling. Brody found himself smiling for the first time during their conversation. Yes, Charlene knew when to call his bullshit. His office door creaked open and Travis poked his head in. "The photographer's here."

A spread in a magazine that had already trashed them? Would those same readers even give a damn about the Golden Glove's new, toned-down decor? Or that the new chef had introduced inventive, unique items to the menu? In Brody's experience, once diners had a bad meal at a restaurant, they weren't likely to return. Not only that, they'd probably tell everyone within earshot to stay the hell away from the place. His father had already pitched a fit about the first bad review. Even though Brody ran the place, Martin was a perfectionist who took insults to his restaurant personally, although normally he didn't take reviews too seriously. In the light of the place's recent dwindling numbers, his old man was paying extra attention to any sort of negativity. Brody's working relationship with his father had already been on thin ice because of the downturn in business. Once Martin read the latest review, Brody was likely to be exiled. His earlier fear of his and Tyler's futures returned with a wicked vengeance. How would he pay for his son's college if he was unemployed?

"Brody?" Charlene asked after he'd failed to move from his chair. "You're on board with this, right?"

He blinked at her. "On board, right. Yeah." He pushed himself out of the chair and followed Charlene and Travis downstairs.

Okay, he'd be on board with this.

The dining room, recently redone to be more appealing to families and less to rowdy college students home from school, had been mostly cleared for today's shoot. The

tables and chairs had been pushed aside to make room for
the "shooting area," as Charlene had described it. "It'll be
short and simple," she said.

Except it wasn't. The area that used to be the dining
room now looked like a professional photographer's stu-
dio. In the middle of the room, surrounded by several
tall lights and mirrors, were tables draped in dark brown
tablecloths. Travis walked ahead of them and disappeared
into the kitchen. Several seconds later he reappeared with
plates on each hand. He lowered them carefully to the
tables, added garnishes, wiped the rims, and spun them
around until satisfied they looked presentable.

After his inspection, he went back into the kitchen.

"Is all this really necessary?" Brody asked Charlene.

Charlene shot him a narrow-eyed look. "You can't just
come in and take a few pictures of the food the way we
would normally serve it. You have to doll it up and make
it look attractive."

He lifted a hand toward the shoot area. "But we don't
serve our dishes on brown tablecloths with wineglasses.
Isn't that a bit misleading?"

They stopped next to one of the tall light things.
"Brody, do you trust me?" Charlene asked.

His eyebrows pulled together at her question. "I'm not
sure."

She patted him on the arm like one would a small child.
"Well, you're going to have to this time. Besides, this is
the way food is photographed. And Elisa knows what she's
doing."

He shot her a glance. "Elisa?"

"The photographer."

Bright morning sunshine shone in when the doors to
the restaurant opened. A tall woman, with hair the color of

a moonless night hanging halfway down her back, floated across the parquet wood floor. Her attention was on a spiral notebook, which was cradled in long, thin arms. A loose-fitting, flower-printed blouse covered petite shoulders and disappeared beneath the waistband of wide-legged, light gray slacks. She was as professionally dressed as any person in a corporate office, yet the gentle sway of her hips exuded a magnetic sexuality that had blood rushing to Brody's groin.

His eyes followed her every move. "Did we hire a model for this shoot?"

Charlene had started to walk toward the woman. She glanced back at him. "What?"

He jerked his head in the Amazon's direction.

One corner of Charlene's mouth curled up. "She's the photographer."

"Are you sure?" he asked. The woman who looked like she should be posing in front of the camera was behind it instead?

"Quite sure." Always-present amusement lit up Charlene's eyes.

Brody sauntered over to focus on the tables with the food only because he didn't want to stand around looking like he had his thumb up his ass.

Travis had prepared a wide variety of dishes and ones that were more popular with their diners. Chinese chicken salad, minestrone soup, a barbecue bacon cheddar burger, and grilled chicken penne pasta with a garlic breadstick sat on pristine white plates. Charlene may have organized the photo shoot, but Brody had hand-picked the dishes. Two of them were Travis's signature meals.

"You're in my light."

The husky, let-me-seduce-you voice came from directly

behind him and danced over his skin. Brody glanced over his shoulder and locked gazes with the willowy Amazon who already had certain parts below his belt stirring. The woman either found time to visit a tanning salon on a regular basis or had a natural olive complexion. Almond-shaped eyes accented by thick, black lashes gazed back at him. The corners of her full, pillowy mouth were turned up ever so slightly.

"Sorry," he managed. For hell's sake, he ran a success-ful business, dealt with servers, chefs, and customers, on a daily basis, and now he could barely manage a two-syllable word. He'd really been out of the dating game too long.

When he stepped aside, she continued adjusting the mirror her ring-adorned fingers were wrapped around. The smooth skin of her forehead furrowed as she concen-trated on her task.

"Is this going to be enough light?" he asked her.

Her attention remained on the food as she tried to achieve the right angle with the mirror. "Windows are best, but I can make do with the skylights." She extended her hand to his. "I'm Elisa, by the way. Cardoso," she added.

Brody allowed his eyes to drop down to her mouth one more time before wrapping his hand around hers. Her fin-gers were long and thin, and the silver rings she wore were cool against his palm. His hand lingered in hers, prob-ably longer than necessary, but what the hell. Her hand felt good in his, a perfect fit. And he liked the way her hand felt wrapped up in his, small and feminine. A sud-den image of them on his skin, exploring intimate parts of his body, slammed into him and assaulted his senses.

"Brody." Another two-syllable word he had trouble

forcing out of his mouth. What was wrong with him today? He'd always been able to hold a semi-intelligent conversation with an attractive woman before. Then in comes this exotic beauty and his brain ceases to function. "McDermott," he threw in.

"Nice to meet you," she replied with a playful gleam in her dark brown eyes. Before he was ready to let go, she slipped her hand from his and continued adjusting all her lights, mirrors, and other props.

Thirty minutes went by before she actually started snapping pictures. The first dish was arranged on the brown cloth-covered table with silverware and napkins placed casually about as if an actual diner had been sitting there. Elisa had picked up and moved the wineglasses half a dozen times before she was satisfied they were in just the right spot. After giving the setup one final glance, she took an expensive-looking camera out of a bag and dropped to her knees directly in front of the table. With her elbows resting on the table, Elisa cradled the camera in her hands and started snapping pictures rapidly, one after the other.

"She sure is thorough," Brody muttered to Charlene.

"I told you she was good."

Not only was she good with the camera, her ass looked damn fine in those slacks of hers, round but petite at the same time. The same image of her hands roaming over him continued, only this time her derriere took a front and center role. He bet it would feel damn good cradled in his lap rubbing against his thighs...

*Okay, you're supposed to be saving your restaurant here, and all you can do is admire the photographer's ass?*

Time to be professional.

"You might want to keep your eyes on a place that won't get you sued for sexual harassment." Charlene had the nerve to actually smirk.

He tossed her a narrowed-eyed look. "You're not funny."

As usual, Charlene ignored his surly remarks. "She could be a while. I'm going to work on next week's schedule." And with that, Charlene left him alone with the woman who made him stumble over two-syllable words. And had a great ass. *And* had soft hands.

Over an hour passed and Elisa had only done two dishes. Her camera would click rapidly, then she'd stop to make an adjustment with one of the mirrors or point the lights in a different direction. Call him ignorant, but Brody had no idea so much went into taking pictures of food. He'd thought Travis would cook some dishes, place them on a table, and he would take some pictures with his digital camera. Charlene had rolled her eyes like a teenage girl when he'd told her that. "Why don't you let me take care of this?" was what she'd said to him.

Gladly. He'd had enough on his plate at the time, with having to decide which employees had to take fewer hours in order to cut back on costs.

Elisa lowered her camera and rolled her head from side to side.

"Do you need a break?" he asked her.

She craned her head over her neck and then stood. "No, I'm fine. If I stop I might lose momentum."

"I was thinking the soup would look better with some steam coming out of it."

Elisa set her camera down, then pulled her hair back in a high ponytail, revealing a long neck. One that was perfect for dropping light kisses. "I always digitally add steam in later. If you want it."

His eyes danced over her neck. He'd never paid attention to such a thing before, so why was he starting now? "Won't digital steam look fake?"

"Charlene said you'd never done this before," she said with an alluring smile. "Digital steam looks just as good as the real stuff. Besides, real steam is too much of a variable. The slightest breeze can make it curl in an unattractive shape."

Suddenly he found himself interested in the art of photographing food. Who knew? "And all the mirrors? What are those for?"

She planted her hands on her slim hips and ran her tongue along her lower lip. It was full and looked good enough to nibble. "They deflect the light in different directions. Different foods need light coming from different angles." She gestured to the table. "Like with the salad, I had the light coming from behind so you can see the veins in the lettuce. But the soup needed light coming from above so you can see the reflection on the surface of the liquid. With the hamburger, I'll probably have the light coming from behind so we'll have some cool reflections on the plate and also have some translucency in the tomato…" Her deep eyes lit on his. "Sorry. I tend to get carried away when people ask me about taking pictures. Most people don't realize how technical this all is." Her laugh was melodious and sent blood rushing down to his groin.

He barely managed not to adjust himself around her and glanced at the staging area. "Very technical, I can tell."

Her teeth nibbled her lower lip.

If she didn't stop that, he'd do something to seriously embarrass himself.

"I'm boring you, aren't I?" she said. "It's just that you're the first client to ask me questions. Most don't care about the process, only the end result."

His eyes stayed on her white teeth, which were still worrying that delectable lower lip. "It's not boring at all." Well, he wouldn't go that far. It *was* a little boring. But the light in her eyes alone was reason enough to keep asking her questions. "This is all new to me. I just thought I'd be able to take pictures with my camera and send them to the magazine."

"That's what most people think. But you would have ended up with yellow food." When he lifted a brow, she continued. "Light is very important to photographing food. If you don't have enough light, the food in the picture will look yellow. Not very attractive to potential customers."

He nodded his understanding even though the science of it still eluded him. "That makes sense."

Elisa's eyes roamed down to his mouth before she cleared her throat and picked up her camera again. Was she checking him out? Could he possibly be having the same effect on her that she was having on him?

"After you're done, you should stay for something to eat." *Now, why would you go and say that? Isn't it bad enough you've been staring at her ass, now you have to come on to her?* "You're taking pictures for us. The least you could let me do is feed you." *Okay, that sounded much more reasonable; not like you're trying to hit on her while she's doing a job for you.*

She gazed at him over her slender shoulder. "I'll have a Caesar salad with grilled chicken."

# TWO

ELISA SCOOPED HER FORK BENEATH a piece of soggy lettuce and tried not to stare at the man sitting across from her. She wasn't even hungry, but the fact that an attractive man asked her to stay for a meal had her agreeing. Well, he was more than attractive. He was downright otherworldly. During her modeling days, she'd been up close and personal with some of the most handsome men on the planet. Had any of them made her heart go all pitter patter and her mind conjure up images it shouldn't have? That would be a negative.

Brody was what Elisa considered a double threat. Not only did he have devastating looks, but he had an engaging personality to go along with it. When the chef had dropped off her salad, Brody had eyed it like it had worms and said she should be adventurous and eat a burger. Then she said she'd been adventurous enough that morning with the cinnamon roll she'd eaten. The comment had earned her a wicked grin, causing a shallow dimple to appear in his left cheek.

Brody could do some major damage if a woman wasn't paying attention. Fortunately for her, she had both her eyes wide open.

"So, why food?" he asked after taking a sip of his water.

She paused with the fork halfway to her mouth. "Because you asked me to stay for a meal."

Another slow grin broke across his face. "Why photograph food?"

Before answering, she slid the fork in her mouth and tried not to wince at the amount of dressing weighing down the lettuce. "I started off photographing landscapes, which is my real passion. If I could, I'd be out there right now taking pictures of anything in nature. Then I realized the world does not need another generic landscape photographer. So I got into food. It's more lucrative."

"When you say you'd rather be out taking pictures of nature, what does that mean exactly?"

She pursed her lips and thought about her answer. "Spending time indoors and taking pictures of food was never my ultimate dream." She gestured toward where she'd snapped pictures earlier. "I mean, I love being behind a camera no matter what, but..." She lifted her shoulders. "It's just not what I imagined myself doing."

"So, what happened? Why aren't you out there taking pictures of sunsets, or whatever?"

His question made her grin. "When I first got into the field, I was. But landscape photography is extremely competitive. And although I loved what I was doing, I wasn't making enough money. I needed to switch my focus to something more practical."

Brody tilted his head to one side. "So, if you could you'd be out traveling the world with your camera?"

Was that disappointment she heard in his voice? And if so, why did that make her happy? "Absolutely. When I first got started I traveled the U.S. to build my portfolio. My ultimate dream is to photograph a collapsing ice shelf in Alaska or a migrating heard in Africa. If I could get my photos published in *Time Magazine* or *National Geographic*, I would die a happy woman." She pushed her food around her plate before stabbing a piece of uncharred chicken with her fork.

He stared back at her with admiration coloring his spectacular eyes. "You sound like you're a woman who knows what she wants."

"I am."

When he shifted in the booth, his leg brushed hers. The heat coming off him was palpable.

"If you're half as good out in nature as you were in here, I'd say you could make a good career for yourself."

His compliment warmed her in a way nothing had in a long time. Why did his approval mean so much to her? "Most people don't realize how scientific and professional photography is. It can take hours to get one good shot."

Brody glanced at the dining room, now put back together. "Yeah, I noticed that."

The dry humor in his deep voice didn't go unnoticed on her part.

As he took a sip of his water, his stormy-gray eyes burned into her over the rim of the glass. Something close to butterflies skittered around her stomach at the way he looked at her, as though his mind had conjured a naughty fantasy involving the two of them. Damn, she'd just met the man, and already he had her hormones in disarray.

And Elisa had never seen eyes quite that shade before. They couldn't really be considered blue; they were too light. The penetrating gaze accompanied by hair as black as her own made for a knee-weakening effect she wasn't used to, nor was she comfortable with. She'd only met the man a few hours ago, and she already felt like she wanted to come out of her skin.

With his eyes still on hers, he lowered the glass and wiped a bead of moisture off his lip.

His gaze ran over her face, then dropped down to her plate. "You're not eating much of your salad. Is part of being a health freak not eating a whole meal?"

Elisa followed his attention to her meal. Let's see, drenched lettuce, overcooked chicken, and questionable tomatoes? She'd done the salad more justice than it deserved, which was a shame considering the one she took a picture of had been damn near immaculate. This one looked like it'd been thrown together by a six-year-old.

"Well," she started, not sure how to tell Brody the meal was subpar. "Would you like me to be honest?"

He lifted a hand off the back of the booth in a please-do gesture.

"The salad's not that good. There's way too much dressing and the chicken is overcooked. Quite frankly, it's almost inedible."

One of his large hands pressed against his chest. "Wow. Don't tiptoe over my feelings or anything."

She picked up her water glass. "You asked me to be honest. I didn't think I'd be doing you any favors by lying."

Something darkened those beautiful gray eyes. "Trust me, you wouldn't be. Believe it or not, I appreciate the honesty."

Elisa pulled in a breath and pursed her lips. "I didn't want to say anything at first, but the food he brought out for the shoot looked amazing." She picked up her fork and pushed at the lettuce. "Not at all like this."

Brody drummed his fingers on the leather booth. "Travis has a bit of a problem with consistency. It's something we're working on."

"I've photographed a lot of food over the past few years, and he definitely shows some promise. It might be an age thing. How old is he?"

"I think he's a few years younger than me." Brody ran a hand over the dark stubble on his chin. "Twenty-seven, twenty-eight maybe."

So Brody was older than she was. He looked about her age, but she was twenty-eight so he had to be at least thirty or thirty-one. "He'll get there," she said. "Maybe he just needs some more experience."

"Maybe," Brody muttered while staring at a point over her shoulder. "I'm sorry about the meal. Every diner deserves top quality. Not..." He lifted a hand toward her dish. "That."

She dropped her attention to the salad. "To be honest, I wasn't that hungry."

Her heart tattooed against her rib cage while his eyes continued to burn into hers. Oh yes, Brody could very well be dangerous to her and the quiet life she'd built for herself. Elisa wasn't inexperienced or anything, but she generally stayed out of the dating scene. After her last disastrous relationship in college, she'd placed a nice little bubble around herself so as not to experience anything like that again. She had her quaint house big enough for just her and her photography. That was all she needed to be happy, thank you very much. The man sitting across from her had the potential to send all that to hell in a handbasket. It might be a fun ride down, but she'd been there and had no desire to go again.

"So, why'd you agree to stay if you weren't hungry?"

His bedroom voice pulled her out of her thoughts. Yes, why had she? Because he was nice to look at? Okay, way more than nice. So, she'd succumbed to the chemical reaction he had on her. Big deal. She could hardly say that to him, though.

*I just wanted an excuse to look at you because you're so darn good looking.*

Yeah, probably not a good thing to say. But it was all she had. So she lied.

"I guess I wanted to taste some of the food that looked so good."

He tilted his head to one side. "Except it wasn't that good."

Her teeth plunged into her lower lip. "Well, no. But if Travis can make every dish like the ones I photographed, then you guys are all set." When Brody didn't respond she added, "You're not sure, are you?"

"That's a terrible thing, isn't it?"

Elisa glanced at their surroundings. The place had been well decorated, she'd give him that. The plethora of sport-themed photographs was a nice touch and added a homey feel to the place. The rumor mill around town said that the Golden Glove had a tendency to get a bit rowdy, which kept away most families. Elisa didn't have a hard time picturing that as she ran her eyes across the long bar on the other side of the restaurant. As she'd told Brody, she'd never been here, partly because of the name the place had made for itself. Not that she'd tell him that. She had the sneaking suspicion the Golden Glove was his baby. With the steady downhill descent of the restaurant, Brody had to be racking his brain about how to bring the place back to glory. And she could begin to imagine the stress he must be under. As the general manager, the ultimate responsibility of the restaurant landed squarely on his shoulders. Having a spread in a local magazine was a start. The key, however, was having at least a three-star chef in this little town. Was Travis one of those? Elisa wasn't convinced.

"I wouldn't say it's terrible," she answered. "You're cautious, as you should be."

His mesmerizing eyes narrowed at her. "What exactly have you heard about this place?"

"Nothing bad," she assured him. "Well, I heard the food isn't as good and it's not as family friendly as it was a few years ago."

"That's kind of bad." The smile creeping along his kiss-able mouth had her toes curling in her too-pointy shoes.

*Just remember the bubble.*

What kind of person was she? First she told him the food wasn't good, after they'd prepared it for her, then she told him his restaurant had a bad reputation? Maybe she should have declined his invitation so Brody wouldn't feel the need to go hang himself.

She reached across the table and placed her hand on top of his. Her first thought was how big and warm he was. His fingers were long and thick and felt oh-so-nice beneath hers. Way too nice, actually. She pushed the thought aside. "It's nothing that can't be fixed. Photo shoots like this are a good way of getting a place back on its feet."

Big mistake touching him. His big, warm, hard hand was a quintessentially male thing that Elisa had fallen victim to in her youth. The veins beneath the surface of his skin pressed against the inside of her palm. Her index finger actually itched to trace each vein over his hand and up his arm until she reached his shoulder.

Okay, time to leave. She needed to leave now.

Brody left his palm under hers. "I'm sorry about the meal."

Reluctantly, Elisa removed her hand from his. "It wasn't that terrible. The nonburned pieces of chicken were actually pretty good."

"Is that supposed to make me feel better?" The smile that had been playing across his mouth grew wider.

The butterflies from earlier returned and danced all over her stomach. When was the last time she'd reacted this way to a man? Like she wanted to crawl across the table and settle herself on his hard thighs.

She found herself smiling along with him. "That's the general idea, yes. Is it working?"

He waited a second before answering. "That depends on whether or not you're willing to come back."

*Remember the part about leaving? Now would be a good time to do that.*

Oh, but how could she leave this booth when the man across from her stirred things inside her she'd never felt before? Why would she deny herself that? Yes, it was smart to protect herself, which she worked very hard at.

Brody glanced at his silver watch. "Not that I'm trying to rush you or anything, but I have to get back to work. How about I walk you out?"

The invitation sounded so much more seductive than it should have been. As though walking her out would turn into some forbidden tryst that would leave her boneless.

*And what if it did? You know you'd jump at the opportunity. You're already lusting after him.*

On the other hand, Elisa needed to tread carefully. If the opportunity to travel the world for a major magazine presented itself, she'd take it in a heartbeat. How would that work if there was a man in her life? A man she could easily develop some very deep feelings for?

Simple answer: It *wouldn't* work.

Perhaps she could indulge herself just this once. After all, it's not like he was down on one knee. He was doing the chivalrous thing by escorting her to her car. What harm was there in that?

"Okay," she found herself saying.

He led her outside, and she didn't protest when he placed a hand on the small of her back. Not only didn't she oppose, but she kind of liked it. Liked it a lot, actually. His touch made her bones feel all gooey, and a warm feeling skittered up her spine. And was he walking so close to her on purpose? Because she swore she could actually smell him—some kind of woodsy bar soap that was nothing but cleanliness and masculinity.

Low-lying clouds drifted across the sky in the gentle breeze and hid the sun. Wind in Wyoming could often be an issue, especially in their area. At times it blew nonstop and often posed problems when she went out to take pictures. Luckily today it was pretty tame. With the low winds and cloud cover, it was actually a pleasant day.

Elisa led Brody to her compact SUV, parked on the side of the building. Before lunch, she'd taken the time to load all of her equipment in the back of the car.

"When I get home, I'll upload the photos to my computer and put together a proof sheet for you. From there, we will go over the pictures together, choose what you want, and then they have to go to the magazine for approval."

He nodded his understanding, even though he looked like he wasn't interested in their conversation. Elisa could safely say that he looked interested in something, just not what she was saying. He tilted his head and dipped his gaze downward, touching every part of her until she felt exposed. How could a man have the ability to make her feel naked? And why did she like it so much?

"Okay," he said noncommittally, as though he were commenting on the weather. He took a step closer to her, but she didn't back up, mostly because he smelled so damn good. "What do I have to do to get you to come back here? I'll even cook the meal myself."

The huskiness of his voice bushed over her skin and left her breathless. A man hadn't come on to her like this in a long time. Oh sure, they flirted with her. But this was more than flirting. This was outright seduction. The tone of his voice held all sorts of promises, the kinds of promises that led to screaming.

For a moment she couldn't say anything, because she was literally speechless. Not only was Brody gorgeous, but he was so easy to talk to. He was the kind of guy she could spill her guts to, tell things she hadn't shared with anyone. She ought to say no. She *really* wanted to. No, *needed* to. But jumping into a relationship with him could be exhilarating at the very least.

*Then what happens when you leave?*

As she'd told him earlier, her ultimate dream was to travel the world and capture some of its wonders through her camera. Life in Trouble was nice...but lacking. In her mind it had always been temporary, until that one dream job came along.

Until now.

With Brody standing in front of her, smelling so good, big and wide and so masculine, it didn't seem all that lacking.

"Just for drinks," he continued when she hadn't accepted his invitation. "You don't even have to eat anything. Because after that meal I wouldn't blame you."

She giggled despite the tension humming through her body. *Just do it! Go out with him and have all sorts of wicked sex.*

And then he touched her. If she thought herself incapable of speech a second ago, now she was practically paralyzed. She just stood there like some fool while he cupped her cheek with one warm hand. His hand was callused but felt divine on her skin. He rubbed his thumb in small circles over her earlobe. She'd never thought of her ear as an erogenous zone, but her eyes almost rolled back in her head. Had any man ever paid such attention to her ear before?

She sucked in a sharp breath when he skimmed his thumb just along the edge of her jaw.

"You think you can stay away from me, but you can't," he stated in a low voice. "Even if you don't come back here, we'll see each other again."

She barely managed to peel her tongue off the roof of her mouth. "Is that a warning?"

He stepped closer and bent down so his lips were against her ear. "Just a promise," he whispered.

Without another word, he sauntered away as though pleased with himself for throwing her off balance.

The rapid ticking of the egg timer echoed in the quiet darkroom. A steady stream of water ran from the faucet and cleansed the photo paper resting in the holding tank. Cleaning the paper of the chemical it just sat in would take thirty minutes. Elisa used the time to mix some new chemicals for her next batch of photos.

Since the digital age, developing your own photographs was becoming a lost art. No one used film cameras anymore. Even she didn't use them that much, except for her landscapes. Why would people use film cameras when they could take the pictures and immediately upload them to their computer? Why waste all this time mixing, stirring, cleaning, scraping, and in the dark no less? Honestly, there was nothing more therapeutic for Elisa. In her darkroom, it was quiet. She was alone. Nothing but her and the photos—photos she'd captured with her camera and created on paper. The best part of the developing process was being able to watch the image appear on the paper, the fruits of her labor slowly emerging before her eyes. The results gave her satisfaction like nothing else could.

Plus being in her darkroom gave her time to think, which she did a lot of.

The meal she had at the Golden Glove a few days ago might not be worth remembering, but the man she ate with was. His deep voice, like magical fingers caressing all her sweet spots, had been inside her head since departing from him. Like a forbidden promise she had little will to deny. He could be very dangerous if she spent too much time with him. His smile alone could chip away at the protective barrier she'd built around herself. Would he be worth coming out of that shell for?

*You think you can stay away from me, but you can't.*

She'd thought Micah had been worth it. After that fiasco, she'd gotten back to reconstructing her life, this time taking extra care to keep herself even more protected. But a friendship would do no harm, would it? Brody had asked her to come back. Then proceeded to make her pulse race and give her erotic dreams. Would it really hurt her to eat out every once in a while? There had to be something on the menu worth eating.

However, once the photos got sent to the magazine, she had no reason to see him again. Unless it was on her terms. That she could do. Plus she deserved a little eye candy every once in a while. And why not a date? She hadn't made it a priority since moving to Trouble, since she'd wanted to focus on her career. Some women would consider a few years to be a major dry spell. Elisa considered herself career driven. If the right guy came along, she'd go out with him. However, although she loved Trouble, there didn't seem to be that many eligible men here.

The metroplex of Dallas/Fort Worth, where she'd gone to school at Texas Christian University, had plenty of young men for her to choose from. But Elisa had never really been at home in Texas. Years before her parents' deaths, they'd taken a driving trip through the West to see the countryside. They'd explored Wyoming and had stopped in Trouble for lunch. After college and her parents' deaths, there had been nothing to keep her in Fort Worth—just the memories of the family she used to have. On a whim, she'd packed her things and relocated from north Texas to southern Wyoming. Unexpectedly, there were things she missed about Texas: the breathtaking sunsets and blue sky that went on forever and ever. But Wyoming had its own beauty, and Trouble was a rare gem of a small town that could hardly be found across the U.S. Very quickly, she'd fallen into a pleasant routine, bought a house, and had been working on her photography. All in all, she'd never been happier. Even if she knew she'd leave in a heartbeat if the right job offer came along.

All it would take would be a phone call from her former college professor, who'd also been her mentor, asking her to accompany him on a shoot. Professor Samuel Harper had been her advanced digital photography teacher and had previously traveled the world shooting for some of the biggest magazines, including *National Geographic*. Some of his work had hung in his classroom, and Elisa had fallen in love with it immediately. He'd displayed some of his most spectacular work, such as snow blowing off the peak of Mount Everest, and the migration of gray whales in Alaska's Nelson Lagoon. The man was an absolute genius behind the lens, and Elisa had known she'd wanted to be just like him.

Right after graduation, he'd pulled her aside and had given her the best piece of news she'd ever heard.

"Sometimes, if the right offer comes along, I'll go on an assignment for *National Geographic*," he'd told her. "*And* if they're generous enough, they let me bring a team with me. If and when that happens, I'll give you a call."

Too stunned to speak, Elisa had just shaken her head in disbelief. "You'd do that for me?"

He'd placed both hands on her shoulders and looked her in the eye. "You're an incredibly fast learner and one of the most talented photographers I've seen in a long time. I'd bring you with me in a heartbeat."

Only once since then had he called her. It had been for a shoot in Australia, covering the Ningaloo Reef. To her ultimate frustration, the timing hadn't worked. She'd already purchased nonrefundable tickets to see her brother during the time when Professor Harper needed her to go. She'd been so torn over her inability to pursue her dream. But Marcello had been and always would be more important than anything. She didn't regret the decision to travel to South America to see her little brother, because she so rarely got to see him.

Despite that, she still held out hope she'd hear from her old teacher, inviting her to globe-trot for *National Geographic*.

After mixing the fixer solution, she placed it on her supply shelf and waited for the photo to finish rinsing. When she first started working in a darkroom, she made the mistake of being impatient and leaving the room during the rinsing process. Even the tiniest filter of light would cause a photo to turn gray. Nothing was more disappointing than watching a picture, which she'd worked painstakingly on to get just the right angle, turn gray. Gray pictures didn't sell. Gray pictures ended up in the trash. She'd thrown away a lot of gray, streaky, and spotty photos over the years. Not only was it disheartening; it was an incredible waste of supplies. Things like paper and solution weren't cheap.

When the thirty minutes was up, Elisa shut the water off, grabbed the paper by the corner, and hung it on a drying clip. Then she ran a small sponge over the photo to remove excess water. When the whole process was finished, she had a breathtaking shot of the moon edging just above a ridge of foothills. It had taken her a long damn time to get this. Each evening she'd go out, hoping to catch the moon at just the right time. To her disappointment, the sky would either be too light or she would arrive too late. In her mind, she knew exactly what she wanted and would settle for nothing less.

Brilliant daylight pouring in through the windows practically blinded her when she left the darkroom. Elisa was just about to pick up the phone and make her weekly call to her brother when the doorbell rang. She swung the door open, and on the other side stood one of her neighbors, Kelly. Whenever Elisa thought of Kelly, images of Tinker Bell flashed through her mind. The other woman was five foot four at best and sported a spiky hairdo that made her look like she was about fifteen. Elisa's trained eye always spotted professionally done hair. Every varied shade of blond woven into the pixielike cut wasn't cheap.

"Hi," Elisa greeted her visitor. She stepped back and let the other woman enter.

Painted red toenails encased in silver-jeweled sandals stepped over the threshold. Elisa led Kelly into the kitchen.

"Would you like something to drink?" she asked the other woman.

"No thanks." Kelly grabbed her sunglasses off the top of her head and dropped them in her snakeskin bag. "I came by to ask you a huge favor. I wasn't interrupting your work, was I?"

Elisa shook her head and took a seat at her farmhouse-style breakfast table. "I just finished up."

Kelly's jade green eyes danced around the room and landed on some pictures. "Are those your latest pictures?"

Elisa followed her attention to the black-and-white photos propped on the mantel. "Yeah, I did those a few weeks ago."

"This one is stunning." Kelly picked up a photo of an old windmill.

"That one took me all day to get."

Kelly glanced at her. "All day? For a windmill?"

"I needed the right light," Elisa answered with a shrug. "You can have it if you want it."

"Really? How much to you want?"

Elisa had given Kelly several pictures over the past year, and the woman still tried to give her money. "I do those for fun. Just take it."

Kelly's eyes lit up with delight. "Thanks. I think I'll frame it and put it in Colin's office. He loves this stuff."

Elisa waited until the other woman joined her at the table. "So how's it going?"

"Not so well, actually." Kelly's fingers ran over the edges of the photo. "My mother fell this morning and broke her hip. She has to have surgery. And since she lives alone and has no other family except me, and Colin can't take a lot of time off work, I have to go and stay with her for a while and take care of her, at least until we can find a live-in nurse. Then we'll probably have to start researching places for her to live."

"I'm sorry. That's never an easy thing to do." Elisa's parents died before she had to make that kind of decision. Her heart squeezed painfully whenever she thought of the emptiness their deaths had left in her life.

Kelly fingered her pearl earring. "She's getting up there in years anyway—she had me when she was older; I was a surprise baby. And she hasn't been moving around that well. I don't know if she'll be able to walk after this." Sorrow darkened her eyes. "Colin left first thing this morning, but can't stay there for more than a few days. I had some things to do before I head out there this afternoon. My dilemma is Tyler. I can't take him out of school that long, and his dad can't get off work that early to pick him up."

Kelly hardly ever brought up the subject of her exhusband. All Elisa knew was that Kelly had divorced the man a few years ago and had joint custody of Tyler.

"Do you need me to pick him up and take him somewhere?" Elisa had been around the boy a few times. Hair as blond as his mother's was always a bit too long so that it curled just over the top of his ears. Mother and son were equally well mannered and soft spoken.

Kelly twisted her wedding ring around her finger. "That's the other thing. No one he's comfortable with is home during the day. There would be no place to take him. Since we live so close together and he's used to walking anyway, I was hoping you'd be okay with him walking here after school and hanging out for a few hours. It would only be for a few hours after school during the week. And it would only be for a few weeks, a month tops," Kelly rushed on as though she suspected Elisa would object. "And I would be happy to pay you."

Elisa shook her head. "I don't want your money, Kelly. You have enough to deal with."

"Please let me. It would be the least I can do." The pleading look in Kelly's green eyes told Elisa she wouldn't accept anything less.

"We can talk about that later," she replied.

Though she'd met the boy on a few occasions, she didn't really know him that well. He always called her Senorita Cardoso because he'd heard her say something in Portuguese once and mistook it for Spanish. The nickname had been given so innocently, Elisa hadn't had the heart to correct him. A sweet smile always lit up his green eyes when he addressed her that way.

"Would Tyler be okay with that? He doesn't know me that well," Elisa added.

"I've already talked to him and he seemed to be pretty excited." Kelly leaned forward over the table. "Just between you and me, I think he's sporting a little crush on you. Something about the whole foreign-language thing has him intrigued."

Ah, youth. A giggle bubbled up in Elisa's throat. "Maybe I'll teach him some Portuguese while he's here. We could have our own secret language."

"Just don't teach him any curse words. His dad would kill me."

Elisa couldn't help but ask. "Speaking of Tyler's dad, would he be okay with Tyler being here?"

Kelly leaned back in her chair and lifted her eyes to the ceiling. "Trust me, he'll be okay with it. The hard part will be talking him into leaving work a little early. He has a habit of disappearing sometimes."

Was that resentment Elisa heard? Without any information on the man Kelly was once married to, it was difficult to make an assessment. Maybe he was a workaholic who ignored them, and that's why Kelly divorced him? Or maybe he'd cheated? Kelly was around Elisa's age, so she could only guess that she'd been young when she'd had Tyler. She could imagine a scenario in which she and Tyler's father had married out of obligation.

"If you're sure everyone's okay with it, I'd be happy to help." Plus Kelly had come through for Elisa big time when she'd been in a major predicament. About six months ago Elisa's car had been making a funny noise, which had landed it in the shop. Turns out the thing had needed a major repair, and the mechanic had needed to keep it for three days. Unfortunately they hadn't had a loaner car, and Elisa had needed transportation to get to a photo shoot for a recurring client. Kelly had swooped in and saved Elisa's backside by lending her her car. She'd told Elisa to use it for whatever she'd needed. And she'd even driven Elisa back to the mechanic to pick her newly fixed car. For a long time after that, Elisa had tried to think of a way to repay the woman for her generosity. This was her chance.

Kelly's slim shoulders slumped over in relief. "You are literally saving my life. If you wouldn't be able to, I'd probably have to withdraw him from school then reenroll him after I got back. Then his dad would really kill me." The woman turned her wrist over and gave her slender gold watch a glance. "I'm on my way over to talk to him right now. It'll be fine with him, but if there are any snags I'll let you know." Kelly stood from the table and gathered the picture along with her purse. "My plane leaves at six, so I'll pick Tyler up from school so I can explain things to him, then I'll drop him off here. Oh, I almost forgot." She pulled an envelope from her purse and passed it to Elisa. "This is my contact information just in case anything comes up. I also gave you the number for Tyler's doctor and his dad's cell phone number."

Elisa felt for Kelly. It could not have been easy making a decision to put a parent in a retirement home. A lot of children must feel like they were letting their parents down by entertaining the idea of community living. Elisa's heart went out to the woman.

"There's just one thing," Elisa started before Kelly let herself out the door. "There will be afternoons when I might have to go on a photo shoot or just out taking pictures. I just want to make sure it's okay with you to bring him along. I wouldn't feel right leaving him here alone."

Kelly slid her aviator sunglasses over her green eyes. "As long as you don't mind him tagging along. In fact, it might interest him." Then, as if on second thought, she reached her arms out and wrapped Elisa in a tight hug. "I really appreciate this," she whispered in Elisa's ear. "I don't know what I would have done." She stepped back, retrieved a tissue from her pants pocket, and dabbed it beneath her sunglasses. "Sorry. I've never been apart from Tyler this long before, and it's making me crazy." She waved the wadded-up tissue in the air. "I mean, I know he's in good hands and everything. I just can't stand the idea of being three states away from him. Plus I'm so worried about my mom." She made a mad dash to wipe away some tears that rolled below her sunglasses

"Don't apologize," Elisa replied, feeling heartsick for

the woman. "I don't have kids but I can imagine how you feel. Tyler's dad and I will keep everything under control." She closed the door after Kelly left. With no work to do, now was the perfect time to place a call to Marcello. He probably wouldn't answer, but just hearing his voice on the answering machine was enough for her. Just as she was about to pick up the phone, it rang. Again.

With a groan of annoyance, she snatched it off the base and muttered a cheerful hello.

"Did I drag you out of your darkroom?"

The familiar voice on the other end sent a zing of excitement through her. "Professor Harper?"

"What have I told you, young lady?" he scolded in that typical way of his.

She grinned and sank to the couch. "Sorry, Samuel. It's an old habit."

"Hey, don't mention it. Listen, I don't have a lot of time to talk, so I'll get to the reason I called. I've been offered a job by *Time Magazine* in Mongolia. They're doing a piece on the nomadic shepherds who herd through the Mongolian steppes. It's a huge job that I won't be able to do on my own. Would you be up for that?"

Would she be up for that? This was only what she'd been waiting for since college. To shoot photographs in countries like Mongolia for *Time Magazine* was every photographer's dream. How could she pass up an opportunity like this?

"Of course I'm up for it," she replied. "When are you supposed to go?"

"Not until the end of summer. I wanted to give you enough time to update your passport, if you need to, and get all the necessary vaccinations. I also wanted to give you time to clear your schedule. The whole piece will take several months to complete. Will you be able to be gone for that long?"

Several months in Mongolia? Even if she had some pressing issue, she'd clear her schedule for this. She'd already passed up an opportunity with Samuel once. No way would she walk away from this.

"I'll make it happen," she promised.

# THREE

THE SOUR, I-JUST-SUCKED-ON-A-LEMON look on Reginald Buchanan's face didn't lift Brody's spirits. The man had ambled into the restaurant on legs so thick they resembled an elephant's. The light blue polo tucked into black slacks was barely able to contain his round, sagging belly. His appearance alone told Brody that he'd been a food critic likely since leaving the womb. Martin, Brody's father and the restaurant owner, had gotten a referral who said he had a habit of being one of the milder, more forgiving critics. Brody wasn't sure he wanted a critic who was "forgiving." After all, what good would that do them?

The situation had shown promise when Reginald nodded his bloated head and tilted one corner of his mouth in what Brody thought was a smile. That was after slurping his loaded baked potato soup so loudly, Brody's stepmother, Carol, would have slapped the man upside the head. After that, the meal had taken a turn for the worse. His eyebrows, which looked like overgrown caterpillars, lowered in distaste after he saw the fried chicken. The man shoveled two impressively large bites into his mouth before shoving the plate away from him. The poor harried waitress endured grumbling and groaning from Reginald as she carted away his food.

Brody held out little hope for dessert.

"I don't know how much more of this I can take," Charlene muttered next to him. She'd been uncharacteristically nervous during their critic's stay. In the past she would breeze past Brody, pat him on the shoulder, and say, "Don't worry about it. It's only one person's opinion." Okay, now they were working on their third, and things were not looking up.

"Maybe we should offer him a discount," she suggested.

Brody's gaze never left the critic's table. "That would only look desperate." Plus critics tended to frown on that sort of thing. They didn't want to feel like they were being bribed into giving a good review.

The waitress hurried back to Reginald's table and set down a berry cobbler à la mode. Reginald's beefy fingers wrapped around a fork and attacked the dessert with gusto. The thing disappeared faster than gold in the Yukon.

Charlene glanced at Brody. "He seemed to like that."

Brody snorted. "I think he likes all desserts."

When the whole painful experience was over, the critic paid his bill and somehow managed to lever himself, after several attempts, out of his booth. Charlene offered him a professional, friendly smile and asked him to come back soon.

His response was a discouraging "Don't count on it" muttered through lips bracketed by deep lines.

"He's supposed to be forgiving?" Charlene asked, but Brody ignored it as he approached the waitress who'd served Reginald.

The young woman, Theresa, gathered the dessert plate and silverware in her hands.

"What did he say to you after eating the chicken?" Brody asked her.

"Trust me, you don't want to know," she answered.

He forced his voice to come out calm and not show the frustration and borderline hysteria bubbling inside him. "Yes, I really do."

The girl turned her brown eyes to his. "He said it was too salty. In fact, his exact words were 'I wouldn't feed that to my dog.'" She held up a wad of cash. "But he gave me a decent tip."

Brody managed to grace the waitress with a tight-lipped smile. "You did a good job handling him." He left her to clean up and headed to the kitchen. There were some words that needed to be exchanged between him and Travis.

The chef was tossing pasta in a skillet, the noodles lifting up into the air without sliding over the edges and falling to the fire beneath them. "Is his highness finished with his meal?" Travis asked without taking his attention off his task.

"Yeah, he's gone. The appetizer and dessert went well. The main course, however, is a different story."

The muscles in Travis's jaw hardened. "Theresa mentioned he didn't like it."

Chefs were temperamental creatures who tended to take criticism of their food personally. Travis was no different. If Michael had received feedback like that, he'd have chucked a meat cleaver across the kitchen.

Heat from the stove only exacerbated Brody's rising body temperature. "Tell me you tasted the dish before you sent it out there."

Travis threw him a borderline murderous look. "Of course I did. Either that guy's taste buds are off or he was just having a bad day."

So it was the critic's fault? "No matter the guy's mood, he's now going to give an honest opinion about his experience. Which wasn't good," Brody added in case Travis didn't seem to understand the severity of the situation.

The pan settled on the stove with a loud *clang*. Travis turned to face Brody. "Look, I tasted that dish and it was perfect. Get another reviewer in here and I'll show you. Those other two clowns don't know what they're talking about."

"Travis, when a possible customer is reading a review, they're not thinking about whether or not a reviewer knows what they're talking about. All they see is that this person had a bad experience. A bad review can have more of an effect on a restaurant than a good review can."

The man turned back to his food. He picked up the pan and dumped the pasta dish onto a plate. "I'm fully aware of that." Then he handed the plate over to Maria at the garnish station. Travis turned back to Brody. "I've already had the shit come down on me from your father." The chef's voice lowered a notch. "He said if this guy had anything negative to say, he'd fire me."

Now, that was a real problem for both of them. Usually Brody took care of hiring and firing people. However, this was Martin's place, and if he wanted to fire the chef, that was his prerogative. There'd be little Brody could do to stand in his old man's way.

He pinned the chef with an aggravated look and forced his words to come out calm. "Your ass isn't the only one on the line here, Travis. I have a son to think about."

He left the kitchen and Travis to his work. When he'd first

hired Travis, the man had been pretty good. The restaurant had just gotten rid of Gary and had been desperate to get someone back in the kitchen. Martin hadn't been thrilled with the man and had compared his food to a low-grade buffet. Not a high compliment for a head chef. Fortunately for Travis, he was surrounded by excellent sous-chefs who did their best to cover up his inconsistent food.

Even though Martin hadn't said so, Brody had a feeling Travis was his last chance. They may be father and son, but his old man was a hard-ass when it came to business. Brody had no doubt Martin wouldn't hesitate to fire him if things didn't pick up soon.

He was running out of options. Fast.

Charlene broadsided him the second he pushed through the kitchen doors. "This will be the third bad review we've had under Travis."

He continued to walk past her. "We don't know the review will be that bad." Well, he actually did. But he didn't need Charlene to be negative in addition to him and his father. Charlene was this restaurant's sunshine.

She fell into step beside him. "I guess we'll have to see. Kelly's here, by the way."

Just what he did not freakin' need right now.

There had been a time when he'd loved Kelly very much. Her bright smile and willowy body had attracted him when he first met her. Her pregnancy had been completely unexpected, leading to a rushed marriage. Then she had Tyler, and over the course of their marriage, they'd gone from being a married couple to simply existing with each other. Kelly deserved better than that. She'd deserved to be with a man who could worship her the way she should have been worshipped. Brody just hadn't been that man.

He came to a stop in front of her. "I can't really talk right now."

"This can't wait, Brody. I have to leave this evening."

A weary sigh flowed out of his lungs. "All right." He turned and led her to his office so they could speak in private. Sometimes being on the floor gave him a headache. He'd been having a lot of those lately.

"I don't know how I feel about you leaving our son with a woman I've never met," he said after Kelly told him about having to leave town to take care of her mother. He completely understood the reason for she and Colin to leave. Brody would have done the same thing for Martin or Carol. Unfortunately, Brody couldn't leave the restaurant every day for long periods of time to pick up Tyler, and he couldn't bring the boy back here—especially with all the tension in the restaurant. But some stranger Brody knew nothing about? He didn't love that idea either. For all he knew, this woman could be some witchcraft-practicing basket case who would have his son worshipping Mother Earth within a week. No thank you.

Kelly crossed one leg over the other. "I know her, and Tyler knows her. She lives right down the street from us. I trust her."

Brody swiveled back and forth in his leather chair. "Okay, point made. But that doesn't remedy the fact that *I* don't know her."

Her green eyes lifted to the ceiling. "What suggestion do you have, then? What about Lacy? She's home during the day with Mason."

Lacy was married to Chase, Brody's older brother, and had always been like a sister to him. And normally a very wise choice. But not this time. "She's also eight months' pregnant and on strict bed rest."

She threw him her famous you-are-so-frustrating glare. "What about Noah's wife, Avery?"

"Avery already has her hands full with her own daughter and watching Mason while Chase is at work." While Lacy was on bed rest, Brody's other sister-in-law Avery, who was married to Brody's oldest brother, Noah, had volunteered to watch Lacy and Chase's son, Mason.

Kelly tossed her hands up in the air. "See, all you're doing is proving my point for me. Everyone I know either works or Tyler doesn't know them. She lives right down the street and Tyler can walk there after school and I just need you to pick him up when you leave here." She pointed a finger at him. "And not at midnight either. You'd need to be there in time to feed Tyler some dinner."

One side of his mouth kicked up. Kelly always had a little temper on her. "Sounds like I don't have much of a choice."

Both her fair eyebrows shot up her forehead. "I didn't come here to get your permission. I just needed to fill you in on the situation."

"Point taken."

She stared at him. "I'm serious about the midnight thing."

"I hear you."

"Because I know how you like to work late."

"I'm aware you do."

Her eyes narrowed at him. "Why do I get the feeling you're mocking me?"

"Because I am."

She chose to ignore his last comment and glanced at her watch. "I have to go pick Tyler up before I leave." She stood from her chair and headed to his office door. "Please try to pick him up at a reasonable hour."

This time he couldn't help but smile. "Heard you the

first time, Kel. Wait," he said, then stood and came around the desk toward her. "I'm sorry to hear about your mom. I know the two of you are close." Kelly was so much shorter than he that she had to crane her neck when he stood in front of her. "I hope she'll be okay."

Her mouth turned up in an understanding grin. "Thanks. I'll call in a few days and check on things."

Elisa was ninety-nine point nine percent sure she knew absolutely nothing about eleven-year-old boys. Were they too young to be interested in girls? Too old to play board games? These things were not a part of her common knowledge, because it had been way too long since she'd been around a boy Tyler's age. The fact that she didn't know much about Tyler didn't help either.

After his mother dropped him off, he sat down at the table and started working on math problems far beyond her comprehension. Just to strike up a conversation, she'd asked him if he needed help. Not that she'd been able to help him anyway. Fractions were not her friend.

His only reply had been a soft "No thanks." Their conversation had been limited since. Soon Tyler slid the thick math book into his backpack and took out a history one. If math was uninteresting, then history was even less interesting. Her father had been an enormous history buff, which was probably one of the reasons he chose to be an investigative reporter. Anything that would give him a little history lesson had always made him giddy. Unfortunately, reporting the world's news took him away from home for long periods of time. Every once in a while, her mother would fly out with him, leaving Elisa and her little brother to stay with friends. Then eight years ago, they'd flown on their final assignment and never came back...

During her childhood, she'd grown used to her parents' flightiness. They certainly hadn't been bad parents. When they were home, they were very loving and involved with both their children. They'd taken many camping trips, road trips, and holidays away. Every once in a while a story too good to pass up would pop up on the other side of the globe and her father would jet away. Elisa had always understood her father's work was what had paid for their house, the food on the table, and Marcello's soccer lessons. Would she have liked to have her father around more than he had been? Of course, what little girl wouldn't? But Elisa had never held anything against him.

Marcello was the one who'd had the issues. Not anything worrisome. Just a small boy who didn't understand why Daddy wasn't around more or why he had to go live with his grandparents in South America after their parents died. That wasn't a decision Elisa had come to easily, but it'd been her only choice. A college student could hardly take care of a twelve-year-old boy by herself.

Five years, six months, and twelve days. That's how long ago she'd seen Marcello. A round-trip ticket to Rio de Janeiro was enough to put anyone in the poor house. Luckily for her, she'd been there for a fashion show. It was better than nothing, but she'd barely had enough time to see him.

Oh, how she missed him.

"Why do you have a picture of yourself up there?"

The question was unexpected and came out of nowhere. Elisa glanced up from her proof sheet and looked at Tyler. He'd taken his attention off his homework and focused it on a framed picture of her on the wall. That was a good question and one whose answer she was already beginning to regret. Why *had* she put a picture of herself up there?

Elisa rested her elbows on the table. Would an eleven-year-old understand this?

"That picture was taken about six years ago and was the first time I'd been on the cover of a magazine. I hung it up because it reminded me of a big accomplishment I'd made." He probably still wouldn't get it, but that was the best she could do.

Tyler's eyes remained on the framed cover. "But how'd you get to be on the cover?"

"Because they asked me."

"Why?" The boy's eyes flickered back to hers.

An amused laugh bubbled out of her. "You know, that's a good question."

The number two pencil in the child's hand tapped a rapid rhythm on the table. "It's kind of a funny-looking picture. How come you're wearing that big dress? It doesn't look comfortable."

Okay, maybe he understood a lot better than she gave him credit for. That shot for a famous Italian magazine had been done in South Africa. In the middle of the country's summer. The magazine had dressed her in that horrible, way-too-heavy period dress. The thing came accented with a full petticoat and had about a thousand billowy layers that had practically swallowed her up. The South African sun had been wicked and unforgiving. In between each shot, the stylist had to blot Elisa off then reapply makeup. Overall, the shoot hadn't been fun. But she'd done her job, received quite a nice check, and had flown off to her next location. Flying from one country to another was not something she missed.

Elisa realigned her mind to Tyler's observations. "That dress had been the magazine's choice. And you're right. It was really uncomfortable."

Tyler tilted his head to one side. "You look really pretty in it, though. I bet my mom would like that dress."

Elisa would bet not if Kelly had to put the thing on.

The boy may have been a quiet, reserved child but he sure was observant. He was probably one of those people who absorbed everything around him like a sponge. Tyler could probably sit in a room full of people, disappear completely, yet be able to tell a story about every person in the room. Marcello was like that. He'd always been a silent observer, even as a child. He could go hours without conversing with a single person and still be able to tell everything everyone around him was feeling: a trait that would no doubt one day make him an excellent doctor— something he was currently going to school for.

"Was that the only magazine cover you were on?"

"No, I did a few others, but that's the only one I framed." The other two were in the top of her closet. Elisa didn't really care much about that stuff anymore. Those days had only been to pay for college after her parents died. After graduating, the excitement and purpose had worn off. She'd continued modeling for one more year, but only to fulfill her contract with her agency. They'd asked her to stay on, saying they'd make her a big star one day—the next Adriana Lima was what her agent called her. But Elisa had always been more interested in what went on behind the camera than in front of it. She would still love to travel the globe, but only if she could explore and take her own pictures. Like in Mongolia with Samuel Harper. Just thinking about it brought an exciting jitter through her midsection. She couldn't think of any reason not to take the job. Just the fact that *Time Magazine* would be covering all the expenses was reason enough to accept it. Her passport was up to date, and all she needed were a few immunizations.

The details that Samuel had faxed over had been overwhelming but thrilling. Five months trekking through the Mongolian steppes, documenting the life of nomadic shepherds...what more could she ask for? She'd finally struck gold, and nothing would keep her from this trip.

Elisa pursed her lips and pulled a deep breath into her lungs. "You should finish up before your dad gets here," she said. Thinking about her parents always brought back the old ache. "Do you need some help?" she offered.

He picked up his pencil and tapped on the textbook. "No thanks. I can do it." The boy lifted his scrawny shoulders. "My dad will probably be late anyway."

Elisa stared at the top of his blond head. "Your mom said he'd be leaving work early so you can have dinner with him."

The pencil flew over the worksheet as the boy wrote down answers to questions. "He's always late."

Elisa could feel his back-off vibe. Something about Tyler's father made him shut down. He freely spoke of his mother, talked about how she cried at the death of his grandfather. At the mention of his father, he practically placed a lock over his mouth and threw away the key.

Elisa knew when to let well enough alone. She didn't like answering questions about her parents either, so she understood the feeling. Kelly once mentioned the divorce had been particularly hard on Tyler, but she hadn't said anything about him not having a good relationship with his father. None of this was Elisa's business anyway, however, but curiosity nagged at her.

She left the table to give Tyler a chance to concentrate on his homework. For the next hour, she worked on proposals for stock agents, someone who could represent her and help her nab those higher paying jobs.

A major job like the one in Mongolia could open a lot of doors for her. Her hope was one day she wouldn't have to do dead-end, small-scale shoots that could barely get her through to the next paycheck.

"Are you finished?" Elisa asked Tyler after he'd cleared all his books away in his backpack.

"Yeah. But I'm getting kinda hungry."

Elisa glanced at her watch. Half past seven. Kelly said Tyler's dad should be stopping by no later than seven so Elisa wouldn't have to worry about feeding the boy dinner. Tyler wasn't a bother, and Elisa would have no problem fixing him a meal. Unfortunately, all she had to eat were things like whole wheat pasta and smoked salmon. Something told her an eleven-year-old wouldn't be too excited about those choices.

"Your dad should be here any minute. Your mom said he'd feed you dinner."

Tyler shrugged a shoulder and put his pencil in a small front pocket of his backpack. "I told you he'd be late."

Just when Elisa was about to ask Tyler to elaborate, her doorbell rang. "There's your dad. Now you can finally get some dinner, right?"

Tyler didn't respond. Either he didn't hear her or wasn't all that excited to go home with his dad. The latter bewildered her a bit as she walked to the front door.

When she swung the door open, her heart did a triple beat then plummeted to the bottom of her stomach.

"Elisa?" The expression on Brody's face mirrored her own surprise and confusion. He glanced down the street then looked back at her. "Do I have the right house?"

The magnificent sight he made, a black button-down shirt tucked into a pair of stone-washed khakis, very nearly pushed aside her bewilderment. "Uh…" His slate-gray eyes landed on hers. "Did you come here to look at the proofs?" A client had never come to her house to look at a proof sheet before. And she hadn't even had a chance to scrutinize each one before showing them to him.

Brody stared at her with a blank expression as though her words didn't make sense. Then his thick black brows tugged together. "Proof sheet?" he echoed.

"Yeah, from the pictures I took." She gestured over her shoulder with her thumb. "I have them here if you want to— Wait a minute." She planted her hands on her hips. "How did you know where I live?"

Something that looked very close to suspicion clouded Brody's eyes. He dug his hand into his back pocket, then withdrew a slip of paper. "Well, I have this address but—"

"Hi, Dad."

Tyler's thick, navy blue backpack was slung over both shoulders when he came to a stop next to her. *Hi, Dad?*

The perplexity on Brody's face melted away. In its place was an ear-to-ear grin that brought the light back into his eyes. "Hey, buddy." He ruffled the sandy-colored strands on the boy's head. "Did you get all your homework done?"

"Yeah."

"Good. Why don't you go wait in the car for me?"

"'kay." Tyler turned his green eyes up to her. "Bye, Elisa. Thanks for letting me look at your pictures."

She placed a hand on the boy's small shoulder. "Anytime. See you tomorrow."

Both she and Brody were silent until Tyler got out of earshot.

"*You're* the babysitter?" Brody asked her.

*You're Tyler's dad?* Elisa's eyes danced over Brody's face and picked up on the similarities between him and

Tyler, which were few. They both had the same straight nose and square jaw. Other than those two small details, the man standing in front of her didn't really resemble the boy she'd spent the afternoon with. Brody's midnight hair was at the opposite end of the spectrum from Tyler's tow-headed coif. They both had light-colored eyes, but Tyler's were the color of freshly cut grass and Brody's resembled a stormy sky.

"I didn't know you and Kelly knew each other," Brody said when Elisa hadn't spoken.

She couldn't help the tilt of her mouth. "Ditto." Now, wasn't this just great? She'd finally found a guy, an enormously handsome guy she pictured herself spending time with, and he turned out to be Kelly's ex-husband. Not that Kelly had specifically said "Stay the hell away from my ex." But something about getting involved with a friend's ex-husband didn't sit right with her.

"Kelly gave me your address, but she forgot to mention the name." Brody crossed his arms over his chest. "Kelly didn't mention me?"

"Not by name. I had no idea the man I met at the restaurant and the man who'd be coming here tonight were the same person."

He waited a second before asking, "Would you have agreed to do this if you had?"

"Of course." *But I would have thought much harder about it first.*

The smile that turned his mouth up looked a little too much like satisfaction. "Actually, now that I'm here, there's something I need to run by you."

His grin affected her more than she was comfortable with. Her once even heartbeat did a little jig. "What's that?"

The delight on his face faded. "I called the magazine and postponed the article. We've decided to wait a bit longer before going forward with it."

Concern had Elisa taking a step closer to him. "Why? I thought doing that article was a brilliant idea."

"We're still doing it. Just not with Travis as our chef."

Realization dawned. Elisa crossed her arms over her chest. "You're letting him go," she concluded.

He must have taken her tone as disagreement. "You think that's a mistake?"

"It's not my restaurant. I think with time he could have been a great chef."

He wagged his index finger at her. "*Could* is the key word there. And I don't have time for Travis to become a great chef. I need someone great now. Look," he said with a glance at his black watch. "I can't go into details right now because I've got to get Tyler home and get him fed. Can you come back to the restaurant on Friday so we can talk about doing another spread? I've decided not to rush into running pictures in an article, but still would like to get some shots done. I'll even have Travis prepare the selected dishes for you. That way you can give your honest opinion on the appearance and taste."

Go back? Seeing him here for a few seconds in the threshold of her doorway was one thing. Being on his turf, watching his long legs eat up the ground beneath him and the way his shirt fit over broad shoulders, was *not* the same thing.

"Brody—"

"I'll double your fee," he offered.

How could she tell him it wasn't really about money? How could she say being near him and getting to know him was what scared her? Especially if she wasn't going to be in Trouble that much longer?

However, compassion for his situation had her agreeing. "All right. Have whatever dishes you plan on using ready so I can see them and get a feel for what equipment I'll need."

"Yes, ma'am. And don't be afraid to be brutally honest. Travis could certainly use it." The same disarming grin he'd used on her during their lunch broke across his face. He started to turn and then stopped himself. His gaze connected with hers, then he took a step forward and fixed his mouth over hers. At first she was too stunned to move, but at the same time his lips were soft and felt so right against hers. It was over too quickly, yet it had been enough for her heart to kick start in her chest. "I told you you couldn't stay away from me," he said in a husky voice. With cocky grin playing at his sexy lips, Brody McDermott strolled down the walkway, leaving her bewildered and more turned on than she'd been in a long time.

# FOUR

"WE HAVE A PROBLEM."

The pep in Brody's step fizzled away at Charlene's words. He came to a stop in front of her and took in the troubled expression on her face. Her teeth were worrying her bottom lip, which was never a good sign. Just before entering the restaurant a few moments ago, he told himself today would be a productive day. No thinking about bad reviews and whether or not he'd have a job in six months. With the exception of having to let go of Travis, Brody had started the day on a decidedly high note. Then Charlene burst his bubble.

He pulled her aside. "What's the matter?"

Charlene's worried eyes glanced around them as though she were afraid someone would overhear them. "Your father just fired Travis."

Brody stared at her for a second before responding. "He did *what*?" Why in the world would his father fire their chef without consulting Brody first?

His assistant manager placed a hand on his arm and led the two of them to the back offices. When the door closed, Charlene turned to face him. "Over the past few days, some diners have posted unfavorable reviews on websites."

"Yeah, I know." Even though Brody had tried his hardest to ignore them, they'd been particularly damning. One diner had even gone so far as to say the food was so horrible, they'd never return again. While Travis did have potential, he was still inconsistent. Brody knew the man's days were numbered. Reading those online reviews had only sealed the chef's fate, and possibly Brody's.

"Anyway," Charlene continued. "I don't know how he knew, but somehow Martin learned of these reviews and came in this morning specifically to fire Travis. Judging by the look on Travis's face, it didn't go well. He stormed out of here like his ass was on fire. Now your dad's in the kitchen handing the reins over to the sous-chefs. And he mentioned that he wanted to speak with you."

And what the hell was he supposed to do with Elisa? She was due in today to check out Travis's stuff for the upcoming shoot. Should he have the sous-chefs take care of it or call Elisa and cancel? Even though he wasn't totally sure Vic and Stanley, the sous-chefs, could handle all that, plus prepping for the day, the idea of canceling was even less appealing. The desire to see Elisa and watch her eyes light up with fire for her work overrode everything else.

Brody ground his back teeth together. A headache was already forming, making the back of his skull feel tight. "Hold the fort down for me." He spun around and shoved the kitchen doors open with the heel of his hand.

At the age of sixty-seven, Martin McDermott had a head of thick, cotton-white hair and a paunch belly. He had passed on his impressive height to all three of his sons. He still managed to work forty-plus hours a week. The third restaurant he'd opened a few years ago was thriving like well-oiled machine. In fact, the only time his father showed his presence in the other two restaurants was when someone needed an ass-kicking. That didn't bode well for Brody.

Brody waited until his father concluded his discussion with the sous-chefs. Then Martin turned his steel-gray eyes to Brody. "I can only guess what you want to talk to me about."

"Can we go somewhere more private?" he asked his father. Brody didn't expect this conversation to accomplish anything. Martin McDermott was a force to be reckoned with and rarely could be stopped once he got started. He'd built all three of his restaurants in Trouble from the ground up beginning in the 1980s and still wielded a large portion of control, despite doling some daily control out to his sons.

Once they were in Brody's office, the two men squared off and Brody jumped in first. "I know you fired Travis this morning. I just wanted you to know that I had planned on letting him go, but I don't appreciate you executing that decision without letting me know first. And I really needed him today."

One of Martin's white brows lifted. "Last I checked, this was my place and I was free to do as I see fit."

"I didn't say you couldn't. But I'm supposed to be running this restaurant, and I can't do that properly if you don't include me in these things."

"Travis needed to go," Martin stated.

Brody nodded. "I agree. But now we're minus a chef, plus we still have a photo shoot to do. I wouldn't say that was any better than where we were before."

"Actually we are. Vic and Stanley can handle things until we find someone to replace Travis."

The oncoming headache Brody felt before was now full-fledged. "And do you plan on excluding me on that as well?'

"Of course not." Martin placed a weathered hand on Brody's shoulder. "I'm not trying to do your job for you, son. I know you're under a lot of stress and things haven't been going well. Frankly, I thought I was doing you a favor by firing Travis. Letting an employee go is never an easy thing, but this place has been going downhill for too long. It was time to take some action. And that's another thing we need to talk about."

Even though Brody's head pounded like nobody's business, the tension in the rest of his body eased slightly. His father had a point. His impending discussion with Travis had weighed heavily on him since he'd made the decision. It'd been like an elephant on his back. Normally, Brody didn't appreciate his father making him feel like he didn't know how to do his job. In light of the situation, Brody was willing to give his old man the benefit of the doubt.

But his father's last words created a pit in his stomach.

"Brody, I'm not sure what's been going on. And maybe I've been too ignorant of the situation here. After all, I am the owner and I am ultimately responsible for this place."

Martin paused and Brody felt an enormous "but" coming on.

"But I've been watching and waiting for you to turn things around, and they don't seem to be. I didn't want to do this, but if things don't start to turn around in the next sixty days, I'll have no choice but to replace you."

Knowing it was coming and actually hearing the words were worlds apart. The restaurants had always come first in Martin's world, and quite frankly Brody didn't expect anything less from him. He'd never expected special treatment because he was the owner's son. And if Brody had owned the business, he would have done the same thing. In fact, he wouldn't have given the situation this long. He would have fired all responsible parties right away. So, no, Brody didn't blame his old man for the ultimatum.

On the other hand, the severity of Brody's circumstances were now staring him in the face. He had two months to come up with a solution. Sixty days to find a new chef and prove to his father that he was worth keeping around. Otherwise he'd be out on his ass. With the local job market, he was likely to end up as a shift manager at the Greasy Spoon. Brody wouldn't be able to look his son in the eye if he hadn't done everything possible to secure both of their futures. Though he'd managed to save enough money to live off of for several months, he'd still need to find another job.

Before Brody could respond, Martin continued. "I understand that when I brought you here, you knew almost nothing about running a restaurant. And you are a major part of the reason this place got off the ground so quickly. You fired the original chef and found Michael. It was your idea to have a happy hour, and you brought in RJ. You've shown you can do this, Brody. But something's just not working right now, and I'm giving you one last chance."

Although Brody appreciated the uplifting words of his success, his impending demise outweighed the feeling.

"I understand" was all he could say.

"Charlene told me you've decided to hold off on the article in the magazine. I think that's a smart choice. We need to highlight whoever our new chef is going to be."

Brody paced his office and plowed a hand through his hair. "I still wish you would have waited until we'd found somebody new before firing Travis."

"I know you don't agree with the way I handled this. But Travis isn't the first chef I've had to fire. I honestly think we're better off with the sous-chefs in the kitchen than we were with Travis." Martin paused before continuing. "I wouldn't have let Travis go if I thought otherwise."

Brody glanced at his father. "I want you to promise me you'll let me find a replacement on my own. I don't want to come in here tomorrow to see someone I haven't even met before barking out orders in the kitchen."

The twitch of Martin's mouth almost looked like a smile. "You have my word. Now I need you to make me a promise."

"What's that?"

His father took one step forward. "Before you hire anyone, I want to meet them and taste the food. With the state of this place, I need to be a part of the hiring process."

Brody gritted his teeth at having to relinquish part of his control. He wasn't used to, nor was he comfortable with, having his father lurking around. Given the circumstances, however, Brody agreed. "All right. I'll get started finding someone today." When Brody had gotten up that morning, he hadn't imagined his day going like this. Admittedly, he was relieved at having the burden of firing Travis taken off his hands. Only now he had to deal with his father scrutinizing his choice of chef.

"Remember what I said. If the replacement doesn't work out, you'll be shown the door along with him," Martin said ominously.

Brody didn't reply because there was really no need. They both knew that Martin always made good on his word, even if that meant firing his own son.

Elisa arrived at the Golden Glove ten minutes early. Her early arrival had nothing to do with the fact that she was eager to see Brody. Because she wasn't. Really. The jitters in her stomach had nothing to do with the man's hypnotic voice or the way his eyes burned down to her soul. Or the kiss that had knocked her off her feet. Yessiree, the only reason she came was due to Brody's generous offer to double her fee. That money would go a long way to helping her get by until she landed a contract with a stock agent.

Or, better yet, helping her save for traveling.

Last night after Brody left with Tyler was the most conflicted she'd felt in a long time. Brody was the first guy who'd sparked a real interest in her. Even though she was already fighting her attraction to him, deep down she'd hoped for something more with him. Lazy Sunday afternoons and weeknight dinners at home. No, she couldn't let herself keep going down that path in her mind. Knowing that he was Kelly's ex-husband had put a damper on her feelings. Some women were kind of funny about their ex-husbands dating friends of theirs, and others were downright cruel to the woman treading on their territory. Elisa didn't know Kelly well enough to know for sure how she'd react, and she was never one to risk a friendship for a fling that would likely trickle out soon enough. Plus, watching Brody's son during the day would make things even stickier. Elisa already knew his parents' divorce had been hard on him. She didn't want to add to the child's confusion by engaging in a relationship with his father, only to have things not work out. No matter how devastating or appealing the father was. No, it was best for all parties involved if Elisa kept her distance from Brody. She would meet with him today, come back and take more pictures, and that would be the end of it.

Today would have to be the end of it, because she was

leaving Trouble in several months. Spending five months away in Mongolia was sure to put a damper on whatever relationship they'd develop. As for coming back to Trouble? Elisa always loved it here, but making a career for herself here seemed like less and less of a possibility. If she was serious about being a photojournalist, surely she'd have to travel. Taking pictures of food was okay, but it didn't fully satisfy her. She could not allow herself to fall for Brody, knowing she was leaving. Her heart couldn't handle that.

Her attention honed in on the man of her fantasies the second she walked into the restaurant. He stood at the bar next to Charlene, who held a handful of papers. Elisa didn't so much as spare the other woman a glance. Brody's spectacularly hard ass, encased in a pair of black slacks, held her attention so well that she damn near tripped over her own sandals. She moved her eyes upward, only so she could place one foot in front of the other like a competent human being. That view didn't help matters either. Wide shoulders filled out a baby-blue collared shirt, which accented his midnight hair. The strands were clipped short and close to his head, the tips not even reaching his ears. During her modeling days, Elisa had grown an affinity for men with long hair. Something about the roguish way the long strands would fall over a man's collar like he just didn't give a damn made Elisa weak. Brody was the antithesis of every man she'd known during her modeling days. This was the first time in her life short, spiky hair took her breath away.

As though he sensed her presence behind him, Brody turned his attention from Charlene to Elisa. His gray eyes met hers from across the room and then swept down her body with slow appraisal. When she'd put on the knee-length skirt that morning, it hadn't felt too short. Now she had to resist the urge to tug at the hem with the way his eyes lingered on her legs.

He lifted his gaze back to hers and turned from Charlene. His long legs ate the distance between them with purposeful, confident strides. Elisa felt like the prey to his predator. Suddenly, she couldn't remember the reason for staying away from him.

Oh, yeah. He had the potential to completely shatter her heart.

Brody came to a stop in front of her. "I was kind of thinking you weren't going to show."

"Well, you *are* paying me," she said with a reluctant smile.

"That's not the only reason you came."

She decided to let the comment go, even though he was totally right. How did she manage to give herself away? She cleared her throat and tried to refocus her attention to the reason why she came. "Are you ready for me?"

One of his dark brows crept up his forehead.

A laugh bubbled in her throat when she realized how her words sounded. "With the food," she spluttered out. "To take pictures, I mean." *Geez, that was articulated like a five-year-old.*

"I know what you meant," he replied. He tilted his head. "Are you sure *you* know what you meant?"

Well, now she wasn't. Being around this man took away all ability to think coherently. Did she really need the money from this job that badly? Was it worth screwing with her sanity? The jury was still out on that one.

*Okay, steer the conversation back on track.* "So, where are we doing this?" Did every word that came out of her mouth have to have a double meaning?

This time Brody's mouth turned up in a slow melt-your-bones grin. "We'll go into the kitchen," he finally said.

Oh, good. They'd be around other people. She wouldn't be in danger of spontaneously jumping his bones.

# FIVE

BRODY COULDN'T THINK STRAIGHT.

Every time Elisa moved, the dark strands of her hair fell over her shoulder like pieces of silk. Too many times to count he'd had the urge to tunnel his hand into her curtain of hair to see if it really was that soft. Her almond-shaped eyes lit up with delight when they landed on the dishes the sous-chefs had prepared for them. The reaction was equivalent to a person who'd just struck gold.

Then, as though she'd just realized the situation, she'd shot him a questioning glance. "Where's Travis?"

"My father fired him."

Both her dark brows shot up her forehead. "Uh…" Her gaze glanced around the kitchen, touching on the chefs flying through their usual motions with efficient but rapid ease. "How's this going to work with no chef?"

Brody touched one of the plates that Elisa had already scrutinized. "Let's take a closer look at these, then you can tell me for sure."

She tilted her head to one side, revealing a tiny pearl earring in her ear. "Well, they look great. Aesthetically pleasing. Nice balance and color."

When she finished snapping the photos, she placed the camera back in the bag and gathered her notebook. Brody forced his eyes to stay above her waist. Elisa had the sort of legs that went on for miles. The skirt that fell to her knees left plenty to his overactive imagination. His mind had no trouble thinking up ways Elisa could use those babies.

*She's doing a job for you and babysitting your son. Watch yourself.*

Brody never had a problem controlling himself around a woman. Not even when he first met Kelly. Something about Elisa brought an animalistic side of him, like he needed to drop to his knees and howl at the moon. That or claw her clothes off.

She caught him staring when her gaze darted to his. Her eyes held his for one moment, then she flipped her notebook closed. "I think I'm done here."

Brody peeled his tongue from the roof of his mouth. "Why don't you go find a place to sit?" he suggested. "I want to have a quick word with the guys, then I'll come find you."

She nodded and turned from the kitchen. With miraculous willpower of steel, Brody kept his eyes off her ass. Mostly because he didn't want his employees to catch him ogling her. What kind of dirtbag would that make him? A horny one, that's what.

Vic was slicing mushrooms with lightning speed when Brody approached him. "Hey, I just wanted to say great job with that. I know I kind of sprung this on you, but you guys came through for me."

The young chef glanced at Brody. "I saw her smiling. I take it we passed her inspection?"

"So far," Brody answered with a nod. "For now let's

take it one step at a time. But I will try to get someone in here soon to alleviate some of the pressure."

"As long as he or she has more experience than Travis had," Vic muttered.

Yeah, he didn't have to tell Brody twice. He nodded and glanced at the kitchen doors, as though expecting Elisa to be standing there. Damn, his desire for her was so strong that he couldn't keep his mind on one simple conversation with one of his chefs. "In the meantime, throw together some dishes for us, will you?"

"Sure, what'll it be?" Vic asked without glancing up.

Brody turned and started toward the kitchen doors, so damn eager to be near Elisa again. "Surprise me," he said over his shoulder.

He spotted her right away, sitting alone in a booth with the light overhead catching on the dark strands of her hair. Her head was bent over a menu and her teeth stabbed into her lower lip, accentuating its fullness. The action made him want to curl his hand around the back of her neck and yank her mouth to his. Then he'd see for himself just how full and luscious her lips were.

A shot of heat bolted down to his groin.

She glanced up at him and smiled when he approached. "Is everything okay?" she asked.

"Yeah, we're good." He lowered to the booth and stretched his legs out. "This all sort of got sprung on the chefs at the last minute."

"Well, they did a great job. The guy with the dark hair has good technique." She eyed him from across the table. A little too closely, but hey, who was he to complain? "He might be a suitable replacement for Travis."

Yeah, he'd thought about that, but Vic was more valuable where he was. "Vic? The thing is, he's an excellent prep cook, but he lacks the imagination of a head chef. I'm not convinced." Though he knew Vic would jump at the opportunity to run the kitchen, Brody wasn't about to hand that job over to just anyone. Not again. Not with so much at risk. Whoever he brought on essentially held Brody's future in his hands.

"You're still kind of gun-shy, aren't you?" Elisa asked with a grin.

Damn, she glowed when she smiled. "Hell yeah, I'm gun-shy. Right now I'm oh for two, and no way in hell will my father let me get to oh for three."

Elisa folded her arms on the table. "So, what happens now? Do we still postpone the shoot?"

He glanced around and thought about just having Vic or Stanley whip something up for Elisa to photograph. After all, she'd said herself they'd done a good job with the dishes, that she'd gotten some promising shots. But why rush? In the past, rushing was what had gotten him in trouble. No, best to take his time. Even though they weren't running the article right away, Brody had been curious to see what Vic's plating would look like on film. When he'd found out about Travis getting the boot, he'd contemplated calling Elisa to tell her not to come. But any excuse to see her was good enough for him.

"For now, yeah. It needs to get done right."

She nodded and tucked a strand of hair behind her ear. "I understand that. Just consider me on standby. In the meantime," she held the digital camera up. "I have these as a reference."

*Yeah, she's got you figured out, pal.*

Brody's eyes dropped down to her mouth, as he imagined, for the second time, what it would be like to kiss her. Really kiss her. Tongue-searching, breath-stealing, backseat-of-a-car tonsil hockey. When was the last time he'd made out with a woman?

He rubbed his hand over his jaw and grinned. "Honestly? I just needed an excuse to get you back here. Plus, I like watching you work."

Her chuckle danced over him. "I should have known." She tossed the camera back in the bag, then glanced at him and a slow grin broke across her face. The type of grin that slowly crept along her cheeks and formed shallow laugh lines at the corner of her eyes. "What're you thinking?"

"Are you sure you want to know?" he asked in a low voice.

"I wouldn't have asked otherwise."

"I was thinking that I want to kiss you." *Or, better yet, take you to bed.*

The smile on her face froze, then fell a fraction. Had he shocked her? Said too much and scared her away? Maybe he should have blown smoke and pretended that she didn't affect him. Pretend that he didn't want to wrap those long legs around his hips.

*Yeah, right. You couldn't pretend otherwise if you had a gun to your head.*

"So now tell me what *you're* thinking." He silently prayed it was along the same lines as his thoughts, so he didn't sound like a creepy bastard.

Elisa leaned back in the booth and gazed at him from beneath long lashes. "I'm thinking that you're a very dangerous man, Brody McDermott."

*He* was dangerous? She obviously had no idea of her own power.

But before either of them could say anything else, or before he could drag her from the restaurant to a dark corner somewhere, their food was delivered. The server set a chicken Caesar wrap in front of Elisa.

Brody glanced at the dish, then up at Theresa. "Where did this come from? We don't have wraps on the menu."

Theresa shrugged her shoulders and set Brody's dish down. "Anthony made it." She spun on her heel, but Brody made a rapid grab for her arm, stopping a hasty retreat.

"What's Anthony doing in the kitchen?" he demanded. Anthony was the bartender slash mix master. The man really had no reason to be in the kitchen.

"I think Vic and Stanley needed help and Anthony stepped in. He threw these together for you." She gave a pointed look at his hand wrapped tightly around her forearm.

Brody loosened his grip. "He's in there right now, cooking?"

"Yeah."

He shot a look at Elisa, who slowly chewed a bite and swallowed. "This is incredible," she stated. "Try some."

She held the food across the table, offering to feed him like they were on some romantic date. Maybe he'd bypass the wrap and take a nibble out of her hand. In order to seem like a normal guy and not some obsessed psycho, he took what she offered, getting a piece of seasoned chicken, tomato, and crisp lettuce. The dressing was tangy but not overwhelming.

Overall, incredible. Just as Elisa said.

"Can I go to my other tables now?" Theresa asked with a thumb over her shoulder.

"Yeah, sorry. Go ahead," Brody said absently. He grabbed Elisa's hand, noting how much softer and smaller it was than his. "Come on," he said to her as they exited the booth and he tugged her along beside him to the kitchen.

Her long legs ate up the ground as quickly as his did. In the kitchen, he immediately spotted Anthony, doing something with a sweet potato. Was he making sweet potato fries? How in the world did he even know how to do that? The man had never shown any inclination for food or cooking.

Brody kept Elisa's hand in his, because, really, he didn't want to let her go. It felt right to have her tucked so close to him.

Anthony glanced up when they approached. Was that a flicker of alarm that flashed in his eyes? "Sorry, man. I'll be out of here in a minute. Vic needed a hand, then I wanted to make myself some lunch."

"So Vic asked you to make our meals just now?" Brody asked.

The bartender shot him a look out of chocolate brown eyes. Beads of sweat dotted the man's smooth head. "Uh, yeah. I hope that's not a problem."

A problem? He thought throwing together a wicked tasty chicken Caesar wrap was a problem? Brody reluctantly dropped Elisa's hand and crossed his arms over his chest. "The only problem is that I had no idea you could cook like that."

Anthony's hands stalled for a brief moment. He shot an uncertain look at Elisa, then at Brody. "You liked it?"

Elisa stepped forward. "It was delicious. And where did you learn how to spiral slice a cucumber like that?"

The other man's thick shoulders lifted and fell in a shrug. "Just taught myself."

After RJ's departure from the restaurant, Brody had put out an ad for a new bartender, which Anthony had answered within days. Brody later had learned the burly black man was an ex–air force pilot with a quiet disposition and swift hands. Over time, Anthony had proved himself a reliable and valuable employee, one whom Brody was proud to have on staff.

"Did you learn how to do that in the military?" Brody asked the man.

"Nah," Anthony replied with a shake of his head. "When I was young, my mom worked two jobs, which left me at home in the evenings by myself. I started experimenting with food and just sort of learned as I went along."

Was he serious? The kind of food he'd just served them wasn't something someone just taught themselves how to do. The man had some serious skills.

"Have you ever worked in a kitchen before?" Elisa asked.

"Just at home," Anthony answered.

"But here you are, helping out Vic and Stanley," Brody pointed out. "Do you do that often?"

"No. Well, Travis used to let me sneak back here and make myself some lunch."

Elisa picked up a sweet potato. "Are you making sweet potato fries?"

Anthony stopped peeling the potato and glanced at Elisa. "Yeah. I made them at home one day because I didn't have any regular potatoes. They turned out pretty good."

If his wrap was anything to go by, "pretty good" would be an understatement.

Brody gestured toward sliced tomato and marble rye bread. "And what are you doing with this?"

"I'm making a BLT," the other man answered.

Elisa lifted a brow. "On marble rye?"

Brody didn't even think it was possible, but the big ex-pilot actually blushed. "I know it's not usual for a BLT, but it's really good."

"You put avocados on it?" Brody asked with a nod toward the green vegetable.

"That's for guacamole." Anthony glanced at Brody, then Elisa. "And I spread some cream cheese too."

"Cream cheese and guacamole?" Elisa repeated.

Brody wasn't sure yet, but he could be sitting on a gold mine. In the form of a soft-spoken ex–air force pilot who poured drinks for a living.

"Can you plate this so Elisa can take some pictures?"

A startled look passed across Anthony's face. The guy looked like he wanted to bolt in the other direction.

Elisa, bless her gentle heart, placed a hand on the other man's arm. "I promise the pictures won't get published. I just want to see what they look like on film."

Anthony hesitated, then gave a slow nod.

Elisa's face broke out in a triumphant grin, right before she spun around and pushed through the kitchen doors. She returned a moment later with her camera bag. "All ready," she said, a little breathless.

Was she as eager as Brody to see what else Anthony had up his sleeve?

One side of Brody's mouth kicked up. "You're on, bro."

He and Elisa stood while the bartender went to work, with slightly trembling hands, Brody noted. Was it possible Anthony was nervous? What could cause nerves like that when the man was such a natural with food? At the same time, he moved through the motions like someone born to be in a kitchen. He flowed with effortless grace that amazed even Brody, and he'd worked with a lot of chefs. A tiny glimmer of hope sprang in his chest as he watched Anthony plate the sandwich, arranging it just so, then adding the sweet potato fries he'd made.

"Wow," Elisa breathed, as she turned the plate and

inspected the dish. "You've really never had professional training? This is all self-taught?"

Anthony moved one shoulder in a restless shrug. "Took a lot of years. And it's something I'm still working on."

"You know my father just fired Travis, right?" Brody asked him. When Anthony nodded, Brody pressed on. "So, we're shorthanded in the kitchen."

Anthony rubbed a hand along the back of his neck, while Elisa snapped pictures. "Yeah, but I don't think—"

"Anthony, you're good," he encouraged when he sensed the other man's hesitation. "I don't think you realize how good you are."

"I've never cooked for anyone before." Anthony shook his head, and Brody could practically feel the other man's panic. "I-I wouldn't know what to do."

"What else can you make that isn't on the menu?" Elisa asked in between shots.

"Uh…well, I have a recipe for cream of sweet potato soup."

Elisa set the camera down and leaned against the prep counter. "What if Brody were to put that on as a special tonight? And that could be your thing? You make only the soup, and that way you wouldn't feel overwhelmed by doing too much too soon. You could pretend you're cooking for yourself."

Damn, but Brody could kiss her. And he would have if they hadn't been in the middle of the kitchen. Her suggestion was freakin' brilliant, and he was kicking himself for not coming up with it on his own.

"What do you say?" he asked Anthony.

The big man's chest puffed out as he considered his options. And Brody held his breath as though waiting for a life-changing decision. Well, considering the mess he was in, he supposed one could consider it sort of life changing.

"I have no training in a professional kitchen," Anthony started with a shake of his head. "I don't know how stations work or how to read tickets..." His words trailed off as more dots of sweat bubbled on his shaved head.

"Don't worry about any of that." Brody placed a hand on Anthony's shoulder, which was hard with tension. "All you have to do is make soup. Think you can handle that?"

Anthony shot a look at Elisa, who nodded and graced him with a smile of encouragement. Jesus, the woman pinched his heart.

"Yeah, I can handle that."

# SIX

B RODY PULLED HIS TRUCK INTO Elisa's driveway and cut the engine. Just as he'd been about to walk out of the restaurant, Charlene had tried to get him to approve next week's schedule. Even though their business had picked up slightly, things were still in the red. Because of that, he'd had no choice but to cut some people from the upcoming schedule. A few servers and busboys had taken a hit on hours. Also, Vic had agreed to work five less hours a week than he had been working. It wasn't much, but every little bit helped. But he'd had to call his brother RJ, who'd been the bartender before he'd left to open his own auto shop. With Anthony spending time in the kitchen, Brody had needed someone ASAP to lend a helping hand behind the bar until he could find a suitable replacement. RJ, being the cool guy he was, agreed to spare a few hours in the evenings.

Seeing Elisa when he came to pick up Tyler had become a highlight in the last week. He'd only known her a short time, but the woman already had him tied up in knots. But those damn knots that churned in his stomach had more to do with the effect she had on him. Her friendship with his ex-wife and newfound relationship with his son made for a trickier situation than he'd had with any of the other women he'd been on first dates with. His romantic feelings for his ex-wife had subsided well before their marriage had ended. Sure, when they first divorced, he'd had a hard time imagining himself in another relationship. Now, years later, Kelly was remarried and Brody had more than moved on. He certainly had never felt the need to clue her in on any relationships he'd been in over that time. He'd also been very careful not to let any girlfriend become acquainted with Tyler. As long as Kelly knew he was being respectful, she'd kept her nose out of that aspect of his life. But then again, none of the women he'd dated had given him that feeling of permanence. The last thing either of them had wanted was their son becoming confused when his father brought women into their lives, only to have them exit. Eleven was such a pivotal age, and Brody needed to devote as much time to Tyler as he could. The boy needed his father to teach him right from wrong, to teach him how to be a man. That was more important to Brody than anything else. But perhaps the most disturbing thought was Brody's inability to relate to his son on the same level. They'd always understood each other better than anyone else. As Tyler had grown older, he'd changed and matured, and Brody found himself losing ground with his only child. He'd slipped into that preteen moody world that Brody struggled to understand. And he had a feeling that Tyler was as aware of the complication as Brody was. His boy had always come to him with problems. Now Tyler was nearing that age when he kept his thoughts and feelings more secret.

Brody felt like he was on the outside, looking in, watching his son change with no way to keep up.

As he neared the door, his thoughts shifted to the

woman inside the house. More important, his eagerness to see her.

All sexiness aside, she was incredible behind the camera. And, yeah, he got that photographing food probably didn't light her fire. But she was good at it. No, more than good. She made the food come alive. Her creativity with the dishes astounded him, and he'd been working with food for a long time. Her photographic abilities were just another thing that added to her layer of desirability. The thought had him grinning when he pressed the doorbell.

A second later Elisa swung the door open with a wide smile and her long, dark hair falling over both shoulders. "Hi," she greeted him.

"Hey." He stepped over the threshold after she gestured him inside. He let his eyes linger on her a moment longer before glancing around at her home. The house was fairly new but not terribly big. The kitchen, small breakfast nook, and living room were all basically one area designed like a great room. To their right, a narrow hallway led to the rest of the house. Flowery curtains adorned the windows and sliding glass door. Different-colored, mismatched throw pillows were tossed about on the denim couch where she'd likely been curled up earlier. The home was girly and welcoming, much like its owner.

When he glanced back at Elisa, her attention wasn't on his face. Her deep brown eyes bounced from his chest, down his legs then back up. The pink hue that had once brightened her cheeks turned deeper when her gaze locked with his.

The soft lighting of the table lamps picked up flecks of red in her hair. Dark eyes encased in thick black lashes stared back at him. Brody ran his gaze over her olive complexion as something Tyler said to him several months ago came back to him. "You wouldn't by any chance be Senorita Cardoso?" Tyler had mentioned the name to him a few times, but Brody had never given it much thought.

Her entire body seemed to go still. "Tyler's mentioned me before?"

Brody lifted one shoulder in half a shrug. "He's talked about the pretty, dark-haired lady down the street a few times."

Her teeth stabbed into her lower lip at the same time pale pink colored her high cheekbones. The woman was even more beautiful when she blushed. "Why does he call you senorita?" Brody asked.

Elisa giggled and fiddled with the rings on her hands. "The first time I met him, I said something in Portuguese to him and he thought it was Spanish. He drew me a picture and wrote *Senorita Cardoso* on the top, but spelled it the Spanish way. Every time he sees me he refers to me as Senorita Cardoso, thinking I'm Spanish."

"And you're not?"

"I'm actually Brazilian on my father's side. A lot of people make that mistake because the languages are so similar. I thought it was so adorable that I just never corrected him."

"And how would you write it in Portuguese?"

"It's almost exactly the same in Portuguese but it's spelled with an *h*. S-E-N-H-O-R-I-T-A. He spelled it without an *h*." She shrugged her shoulders. "It's a common mistake."

He took a step toward her. Every time he spoke to this intriguing woman he learned something else he liked about her. For the first time in a long time he found himself genuinely interested in what a woman had to say. Not the kind of interest that made him want to get her into bed ASAP—though he wouldn't turn down the invitation. No, he wanted to peel back the layers of Elisa Cardoso and see what made her tick.

"So your father is originally from Brazil?" he asked her as she ran her tongue along her lower lip. If she didn't stop that he'd lean toward her and do the licking for her.

"Yes," she answered. "My father and his family are from Sao Paulo. We moved here when I was three."

His eyebrows shot up his forehead. "You were born there? Do you speak Portuguese?"

"Fluently. My father always used it in the house, and taught us the language from a young age."

He leaned closer to her. "Say something."

Her deep gaze bored into his before dropping down to his chest. Her long black lashes swept back up. "*Você tem graxa em sua camisa.*" The Latin lingo rolled off her tongue like sweet honey.

Just the sound of the foreign language coming from her had blood rushing below his belt. Certain male parts, parts he hadn't used in quite a while, came to life. He cleared his throat so his voice would come out normal. "What's that mean?" To him, it sounded like some forbidden words of seduction.

One corner of her pillowy mouth crept up. She leaned closer to him and dropped her voice to a whisper. "You have grease on your shirt."

Brody barked with laughter. Seductive *and* sassy. What a dangerous combination. "Unfortunately, that's one of the hazards of working in a restaurant," he said after his laughter subsided. "Are your parents back in Brazil now?"

Her smile faltered and then lowered just a fraction. "No, but my father's whole family is now in Rio de Janeiro. How did Anthony end up doing?"

Okay, she didn't want to talk about her parents. Brody

could take a subtle hint. "Like a champ. I don't know why that man isn't cooking at the Four Seasons. Or owning his own restaurant. A guy with that kind of talent shouldn't be behind a bar."

"I agree. Do you think he can handle a photo shoot?"

Brody considered the situation and remembered the way Anthony had been in the kitchen. Several orders for his soup had come through, and he'd flown through them like the talented freak he was. The hope that had coursed through Brody's body almost had him offering Anthony a job on the spot. But that's what he'd done with Travis, and it had come back to bite him in the ass.

"I think Anthony has confidence issues. He's unsure about himself, and that makes me nervous."

"But he's got natural talent. Confidence will come with time."

Brody rubbed a hand over his jaw. Damn, he needed a shave. "Yeah, but how much time?"

Elisa took a step toward him. "I know you're hesitant because of what happened with Travis. But I think with enough work and training, Anthony could be your guy. I see something in him."

So did Brody, but he was already on thin ice with his father.

"I think you should go ahead with the shoot anyway," Elisa went on. "And you already know he can plate a dish like nobody's business. Maybe just have him work with Vic during lunch when things aren't so busy. The sous-chefs can teach him how the kitchen runs."

"That's not a bad idea," he mused. His gaze ran over her face. "Is there anything you can't do?"

Her mouth turned up in a small smile. "I kill flowers. I'm a terrible gardener."

The comment prompted a chuckle from him. "Where's Tyler?"

She cleared her throat and ran her tongue along her lower lip. "He's in my darkroom."

Both his brows lifted in amazement. "You have an actual darkroom in this house?"

She gestured with her thumb over her shoulder. "It's down the hall. I made some rearrangements to my laundry room."

Sexy and resourceful. "No kidding?"

"It's the biggest room without a window."

He slid his hands in his pockets. "And you trust an eleven-year-old in there by himself?"

Elisa glanced down the hallway, then back at him. "Yeah, I do. He's a quick learner."

The compliment warmed him from the inside out. "Yes, he is. What's he doing in there?"

"Right now he's cleaning. Earlier we were developing the pictures he took."

Brody's mouth turned up in another smile. His son, the boy who slept with his baseball glove, spent the afternoon taking pictures?

Elisa ran a hand through her hair. "To be completely honest, I don't know much about boys and even less about things they like. He seemed kind of bored and I couldn't really think of anything else to entertain him."

The uncertainty radiating off her was so endearing, Brody wanted to envelop her in a hug. Of course, that wasn't the only reason. The need to feel those womanly curves pressing against him almost had him reaching for her.

She'd willingly given up her afternoons to look after someone else's child, and a child she didn't know that well, to boot. Instead of letting Tyler sit around a house that had nothing to offer him, Elisa engaged him. She showed his son the only thing she knew, even if those things didn't particularly interest Tyler. Brody appreciated her effort and affection toward his son.

"I'm sure he had a good time." He tried to put her doubt to rest. "And just so you know, he's really into baseball."

"I know," she said with a grin. "He mentioned..." She paused and her smile faltered. "He said something about going to the baseball fields."

Playing catch at the baseball fields had been a special tradition Brody and Tyler started years ago. On his days off, the two of them would ride their bikes and toss the ball back and forth. Since the divorce their routine had shifted. Unfortunately, on some of Brody's days off, Tyler had been with his mother or at school. In those cases, Brody would sometimes go into work anyway. Providing a good life for his son was the most important thing to him. Before he knew it, several years had passed since they'd gone to the fields. Brody didn't like to talk about the divorce or how the situation had affected Tyler. The subject was a sore spot for Brody, knowing he'd been unable to keep his family glued together. He'd felt as though he'd let his only child down, and he'd walked away from his divorce feeling like he'd lost a piece of himself. That particular chapter of his life had closed and was one he didn't often share. Hearing Elisa mention the past times he and his son had shared made Brody wonder. Had Kelly or Tyler said other things to Elisa? Things about the divorce Brody wasn't proud of?

He cleared his throat. "What else did Tyler mention?" he asked, trying not to sound anxious.

Elisa tilted her head and some silken hair slid over her

shoulder. "Not much. Just that the two of you used to go there." Her bottomless brown eyes studied him for one intense moment. "He really enjoyed the time out today. I think he'd probably like to go back."

Brody nodded. "I'm glad. Maybe the two of you can go back tomorrow."

Her lips twitched in a hint of a smile. "Actually I think he would have more fun if you took him."

Tyler had outgrown the playground years ago. The last time Brody mentioned that place Tyler's response was "Dad, the park is lame."

"Tyler isn't really into the playground," he said to Elisa.

She took a step closer to him. "I wasn't talking about the playground. When he mentioned the baseball fields, there was something wistful about him, almost sad. Like he really wanted to go back but..."

Her words twisted in his gut and made him feel almost nauseous. "But I'm too busy to take him."

Elisa placed a hand on his arm. Her soft skin burned him up from the inside out. "I didn't mean to imply anything. I just thought—"

"It's okay." He tried not to show the effect her words had on him. Guilt. Worst father in the world. Yeah, he was definitely feeling those right now. He cleared his throat again. "I know how much my work takes me away."

Elisa took a step closer to him. Her womanly cinnamon scent tickled his nose and clouded his brain. "I'm sure he's—"

A door down the hallway opened before Elisa could finish her sentence. Tyler's striped polo hung loose over his grass-stained blue jeans. His brand-new black and white Nikes scuffed down the white-carpeted hallway. Over the past year Tyler had shot up over two inches in height. His hair, once as white blond as his mother's, had darkened to a deep honey. His boy was growing into his own. Sometime when Brody hadn't looked, Tyler had started to resemble a young man. The last thing he wanted was for Tyler to suffer because of the long hours Brody worked. He had to admit, he'd really begun to miss some of the things they'd usually done together.

Brody's heart squeezed in his chest when Tyler's green eyes landed on his. The boy smiled, then his smile grew even wider when he glanced at Elisa.

"How'd they come out?" Elisa asked Tyler.

Tyler shifted the papers in his hand and showed them to her. "This one is kind of streaky but the others are pretty good."

Elisa placed a hand on his son's shoulder. "Don't feel bad about that. I messed up a ton of photos when I first started."

The woman was a natural nurturer. Her face softened and her pouty, full mouth turned up in a reassuring grin. She gave Tyler her undivided attention as they went over each photo.

Elisa handed one to Brody, letting her hand linger on his arm while her left did the reaching. "Didn't he do a good job?" She asked the question as though both she and Tyler had been waiting for him to say something. How long had he been standing there just watching them?

He took the picture and allowed his fingers to brush along Elisa's softer ones. Pure fire shot up his arm like a jolt of electricity. His brain did a pretty good job of trying to ignore the sensation, while other body parts had a mind of their own. Brody summoned his iron-clad willpower and forced his eyes to the photos. Never in his life would he have imagined his eleven-year-old son enjoying taking pictures.

Apparently not, given the ear-to-ear grin on Tyler's face and the way he practically hopped from one foot to the other with excitement. That was what astonished Brody the most—not the fact that the pictures were semigood. The activity Elisa had introduced to Tyler this afternoon had made an impression on the boy. Brody couldn't remember the last time his son had been this enthusiastic about something.

Brody's mouth turned up in a proud grin as he shuffled through the black-and-white pictures. "You took these all by yourself?" he asked after he'd found his voice.

Tyler shrugged a bony shoulder. "Well, Elisa helped me."

Elisa placed an arm around the boy. "All I did was show him how to use the camera. After that it was all him."

Brody held up the picture of the well. "Do you mind if I frame this one and put it in my office?"

"Sure." Tyler took one of the photos out of Brody's hands. "I want Elisa to have this one."

She took the picture and gazed at it with a small smile. "That's very nice of you, Tyler."

Brody needed to get out of there before he started kissing the hell out of Elisa in front of his child. The urge was getting stronger and stronger, and he needed to eliminate the temptation altogether.

"Tyler, why don't you get your stuff so we can go get some dinner?"

"Okay." Tyler gathered his backpack from the front door and hugged Elisa good-bye. His long, skinny arms wrapped around Elisa's narrow waist as though he didn't want to let go. Hell, Brody knew the feeling.

"See you tomorrow, Tyler," Elisa said as the boy opened the front door.

Brody stepped through after his son and turned to face

the beautiful woman who had his guts tied in knots. The casual khaki pants and baby pink polo was just as sexy on her as the slacks and floral print blouse she'd had on the first day he met her. Her hair hung free over her shoulders and halfway down to her waist. The sight reminded him of those cartoon mermaids who had nothing to cover their bare breasts except their long hair. He took a step closer to her just as an image of water cascading over her hair and down her bare breasts invaded his mind.

"Dad, I'm hungry."

The words spoken behind him were like a bucket of ice-cold water thrown over his head. Nothing like the presence of his son to pull him back to reality.

"Is something on your mind?" Elisa asked in that soft, bedroom voice of hers.

"Uh, no," Brody managed to get out without making a complete ass of himself. He'd come close to doing that too many times around her. "I just wanted to thank you for taking him out today."

Her face softened again and her mouth spread into a grin. "It's always a pleasure with him. Are we still on for tomorrow to take pictures?"

She was supposed to take pictures? Of what?

Elisa straightened from the door. "You still want to do the shoot, right?"

Oh, the restaurant. He was supposed to be concerned with saving the place, and all he could think about was mermaids and Elisa's hair. He was in trouble.

"Yeah," he muttered like an idiot. "But I think tomorrow is too soon. I'd like Anthony to work in a kitchen a bit more before I dump this on him. Let's shoot for next week."

*And that will give me plenty of time to be around you*

*and hear your beautiful voice. You know, basically be obsessive.*

"Dad…" Tyler's once-patient voice had taken on the quality of a four-year-old's whine.

Brody glanced at Tyler over his shoulder. "I'm coming. Thanks again," he said to Elisa.

"My pleasure," she said in a low voice. Her tongue swiped across her lower lip, leaving it sinfully moist and kissable.

This time he gave in to his urge to touch her. Her smooth skin had been calling out to him all day. Would it be as soft as it looked? To answer those burning questions, Brody skimmed the back of his index finger just along the edge of her jaw. His suspicions were right. He hadn't felt anything that soft since Tyler was born. His satisfaction piqued when her teeth stabbed into her lower lip. To get even more of a reaction out of her, his finger journeyed up her cheek then tucked some hair behind her ear. If her skin had been soft, then her hair was even softer. Like spun silk sifting through his fingers.

Intensely aware of his son marching toward the car only several feet behind him, Brody dropped his hand and walked away without saying a word to her. Maybe tonight her dreams would be just as torturous as his had been since he'd met her.

Even after ten minutes and after putting considerable distance between him and the forbidden fruit, Brody still couldn't calm his raging hard-on. What's worse is that he was trying to adjust himself while his son sat, without the faintest clue, in the car seat next to him. This was definitely a new low.

He might as well come out and say "Hey, son, I want to screw your babysitter."

His knuckles ached and turned white as he wrapped his hand tighter around the leather steering wheel. Brody came to a stop at a red light and glanced at Tyler. The boy sat quietly in his seat, staring out the window. He reminded Brody so much of himself at that age; the similarities almost frightened him.

Tyler was a quiet boy but also a deep thinker. He'd never been one to rush a decision or fly by the seat of his pants. Even selecting a candy bar at the store took him longer than a typical person. Those qualities ran strong in Brody. Take his divorce, for example. It had taken him over a year to decide he'd wanted to end his marriage.

All the time he'd been spending at work was having a negative effect on their relationship. Was that why Brody always felt a strange void between them? He hoped to God his only child didn't resent him. Living with the knowledge that Kelly had resented him all those years was bad enough. He'd moved her far away from her family, to a town she'd never been to, and in return he'd drowned himself in work and hadn't been a good enough husband. She'd given up a lot for him so he could work, and he'd been emotionally distant.

Brody eased off the brake when the light turned green. He glanced at Tyler again. "What did you do at school today?" *Is that the best you can come up with? Why don't you ask him about the weather next time?*

Tyler's gaze remained fixed out the window. "The same thing we always do, Dad."

O-kay. And what was that? Was it the same things Brody used to do as a kid? How did he not know this stuff? He suppressed a sigh. "Can you be more specific? Did you learn anything new?"

Tyler shifted his legs in the seat. "We learned about

more fractions. Those are so boring and I'll probably never use them."

Ain't that the truth? Tyler clammed up after that and returned his attention to the window. Brody steered his truck through the town and toward his neighborhood.

After the divorce, Brody gave Kelly the house, and he moved to a newer one in a nearby neighborhood. They wanted to stay close to each other for Tyler's sake. It had been imperative for them to keep things as normal as possible. Then Kelly married Colin, who moved into the house Brody had once lived in. Tyler spent the majority of his time in the house he grew up in, with the exception of every other weekend with Brody. He hadn't wanted to take every single weekend away from Kelly, so the two of them agreed to two weekends a month.

Even with that, seeing his son only four days a month was hardly satisfying. The boy's absence during the week had carved a gaping hole inside Brody's chest that nothing else could fill. The weekends they had together went by far too fast for Brody's liking. Sunday nights always ended with an empty house and an even emptier heart.

He turned the truck into his neighborhood. "So you really enjoyed taking those pictures today? You did a great job with them."

"Thanks," the boy muttered. "I miss Mom. I wish she was coming back soon."

Kelly had only been gone for a week, and Tyler was already asking for her. Brody didn't want to know the answer to whether Tyler asked for him after a week too.

*Why is this hitting me now? You'd think four years would be enough time to get used to this.*

"To be honest, buddy, she's taking care of a lot right

now, and I'm not sure exactly when she'll be back. And we're having fun, right?"

Tyler turned in his seat to face Brody. "Yeah, sure, Dad. But can we go back to the park this weekend? To take more pictures?"

The question threw Brody off guard. Well, he'd watch paint dry if it meant spending uninterrupted time with Tyler. "I don't have a sophisticated camera like Elisa does." He glanced at Tyler. "But I suppose we can make do."

Tyler grinned. "Maybe Elisa can come with us. She's really good at taking pictures. And she has a cool camera."

That wasn't the only reason that Brody got so excited. He'd take any excuse to be near her, smell her, hear her soft voice. He turned the truck onto the driveway, cut the engine, and faced his son. "You like Elisa, don't you?"

Tyler nodded. "She's really nice. And she has pictures of herself in her house. She's wearing a funny-looking dress in one of them. She told me the dress was uncomfortable but she looks pretty in it."

That was just about the strangest thing Brody had ever heard. Why would Elisa have pictures of herself? "What kind of pictures?" he asked.

The boy shrugged both his shoulders. "I dunno. She's wearing a bathing suit in one of them and has sand all over her skin."

Brody just about went into apoplectic shock at the image his brain generated. Hmm, pictures with a funny-looking dress and swimsuit with sand all over her? Something told Brody there was a lot more to Senorita Cardoso than he originally thought.

"Where's Mongolia?" Tyler asked.

Brody blinked at his son. "Mongolia? Did you learn about it in school?"

"No. Elisa was helping me with some geography home-work and she was showing me all the countries she's been to. Then she said she's going to Mongolia. But I couldn't find it on my map."

Mongolia? Surely Tyler heard her wrong. "Do you mean she went to Mongolia in the past?"

Tyler shook his head, adamant he had the correct infor-mation. "No, she said she's going there in a few months to take pictures. She said she'll be gone a long time and that she might have to sell her house."

What the hell? True, the two of them had just met, but he'd already started to feel things for Elisa he hadn't felt for other women before. Unless he was completely on another planet, he was pretty sure she felt the same things for him. When he'd kissed her the other day, she'd definitely reacted. Traveling to the other side of the planet for a considerable amount of time seemed like a pretty important piece of information.

Why hadn't she said anything? Just the other day they'd spent a good amount of time discussing her career and what she had hoped for her future. Had Brody completely misread the signals from her?

# SEVEN

"YOU NEED A HAIRCUT, HENRY Cavill."

Courtney Devlin, Brody's outspoken and vivacious stepsister and Carol's daughter, walked through the doors of the Golden Glove with a purposeful stride and yet another wild shade of hair. Normally she kept her hair short, probably because she didn't want to bother styling it. Or she thought the cuts were edgy. Knowing his sister, it was the latter.

Today she'd changed things up by adding some kind of extensions that had some weird fading going on. The top of her head was almost black, then slowly transitioned to hot pink. Personally Brody thought it looked like she'd dipped the ends of her hair in a pitcher of Kool-Aid.

"I've asked you before not to call me that," he warned her as her gaze continued to scrutinize his locks. The two-tone princess was really going to criticize his style?

Courtney elbowed her friend Rebecca, who'd accompanied his sister into the restaurant. Although Rebecca had yet to look up from her phone, where she'd been texting...or something.

"Don't you think Brody looks like him?" she asked her friend.

"I don't even know who that is," Rebecca said without looking up from her cell.

Court rolled her eyes. "Hello? *Man of Steel*?" She tossed a look between him and Rebecca. "*The Tudors*?"

Rebecca shook her head, sending her red curls flying. "Nah, I got nothin'."

"You're both lame." Court took her patchwork-quilt sling-style purse off her shoulder and set it on the bar top. Lately she'd been going through some weird hippie phase, and Brody could only guess she was having some kind of identity crisis.

"Who the hell are the Tudors?" RJ, who'd been coming in lately to fill in for Anthony, strolled behind the bar with a long-legged stride that was more lazy than slow. Courtney's older brother had an affinity for ripped jeans, borderline-inappropriate T-shirts, and old cars.

Oh, and Rebecca. Although that wasn't really an affinity. More like a love/hate/drive-each-other-crazy...thing.

Over the years, Brody had never been sure if RJ had wanted to kiss the hell out of the redhead or wring her neck. At the same time, he wasn't sure if Rebecca would protest the former.

At RJ's appearance, Rebecca stopped her texting and glanced up. She moistened her lips and followed his movements behind the bar, her shoulders stiffening noticeably. Brody's stepbrother fixed his gaze on her for a brief moment but didn't say anything. Probably for the best. RJ had an odd sense of humor that often turned sweet Rebecca into...well, not sweet.

Courtney shot her brother a narrowed-eyed look. "I wouldn't expect someone like you to know what that is."

One of RJ's blond brows shot up his forehead. He withdrew a protein bar from the back pocket of his jeans. With slow movements, he peeled the wrapper open then ate practically half the bar in one bite. "You mean someone with a life?" he asked after swallowing.

"That's debatable," Courtney countered. "Why are you even here? Don't you have, like, grease to get your hands in?"

RJ chewed and looked back at his sister. "Helping a brother out," he responded with a nod toward Brody. "Because I'm a nice guy like that."

Rebecca, who'd otherwise remained silent, which was odd in RJ's presence, snorted. The sound had RJ drilling his blue gaze into her. A muscle in his jaw ticked, then one corner of his mouth kicked up.

Sick bastard.

Courtney grinned, because she always got shits and giggles out of RJ and Rebecca's relationship. "This one disagrees with you."

RJ finished off the protein bar, chewed, and swallowed. "She's biased."

"That's not what I'd call it," Courtney countered.

His brother crossed his arms over his chest and leaned back against the wall, as though having the time of his life. In all honesty, Brody wouldn't be surprised if that was the case.

Yeah, definitely a sick bastard.

"Why don't we hear what Rebecca calls it?" RJ wanted to know.

Rebecca, who'd done an outstanding job of otherwise ignoring RJ's presence, which wasn't an easy thing to do, slid her phone into the back pocket of her jeans. She focused her attention on him and went several seconds without blinking.

Uh, yeah. They were having some kind of weird staring contest that made Brody feel like he needed to give them privacy.

"You don't want to hear what I'd call it," she finally said in that soft voice of hers. Then she turned her attention to Courtney. "Can we go now?"

"I haven't even gotten to the reason for my visit yet," she argued.

Brody heaved a sigh and counted to ten. He loved his sister to death, but, man, she could be taxing. "Please get to it then. I have work to do."

"All right, already." She sucked in a deep breath, and blew it out. "I need a job."

"What?" RJ tossed out.

"But you have a job," Brody reminded her, while ignoring his brother.

"Yeah, but it's not exactly paying the bills. Plus my mom's all up in my biz."

RJ lifted his shoulders, then let them fall. "So tell her to back off."

Court shot her brother a droll look. One she'd perfected by the age of ten. "What a great idea. Why didn't I think of that?"

Brody slugged his brother in the shoulder. "Stop talking."

"I've tried that tactic before," Rebecca said. "It doesn't work."

"Ooh, she burned you," Courtney remarked with a sly grin.

Someone just kill him now and put him out of his misery. Brody pinched the bridge of his nose. "What kind of job are you looking for?" he asked in an attempt to steer the conversation back on track. If one could even call it that.

"Anything," his sister answered. "I'll clean toilets if I have to."

RJ tossed his head back and howled with laughter. "I'd actually pay money to see that."

"Pay it to me then, because I seriously need some cash," Courtney urged.

Brody stepped forward and ignored the banter between brother and sister. Honestly, those two were worse than bickering toddlers. "Court, I can't hire you."

She slapped her hand on the bar top. "Why not? And don't tell me you can't hire family when you've got this guy here." She finished her demand with jabbing her finger toward RJ.

Brody shook his head. "It's not that. The restaurant's struggling right now, and we're having to cut back on hours and let go of a few employees. Besides, RJ's not being paid."

"See, I really *am* a nice guy," RJ said with a lifted brow toward Rebecca.

She ignored him. Smart girl.

"You're only here because the women fall all over you like you're freakin' Chris Hemsworth," Courtney shot out.

Rebecca shook her head. "Where do you come up with these names?"

"You *have* to know who he is!" Courtney argued with a hand waving in the air.

RJ shook his head and pushed away from the wall. "I can't take any more of this nonsense."

Courtney shot furious glares at her brother's backside as he ambled away from them. Lucky bastard.

"Okay," she said to Brody. "There isn't anything you can pay me to do? I'll take minimum wage if I have to."

Ah, shit, she was doing the lip-biting bargaining thing. Courtney may have been able to bring on the drama that would knock Sally Field on her ass, but, man, she could yank sympathy like nobody's business. Must have been a special talent of hers.

"Court," he said on a sigh, because he really wanted to help her. He just couldn't. "I'm sorry, but I can't. Do you have any idea what Dad would say if he found out I hired you?" He held up a hand when she opened her mouth to argue. "And it's nothing personal against you. It has nothing to do with whether or not I think you're responsible, because I do." He had to throw that little disclaimer in there because he knew her too well. "It's just a matter of economics."

When the defeat finally hit her, which was never an easy thing with Courtney Devlin, her shoulders slumped and her eyes dropped closed. And, yeah, he felt bad. Like just-kicked-a-puppy bad. A crippled puppy.

She picked up her purse and slung it across her torso. "Fine," she said on a low voice. "But if you find my lifeless body because I died of starvation, I'm going to say I told you so."

He narrowed his eyes at her. "That doesn't really make any sense."

"And now you just killed my punch line. Thanks for kicking me while I'm down."

Until now, Brody never thought it was possible to look sexy in a pair of torn sweatpants and a threadbare T-shirt with a suspicious green stain. The pants practically swallowed Elisa's slim waist and incredibly long legs. Not every woman could throw on such a mismatching, homey outfit and look good enough to lick. Elisa pulled it off with effortless ease. He had visions of her long, swinging ponytail tickling his chest as she straddled his hips and leaned down for a kiss. Hell, he'd had dozens of visions about her, and half of them were a lot more X-rated than that. The sad thing was that his brain could no longer filter them out at the appropriate times.

Earlier today, he'd been distracted from the payroll because the numbers on the checks had turned into erotic fantasies, one of which involved her licking chocolate off his chest. What kind of man had fantasies like that?

The kind that was half in love with a woman he'd just met. Brody didn't make a habit of falling for women he'd known for less than two weeks. Even Kelly hadn't captured his heart that fast. The final nail in his coffin was how she treated his son. Tyler was a mama's boy who missed his mother like nobody's business. The occasional hand on the shoulder or the affectionate hug Elisa gave him was a good temporary replacement for the motherly love Tyler needed, and Brody was grateful for that.

The good thing was that she offered a distraction to a shitty end of his shitty day. Another disagreement with his father had created a massive storm cloud over his head. The thing had followed him from work and had damn near forced him into a serious case of road rage.

Not to mention the cloud of guilt he'd been carrying around for having to turn his sister away empty-handed. It killed him, knowing she was struggling and thinking she could turn to family for help. Not being able to offer that help had made him feel like his hands were tied behind his back. Maybe he could pay her out of his own pocket. Even though Court was his stepsister, because her mother was married to his father, he loved her like she was his blood. As well as RJ. The two of them had come to the

McDermott family, and may have carried a different last name, but they'd fit in like they'd been born McDermotts.

He rang the bell, and after allowing him in the front door, almost an hour later than he'd been last night, Elisa led him into the house.

"Where's Tyler?" he asked after seeing an empty kitchen and living room.

Elisa straightened some papers on the table. "He's in my office using the computer. He's got a history project due tomorrow and needed to get it typed."

Brody glanced at Tyler's school stuff. "He didn't mention anything about a project." It wasn't like his son to leave such a thing to the last minute and not even bring it up.

Elisa's mouth turned up in an amused grin. "I think he waited until the last minute because he didn't want to do it. I tried to help him as best I could, but I don't really know my history."

"You and me both," Brody replied. "His mother was always good at research. She usually handles this kind of thing."

"He mentioned that," Elisa said as she threw some trash in the garbage.

His eyes followed her graceful movements around the room. The gentle sway of her hips and high, swinging ponytail had his tongue sticking to the roof of his mouth. "What else did he say?"

She glanced at him and paused before answering. "Nothing much."

"No, that's not all." He came around the table and walked toward her. "What else did he say?"

Her full, kissable lips pursed together. "He just said he misses his mother."

Kelly and Tyler had had an hour-long conversation last night before bedtime. Tyler told her about staying with Elisa, taking pictures, and getting a B+ on his vocabulary test. If Brody hadn't overheard the conversation, he wouldn't have known about the test.

"You look like you could use a drink," Elisa said, pulling Brody out of his brooding thoughts. Did he look as bad on the outside as he felt on the inside? As if he'd been through the gauntlet of relentless fatigue and stress? Apparently so. If things didn't turn around soon, his ass could be grass. In other words, Brody's future was hinging on Anthony's ability to bring customers back.

"Will white wine do?" she asked after he failed to answer her first question. Drinking wine, alone with Elisa when she turned him on more than he even thought possible? Why the hell not?

Under normal circumstances, Brody wouldn't be caught dead with white wine. His brother Chase always called it a girly drink no man should ever touch. Considering it was all Elisa had, though, Brody accepted the glass and followed her to the couch. They sat down next to each other and sipped their drinks for several quiet moments. Elisa curled her long, fantasy-worthy legs under her and cradled her glass in her feminine little hands. Deep brown eyes gazed at him from underneath thick black lashes. Something about the way she looked at him made him feel vulnerable and exposed, like she wanted to know his deepest, darkest fears. If she knew those, she'd run screaming for the hills.

He glanced around the room and his eyes landed on papers on the coffee table. One set of papers were photos. The other set was a sizable stack, and the paper on top had the word "Mongolia" on it. Suddenly, Tyler's announcement from the other night came back to him.

Brody jerked his head toward the papers. "Seems you have plans to do some globetrotting."

Elisa lifted her glass to her lips but paused before taking a sip. Her gaze darted to the papers. "Yeah, I was offered this amazing opportunity to travel to Mongolia and take photos for *Time Magazine*. The piece covers nomadic shepherds." She waved a hand in the air. "But it's still a long way off. In fact, I haven't totally decided on whether or not to go."

He studied her for a moment, trying to ignore how luminous her skin looked, and focused on the wistful look on her face when she talked about the opportunity.

"Tyler told me you said you were going." And why did that bother him? Why did the idea of her leaving and going so far away create a pain in his chest? He should be happy for her. Just the other day she'd admitted how much she desired this very thing.

She tugged on her earlobe. "To be honest, I've gone back and forth. If I go, I'd be gone for about five months. I'd most likely have to sell this house and..." Her words trailed off, and Brody suspected there was more.

"And what?" he pressed.

Her teeth worried her lower lip. "And then there's the question of whether to come back at all."

He stared at her, unsure of what to say, because the thought of Elisa leaving for good was like someone carving out his stomach with a spoon. Hell, he'd only known her for a short time, but he'd already developed a connection with her. A part of him had been hoping for something more than what they currently had. Even though Brody didn't think himself capable of more, a part of him wanted to try.

He took a sip of his wine and tried not to let the

disappointment show in his voice. "When you say 'not come back,' do you mean staying in Mongolia?"

She pursed her lips. "Not specifically Mongolia. But how can I be serious about having a kind of career that I want from Wyoming? The most successful photographers travel constantly."

"And that's what you want? To travel?"

Her delicate shoulders lifted in a shrug. "I think so, yes."

"Are those the photos from the other day?" He changed the subject because the conversation was depressing him. After his disagreement with his father, Brody needed something harmless to concentrate on.

She glanced at the coffee table where several sheets of pictures lay. "Yeah. Do you want to see them?"

Did he have to answer that honestly? What he wanted to do was take her hair down, peel those hundred-year-old sweats down her lean hips, and lose himself inside her. Probably best not to make her think he was some obsessive psychotic. "Sure," he said in a gruff voice.

She set her wineglass on the table and picked up one of the sheets. "They came out way better than the last ones. Anthony's plating is so much simpler than Travis's was, but it works. In fact, they make for better photos."

They were better? Brody couldn't tell anything past how good she smelled. The woman was going to send him comatose. He gulped his wine down faster than he should have, and some got caught in his throat. He coughed to force the liquid down.

"Are you okay?" she asked after replacing the sheet on the table.

"I'm fine. It just went down the wrong pipe." That was nice and plausible and made him sound less pathetic.

"You've had a tough day, haven't you?" Concern had her brows lowering over her eyes.

Tough day? Most people who had days like his went to bars and got shitfaced. In his youth, he would have. Now he had no choice but to leave his work at work so he wouldn't come home grumbling like an ogre. His father had a way of sucking the humanity out of Brody. Going back and forth with him over whether or not Anthony was capable of handling the kitchen had done Brody in.

"Do you want to tell me about it?" Elisa asked when Brody still failed to speak like a normal person.

He gazed into her worried eyes and found himself spilling his guts. "I told my father about putting Anthony in the kitchen and he's not happy."

"Maybe he's just concerned about his business and doesn't know how else to handle it."

"I know he doesn't know how. That's why he's been there all the time. He doesn't know what else to do. On the outside he acts tough, but on the inside he's worried."

Elisa looked at him over the rim of her glass. She took a shallow sip before speaking. "And he's projecting that onto you, right? Are you still worried about losing your job?"

Sharing his fears and concerns had never been comfortable for Brody. In that way he was more like his old man than his two brothers. But, sitting next to Elisa, sharing wine, he found himself in unfamiliar territory. Strangely enough, Elisa took the uncertainty away, just by talking to him. And she was leaving in a few months.

"Oh, yeah," he admitted. "In fact, he told me that if Anthony doesn't work out I'll find myself without a job."

"So, he's still serious about letting you go," she stated. "I'll do what I can with the pictures, and the next photo shoot should be better. But I feel like I should be doing more."

Brody glanced at her. Her knees were pulled to her chest, her chin resting on top of them. Her olive skin had a healthy glow like she'd spent the day in the sun. Had he ever laid eyes on a more beautiful woman?

"You've already done a lot. In fact, just talking about it has helped." Shit, his life had become such a mess. He'd been irresponsible and gotten his college girlfriend pregnant. Then he couldn't hold his family together, and now the business was on a rapid slide down the tubes. His father had never said as much, but Brody had the feeling the old man placed the majority of the blame on him. And he deserved it. Somewhere along the way, he'd lost himself and other things in the process, his son being one of them. As long as he was still Tyler's hero, nothing else mattered. Even though he felt far from anyone's hero.

"You don't want to talk about this, do you?" Elisa asked in a soft voice. "It's okay if you don't."

How did the woman read him so well? Kelly had always complained that Brody had been a closed book and she never had any idea of what went on inside his head. The lack of communication had been the ultimate downfall of their marriage. One of the last things she'd said to him as his wife had been "If you don't learn to open up, you're going to end up alone."

Elisa got him. He had no clue how, and a part of him wasn't entirely comfortable with it. But somehow she *knew*, like she had some extrasensory radar.

"Are those your parents?" he asked when his attention landed on a photograph of two forty-something people.

Elisa glanced at the picture. "Yeah."

"Do they live close by?"

Her attention shifted back to him. "They died in a plane crash."

"I'm sorry." Didn't he feel like the asshole? "I know what it's like to lose a parent. How old were you?"

Elisa sipped her wine and waited. "Eighteen," she finally admitted.

He studied her and noted the way her eyes had clouded over. Damn, he hadn't meant to suck the light out of them. "You were close with them, weren't you?"

"Yeah, they were..." She nibbled her lower lip. "They were really good parents. My dad was gone a lot, but when he was home, he was very attentive."

"What did he do that made him travel a lot?"

"He was a freelance reporter." Elisa tucked her legs beneath her. "He used to get job offers all over the world. The traveling was his favorite part. I mean, he hated being away from his family, but at the same time he craved the adventure of going to places or situations most people didn't want to go."

"And your mother was a reporter also? Is that why they were both gone?"

"Sort of. She started off in a Dallas news station, basically at the bottom of the tier covering things like a high school championship football game. But over the years, she'd slowly worked her way up, and eventually she was offered an opportunity to cover riots that had broken out in Sao Paulo. That's how she met my dad."

"So, how did they end up back in the States?"

Elisa pulled a sip of wine. "Well, my mom loved Brazil so much that she decided to relocate there. She learned Portuguese and took a job at a local TV station. A few years later she had me and quit her job, but with Dad traveling all the time, my mother got lonely. She had no family around and not many friends. So, my dad agreed to move my mom back to Dallas. Since he was freelance, the move was easy for him.

"Anyway, Mom still liked to travel so she would sometimes go with my dad when he'd go on an assignment."

"And that's why they were on an airplane," he guessed.

Elisa nodded and stared down into her wineglass. "Yeah. They were on a twin-engine commuter plane in Panama."

Brody tried to imagine losing both parents so suddenly and in such a tragic way. To have them there one day and gone the next. Not having a chance to say good-bye or prepare for their passing. "That must have been hard" was all he could think to say.

Her lashes lowered and she gazed into her wine before responding. "It was one of the hardest things I've ever been through."

He tilted his head and looked at her for a moment. The death of her parents had scarred her. That much was painfully obvious just by the tone of her voice and the look in her eyes when she glanced at their picture. They'd been close, and she'd just been a kid when they'd been taken from her. This was another layer of Senorita Cardoso being peeled back for him to examine.

"How did you manage on your own after they died?"

She lifted her eyes to his and ran her tongue over her bottom lip. "It wasn't easy. My parents didn't leave us with much. But I was lucky enough to land a modeling contract that paid for the rest of my college tuition."

Modeling? He knew it. She was tall enough, beautiful and ethereal enough to be good at it. "That's what Tyler meant about the pictures," he said more to himself than her.

"Pictures?" she asked.

He stretched his arm along the back of the couch and his fingers came within millimeters of touching her hair. "He said one day that you had pictures of yourself around your house. I wasn't sure what he meant."

A slow, sweet smile broke across her face. "Oh, my covers." Her cheeks turned a beautiful shade of pink. "I can't believe he mentioned that."

If it was possible, she was even more gorgeous when she blushed. The color in her cheeks made him want to trail the tip of his index finger across her face. Would she allow him to touch her again? Would she blush even more?

"Being on the cover of a magazine is quite an accomplishment. You shouldn't be embarrassed about that."

Her teeth stabbed into her lower lip. "It's not that I'm embarrassed. It's just...I was never totally comfortable with the attention I got as a model. I was good at it, but I didn't love it. That's why I quit and turned to photography. I'd much rather be behind the camera than in front of it."

Most women would have walked around with their nose in the air and a you-can't-touch-me attitude. He'd been around a few women like that in his life. Their attitude alone made him turn the other direction. Elisa's humility was an endearing trait. She'd lost her parents at a young age but she'd made the best of her situation by taking care of herself. Brody wished he had half her courage.

He lost his will and trailed his finger over a chunk of her hair. It really was as soft as it looked. Touching the weightless strands had more of an effect on him than when he'd touched other women in his life. Something about this one had him tied up in knots. She had a strange magnetic pull over him he was powerless to resist.

He set his wineglass, then hers on the table so there were no hindrances between them.

"Brody," she said on a half sigh, half moan when his hand went farther into her hair.

"What is it about you that makes me feel this way?" he murmured.

"Like what?"

He trailed his finger down the column of her neck. "Not like myself. Like I'm having an out-of-body experience."

Her lips quirked. "I'm not sure if I should feel flattered or insulted."

"Trust me, there's no insult in that. I'm just not sure how to handle what I'm feeling."

She sat perfectly still while he continued his feather-like caress. "And what's that?"

He just barely grazed her lower lip with the tip of his finger. "I don't know. That's what scares me."

"If you're scared then I'm petrified."

Her tongue darted out and caught his finger. The cool moisture sent waves of fire through his blood. He had a sudden, animalistic urge to flip her beneath him on the couch and strip them both of their clothes. She had the sort of body a man could get lost in. All that softness and those curves had the potential to turn him into a babbling idiot. Hell, he was halfway there and they were still clothed.

"Dad?"

The voice came from behind Brody and had Elisa pulling away from him. He dropped his hand from Elisa's mouth and stood up from the couch.

"Hey, buddy," he said when Tyler stood in the kitchen, staring at Brody and Elisa. "Did you get your report finished?"

"Yeah. Can we go home and call Mom?"

Brody wanted to spend a little time with his son, talking about his day at school, before getting on the phone with Kelly. "Why don't we go get some dinner first?"

"Elisa made me a sandwich, so I'm not that hungry."

He glanced at Elisa, whose attention volleyed back and forth between him and Tyler. "It was just a grilled cheese," she said.

"Thanks for doing that. I really didn't mean to be late. With the state the restaurant is in, it's hard for me to get away on time." Every moment not spent with Tyler was like a rusty knife in his gut. The boy deserved every second of his undivided attention. Sometimes he felt like he needed to split himself a dozen different ways to please everyone in his life. In the past, Tyler had always come first. Lately Brody had been slacking in that department and needed to change it.

Elisa stood from the couch and walked them to the door. "You weren't that late. Besides, Tyler had plenty to keep him busy. Didn't you?" she asked as she placed a hand on the boy's shoulder.

Tyler wrapped his gangly arms around Elisa's midsection. "Thanks for all the help. And thanks for letting me use your computer."

Brody's heart clenched as Tyler held on a moment longer before letting Elisa go. He wanted to repeat Tyler's actions with a hug of his own but settled for a light touch to her cheek. Like the night before, Brody grazed her soft cheek with one knuckle. "I'll see you next week for the shoot."

"Do you think Anthony's ready for that?"

"I've been working with him in the mornings before we open, and he's learning from Vic and Stanley. And I honestly don't think throwing together some dishes for a camera will be a problem for him."

Elisa nodded. "Okay. When should I be there?"

"Tuesday. Seven-thirty a.m." Then Brody and Tyler left her standing in the front doorway.

# EIGHT

"WILL LILY BE THERE? WILL LACY be able to get out of bed when we get there?" Tyler continued to pepper Brody with questions as he drove toward Chase's house. First he wanted to know if Mason would be napping, then he wanted to know if his uncle Chase would be there. This was the chattiest Tyler had been in several months, and Brody planned to take advantage.

"I'm pretty sure Lily will be there. But Lacy can't get out of bed. You know that." He tossed Tyler a glance. The boy had lost interest in his handheld gaming system, which now lay on the floor by Tyler's black-and-white Nikes.

Lacy was just six weeks shy of her due date and had been restricted to bed rest since her second trimester. Chase told Brody this was a common thing among women who carried twins. He'd also told Brody that Lacy had not been shy about her distaste for lying on her backside twenty-four hours a day.

Her hobby of selling her sketches had just started to take off in the past year. Unfortunately, she hadn't been able to draw as much as she'd like thanks to severe morning sickness and fatigue.

Chase and Lacy's house came into view and Brody turned his truck onto the driveway. The vehicle hadn't even come to a complete stop when Tyler threw the door open and ran into the house. When Brody ambled through the door a moment later, Tyler already had nineteen-month-old Mason in his lap. Two-and-a-half-year-old Lily bounced up and down on the living room floor, her dark curls springing in perfect synchronization to some musical cartoon. Avery walked out of the kitchen with a sippy cup in one hand and a package of crackers in the other.

Her friendly eyes lit up when she saw him. "I thought I heard someone come through the door. What're you two doing here? I thought you normally worked on Saturdays?" Avery's hair had darkened slightly over the past few years and brushed the edges of her jawbone. The cut suited her perfectly, practical yet sophisticated.

"Every other Saturday, but Kelly had to go out of town for a little while so I'm taking the weekends off until she gets back." Brody followed Avery into the living room. Lily still hopped up and down on two feet with boundless energy two-year-olds were so famous for. Mason had left Tyler's lap and directed his attention to the cartoon. "Looks like you've got your hands full."

"They're really good at entertaining themselves. Except when Lily is having a terrible-two moment or Mason won't take his nap, like he's supposed to be doing right now."

The tow-headed mini-version of Chase tried to mimic Lily's bouncing but was much less coordinated on his stubby legs. Tyler picked up a toy football and tossed it in Mason's direction, hoping to snag the toddler's interest. Mason spared the ball a quick glance before returning his attention to the television.

"I came by to see Lacy. How's she doing?"

Avery handed the cup to Mason and the crackers to Lily. "She took about a two-hour nap this morning. I think she's drawing right now." An amused grin lit up Avery's face. "I feel so bad for her. I know she's dying to get out of that bed. And I know it's killing her not being able to take care of Mason."

Brody settled on the ottoman in front of the couch. "I'm sure she appreciates all you're doing, though."

Avery glanced at the children. "It's the least I could do. Besides, I know she'd do the same for me."

The two women had hit it off as sisters-in-law. Lily had only been about a year old when Mason had been born, and the two children had fast become good playmates. Then Lacy got pregnant with twins on hers and Chase's belated honeymoon, and Avery selflessly offered to help out with Mason while Chase was at work.

Mason let out an ear-piercing squeal when Lily took the toy football right out of his hands. Big, fat tears rolled down the boy's face. Avery dropped to her knees in front of her daughter. "We talked about how to play nice, remember, Lily? Mason had the ball first and you need to wait your turn. And we ask; we don't just take." She turned Lily to face her bawling cousin. "Now give the ball back to Mason like a good girl."

Mason reached his chubby little fingers out to swipe the ball from Lily's grasp. The two-year-old held the ball just out of Mason's reach and stuck her bottom lip out. Mason's white-blond eyebrows tugged together in a thunderous scowl. He stomped his feet and tried once again to get the ball back.

"Lily," Avery commanded in a firm voice. "If I have to start counting, you're going to lose a sticker on your chart today. You know what happens when you lose all your stickers."

Lily dropped the ball on the carpet and walked to the couch so she could bury her face in the cushions. She sobbed like her poor little heart had been broken in two from having to give up a ball neither of the kids had been interested in a moment ago. Brody chuckled when Avery rolled her eyes.

"Maybe Noah and I won't be having more kids after all."

"Why are they so cranky?" Tyler asked Avery.

Avery glanced at her daughter, who still had her head buried in the couch. "They haven't had their naps today. Lily thinks she's too old and I can't get her to lie down anymore. Mason screamed for twenty minutes before I got him up."

Brody's gaze followed Tyler as the boy wandered into the kitchen for something to eat. "That must have been rough, dealing with two cranky kids."

Avery lifted one shoulder in an elegant shrug. She pulled Lily into her lap when the girl finally calmed down. "I can handle it. My main concern is keeping the peace for Lacy. After the twins come she won't have time to lie around anymore."

"Something tells me Lacy will welcome it." Brody left Avery to the two kids while he walked down the hallway to see Lacy. His sister-in-law was propped against the wooden headboard with a sketch pad resting on her enormous belly. The pencil in her hand flew over the paper as she drew whatever image was in her mind.

As teenagers they'd been close friends and had developed a brother-sister bond. Being gone from Trouble for college hadn't weakened their bond one bit. After Lacy had returned to Trouble several years ago, the two of them had instantly reconnected. Lacy understood him probably better than anyone else and was the only person who saw through him. At first, he'd been taken aback when he learned of her relationship with his brother Chase. But he'd gotten over that quickly and had nothing but happiness for them when they'd married a year and a half ago, after Mason had already been born.

"Hey, kiddo," he said when he walked through the bedroom door.

Her eyes lifted to his and an ear-to-ear grin broke across her face. "It's about time you came to see me. What was all that screaming about?"

He sat next to her on the edge of the bed. "Just a domestic dispute between two cousins. How're you holding up?"

She set her sketch pad aside. "Let's see, I feel like a beached whale, I don't sleep worth a damn, and I have never-ending heartburn. Other than that, I feel great."

He flicked the tip of her nose. "You're such a ray of sunshine."

Her grin widened. "I know."

"Maybe you should go on birth control." The twins she carried had been a surprise, along with their older brother Mason.

"I was on birth control when I got pregnant with the twins. It didn't work." She picked at the balls of lint on the ancient blanket covering her belly. "I blame your brother completely."

Such was the way with women. This was what Brody needed to keep his mind off Elisa: a little dose of a cranky pregnant woman.

"I feel bad that Avery has to sit here day after day dealing with my cantankerous son."

"I don't think she minds."

Lacy shifted her position on the bed and rested both her hands on top of her belly. "I know, but she's giving up so many hours at the youth center to help me out. I honestly don't know what I would do without her."

Brody smiled to reassure Lacy. "I guess it's lucky for you she's on a volunteer basis. Avery says the kids keep each other entertained."

The mother-to-be sighed. "I'll be glad when this one's over. I am not having any more kids for a while."

He tugged on a strand of her long hair. "That's what you said after Mason was born. I give you six months before you're pregnant again."

She slapped his hand away. "No way. I had good intentions though."

He lifted a brow. "So did I. Good intentions only get you so far."

"Not everything is your fault, Brody." She placed a comforting hand on his arm. "You did what you could."

Doing everything he could hadn't been enough. He hadn't been able to keep his family together, and he was struggling to keep the restaurant afloat.

"What's eating you?" Lacy asked him.

"What do you mean?" Were all the past weeks of stress and sleepless nights starting to show on the outside?

"Something's on your mind." When he didn't answer her, she pressed on. "Chase said things at the restaurant aren't going well."

"Actually I think they're taking a turn for the better. We filled more than half our tables last night." They hadn't had that many diners in more than two months. Brody only hoped it was a sign things would get better. He filled Lacy in on what Chase hadn't already told her, about promoting Anthony and the disagreement with his father. "Now I just don't know how to spread the word about the new menu. I can't seem to get another reviewer in there."

Lacy leaned her head back against the headboard. "You know, Avery mentioned earlier that she's organizing a fundraiser for their summer camps. She said she's been having a hard time finding a caterer."

He studied his sister-in-law for a moment. "Are you saying you think we should cater for the youth center?"

She shrugged one shoulder beneath her old shirt. "Their fundraisers are always a pretty big deal. The last one I went to had half the town there. It could be a good way to spread the word about the new food."

He considered the option for a moment. The youth center where Avery volunteered was the only one in town and generally got a lot of recognition and donations from people. And Lacy was right; its fundraisers usually had a pretty good turnout. If the Golden Glove provided the food for one of those all-day events, they could potentially make a favorable impression on half the town. He'd have to convince Avery, then pitch the idea to his father.

"That's not a bad idea," he told Lacy.

She rubbed her belly like it was a Buddha statue. "See? I am good for something other than birthing children."

"Dad, look at Mason." Brody walked back into the living room just as Tyler gestured toward the couch and then disappeared in the kitchen again. Chase and Lacy's hell-raiser son had crawled onto the couch and passed out cold, with one chubby leg hanging off the edge. The corner of Brody's mouth turned up at the sight that reminded him so much of Tyler at that age.

"Knocked himself out, did he?" Brody asked.

"Just as I knew he would." Avery perched on the edge of the couch and ran a hand through Mason's baby-fine hair. "He's a sweet boy."

Brody stood in the middle of the living room and studied Avery as she stroked the boy's hair. She was so patient and natural with kids. The dispute between Lily and Mason could easily have escalated to full-blown tantrums. She'd diffused the situation as though she hadn't given the problem a second thought.

"When are you and my brother going to be adding to your family?"

Avery kept her attention on the sleeping toddler. "Whenever nature decides to bless us with another."

Brody's eyebrows shot up his forehead. "So you're trying to have another one right now?"

She dropped her hand from Mason's head and turned her gaze to Brody. "We've been trying for over a year."

A year? Couples who went that long usually sought out the help of a fertility specialist. "You and Noah aren't having trouble conceiving, are you?"

"It took me seven months to get pregnant with Lily."

Brody had no idea the two of them were having such a difficult time. "I had no idea." What a stressful and frustrating situation for anyone to go through. And now a year to have another one?

"That's because we didn't tell anyone." Avery smoothed a hand down her knee-length skirt. "Noah would absolutely kill me if he knew I was about to tell you this, but…" She inhaled a deep breath. "About six months ago I miscarried."

A piece of Brody's gut twisted at the agony his brother and Avery must have gone through. To try for so long, then have it end like that…Brody wasn't sure how to console her. He had no clue how she must have felt, how confused and desperate Avery must have been. His heart cracked open for his brother and sister-in-law. He took a step closer to her and placed a hand on her shoulder. "I'm so sorry, Avery."

Her shoulder moved underneath his hand. "I was only a few weeks along. But we'd already been trying for several months. And now six months later, we're still not having any luck. Noah thinks we should go see this fertility doctor in Casper."

"What do you think?"

She tilted her face to his. "I think if it's meant to happen, it'll happen."

He squeezed her shoulder and offered her a comforting smile. "It'll happen."

Out of nowhere, Tyler ran from the kitchen and toward the front door. "Dad, Uncle Chase is home."

The boy threw open the front door and started pummeling Chase with weak punches to the arms and midsection. Chase dropped his bag and grabbed Tyler in a headlock as he practically dragged the boy away from the front door and into the house.

"You'll never be stronger than me, kid," Chase said as Tyler struggled to remove himself from Chase's steel-like grip. Tyler wrapped his hands around Chase's forearm in a weak attempt to get free.

"You just wait. Someday I'm gonna overpower you," Tyler said in a strangled voice as his feet dangled off the floor.

Chase's grin turned evil when he dug his knuckles into the top of the boy's head. "Let me hear who your favorite uncle is, then I'll let you go."

Tyler giggled and continued to struggle. "Uncle Noah," he replied.

"That's it." Chase picked Tyler up, slung the boy over his shoulder, then dropped him onto the loveseat. Tyler bounced once then rolled onto the floor, laughing even harder than he had a moment ago.

"You're going to wake Mason up, then you'll really be sorry," Avery scolded.

Lily ran to Chase and wrapped her arms around his legs. "Dat's not nice!"

"You want some too?" Chase picked the girl up, dangled her upside down, then set her back on her feet. Lily giggled until she had tears coming out of her eyes. "How's my wife doing?" Chase asked after the children had calmed themselves down.

"Cursing you to hell and back," Brody answered.

"You mean like she does every day?"

"I'd like to see you carry two babies," Avery said as she gathered baby toys from around the room.

Chase ignored Avery's comment and kissed Mason's sweaty forehead. The boy didn't so much as twitch an eyelash. He was out cold.

"Since my work here is done, I'm going to go home and cook my husband some dinner." Avery took Lily by the hand after the girl gave everyone in the room kisses bye-bye.

"I'll walk you out," Brody said to Avery as she headed toward the front door.

He walked over to Chase and slapped his brother on the back. "Do yourself a favor and rub your wife's feet."

Chase gathered his sleeping son off the couch. "I do that every night. The woman's hormones are unpredictable."

Brody chuckled as he ushered Tyler out the door and followed Avery and Lily to their car. At six fifteen, the sun was already making its way past the horizon. A light but cool breeze tousled the leaves in the nearby trees and whipped the short strands of Avery's hair around her face.

"Mommy, ice cream," Lily demanded as Avery slid

open the side door to her minivan. Brody still had a hard time believing the woman who first drove into Trouble in a hundred-thousand-dollar car was now at the wheel of a soccer mom car. Getting married and having kids had a way of bringing a practical side out of most people.

"Not before dinner," Avery answered as she helped Lily climb in.

Tyler wandered over to Brody's truck and waited for Brody to follow. "Lacy said you're looking for a caterer for the youth center's fundraiser."

Avery glanced at Brody from over her shoulder as she buckled Lily in her car seat. "Yeah, the people we used last year went out of business, and it seems like every restaurant either doesn't cater or the food isn't good enough. I have an appointment with a caterer in Cheyenne next week, but I'm not holding out much hope."

That could be a good thing for him. "Why's that?"

After getting Lily settled, Avery turned around and looked at him. "Their online menu didn't look all that appetizing. But I don't really have much choice. I've kind of run out of options."

He waited a beat before speaking. "What if I did the catering for you?"

She stared at him for a moment, then swiped a strand of hair out of her face. "You as in the Golden Glove?"

He nodded. "Yeah."

"I thought you hated your head chef."

Anthony? Then Brody remembered that Avery probably didn't even know about Anthony. "I never hated Travis. He just wasn't good enough so my father fired him. We have someone much better than him now."

"I didn't realize the Golden Glove was also in the catering business."

"We're technically not. But we're in a bit of a jam, and I need to get the word out about our new menu and head chef. A fundraiser would be a good way to reach a large volume of people in a short amount of time."

Avery gazed at him while her teeth sunk into her lower lip. "I don't know, Brody. I know we're family and everything, but the Golden Glove doesn't have the best reputation right now. And this fundraiser is a high-profile thing. It's a luncheon, and some of the people at the youth center might object when they hear the name."

"I know," he said as he placed a hand on her shoulder. He had to get her to agree. The fundraiser might be the only way to get their momentum going again. "How about this? You come into the restaurant and sample food from our new menu. If it's terrible or you just don't think it's right, then I won't bother you about it again."

Was it sad that he was practically begging his sister-in-law? What was next, going door to door and handing out discount coupons? Avery glanced at Lily for a moment then looked at Brody again. "We can't pay you. Everything is strictly on a volunteer basis."

Brody shook his head. "I don't care about money. I just care about reaching potential customers."

More wind stirred the short strands of her hair. "I'll come by next week."

Brody was still grinning like a moron when he and Tyler climbed into his truck.

# NINE

ELISA WASN'T HUNGRY. SHE DIDN'T need a drink. So why was she driving to the Golden Glove at four in the afternoon with Tyler sitting next to her? That was a good question.

A sane woman would stay away from Brody, especially with the way he touched her. Every time he saw her, he made a point to make some sort of contact. A simple yet devastating caress along her cheek. Threading his long fingers through her hair. These things shouldn't scare her. They shouldn't worry her. They shouldn't make her lose sleep because every time she closed her eyes, she had erotic dreams of him.

Her body reacted to him despite her brain telling it not to.

Tyler's stomach had been growling since he'd walked through her front door. She'd been going stir crazy for most of the day and needed to get out of the house. That morning she'd developed the proofs from the photo shoot they'd done with Anthony. The shots had turned out so good that she'd almost broke out in song and dance to celebrate. But then she'd received a piece of disturbing news that had dampened her mood, and she needed to talk to someone about it. Funny how Brody had become that person.

Somewhere along the way, Brody had become important to her. She felt a deep connection with him she hadn't felt with anyone else, not even Marcello. She wanted to help him save the restaurant. She wanted to help him reconnect with Tyler.

When she'd first gotten the news of traveling to Mongolia, she'd been over the moon. But now, in the wake of her growing feelings for Brody, it scared her. She hadn't been lying when she told Brody about being iffy on the project. One day she thought she wanted to go, and the next doubts clouded her euphoria. What if the job turned into a one-time thing? What if she sold her house, got all the way over to Mongolia, and had no other offers on the horizon? Where would she go from there? She'd have no house to come back to.

And now there was the question of Brody. She instinctively knew she was already on a direct path of falling in love with him. Would she be able to walk away from him when the time came for her to leave? Or was she willing to give up her dream for a chance at love? But what if Brody didn't love her back? What if she gave up everything for him only to have him move on with someone else?

Samuel had told her he'd be faxing some paperwork for her to sign. Week after next, she'd have to make a final decision.

Elisa glanced at Tyler as she pulled her car in the parking lot of the Golden Glove. "Do you have a favorite dish here?" The boy had been quiet as usual.

"I usually get chicken fingers and fries. Mom and I used to come here when her and my dad were still married."

"Your mom doesn't come here anymore?"

Tyler shifted in his seat and placed a hand on the door handle as Elisa cut the car engine. "Sometimes she and Colin come."

"Does your mom ever bring you to have a meal with your dad?" Maybe that's what was missing between father and son, some quality time together.

"Not lately."

The two of them got out of the car and Elisa let the subject drop. She made sure to grab the proof sheets to show Brody. The afternoon sun beat down on them mercilessly, and with each step she took her stomach dipped lower. When had she ever been so nervous to see a man? She thought of his smoky gray eyes and how they always seemed to touch every part of her. Knots formed in her already-quivering midsection.

They approached the double doors, and Tyler opened one for her.

"What a gentleman. Thank you."

He graced her with a shy grin and walked in behind her.

Elisa glanced around her and thought for a moment she'd walked into the wrong restaurant. Almost every table was full with people enjoying meals and sharing conversations. Servers bounced from one table to the next, taking orders and refilling drinks.

"Wow, look at this place," Tyler said next to her.

"I'll say," Elisa replied. She'd never seen the Golden Glove so busy. Had word of their new good food finally reached people?

"What're you two doing here?"

Elisa just about jumped out of her sandals when Brody appeared next to them. His spicy scent surrounded her in a haze of masculinity. And did he always have to look so scrumptious?

"Tyler was hungry and I needed to get out of the house," she said while trying not to let her eyes drop below his face. "Plus, I have these." She held up the white envelope for him to see.

"I've been looking forward to seeing them," Brody replied while rubbing his hands together, then accepted the envelope from her. "And I told Anthony he could see them. Then maybe he'd be convinced about how good he really is."

"Is he still doubting himself?" How could someone with talent like Anthony's ever doubt himself? Someone needed to smack some sense into that man.

"He's getting better. Still a long way to go, though." Brody reached his arm out and wrapped his son in a bear hug. He dug his knuckles into Tyler's scalp, prompting a groan from the boy.

"Dad," Tyler complained after freeing himself.

"So, the two of you are hungry?" he asked with a smile still lighting up his handsome face.

"I'm starving," Tyler announced. "I want a hamburger."

"I think I can get one of those for you." Brody winked at Elisa, then placed his hand on her lower back and led them to an empty table. The spot where his hand lingered burned and set her whole body on alert. Zings of excitement shot through her.

Tyler scooted to the end of the booth and Brody settled next to him.

"Looks like things are taking off in here," Elisa commented after picking up her menu.

"It's certainly better numbers than we've had. But I'm not ready to count my chickens before they hatch."

Elisa glanced at him over her menu. His midnight black hair was combed to perfection and a smile played at his delicious lips. She tried to focus on her selections while he and Tyler chatted about the boy's day at school. This was the most she'd seen the two of them speak to each other. Almost from the moment of seeing the two of them together, Elisa sensed a broken connection between them, as though something had been lost. But beneath Tyler's reserved demeanor was a hero worship for Brody. Elisa felt it whenever she was around them.

The server came by and she and Tyler ordered a meal.

"Aren't you going to eat?" she asked Brody.

His mouth tilted in a devilish grin. "Anthony set me up with a good lunch."

"Dad, Elisa's taking me out to take more pictures," Tyler said.

"I told him we could go out one day next week if he wanted," she told Brody.

Brody turned his attention to Tyler. "You really like taking those pictures, huh?"

When Tyler smiled, he was the spitting image of his father. "I like the developing process the best. Watching the picture appear on the paper is really cool." The kid gasped, as though he'd just been struck by a brilliant idea, and bounced in his seat. "Hey, you could teach my dad how to do it." Tyler pinned eyes on his father. "Dad, it's so awesome. You put the paper in this chemical stuff, then use this sponge thingy and your picture just, like, appears. It's like magic."

"Magic, huh?" Brody responded with a half smile.

Elisa's heart flipped over in her chest. Stupid heart. "Tyler could teach you," she said lamely. "He'd probably be a better teacher than me."

Tyler shook his head and wiggled in the booth. "Nuh uh. You were a really good teacher to me. And you do it so much better."

Brody's clear gaze burned into hers like a couple of heat-seeking missiles. Unspoken but potent tension sizzled between the two of them. The kind of tension that could scorch the clothes right off her back. Not that she'd complain.

"I think I'd rather you teach me anyway," he said in a husky voice. Then, as though to mask the undertones of his words, he nudged his son's shoulder. "Besides, this one is a lousy teacher."

Tyler's eyes lifted to the ceiling like the preteen he was. "He's talking about the time I taught him how to play spoons. He can never beat me because I have better reflexes. But he thinks it's because I'm a bad teacher."

"It is," Brody insisted with a narrow-eyed look at the boy.

Elisa bit back a laugh. "Maybe you just can't handle losing to a kid."

Tyler nodded, but Brody turned his accusing stare toward her. Only the look he gave her wasn't the same as the one he gave his son. No, the look he'd given Tyler hadn't held all sorts of wicked promises and silent dares. But what exactly was he daring her to do? Keep pushing him? Would he push back?

"I think that's it," she said to Tyler while keeping her attention on the addictive man sitting across from her. Yeah, it was definitely fun to push him. With each push, his gaze grew darker and her breath came shorter in her lungs.

"I bet I could teach you a game or two," he practically growled.

"Such as?" she wanted to know.

Tyler looked up at his dad with a furrowed brow. "Yeah, what games to do you know?"

"More than you think," he answered.

"Okay, but games you make up don't count."

This time Elisa *did* laugh, which earned her a satisfied smile from Tyler and a thunderous look from Brody. Thunderous yet... sexy. Interesting. And fun.

"Something tells me Elisa would like my games," he muttered.

She shifted in the booth, trying to extinguish the burning in between her thighs. "Only if you let me win. I'm a sore loser."

His mouth curled up in a devious smile. "These aren't those type of games. You see, these are more about endurance and stamina. There's no stopping until everyone's finished."

Lord. Have. Mercy.

The man was sneaky and underhanded.

*Don't forget sexy. And mouthwatering.*

"I've never heard of games like that, Dad," Tyler said, completely unaware of the weird innuendos and code-talk going on.

"Oh, they're real," Brody answered just as his attention dropped down to Elisa's mouth.

How wrong and sick was it for her to be turned on in front of an eleven-year-old?

Brody's arm stretched along the back of the booth and then he ruffled Tyler's hair. "Is everything okay?" he asked Elisa when she'd been silent a moment.

No, everything wasn't okay. She was falling in love with the man sitting across from her. She was so incredibly turned on that she was about to dump her glass of water over her head. She missed her brother like crazy, and now she had a potential legal mess on her hands.

"I just found out today that an online magazine I sold

some pictures to several years ago has been illegally selling my photos to other websites and even magazines." There, she got it all out. The whole strange scenario still didn't feel real to her. She'd trusted those people, and they'd essentially been defrauding her for the past couple of years. Since letting her contract with them lapse, she'd been eating through the money she'd made during her modeling years. As it stood, she only had enough to live off for the next few months. Had they been honest with her, she could have been making extra income this entire time.

Brody's dark brows tugged together. "What do you mean 'illegally'? Like they've been doing it without your knowledge, or something?"

"Well, it's a little more complicated than that. But, basically yes."

"How'd they manage to do that?"

Elisa glanced at Tyler, who'd pulled his cell phone out and was texting. "About three years ago, I sold about a dozen pictures to them. The agreement I entered into with them gave them one-time use of the photos, for which they paid me a fee. The agreement said that if they wanted to use the photos more than once, they would need to pay me an extra fee. But since I hold the rights to all my own photos, they legally can't distribute them for monetary gain."

Brody's eyebrows pinched in confusion. "So, if they wanted to use your photos again, they'd pay you another fee and be able to use them themselves? What if they sold them and gave you a cut of the money?"

Elisa shook her head. "They don't have the rights to the photos, so they can't sell them. They would have to get in contact with me first and purchase the rights to the pictures, which they never did."

"Are you sure your contract doesn't have a clause saying they retain the rights to the pictures?"

"I had a lawyer look over the contract before I signed it. The rights are mine."

Brody scratched his chin. "So how do you know they've been doing this?"

Elisa couldn't help but smile. "This is where I got lucky. One of the magazine's editors knows me because they purchased some photos from me in the past. She told me when she was contacted, the deal sounded fishy and the man was really hesitant to say where he got the pictures from. Since she's been in the business a long time, she had a feeling they were trying to sell the pictures without my permission. The guy practically clammed up when she asked him to send the pictures over so she could look at them first. He tried to get her to purchase the pictures on the spot."

Thank goodness the scumbag had the balls to contact someone as prestigious as that particular magazine. If not, Elisa might not have known.

"So what can you do?" Brody asked her.

Elisa shrugged and picked up her water glass. "Find a good lawyer, and hope he or she can get the money this website owes me."

Brody glanced at Tyler, then back at her. "My dad has a really good lawyer who handles all the legal business for the restaurants. He might be able to help you or at least give you some advice. Sometimes all it takes is a threatening letter."

Elisa smiled, despite her uncertainty with her new dilemma. "Anything he could do would be great. I'm not even sure where to turn at this point."

"Dad, can I stay the night at Tommy's tonight?" Tyler butted in before his dad could respond to her.

Brody stared hard at his son for a moment before answering. "Can you go another night? I had something planned for us."

Tyler set his phone on the table and pinned his father with puppy-dog eyes. "But, Dad, his mom just got Rock Band and Tommy and I really want to play. And his mom said she would come pick me up at Elisa's house. Please?"

Something dark passed through Brody's eyes as he regarded the boy. Elisa's heart cracked open at the tug-of-war Brody must be going through. Here he was, trying to make an effort to spend time with the boy, and Tyler wanted to hang out with friends. How lonely that must be for Brody. Elisa wanted to comfort him. She wanted to place her hand over Brody's much bigger one and tell him it was okay, that Tyler was bound to reach this phase sooner or later.

Brody ran his hand over Tyler's sun-kissed hair. "All right, you can go. But tell Tommy's mom that I'll drop you off."

"Yes!" Tyler pumped his fist in the air. "Thanks, Dad." His fingers flew with lightning speed over the keypad of his cell phone.

Brody directed his smile at Elisa, but the look didn't reach his eyes. Her hand itched to touch him, but she held back. She was unsure about making a gesture like that in front of Tyler.

The darkness that clouded his eyes a moment ago melted away as he gazed at her. "I'll stop by on my way home to look at those photos."

Brody strolled up the concrete walk to Elisa's front door and tried to ignore his racing heart. Twenty minutes ago, Tyler had been all grins and giddiness when he burst into his friend's house. Rock Band had dominated their conversation ever since Brody had picked Tyler up from Elisa's house earlier. Apparently it was the coolest thing ever. Maybe he was behind the times, but Brody didn't see how pushing buttons on a fake guitar could be fun.

Tyler was only eleven, and Brody was already being ousted for video games. When Tyler had been little, Brody had never imagined a day when he wouldn't have been able to relate to his son anymore. It's like he didn't know the boy. Or Tyler didn't know him. Or maybe a bit of both. Somewhere along the way they'd become strangers to each other. Worst of all, Brody had stopped trying, even though it hadn't been intentional. Work had snuck its way to the top of his priorities, and Tyler had been shoved to the bottom.

The knowledge made him sick to his stomach. As though he were the worst father ever who'd lost all touch with his own child. Maybe he ought to buy a gaming system so they could play Rock Band together.

He took his frustration out on Elisa's door and knocked harder than he needed to. When the door swung open seconds later, the black cloud hanging over his head dissipated slightly. The tension eased from his body when the exotic woman on the other side smiled at him. Her dark eyes practically glowed when they assessed him.

She gestured him inside, then closed the door. "Are you okay?"

Damn, did he have "pissed off" written on his forehead? She'd asked him the same thing when he'd picked Tyler up. This time her words managed to cut through his bad mood like a knife through butter.

He rubbed a hand along the back of his neck. "Yeah. Tyler rarely spends the night with a friend on nights that I have him. It just caught me off guard."

"What was it you had planned to do with him?"

Elisa's breasts smashed together when she crossed her arms, momentarily distracting him from her question. "What's that?"

One side of her mouth kicked up. "Earlier you said you had planned something for the two of you."

Oh, that. Yeah, that had been his last desperate attempt at holding on to his son's childhood.

He lifted his shoulders to feign indifference, even though he didn't feel that way. "I was just going to take him out to play catch. We used to do it all the time."

Elisa's bottomless eyes softened. "That's really sweet."

"Unfortunately, 'sweet' doesn't get you very far compared to Rock Band." Was he already the uncool dad?

"What kid can resist Rock Band? I bet if you offer to take him out tomorrow, he'll go."

Would he though? At one time Tyler would have jumped at the opportunity to play catch with his dad. Now Brody had no one to blame but himself for letting too much time go by. He cleared his throat and tried to steer the conversation in a different direction. "Do you have those pictures for me?"

Elisa regarded him a moment longer with those watchful eyes of hers, eyes that saw way too deeply into him. "Sure, they're over here."

Thankfully she didn't pursue the subject, for which he was grateful. Right now he lacked the words to properly express his feelings. Brody hadn't been born with the ability to put his thoughts into words, which was something Kelly had constantly complained about.

Elisa's knee-weakening flowery scent teased him as he followed her farther into the house. Something about the way she smelled always made him think of wildflowers on the Wyoming prairies.

On her kitchen table was a thick envelope. She picked it up, pulled out several proof sheets, and handed them to him.

"Be brutally honest," she said. "If you don't think they work, we can do them again."

The photos looked like they belonged in a gourmet magazine. Each picture captured the delicious essence and perfection of the dish. This woman really didn't know how good she was. Brody would be damn proud to frame every one of these and hang them front and center in the restaurant.

"These are outstanding," he said as he glanced from one photo to the next.

"I thought they turned out better, but I wanted to make sure you were happy with them."

He took his attention off the pictures and placed it on Elisa. Her teeth worried her bottom lip like a child seeking approval from a parent. Her uncertainty was the sexiest yet sweetest thing he'd ever seen.

"I think you did a perfect job with them," he reassured her.

Her eyes lit up when she smiled. "Thanks. Looks like you were doing pretty good business today."

He nodded. "Our numbers have been slowly climbing over the past week. I just hope it's a sign of things to come and not just a fluke. But as good as these are, we have a little problem.

"Another one?" she answered with a grin.

He set the photos on the table and ran a hand over the back of his neck. "Anthony doesn't want his food photographed."

Elisa blinked her big brown eyes and shook her head. Her disbelief was as evident as his. "Why?"

"I think it boils down to his confidence. And fear." Anthony had had a lot tossed at him in the past couple of days, and thus far he'd handled it pretty well. But when Brody had mentioned publishing the pictures in a county-wide magazine, the ex–air force pilot had become more nervous than a nun in a porn shop.

"What, fear of failing?" Elisa wanted to know.

"I think it has more to do with my father."

Her dark brows pulled together. "He's afraid of your father?"

"Well, yeah, who can blame him? My dad can be pretty intimidating." He leaned against the edge of the table and crossed his arms over his chest. "Anthony knows what's on the line here. I don't think he thinks he can handle the pressure of bringing the restaurant back and have my father breathing down his neck. Anthony saw what happened to Travis."

"So, Anthony is afraid he's putting his job on the line. Basically he wants to play it safe."

Brody nodded. "Pretty much."

"Then maybe you should have the sous-chefs prepare the food for the magazine. Give Anthony more time to ease into things. Maybe it's just too much too fast."

Brody rubbed a hand along his whisker-covered jaw, thinking he desperately needed a shave. It seemed for every one step forward he took, he had to turn around and take two steps back. How many steps backward could he take before his old man gave him the boot? Brody got that Anthony was just as terrified as he, given what had happened with Travis and the chef before him. The bartender had a living to make and couldn't do so if he got fired. Somehow Brody had to convince Anthony that the failure would be on Brody's own shoulders and not on his.

But they wouldn't fail. They *couldn't* fail.

"We could do a mock shoot, then show the pictures to your father," Elisa said as she took a step toward him. "Maybe he could put Anthony's fears at ease. Or you could strike a deal with your dad."

He eyed her as she kept coming closer, bringing with her the intoxicatingly sexy scent that always threatened to bring him to his knees. "What kind of deal?" he asked on a near growl.

For a moment she didn't respond, but hesitated just in front of him. Perhaps she'd picked up on his pulsing desire to scratch all the restaurant talk and just take her already. The table was right there. To hell with a bed. She chewed her lower lip. "I was thinking you could convince your father not to hold Anthony solely responsible if anything goes wrong."

One side of his mouth kicked up. "In other words, you want me to make my old man promise that he'll fire only me."

"Of course, that's not what I want—"

He held his hand up at the wide-eyed look on her face. "That's okay. It's the way it should be."

She watched him for a moment, sweeping those dark eyes in slow perusal down his body as though he were Grade A Choice beef. Maybe she could be his steak sauce and they could just slather all over each other.

"I'm sorry you have to go through all this. I thought maybe you were in the clear."

"So did I," he agreed. "But this is part of my job and I have to figure out where to go from here."

"I bet if you unleash that Brody charm, Anthony will come around," she added with a sly grin.

"You think I have enough charm for that?"

One of her perfectly shaped brows lifted. "I think you know you do."

He graced her with a smile, wondering what else he could get her to admit. How about how much she wanted him? "I know. I just wanted to hear you say it."

"And I just fell right into that trap, didn't I?" Even as she said the words, her cheeks colored. His satisfaction at seeing that eased the tension in his shoulders.

He moved one shoulder in a casual shrug. "Actually, you set the trap up for yourself by bringing my charm into it in the first place." He paused and gave her the same scorching look she'd given him. "Not that I blame you."

Elisa shook her head, but he detected a slight turn up of her lips. "Okay, Mr. Smooth, let's try to keep the conversation on track. Have you thought about advertising? I mean other than running this article."

"I know the place could benefit with a few months of steady promotion. The problem is the restaurant doesn't have a whole lot of extra money to spend right now. But my sister-in-law, who volunteers at the youth center, needs a caterer for an upcoming fundraiser. I asked her to consider the Golden Glove. We wouldn't be paid, but it would be a great way to get the word out to a lot of people."

"I volunteered to do pictures at one of those events a few years ago. They draw quite the crowd. That could be the boost you need."

He ran a hand along the stubble on his chin. "Yeah."

She studied him a moment. "Why do I feel there's a 'but' coming?"

His mouth broke into a grin at her question. The woman was so damn intuitive. "There's just one snag. My sister-in-law, Avery, babysits my nephew for my other sister-in-law who's on strict bed rest. Next week she and my brother are supposed to come to the Golden Glove to sample some food, but Avery needs to find someone to watch Mason so Lacy isn't left in a bind. Both my father and stepmother work, and it just happens to be on a day when Chase has a staff meeting."

"And Lacy is your other sister-in-law who's on bed rest? Is she pregnant or something?"

Brody nodded. "She's carrying twins."

"I could spare an hour or two to watch him." Elisa tucked a strand of hair behind her ear. "Well, I know Lacy doesn't know me or anything. But if she'd be comfortable, I'd be happy to help her out. That is, if it doesn't interfere with rescheduling the shoot."

"I need to work on Anthony before we can take more pictures. But you'd be willing to do that? Watch a child you don't know for someone you don't know?"

Her delectable lips turned up in a smile. "I love kids. And it wouldn't be for that long, right?"

"Maybe two hours. I know Lacy will really appreciate it. Which reminds me…" He set the photos he'd been holding down and took a folded check out of his back pocket. "Just as promised."

Elisa eyed the check but didn't take it. "I can't take that. Just consider what I did a favor. Besides, I haven't technically completed the job yet."

"A favor?" he parroted. "Elisa, you've taken a lot of time out of your schedule to take practice pictures. You deserve to be paid."

Her hands wrapped around the back of one of the dining chairs. "How can I take money from the restaurant when it's struggling? I wouldn't feel right about it."

The woman was trying to be noble. She knew full well the troubles the Golden Glove was having, and she only wanted to help in her own small way. When was the last time he met a woman who was so selfless?

He took a step closer. "The restaurant isn't paying you. I am."

She stared at him, with astonishment widening her deep brown eyes. "I can't take your money," she said with a shake of her head.

"Why? I was serious when I said I wanted to pay you." He grabbed her hand and placed the check in her palm. "Just take it."

Her eyes dropped to his gift, then lifted to him. "Thank you."

"Why do I always get the feeling you're holding back around me?"

Her luscious lips parted and her brow furrowed. "What do you mean?"

"I can't explain it." His finger trailed along the edge of her jaw. "It's like a part of you is afraid of me."

She sucked in a deep breath through her parted lips. "Not afraid, just cautious."

"Why do you feel the need to be cautious?"

She waited a moment, like she wanted to formulate a logical answer. "You make me feel things I'm not used to. I'm just not sure how to handle them."

He stepped even closer to her, so that her sweet body heat flowed around him like a blanket of sexuality. "Like what kind of things?"

The pulse beating beneath her neck sped up when his finger trailed down the column of her throat. "I don't know. But my mind doesn't know how to make sense of them."

His mouth quirked in a small smile. "There's your problem. You should stop thinking so much and allow yourself to feel."

Oh, this woman would be wanton in bed. His finger alone elicited all kinds of reactions from her that had his body coming to life. Her pink tongue kept darting out and swiping across her lower lip, leaving it deliciously wet. After waiting for what felt like a lifetime, he gave in to his craving and leaned down. His mouth lowered to hers with a gentleness that contradicted the raging desire he felt for her. Her lips were soft, full and moist, and even more heavenly than he thought they would be.

She didn't push him away, as he expected her to. Instead, her hand came up to grip his shoulder and her fingers dug into his muscles. The lady wanted him. She clutched at him with a desperation that had to be genuine. The knowledge had him pulling her even closer and slanting his mouth over hers even harder. His tongue probed the entrance of her hot mouth and she eagerly allowed him to enter.

Holy sweet mother. A thousand sensations flooded his wired body when his tongue stroked inside her glorious heat. Her throaty moan vibrated through him. His arms curled around her narrow waist, effectively pulling her flush against him. Her body was even softer and more womanly than he imagined. She had curves and lushness in all the right places. Her breasts, which were flattened against his chest, were full and incredibly sexy. Her skin was smooth and so touchable. Her mile-long legs entwined with his and came within dangerous reach of certain parts below his belt.

When was the last time he'd allowed himself to get this lost in a simple kiss? Or better yet, who was the last woman to kiss him with this much bravado, this much need?

Before he had a chance to take things further, Elisa

yanked herself away from him and took a step back, as though something had frightened her. Had he taken things too far?

She touched her fingers to her lips, as if still trying to feel his mouth there. Her chest heaved up and down as she tried to steady her breathing.

"Elisa..." He tried to close the distance between them, but she backed farther away from him.

"We shouldn't have done that," she whispered.

"Why the hell not?"

She turned to the table and gathered the forgotten photos, completely ignoring his question. "I guess I'll see you next week when you pick Tyler up."

He placed a hand on her arm. "Would you mind explaining to me how you go from hot to cold in three seconds?"

"I can't get mixed up with you." She wretched her arm out of his grasp. "I just can't."

The confusion in her eyes tore his guts up. "What are you talking about, 'mixed up'? It was just one kiss."

*That was a whole lot more than one kiss and you know it.*

"You need to go," she stated out of the blue and tugged on his arm. She marched him to the front door like a damn drill sergeant and practically shoved him through it.

"I'm sorry," she muttered, then shut the door in his face.

What the hell?

The woman kisses him like her life depends on it and then all but throws him out of her house?

# TEN

"THIS IS THE BEST CROISSANT sandwich I've ever had," Avery announced after swallowing a monstrous bite. She picked up one of the potato chips. "Are these homemade?" Her dark hair swung in her face as she reached for more.

Brody couldn't help the grin that broke across his face. He slathered more ketchup on his fries. "Yes, ma'am, they are." For that ingenious idea, he completely credited Anthony. One morning last week, Brody had come to work to find Anthony in the kitchen slicing potatoes. In that deep, baritone voice of his, Anthony said he wanted to try his hand at homemade chips to replace the ones they'd been buying. Brody had just about kissed the man's feet for thinking so practically. Making their own potato chips was much cheaper than buying bags of them, not to mention a whole lot tastier.

"Where'd you find this guy, anyway?" Avery asked.

Brody spread some mayonnaise on his burger. "He was the bartender. Dad fired our other chef, then by chance I tasted some of Anthony's food."

"So you've made him the new chef?" Avery wanted to know.

"Not quite yet. I'm still working on convincing him." That morning, Brody's hopes had skyrocketed when he'd spotted Anthony in the kitchen, already soaking up every word from Stanley, one of the sous-chefs, like a sponge. Then he'd mentioned the word "pictures," and the man's smile had faltered. Although Anthony's proficiency for learning was off the charts, something was holding the guy back. As though his fear of failure outweighed his confidence in his own abilities.

Avery glanced around the restaurant. "Convincing? Does he not want to be a chef?"

"It's not that. He's just a bit apprehensive about running a kitchen."

His brother Noah, Avery's husband, had been quiet as usual sitting in the booth beside her. He swallowed a bite of food before saying "Yeah, how did Dad take you promoting the bartender without consulting him?"

Their father didn't take well to not being consulted on anything. But Brody had done what he thought was best for the restaurant. And he'd been willing to lay down his career for it. "Actually he's not technically the head chef yet. I just made him the interim chef until he has enough confidence to run the kitchen like a pro."

"Sounds like you're kind of stuck in limbo," Noah said.

Brody shook his head. "Limbo between rock and a hard place."

Noah held his hands up. "Just because I'm not involved in the family business doesn't mean I don't have one of these," he said with a tap to the side of his head.

"I'm surprised you were able to get RJ to fill in. I didn't think he liked it here," Avery said.

Brody looked around for his younger brother, but he hadn't entered the bar yet.

"I don't think not liking the restaurant was the problem," Noah answered.

"It wasn't," Brody added. "He didn't want to be just a bartender. For some reason Dad always held him back. Besides," he said with a shrug, "he's happier with what he's doing now. Cars have always been his passion."

RJ went to car auctions and picked out diamonds in the rough. He fixed them up into world-class vehicles and sold them for quite a profit. In the last year or so, word had spread about RJ's fine craftsmanship. People in the area had started taking their clunkers to him and paying him to restore them. Little by little, he'd been able to build a nice business for himself. What Brody didn't know was how his little brother was able to spare time to pour drinks.

"Did you see the seventy-two Mustang he just did?" Noah shook his head and picked up his bacon cheeseburger. "I swear that thing was a piece of art."

Avery picked up her water glass but didn't take a sip. "Noah sulked for a week because I wouldn't let him buy the car."

Brody chuckled. His brother was damn lucky to have such a wonderful woman like Avery. They had a dynamite marriage and were head over heels about each other. Brody missed that—though not necessarily being married. He missed having a companion, someone who could finish his sentences for him and know what mood he was in even if he didn't know himself.

*Elisa knows those things.*

The thought just about scared the shit out of him.

He cleared his throat and grabbed some more fries off his plate. "So Avery, what do you think? Is your dish good enough to serve half the town of Trouble?"

Avery chewed thoughtfully for a moment, then folded

her arms on the table. "I have to admit, I wasn't expecting very much out of the food. I mean, word spreads kind of fast in this town." She paused for a moment and glanced down at her plate. "But I was blown away by this meal. Anthony is a gem and you need to hold on to him."

Brody planned on it, even if that meant risking his father's wrath.

Avery continued, "I think I've tasted enough to know this will be a hit. I'll come by with Lisa next week; she's the one who's coordinating the fundraiser with me. We'll select the dishes together."

Would it be completely wrong of him to jump on the table top and celebrate like he'd just won the World Series? His sister-in-law had just made his entire month.

He placed his palm on top of her hand. "Avery, you have no idea what this means to me."

A sparkle lit up her brown eyes when she smiled. "That's what family does for each other, Brody. This place used to be really great. I want to help you get there again. And you really deserve it. Having just eaten this meal, I promise you I'm not doing you any favors."

"Would you mind removing your hand from my wife, please?" Noah said with a smirk.

Brody ignored him and picked his hamburger up. "So how are things on the baby front? Any luck?"

Noah's brows lowered for a moment, then Avery placed her hand on her husband's arm. "I told him."

His features softened at his wife's words. He leaned closer to her and placed a kiss on her temple. "That's okay." Noah redirected his attention to Brody. "We're going to see a fertility specialist next week to discuss our options."

Brody glanced at Avery, then back to Noah. "As in for fertility treatments?"

Avery pursed her lips and grabbed Noah's hand. "I just found out I have endometriosis. It's a condition that can make getting pregnant very difficult, if not impossible." She paused for a moment and sucked in a breath. "We got very lucky with Lily. It's also why I miscarried."

Noah pulled his wife close to him. "And if she's the only one we have, I'll be the happiest man in the world." He ended his statement with a kiss to Avery's cheek, followed by another one to her lips.

Avery's response was a sad smile that didn't quite reach her eyes. His sister-in-law had such a strong and confident air about her. Brody could tell that she was crumbling inside.

He shifted uncomfortably in his seat. What could he say to them that could possibly be of comfort? "I'm sorry" was all he could think of. And even that seemed inadequate.

A heart-wrenching, melancholy air surrounded Avery. The twitch of her lips was probably meant to be a smile. He'd do anything for his brother and sister-in-law, and he didn't like to feel helpless when someone in his family needed something.

"We haven't told anyone else yet. We've wanted to wait after we see the specialist, so we know what we're dealing with," Noah said.

The food on Brody's plate suddenly seemed unappealing. He pushed the dish away. "Ah, hell. I'm sorry. I didn't mean to be a killjoy." Why couldn't he have given a moment's thought before asking them about their troubles?

This time Avery's smile was a bit stronger, as though she were trying to fake her own strength. "It's okay. I'm going to have to get used to talking about it. People will ask questions when we tell them." She placed her smaller hand on his. Her fingers were cool and soft. "It's okay," she said again.

This woman's courage astounded him. Who knew what sort of internal battles she fought every day due to her fertility issues. Brody couldn't imagine how such an uncertainty was tearing her heart apart. And Noah stood by her side unfailingly. Perhaps someday he would have a marriage as strong as theirs.

In the beginning, he'd thought his and Kelly's marriage was one of those that could go the distance. Not long after leaving college and returning to Trouble, he'd realized he'd been deluding himself. For a while, he'd looked for a reason to blame Kelly. In truth, she hadn't done anything other than love him and be the best wife she could have been. Had he been the best husband possible in return? At the time he'd thought so. Now he could look back and see what he could have done differently.

A heavy silence settled over the three of them. They each ate quietly for several minutes before the voice of their youngest brother finally cut through the tension.

"Why do you get a break, while I'm back there busting my ass?" RJ asked when he stopped next to their table.

Noah leaned back in the booth and eyed RJ. "You don't look like you're busting ass right now."

RJ waved his hand toward the bar. "Jake's covering. I just wanted to come over here and give you shit," he said with a punch to Brody's shoulder.

Brody had learned long ago to ignore his brother's strange sense of humor. RJ often called things as he saw them but had a way of putting his own unique twist on things. He'd been the life of the party ever since his mother, Carol, had married Martin. The scene behind the bar hadn't quite been the same since RJ left. The crowd had become less and less lively over the years.

"So what, the three of you decided to have a little dinner party and not invite me?" RJ asked as he crossed his arms over his chest. A mischievous glint lit up the younger man's green eyes . . . the same light that always had women gunning for him.

"Calm down, RJ," Avery soothed. "We wouldn't dream of having a party and not including you. They would be way too boring." The humor that had been absent from her voice a few minutes ago returned.

"I could never be mad at you, Avery," he said with a quick grin. "I just enjoy giving these two ugly bastards a hard time."

Noah rolled his eyes and shoved a huge bite of burger into his mouth.

"Are you enjoying being back here? Is it kind of like old times?" she asked him.

RJ's smile slipped a fraction. Only someone who didn't know him wouldn't notice the falter. "I guess you could say it's like old times. The tips are nice extra spending cash. I'll just dump the money right back into my cars."

Noah glanced at RJ. "Speaking of your cars, do you still have that seventy-two Mustang?"

Avery slapped her husband's arm.

RJ shook his head. "Sorry, bro. Sold it last week for a nice chunk of change."

"Hey, a guy can dream, right?" Noah muttered.

"Maybe for your birthday I'll fix up a nice little Corvette for you," RJ said as he snagged a fry off Noah's plate.

Noah's brows flew up his forehead. "Would you really?"

RJ chewed thoughtfully for a moment, then grinned. "Nope." On that short but sweet note, their younger brother sauntered away with the confident swagger he was so famous for.

"Ass," Noah muttered.

Brody couldn't help but grin. "Don't sulk. You look like a baby."

"You're an ass too," his older brother said.

Several hours later, Brody's head throbbed like a son of a bitch.

The restaurant had maintained a steady crowd for the rest of the day—not too bustling, but enough to keep the staff on their toes. Brody wasn't sure what had happened, but an invisible switch had been flipped somewhere inside Anthony, who'd proved himself an indispensable part of the staff. He called out every order with the precision and authority of a seasoned chef. He double- and triple-checked every plate that came to the pass, something Travis had done only half the time. Thus far Anthony had impressed Brody in a way he hadn't been since Michael had cooked for them. Seems as though the bartender's time with the sous-chefs was starting to pay off. There were moments when Brody could see Anthony question himself, then he'd snap out of it and get his butt in gear.

Lines of fatigue bracketed Anthony's mouth after a long day's work. A few minutes ago, Brody and his father had called Anthony to the back office for an important discussion. Without a word, Anthony had followed Brody out of the kitchen. Now he stood in Brody's office like a man awaiting execution.

Beads of sweat dotted the chef's smoothly shaven head. A dirty, bedraggled dishtowel was slung over one of his thick shoulders. Every few seconds, he would grab the towel, run it through his fingers, then sling it over the other shoulder.

"Are you nervous, Anthony?" Martin asked to break the silence.

Brody hadn't said a word yet, only because his old man had expressed his desire to deliver the message to Anthony himself. At this point, Brody didn't care who did the talking. He just wanted to get this shit over with so they could get an actual photo shoot done.

Anthony cleared his throat. "Not nervous, sir. Just a bit wired after my day."

Every time the word "sir" left Anthony's lips, Martin practically glowed. Brody had repeatedly told Anthony that referring to Brody's father with such formality was overkill. Anthony's response had been "He's my boss. It's a matter of respect."

Hell, Brody couldn't argue with that.

"I can understand that," Martin answered. "A kitchen is a high-pressure place. Lots of stuff always going on in there. A chef has a lot of people depending on him to get things right. That can be a very stressful thing."

Anthony gave a jerky nod of his head. "Yes, sir. It can be."

Brody glanced at his father and wondered where the hell the old man planned on going with this little pep talk.

*For hell's sake, just put the guy out of his misery.*

"How's your experience been in the kitchen so far, Anthony? Are you working well with the other line cooks? Have you been learning much about how the kitchen works?" Martin pressed.

"Ain't no place I've loved more than to be in the kitchen. Gives me peace." A ghost of a smile played on Anthony's lips. "You have great sous-chefs, and Vic and Stanley have taught me more than I ever could have learned in my mother's kitchen."

Martin nodded his agreement. "Yes, a restaurant kitchen isn't really like anyplace else. It's hot, noisy, and chaotic. Which probably isn't anything you're used to."

Anthony shifted from foot to foot and shook his head. "It's pretty similar to bartending. But it's nothing I can't handle. I'll admit, in the beginning, I didn't know what I was doing, aside from cooking that is. But I think I'm picking it up pretty quickly."

"We know that," Martin replied with a glance at Brody. "And we feel with time, you could run the place yourself. But that's not what we need to discuss."

A look of apprehension crossed Anthony's face. Shit, Brody almost felt sorry for the guy. But his need to get the ball rolling at a much faster pace than it had been overrode any feelings of pity. He'd already put a hold on the article twice. The magazine wasn't going to keep holding their advertising space much longer. They had a short window of time to get the job done.

"The bottom line is, Anthony," Martin said in his no-nonsense tone, which was really the only tone the guy had, "we need to move forward with the photo shoot. And we need you to be in the spotlight."

"He means the food," Brody jumped in with in order to ease some of the panic that had dropped Anthony's jaw. "You personally won't be featured. We just need you to prepare some of your specialties. You know, the new dishes we've added to the menu?"

"Well, yeah, but—"

"And you remember Elisa, right?" Brody interrupted. "The woman who was with me before? She'll be the one taking the pictures."

"Yeah, she was—she was real nice," Anthony agreed with a nod of his head. The man kept wringing the dirty towel around his hands, then slinging it back over his shoulder. "But I'm no gourmet chef." The big man lifted his wide shoulders. "I don't know how to make fancy food like that."

Brody shook his head. "It doesn't have to be fancy."

Martin stepped forward and placed a hand on the bartender's shoulder. "What we're looking for is something simple, which is what you're good at. I've seen the way you prepare and plate food. It's exactly what we want featured for our relaunch."

Anthony shook his head, an argument already forming on his lips. Why did he have to doubt himself so much? Brady wondered. "I can do that, but..." His Adam's apple worked up and down in rapid succession. "Man, I can't afford to lose this job."

Martin's brows pinched together. "What do you mean, Anthony? Why would you lose your job?"

"Well..." He shot a nervous glance between Brody and his father. "After what happened to Travis and Gary, I figured I'd be on a pretty short leash."

Yeah, which was precisely what Brody knew Anthony was going to say. And he didn't blame the guy. Everyone was pretty much walking on eggshells around there, especially when Martin showed up and started casing the place like some bad imitation of a security guard.

Only the other staff didn't need to worry. Not like Brody did. He was seriously putting all his eggs in one basket.

A basket named Anthony.

Martin dropped his hand from the bartender's shoulder, then slid both hands in his pants pockets. "You don't need to worry about that." He tossed a look at Brody that said "*You're* the one who needs to worry."

Yeah, he got that.

Martin continued. "All we need you to focus on is continuing to learn the kitchen and getting ready to have your dishes photographed. And, if it'll make you feel better, you can choose which shots get published. And we won't send them to the magazine without your approval."

Brody wasn't about to go that far, to give the former bartender that much control. But if that's what it took to get Anthony on board, he was all for it. Anything to get the show on the road.

Both he and his father waited for what seemed like hours while Anthony contemplated their offer. In the meantime, more beads of sweat popped up on the big man's smooth head, which Brody took as a sign that Anthony was way overthinking the situation. He kept his patience and remained silent, even though what he really wanted to do was smack the guy upside the head.

"Okay," Anthony finally said.

And Brody felt part of the weight lift off his shoulders.

# ELEVEN

IN THE PAST HOUR ELISA had been peed on, spit on, had food thrown at her, and managed to dodge half a dozen flying toys.

This babysitting business wasn't for the fainthearted, especially with an energetic, outspoken toddler with a shrill set of lungs. Had she known what a hurricane little Mason McDermott was, she might have thought twice before volunteering. About twenty minutes ago, an opportunity for sweet solitude presented itself with Mason's naptime. However, after ten straight minutes of blood-curdling screaming, Elisa had reached her limit and whisked the boy out of his crib.

Her main objective this morning was to give Lacy some rest. How could Elisa do that if Mason's ear-piercing shrieks threatened to bring the walls down?

Lacy had said to turn on some cartoons if Mason was driving her insane. That was all fine and dandy, if Elisa could locate the remote control for the television.

She'd just righted the couch cushions, when she spotted Mason trying to shove Ritz crackers into the DVD player. How had he gotten his hands on crackers?

"Mason, no." Elisa lunged for him a split second before

he could ruin an expensive piece of electronics. She settled him in his high chair and dropped the crackers on the tray. "Okay, you just stay right there," she told him, and continued on her quest for the remote. The thing had to be here somewhere, unless Mason had found it and put it someplace really unorthodox, like the freezer.

She finally located the remote, tucked underneath the sofa. Just as Elisa retrieved it, Mason squealed and slapped his hands on the tray of his high chair, as though celebrating his babysitter's small victory.

Every single cracker she'd given him was now on the floor, in a complete 360-degree radius around his chair. Honestly, how did Avery watch this kid every day and keep her sanity? Elisa hadn't been here that long, and her head felt like it was locked in a vise grip.

After sweeping up the crackers, she pulled Mason out of his chair, kicking legs and all, and settled him on the living room floor. His little round face broke into a toothy grin when she found a suitable cartoon for him.

The bouncing characters on the TV screen wouldn't hold his attention for very long. Elisa used the opportunity to slip down the hallway and check on Lacy. The mother-to-be was on her back, looking decidedly bored while flipping through the TV channels. She expelled a breath and glanced over when Elisa entered the room.

"I never realized how completely useless daytime television is until I got stuck in bed. And I can't sleep because my heartburn is too bad."

Elisa came to a stop next to the bed. "Can I get you some medicine?" The poor woman had to be so uncomfortable, not being able to get up at all.

Lacy grinned and set the remote down. "Thanks, but I've already taken the maximum dosage for the day. I just have to deal." She placed her hands underneath her and scooted herself farther up the headboard. "I'm sorry if Mason's a handful. Cartoons are the best way of getting him to stay still for more than ten minutes."

Elisa offered a reassuring smile. "He's just being a toddler. It's nothing I can't handle."

"I'm shocked Avery hasn't run screaming for the hills by now. The woman has iron-clad patience. And I am so ready to get these babies out of me. But I have no earthly clue how I'm going to handle three kids."

"Brody mentioned you're having twins."

Lacy giggled and ran her hands in circles over her huge belly. "Yes, we're having two more boys. I think I had a coronary when we found out. But my husband, Chase, couldn't stop smiling. He's pretty pleased with himself."

"I think men consider it a personal achievement when they have sons, like it's a sign of their masculinity."

"Let me tell you, the McDermotts have no problems spitting out sons. It would be nice to have some more girls in this family." She ran her green eyes over Elisa in assessment. "So you and Brody are friends?"

Were they friends? More important, was it normal to fantasize about friends?

"I've done some photography work for him, and I watch Tyler after school while his mother is gone."

Lacy nodded and continued to gaze at Elisa. Was the woman fishing for information? How much had Brody told her?

"The reason why I ask is because Brody was kind of vague about your relationship. Not that it's any of my business. I was just curious."

That still left Elisa wondering what he'd told his sister-in-law.

Just because Brody had been vague didn't mean Elisa had to be as well. It's not like they were engaged in a hot, scandalous affair. So, they'd kissed once. So what? People kiss all the time. That didn't mean the two parties involved needed to sneak around, undercover.

"Yeah, I'd say we're friends. I like Brody." Elisa almost said she loved spending time with Brody too. But would Lacy turn around and repeat all this to Brody?

"And you'd like to be with him more," Lacy concluded.

Wait, had Elisa voiced her thoughts out loud? How had Lacy figured that out?

Brody was a man she could lose her heart to. Elisa was fully aware of how devastating he could be to her. For some reason her heart didn't want to listen to her head. The naughty side of her wanted to indulge and see what one night with him would be like.

"I'm going to take your silence to mean that I'm right," Lacy concluded again.

Elisa pulled in a breath. "I don't know," she answered. "It's kind of complicated. If I jump into a relationship with him and it doesn't work out, then that will only confuse Tyler—"

"Why wouldn't it work out?" Lacy interjected.

"Well." Elisa chewed her lower lip. "Have you ever been in a relationship where it didn't work out?"

Lacy laughed. "Okay, you got me there. Judging by the way Brody clammed up, I'd say he likes you."

"What do you mean by 'clammed up'?" Maybe Brody didn't do that with just her?

Lacy paused and ran her tongue along her lower lip. "Brody's divorce left him pretty scarred. Since then he's been really selective about the women he gets close to. And when he does find a woman worth spending time with, he becomes very...reserved. It's like he erects this wall around himself and only shares certain parts of himself with her. I guess gun-shy would be a good way to describe him."

All this time there had been something about the man Elisa couldn't put her finger on, almost like a sense of wariness or fear he couldn't allow himself to overcome. Now she understood his psyche a bit better, thanks to his sister-in-law.

But Elisa still had unanswered questions. Was the reason Brody held himself back because he wanted to explore a further relationship with her?

*Duh, he already made that clear the other night when he kissed you.*

How could she get him to trust her?

Or, perhaps the better question was, how would she handle this with an impending trip around the world? And what rotten timing too. Just when she'd found a guy, a real man who was a genuine threat to her heart, it just happened to coincide with an opportunity of a lifetime.

*But isn't a potential great love an opportunity of a lifetime also?*

How was she supposed to choose between the two? And how could her heart differentiate between two things that she wanted with equal passion? Even more than that, was it possible to have both? Before she'd been so sure that leaving Trouble would be a piece of cake. That she could slap a for-sale sign on her lawn and jet out of town without a backward glance.

Now? A complication had presented itself. A complication named Brody McDermott who'd thrown a pair of steel tethers around her legs and wouldn't let go.

Lacy placed a warm palm on Elisa's arm. "I'm sorry.

I didn't mean to freak you out. I think Brody genuinely likes you." She offered Elisa a comforting smile. "I haven't seen him this clammed up over a woman in a long time. Not even with Kelly."

Lacy's words did something funny to Elisa's insides. Her stomach turned over in uncomfortable knots and her heart did little palpitations.

"Thanks. I should go check on Mason. Can I get you anything?"

Lacy gazed at Elisa, as if sensing there was more Elisa wanted to say. Luckily the other woman didn't press the issue. Elisa was too confused herself.

"I'm fine, thanks. And I don't hear any screaming or loud crashing, so I'm sure Mason's fine too."

Elisa left the bedroom with an odd sort of comfort, yet she wasn't sure what to do with the information Lacy had given her. The comforting feeling was odd to say the least, given the flip-flopping her heart continued to do. Whether or not to take the job she'd been waiting years for or stick around and give her budding relationship with Brody a chance. Because hadn't she been waiting just as long for that?

As a girl, she'd seen the love her parents had for each other and placed that on her list of lifelong goals. To have a life-changing love. What she felt for Brody could easily grow into that. Then again, she'd been living on her own for so long, taking care of herself after her parents had died, that she wouldn't know the first thing about sharing her life with someone. As much as she wanted—no, craved—that kind of deep connection with Brody, Elisa had only known disappointment in the love department. The two people she'd adored more than anyone had been taken from her in the blink of an eye. Then, with the departure of Marcello, she'd lost the last bit of family she had left—her mother's parents had both passed on before Elisa had been born. Since then, she'd been so careful to guard herself against potential disappointment. Potential loss. In the process, Elisa had grown accustomed to being alone. And the idea of losing her heart to someone who could just as easily snatch it from her was almost as terrifying as leaving Brody.

As messed up and twisted as that was.

In such a short amount of time, her life had taken a massive twist. Yet she'd never been so conflicted.

For the first time in several weeks, Elisa had some time to herself. Free time had become such a rare occurrence, she almost didn't know what to do. The idea of completely vegging out with junk food in front of the television almost had her pulling on a pair of comfortable sweats. Plus, didn't she deserve a little down time? Especially since she'd been contacted that morning by *Taste of Home* magazine offering her a small job. It wasn't a huge deal, just some photos for a few featured recipes. An all-expense paid trip to their test kitchen in Iowa would earn her a nice chunk of change. The timing was a bit tight—two weekends before Mongolia—but she'd make it work.

In the meantime, she planned on using today to take some recreational photos. Brody had informed her today was his day off, and he would be picking Tyler up from school. The skies were clear and the wind wasn't howling—perfect conditions for snapping pictures.

Elisa gathered her photography bag and tossed in all her essentials. Next, she packed a light snack and a bottle of water.

Ten minutes later, with her bag slung over her shoulder

and shoes on her feet, Elisa opened the front door. She stopped cold when her eyes landed on Brody strolling up the walkway. Suddenly her peaceful day turned very uncertain. She made a futile attempt to moisten her dry lips. It didn't work.

Why did she have to react to him like this? Being near him always made her feel out of control. And every time she was around him, she questioned her decision to leave, as though she were walking away from something very important.

"Did I catch you on your way out?" he asked in that deliciously deep timbre of his.

Flashes of the other night, of his mouth caressing hers, wreaked havoc with her once-tranquil mind.

She cleared her throat, so she could have a prayer of sounding like a normal human being. "I was just heading out to take some pictures." *And thinking about you.*

He came to a stop just a breath in front of her, so close that his intoxicating Old Spice aroma threatened to make her pass out.

"Want to come?" she blurted out.

*Yeah, invite him along. That way you won't be able to concentrate on anything you're doing. Superb idea.*

Little lines appeared at the corners of his eyes when he smiled. "If you don't think I'll be a distraction."

*Oh, I know you will. But I'm willing to make a compromise.*

"I've managed to take pictures with you there before."

"We weren't alone before," he stated simply.

*All the more reason for you not to have him along! Are you insane?*

For years, Elisa had kept herself sheltered from men. After being burned numerous times in the past, she'd learned to proceed with caution before jumping into a relationship.

Perhaps she'd been too cautious? Had she been her own worst enemy by closing herself off?

She shrugged to feign indifference. "I have nothing to be afraid of."

His mouth twitched in a small smile. "Good."

"Let's go then." She led him to her car, where they both climbed in and fastened their seat belts.

"Where were you planning on going?" Brody asked once Elisa pulled out of her driveway.

"I don't know. But I'll know when we get there."

"What are you going to take pictures of?" he asked her.

She glanced at him and smiled. "I don't know that either."

His low chuckle sent goose bumps along her flesh.

"Do you always do this?" he asked. "Just go without any destination in mind?"

Elisa drove through the town, toward the highway. "Actually, no. But sometimes I like to get back to the reason why I started taking pictures in the first place."

"And why is that?"

The town limits disappeared behind them as she headed east on Highway 80. "Just for the love of taking pictures." She glanced at him, and a jolt of sexual awareness shot through her when her eyes connected with his.

She drove them a short distance before heading north toward the Seminoe Reservoir. Routt National Forest was an absolute splendor of Mother Nature. Elisa had seen a fraction of the area several years ago and had never made it back. Unfortunately, the forest was too far south for just a quick picture-taking trip. She'd have to save that for a time when she could make a day trip out of it before leaving Wyoming. Not when she had the most irresistible man in the world accompanying her.

The red cliffs that dominated much of southern Wyoming soared around them with their entire natural splendor. Elisa had always thought there was something majestic about the steep cliffs that gave way to deep gorges, some of which had been carved out by snaking rivers. She could snap photos up here all day.

"I assume now you know where you're going?" Brody asked after making small chitchat with her for most of the ride.

"We're going to the southern part of Seminole State Park. There's some really beautiful scenery up there."

It was a lengthy drive, about two hours, but they finally entered the park and Elisa found a suitable place to search for something interesting. She parked the car, and she and Brody stepped out. With her bag slung over one shoulder, Elisa headed in no particular direction. Brody's long-legged stride easily kept up with her. The man had a way of walking like he owned the ground beneath him. His confident, loose-limbed swagger was just one of many things that had her constantly going weak for him. And he probably knew it too.

"I think this is a good spot," Elisa announced after they had walked for several minutes. They stood on a low plateau that overlooked a winding river below. Beyond that, the view was clear for miles, nothing but nature's architecture.

"No offense, but this doesn't look particularly exciting. There's nothing here," Brody said.

Elisa tossed him a glance while she retrieved her camera from her bag. "That's the point. Don't you ever just go somewhere where there's nothing around?"

"Yeah, my house," he said with a snort.

His joking exterior didn't fool Elisa. She knew better.

That empty house was like a prison for him. Did he miss being part of a family? Did he regret getting divorced? Was the whole thing his idea or hers? There was a whole other side of Brody McDermott he kept under a tight lock, just like Lacy had told her. She'd attempted to gain access to him before, with questions of Tyler. Each time she was met with resistance.

"Before I forget, I want to give this to you." He extended a white business card, clasped between his index and middle finger.

Elisa glanced at it but didn't take it. "What's that for?"

"My father's lawyer. I'm not sure, but he might be able to help you. At the very least, he could give you some advice."

His blunt fingertips brushed ever so lightly over her knuckles when she took the card from him. A ghost of a smile played along his lips. The man had done that on purpose.

"Thanks." She tucked the card in her back pocket. His intense stare had her heart doing all sorts of tricks in her chest. The deep breath she inhaled didn't calm her racing pulse down.

Instead of taking the moment further, which was probably a good thing, Brody took a step back and said, "You seem like you know your way around here."

Even though the brief connection had been broken, his stomach still turned in knots. She wrapped her clammy hands tighter around her camera. If she wasn't careful, she'd break the thing. "My parents used to bring us up here all the time."

"Us?" he repeated.

Elisa ran her fingers over the delicate switches and buttons of the camera. "My brother, Marcello, and I."

Brody was silent for a moment, looking at her. "You have a brother? I don't remember you mentioning him before."

"He was in middle school when our parents died, and I was in college." The questions in her little brother's eyes, the confusion, when she announced he had to leave still haunted her. He'd begged her to let him stay, so they could be together. It's what Mom and Dad would have wanted. He'd been old enough to understand he had to leave his home—and yet too young to really comprehend why.

"And you're close with him?" Brody asked when she'd been silent.

"As close as we can be." She wound the camera strap around her neck. "He lives in South America now."

"With your father's family," he guessed.

Elisa nodded. Normally she didn't like to talk about her brother and the decision to send him away. For years she struggled with the possibility that maybe she'd made a mistake. Maybe she could have found a way to support her younger brother as a college student. But she'd been living in a dorm room several hours away from where he went to school. After she started modeling, the money started flowing in. The traveling had been the one hurdle she hadn't been able to work around. Her agent had managed to book traveling jobs only during the summer, so she could stay in school. How could she have left a teenager to fend for himself while she traveled all over the world for photo shoots and runway shows?

"How long has it been since you've seen him?" Brody asked as though he sensed her inner turmoil.

"Five years. He lives with our grandparents in Rio de Janeiro."

"And you miss him a lot."

Elisa's fingers continued to fiddle and poke at the camera, simply because it was all she could do not to grab onto Brody. The subject of Marcello was too personal, too raw. Brody had a way of coaxing things out of her, as if she didn't have a choice but to share with him, to lean on him like she hadn't done with anyone else.

He took a step closer to her. "That must have been a difficult decision for you to make."

She lifted her eyes to his.

"You had to send him away after your parents died, didn't you?"

She would not ruin this beautiful day by crying. She'd cried over the loss of her brother for years and had since told herself she'd become a stronger person than the lonely college kid she used to be.

"Even though we're eight years apart, Marcello and I were closer than your average brother and sister. When he left it was like losing my best friend." She'd never forget the feel of his arms wrapped so tightly around her neck, just minutes before he boarded the plane to South America. Then afterward, the emptiness in her heart as she walked out of the airport alone.

"Sounds to me like you made the right choice, though. How could you have taken care of him at that age?"

Elisa tucked a strand of hair behind her ear. "I know I did. My grandparents are very successful people. They've been able to provide him with a life that even my parents couldn't. He lives in a huge house overlooking the city; he went to the best schools. He's studying to be a doctor, for crying out loud. He hasn't wanted for anything down there."

Brody tilted her chin up with his index finger. "Except for you. You can't keep carrying the guilt around. It's eating you up."

His bottomless eyes were so easy to fall into. More than once she'd found herself becoming hypnotized by them, and now was no different.

"How is it you always know the right thing to say?" she asked in a husky voice.

His thumb traced her lower lip. "Because I might have an idea of what you're feeling."

She sucked in a breath, and held it for a second. "Because of your divorce?" She would get this man to open up to her if it killed her. Had the dissolution of his marriage been so traumatic that he couldn't even talk about it?

His gray eyes darkened for a moment, like a cloud of grief. "It's not one of my prouder moments, no."

She tilted her head and studied him. Did he blame himself? "What would you have to be ashamed about? Sometimes things like that are unavoidable."

He stepped even closer to her, so that his body heat wrapped her in a mind-tingling cocoon of sexuality. Day by day, Elisa's willpower grew weaker and weaker. How much longer could she resist him? If he kept touching her, like he was now, she'd be too far gone.

"I can't think clearly when I'm around you," he murmured in a sexy, husky voice.

*He* couldn't think? Her brain was mush.

His mouth hovered just a whisper away from hers, not touching but close enough to drive her out of her mind. "Maybe I should just kiss you and put both of us out of our misery."

Brody was in heaven and hell all at the same time.

As soon as his skin touched Elisa's, his body had come alive like it always did when he touched her. He could no more control his reaction to her than he could stop the world from turning. She had a hypnotic pull over him that he'd never experienced before.

He should have just lowered his mouth to hers, instead of giving her warning. He'd much rather catch her off guard than give her a chance to prepare herself.

Despite that, he kissed her anyway, simply because he wanted to and damn the world. He sensed her hesitancy and pressed himself even closer to her. She tasted exactly the way he remembered, like sweet nectar with a hint of sin all wrapped up in a sexy package.

His tongue darted out, coaxing her mouth to open and allow him entrance. With a soft moan, she obeyed and parted her lips. When his tongue slid inside her mouth, lights danced behind his closed eyelids. All the blood rushed down to his dick, so that it hardened and strained against the fly of his pants. Had he ever grown this hard this fast from just kissing?

Her arms snaked around his neck, effectively pulling him flush against her. The damn camera, which hung around her neck, smashed between them and dug into his rib cage. The piece of equipment was a minor annoyance compared to the pure bliss of feeling Elisa's lips against his.

He molded his hands to her backside, his fingers splaying across the length of her lower back. She sucked in a breath and tangled her tongue eagerly around his. It's like they were made to fit together, like their mouths were designed especially for each other. Perfect was the only word to describe the way she felt against him.

She wasn't nearly close enough. He tried to get closer to her, tried to feel those full breasts against his chest. If it weren't for the blasted camera, he would have achieved his goal. However, it didn't seem to bother Elisa. Her fingers threaded through the strands of his hair, as though she wanted his mouth to be fused even harder to hers. He did the next best thing and changed the angle of the kiss, taking it to a deeper level.

Another one of her sweet groans filled his mouth and consumed him with the satisfaction of coaxing such a reaction out of her.

A shallow gasp left her lips, and she yanked herself away. Oh, no. No way was the woman going to pull the same withdrawing act she had the other night. Brody wouldn't let her.

"What's wrong?" he asked in a gruff voice, a result of what she did to him.

Her eyelids briefly drifted shut, and she skimmed her tongue along her bottom lip. "It's the camera. It kept poking me." Her hand pressed into her chest. "I think I'm going to be bruised."

Relief washed over his wired body. "If that wasn't such an expensive piece of equipment, I would have chucked it over the cliff."

Her lighthearted laugh had his hormones racing even faster.

"I don't think I can concentrate on taking pictures now."

Just because he had to keep touching her, he floated his thumb over her still-moist lips. "Would you be mad if I told you that was my intention?"

Her fingers toyed with the camera strap. "Strangely no. You have a habit of distracting me."

He could get lost in her eyes. They were hypnotic and exotic. Yet they held secrets, things that Elisa kept closely guarded for fear of exposure.

"Give me your car keys," he said as he held out his hand.

Her brows twitched together. "Why?"

"Because we're leaving."

Without a word, she passed them over and followed him to her car. She knew what they were doing. Brody made no attempt to keep his desire a secret.

Thick sexual tension filled the car as he drove them home. Funny how the drive back seemed to take twice as long as the drive there, which already seemed like an eternity. Every few minutes Brody would slant Elisa a look out of the corner of his eye. Her hands were clasped in tight balls in her lap, and she stared straight ahead. The woman had a multitude of layers, each different than the other. One minute she practically tried to climb inside him, and the next she was coiled tight like a spring.

In an attempt to ease her anxiety, Brody placed a hand on her thigh and squeezed gently. Her mouth curled in a seductive smile when her eyes met his. Oh, she wanted him. She just didn't know how to handle it. Well, he'd teach her. He fully planned on showing her how to unleash her inner sex kitten.

Her hand uncurled and rested on top of his. Her fingers were so soft and warm, small and feminine. An image of them trailing over his hot skin followed by her mouth almost had him driving off the highway. Never could he remember being this desperate to feel a woman's naked flesh.

They finally pulled into Elisa's driveway what felt like eons later. His hands shook like a randy teenager when he yanked the keys out of the ignition. The camera equipment was left forgotten in the car as they climbed out and walked silently to the front door.

After several fumbling attempts and some colorful expletives Brody finally managed to insert the blasted key into the lock. His clammy and shaky hands turned the knob and the two of them shoved the door open. Brody kicked the door shut with his foot and dropped the keys on the floor.

Elisa's world-class breasts heaved up and down underneath her shirt. Her full mouth was still swollen from his kisses. The idea that he'd caused her to be out of control filled him with a hefty amount of male satisfaction. He wanted to keep eliciting those same reactions from her.

With a slow lick of her lips, Elisa stepped toward him and placed her hands on his chest. He caught her hands in his and held them before they could slip around his neck. "I need you to be sure," he said.

Her gaze dropped to his mouth. The corners of her lips tilted in a small smile. "I'm sure."

His hands tightened on her wrists, then he backed her to the living room until they came to the couch. A nice, big bed would give him plenty of room to spread out and savor her body. But ever since sitting with her on the couch, he'd had visions of lying her on the soft cushions and covering her body with his. Sexual need hummed through his body when Elisa stared up at him with her bottomless brown eyes. She looked so sweet and expectant, as though she didn't know what to expect next. Well, he'd show her. They had plenty of time to enjoy one another.

She leaned forward off the back cushions and brought her hands to the top button of his shirt. Her tongue darted out to swipe across her lower lip as her fingers made fast work of the shirt. In no time at all, the garment hit the floor and his chest was free for her appraisal. Her teeth stabbed into her lower lip as her attention remained on his midsection. Then her fingers touched him, and every muscle inside him clenched like he'd been shot with a jolt of electricity. As though pleased with his reaction, Elisa grinned then touched her mouth to his stomach.

"Ah, shit." He sucked in a sharp breath and closed his eyes. Her lips were so soft, and felt even more heavenly on his abdomen than they did on his mouth. Her kisses were light and tentative, traveling across his stomach.

Just as he was about to push her back on the couch, her fingers clasped his belt buckle and had it unfastened in record time. Her gaze touched his briefly, then lowered to her task. This was not how he'd planned on things going. He'd planned on seducing her and worshipping her until they were both delirious. Somehow she'd managed to take over and knock him off his feet. Her touch and magical mouth had his head spinning. His Latin beauty was a little minx in disguise.

Brody couldn't bring himself to protest when Elisa pushed his pants down and let them drop at his feet. He quickly shoved them aside.

"Elisa," he said when she hooked her fingers into the elastic band of his boxers.

She dragged them down his legs. "I want to," she replied.

"But I'm naked and you still have clothes on."

The boxers landed on the floor. "I'm sure you'll take care of that. In a minute," she added. She sucked in a breath when her attention refocused on his lower abdomen.

His penis stuck straight out, pointing directly at her. He'd grown so hard from her kisses that it was actually painful, and his balls ached. She stared at him in wonder for a moment, as though she didn't have the slightest clue what to do next. Or maybe she was savoring the sight of him, judging by the hunger flashing in her eyes. She licked her lips, then wrapped her hand around his girth, giving him a gentle squeeze. If he hadn't been so determined to get inside her, he would have come right then and there, just from her touch. It was electric and just about the best damn thing he'd felt in a long time. Her hands applied just the right amount of pressure, gliding from the base all the way to the tip. He had to grab her shoulder to keep from dropping to his knees. And just when he thought she couldn't torture him anymore, her mouth cocooned around him.

"Oh, hell," he rasped out when her teeth lightly scraped the tip of his penis.

Women had done this to him before. But none of them had performed with such passion and enthusiasm as Elisa. Her main focus was to rock his world and show him what a giver she really was.

Her mouth continued to work its magic, gliding up and down his length with a silky slowness that had his eyes rolling back into his head. He threaded his hands through her soft hair, allowing the strands to sift through his fingers, like pieces of satin. She really did have the softest hair, and it always smelled so good. The scent reminded him of the wildflowers that used to grow in his mother's flower bed.

Her pace grew more insistent and his hand tightened on the back of her skull. He'd never had this much pleasure in a woman's mouth before, never known a woman to take such time making him feel good.

She groaned, and he almost shot off into her mouth.

"Elisa, stop." He gently nudged her away from him and

gritted his teeth together at the loss of contact. "I'd rather come inside you."

She licked those sweet, plump lips and waited for him to make the next move. He shoved his boxers aside and lay her back onto the couch, pushing her into the soft cushions. His body was wired so tight from the pleasure she'd given him, it took every ounce of restraint he had not to rip her clothes off and shove himself inside her with the force of a jackhammer. She deserved some finesse and seduction. She deserved the same care and attention she had showed him. Even if it killed him, he'd take his time with her.

Elisa cupped his face with both her hands and brought his mouth down to hers. Her tongue tangled around his in an erotic and mind-blowing dance. Who knew Ms. Cardoso had this much fire and hunger inside her? The wanton woman beneath him was nothing like the woman he'd met a few weeks ago.

Her tongue slid languidly along his, and Brody had grown tired of feeling the clothing between them. Without breaking contact with her mouth, he leaned on one elbow and used his other hand to shove her pants over her hips. How he managed to get them all the way off with one hand, Brody had no clue. Elisa helped by wiggling the garment off her feet, where they eventually fell to the floor. Her legs, endlessly long and smooth as a baby's bare ass, immediately wound around his hips. The move brought her pelvis closer to his. Unfortunately she was still covered by a pair of cotton underwear.

He continued kissing her while trying to slip the panties down her legs. The kisses were too explosive and sexy for either one of them to break contact, but Brody wasn't having much luck getting the things off with one hand. And he needed her bare flesh against his now.

Elisa groaned in disappointment when Brody lifted his mouth off hers.

"There's only so much I can do with one hand," he explained.

"Here, let me," she said, and hooked her hands into the elastic and yanked the underwear down. They disappeared to the floor, then she lifted her shirt over her head and tossed that aside as well.

"Hey, you just took all the fun out of undressing you." Despite that, his gaze ran down her body. Except for the baby pink, polka-dotted bra covering the ripest and most spectacular breasts he'd ever laid eyes on, she was finally and gloriously naked. The cups of her bra barely covered two dark pink nipples, nipples he'd been aching to clamp his mouth over and drive her to insanity.

He just barely grazed the tip of his finger over the swell of her breast. "You know that picture of you over there, in the swimsuit?" When she nodded he said, "I want to put that on you, so I can strip it off with my teeth." He peeled one bra strap over her shoulder and dropped a kiss on the bare flesh there. "And then I'd do this," he whispered, and left a trail of kisses from her shoulder to her breast. Using his index finger, he pulled the cup of the bra aside so he could worship the plump mound. He fixed his mouth over her nipple and sucked on it until Elisa was practically hyperventilating. Her fingers threaded through his hair and held his head steady as he swirled his tongue in rapid circles. She squirmed beneath him, grinding her pelvis into his. His dick was so hard it felt like tempered steel, and her gyrating motions only made his hard-on more painful. But he had to make this last. He refused to take her like an animal only wanting to satisfy a need. Damn if she didn't threaten to blow all his good intentions to hell.

He wound one hand behind her back and unsnapped her bra with two fingers. His mouth remained fixed to her nipple as he whipped the thing away from her and flung it across the room. Finally, after eons of waiting, there were no barriers between them—only their hot skin. Brody lifted his mouth from Elisa's breast and stared down at her.

"God damn, your body is downright sinful." She was long and lean with full breasts and a narrow waist. His dick throbbed right above the entrance to her body, and once again Elisa hooked her legs over his hips. She cradled him in those mouthwatering limbs of hers and lifted her pelvis to his. The two of them were matched up so perfectly that he managed to slip inside her with little effort. Her slick heat surrounded him and fogged his brain in a sexual haze. If someone asked him to recite the alphabet right now, they'd be shit out of luck.

Elisa's eyes drifted shut when he flexed his hips and penetrated her fully. A bead of sweat trickled down his temple as he held himself still. He wanted to feel her satin softness cradling him for one blissful moment before spiraling them both out of control. Her arms wrapped around his shoulders and glided down his back. She dug her nails into his ass cheeks, trying to urge him on.

He buried his face in her neck. "Just hold still a minute." Sweet Lord, she felt so damn good underneath him. He almost passed out from the sheer ecstasy of her muscles clamping around him like a velvety vise.

"Brody, you're killing me," she whispered, and tried again to urge him on with her hands on his ass.

The woman was impatient. After holding himself still for as long as he could, he started the slow slide of retreat. Elisa moaned and clenched her inner muscles around him. A startling thought occurred to him after he felt every ripple of her inner wall. He pushed himself onto one elbow and glanced down to where they joined. How could he have been so forgetful?

"What's wrong?" she asked when he'd stopped and gone completely rigid.

He blinked and lifted his gaze to hers. "I'm not wearing a condom."

Relief washed over her beautiful features. "It's okay, I take birth control."

For one brief moment, Brody seriously thought about abandoning his rule and staying inside her. Nothing else would give him more pleasure than to be able to feel her, skin to skin.

He shook his head and pulled all the way out. "I'm sorry, but I can't take a chance."

"Brody," she protested when he left her side.

"I have a spare condom in my wallet." And thank goodness he did, otherwise he'd have to go against his own code of conduct. Strangely enough, Elisa had been the first woman in a long time to make him consider such a thing.

With shaky, sweaty hands, he yanked the protection out of his wallet and fumbled with the wrapper. "Dammit," he cursed when his fingers kept slipping over the packaging with no success.

"Give it to me," she whispered.

He gladly handed the thing over and settled himself on top of her. Elisa made fast work of the wrapper and gave the rolled-up piece of rubber back to him.

"On second thought, let me." She snagged the condom from him. "I don't think you're in the right frame of mind right now."

"Can you blame me?"

The corners of her mouth turned up in a devilish grin as she reached between the two of them and found his achingly hard dick.

"Jesus." He groaned when her fingers brushed along his length. She managed to fit the latex around him, rolling it all the way down to the very base. It was a damn tight squeeze; it was as if he'd swelled even more in the past few minutes.

"You're barely hanging on, aren't you?" she teased, then gave him a hard squeeze.

"Quit that," he warned.

"But I'm having fun. And you like it."

He swatted her hand away, pinned both her arms above her head, and entered her with a single, deep thrust. She gasped and arched into him.

"Serves you right for torturing me," he rasped. "Now it's your turn." More sweat beaded his forehead at the feel of her heat surrounding him. She was so tight and slick. It was the most exquisite thing he'd ever felt.

He stared down at her as he withdrew almost all the way, until the very tip of him was nestled inside, then rammed himself back in. This time Elisa cried out and clenched her hands into tight fists.

He stilled at the thought that she might be in pain. "I'm not hurting you, am I?"

Her eyelashes slowly swept up, revealing deep brown eyes and dilated pupils. "No," she whispered.

Enough of this slow shit. He'd been patient long enough, and he needed to feel her muscles clamp round him in orgasm.

They developed a nice, even rhythm of him retreating and her lifting her hips to meet his pounding. Her arms remained fastened above her head, but her legs bent higher around him, and she locked her ankles on his lower back. He lowered his forehead to hers as her eyes drifted shut, and she muttered something in Portuguese.

"What's that?" He groaned into her neck.

She gasped when he ground himself into her even harder. "Just that it feels so good."

Her words sent him over the edge. He released her hands so he could hold onto her hips. His fingers bit into her soft flesh and held her hips steady as he pounded into her. Her hands gripped his shoulders, her fingernails biting into his skin, as her inner muscles clamped down on his dick and rippled around him. Elisa cried out her pleasure, gasping and moaning and holding onto him for dear life. Mere moments after that, he followed her, jetting out his release in an earth-shattering orgasm that took his breath away. Brody couldn't remember the last time he came so hard and fast. Through the whole thing, Elisa held him with her limbs wrapped around him and her lips whispering his name.

Brody was pretty sure he'd entered another realm.

He pressed gentle kisses into her neck while their breathing slowed, and they both came back to reality. Elisa pulled in a deep breath and ran her hands up his back. She cradled the back of his head with one hand.

"We can't stay here all day like this," she murmured in a sleepy tone.

"You expect me to move while you're touching me like this? I'm thinking about taking a quick nap."

"It's two fifteen," she said as she ran her hand in hypnotic circles over the coiled muscles of his back.

"So?" he muttered into her neck.

She smacked his bare ass. "So you have to pick your son up in forty-five minutes."

He grinned and nuzzled her hair. "Plenty of time for a nap and another round."

"How about a shower instead? We're both covered in sweat."

He lifted his head and stared down at her. "Only if I get to slather soap on you with my bare hands."

# TWELVE

A FEW MINUTES LATER, THEY both stood naked and wet under the hot spray of the shower. They washed their hair at the same time, then took turns rinsing. Brody couldn't help his eyes wandering to Elisa's slick body and remembering the feel of her beneath him. At the moment, her skin gleamed with water, and shampoo ran down her spectacular breasts as she rinsed her hair. Brody stood directly in front of her and watched as she tilted her head back under the water and closed her eyes. The woman was a freakin' fantasy come true.

"You're staring," she said after she opened her eyes and caught him gawking at her. One of her brows lifted when his penis swelled and rose until it pointed out at a ninety-degree angle.

He glanced down at the muscle, then looked back at her. "It has a mind of its own."

She nodded and ran her fingers through her wet hair.

"Do you always slip into Portuguese like that?" he asked, remembering when she whispered the foreign language in his ear.

An adorable blush colored her high cheekbones. She

giggled and grabbed the bottle of conditioner. "Only when I'm…discombobulated."

He took a step closer to her and wrapped an arm around her smooth, slim waist. "Discombobulated?" he repeated, and brought his head down to her neck. Her skin tasted clean and fresh, like the wildflowers he always smelled on her. His tongue darted out and swirled in a circle, then licked up to her ear. Elisa's head tilted to the side, granting him full access.

"I wonder what else I can make you say," he whispered against her skin. He gave her ear one little nip, prompting a gasp from her.

"You don't play fair," she complained, but allowed him to continue to kiss her anyway.

Taking her in the shower, against the cool tiles, quickly shot to the top of his list of fantasies. He wanted to lift her, wrap her legs around his hips, and pump hard and fast into her. Then he wanted to swallow her cries of pleasure as he kissed her senseless. Instead of following through with that scenario, Brody stepped back from her. He didn't have time to drown himself in a sexual fantasy land starring him and Elisa. Tyler was due to get out of school soon, and Brody needed to be on time.

They finished their shower, in between kisses and intimate touches. Whenever he could, he'd run his hands over her breasts, then cup her firm rear end in his hands. Now they stood on the bathroom floor, toweling off.

"Sorry about the whole condom thing. I'm not usually forgetful like that," Brody said as he wrapped the towel around his waist.

Elisa shot him a glance as she rubbed her hair dry. "It's fine. But it wasn't necessary. I told you I take birth control."

He crossed his arms over his chest and leaned against

the countertop. "So did Kelly." Oh, hell, had he really said that? Rule number one: Do not bring up your ex-wife after you've just been intimate with another woman. Something like that could kill the mood real fast.

Brody risked a glance at Elisa and found her staring at him, paused in the act of towel-drying her hair. A heavy, uncomfortable silence hung between the two of them. Kelly was a subject he rarely touched with other women, especially the circumstances surrounding Tyler. A lot of things happened during his marriage, and the earlier days, that he wasn't proud of.

He shook his head. "I'm sorry," he said. "I'm an insensitive asshole. I shouldn't have said that." He shifted against the hard counter and crossed his arms over his chest. "I don't like to talk about my divorce."

"Because it left you scarred?" she asked in that soft voice of hers.

He lifted his gaze from the floor to her deep, brown eyes. Damn that intuition of hers. He wasn't ready for this. She may want to hear about it, but he wasn't ready to spill his guts like a freakin' woman about the demons he carried around.

A small smile, which didn't quite reach her eyes, graced her lips. "I'm sorry, it's none of my business." She finished towel-drying her hair and grabbed her silk robe off the hook on the back of the bathroom door. "But, you know, accidental pregnancies like that are rare."

Brody watched with regret as she pulled the robe over her shoulders and secured the sash. "Birth control failed me once before. Because of that I never have sex without a condom."

"So you don't want to have any more kids?"

"I don't want to have any more *unplanned* kids. Big difference there."

Elisa nodded but didn't respond.

"Does that bother you?" he asked.

"What, the condom thing?"

He nodded.

She offered him a reassuring smile, one he wasn't sure she meant. There was something in her eyes that said otherwise. "No. I respect your choice."

"Come here." When she remained rooted in her spot by the door, he crooked a finger at her.

She took a few steps until she stood directly in front of him. He framed her face with both his hands, then combed his fingers through her cool, damp hair. His fingers reached the ends of the strands, then he used his index finger to tilt her chin up.

"I think you love me," she whispered.

"How do you figure that?" he countered while running the pad of his thumb across her lower lip. Somewhere along the way, Elisa had started to mean something to him. She'd wormed her way inside his heart and had created a nice little home for herself. No woman had accomplished that since Kelly. During the four years since his divorce, Brody had become very selective with whom he'd allowed himself to get close to.

"I just have a feeling." She touched her lips to his in a tentative kiss, preventing him from responding. Then her tongue darted out, coaxing his lips open. He let her inside and kissed her slow and deep while tunneling one hand through the curtain of her hair.

They kissed for several moments in the silence of the bathroom. The whole time Brody tried to tell himself that she wasn't right.

"How serious are you about leaving Trouble?" he asked out of the blue.

Elisa visibly stiffened in his arms. She lowered her gaze to the floor and toyed with the belt of her robe. "Why?"

*Because I don't want you to leave.* "Is it serious, like update-your-passport serious?"

She looked him in the eye and he saw the torment there, the indecision, as though she were wrestling with the important turn of events in her life. "I think so," she said quietly.

Brody didn't respond, because the terrible pain in his chest had damn near incapacitated him. The thought of her leaving, when he was just getting to know her... well, wasn't that shitty timing?

"What do you mean, you can't help me?" Elisa demanded.

The man in the three-piece pinstripe suit sitting across from her moved his shoulders in a half shrug. He leaned back in his opulent black leather chair and folded his hands on his rounded belly. "Beyond sending them a letter, there really isn't anything we can do for you."

Three days after receiving the business card from Brody, Elisa had been able to attain an appointment with the McDermott family lawyer. At first the man's secretary had been hesitant to allow Elisa time in their office. But after Elisa had tossed Brody's name around, the woman's tone changed. She'd been pretty darn accommodating after that. Unfortunately, now Elisa was receiving a too-bad, so-sad response from the lawyer.

Stephen R. Franks, Esquire, rubbed his hand along his cleanly shaven chin. "Do you want to file an official lawsuit against them?"

"If that's what it's going to take to get the money they owe me, then yes."

His sharp blue eyes bore into hers for a moment. "What evidence do you have against them?"

Elisa blinked back at him. "Evidence?" she repeated.

"Yes, you know . . ." He waved a hand in the air. "Some kind of document that proves this illegal activity they're performing."

She gripped her hands tighter in her lap and forced herself not to stomp her feet in frustration. "I don't have an official document, but—"

"Without anything on paper, there isn't anything we can do." He paused, as if in thought. "Look." He leaned forward in his chair. "You said you have this contact at a magazine who first notified you of this, correct?"

"Yes."

"Get in touch with her, and find out if she documented the conversation. Anything would be helpful: an e-mail she can print out, phone records, a fax she received. Something that has on paper their intent to illegally sell your photographs for their own profit. Without that, all I can do is send a letter. But in order to do so, I'd need some contact information for them. An address and a name would be good."

Elisa gnawed her lower lip. "I can give you the guy's name, but I don't know if I have their address."

"Didn't you once have a contract with them?"

A small amount of relief loosened her tense muscles. "Yes, I did."

Mr. Franks nodded his head. "Find the contract and fax it to my secretary. I can reference it, and their address should be stated somewhere."

She picked her purse up off the plush carpeting and settled it in her lap. "I really appreciate the help. I honestly didn't know where to turn."

His eyes softened. "What they're doing isn't right. I'll do what I can to help you." He patted her hand like a father would his child. "And any friend of the McDermotts is a friend of mine."

"Thank you." She gathered her purse and left the luxury law offices.

Overhead clouds dotted the sky and lent relief from the blazing sun. Elisa slid into her SUV with a small amount of relief washing over her. Mr. Franks had waved a light at the end of her uncertain tunnel. His ridiculous fee for typing a single-page letter would be worth it if he could settle the matter. All she wanted was for this company to pay her the money they owed her. Was that so much to ask?

But more than that, if these jerks didn't pay her the money they legally owed her, she might not be able to scrape together enough to travel around after the Mongolia job, if that's what she ended up doing. And the deadline was coming up. Like, really soon.

Yeah, no pressure there. Nothing important or anything.

If that was the case, then, by default she wouldn't have to choose whether or not to leave Brody and Trouble. She wouldn't have a choice.

Elisa wasn't sure she liked that scenario much better. Call her crazy, but she liked having control over her own life. And, right now, it felt anything but in control.

As she made her way through the town and toward home, Elisa's thoughts drifted from lawyers to Brody. Here she was, supposed to be concerned with this legal mess and potentially not being able to fulfill her dream, and all she could think about was the man who'd all but thrown her into a sexual paradise. What did that mean? How was she supposed to go through the motions of her everyday life, when Brody kept inserting himself into her thoughts?

Definitely not how she'd planned things to go. She was supposed to get her career in order, globe-trot a little, collect a few sizable paychecks, *then* meet Mr. Right. It wasn't all supposed to hit her at once. At least not to the extent that she couldn't focus on a potentially serious matter without her mind wandering to Brody and the magic muscle between his thighs.

Oh, the man was crafty. Crafty little . . . gorgeous man.

And yeah, except he wasn't so little. Big was more like it. No, freakin' huge.

*Stop! Focus, lady!*

She'd gone the weekend without seeing him, but thoughts of him had haunted her for the past several days. Thanks to their lovemaking, she hadn't been able to look at her couch without her muscles melting in desire. Every time she closed her eyes, she saw him, felt him. Never had any man taken such time with her body or paid attention to what made her gasp. Brody had shown her a whole other side of seduction she'd only read about, but never thought could happen to her. She succumbed to his will far easier than she had any other man. Perhaps that was because she was downright and head-over-heels in love with the man. Hell, there was no point in denying it. She loved Brody McDermott with a fierceness she hadn't known she possessed.

And she would have to leave him. Never in her life did she think she'd have to choose between her career and a man she loved.

What the hell kind of choice was that? Would it be impossible to have both? In her world, it would be. And, even worse, she didn't have much time to make the decision.

Hell, if she were to base it on her lovemaking with Brody, the choice would be a no-brainer. To hell with Mongolia. Unfortunately, relationships weren't all naked skin and toe-curling orgasms, as much as she'd like them to be. They were a ton of work and a lot of risk. And sometimes the risks outweighed the good. What was the risk to her?

Missing out on the greatest opportunity to come her way. As of now, Elisa wasn't so sure she'd survive taking that risk.

Elisa turned into her neighborhood and drove down the tree-lined street. She pulled into her driveway and parked the car in the garage. In an hour, Tyler would come through her front door and begin the wait for his father. Then Elisa would see Brody. Would things be weird, as they'd been when he left on Friday? Four days without seeing him felt like forever.

There was so much he refused to share with her. Maybe she wasn't important enough. Maybe, to him, she was nothing more than a fling, and therefore he saw no need to let her in. Had that been his plan all along? Bed her, then cast her aside? Of course, if that happened, she'd have no one to blame but herself. She'd given herself willingly to him without thinking of the aftermath. She'd been so consumed with his bedroom voice and the way he undressed her with his eyes.

She entered the house, and her gaze strayed to the couch, as it always did since they'd made love there. Images of tangled legs, Brody's naked skin, and his voice whispering in her ear danced around in her mind again. She needed to do something productive to take her mind off Brody.

Something like locating her old stock contract. Luckily

for her, organization had become a science for her over the years. Her filing cabinet was filled with important papers she'd been leery of tossing away. Over the next hour, she pored over the contract and underlined phrases she felt would be of use to Mr. Franks. After faxing the document, Elisa got on the phone with Shelly, her contact at the magazine, and drilled the woman with questions. She explained about her visit with an attorney.

"I'm afraid I don't have anything documented," Shelly explained. "We had one phone call."

Elisa gripped the phone harder and paced around her bedroom. "The guy didn't send you an e-mail or anything?"

"I do remember getting something from him, but I'd have to dig through my inbox."

"Okay. What about a phone record, or something?" There had to be something concrete on these people.

Shelly's sigh radiated through the phone line. "I'd have to do some serious digging for that. But, Elisa, even if I got a record of the call, I don't know if that would do you any good."

"Why not?"

"All the record will show is a time and date stamp of the call. It won't show what the conversation was about."

Elisa sank on her bed and stared down at the Berber carpeting.

"Let me see what I can find for you," Shelly said when Elisa didn't respond. "It'll take me a few days."

"I appreciate it, Shelly. Anything you can send me would be great."

They said their good-byes. Elisa set the phone on the bed and lay back on the soft comforter. Her eyes drifted shut as more memories of Brody assaulted her again. For the past two nights, she'd dreamed of him, of feeling his thick length moving inside her with determined and purposeful thrusts. The man knew what he was doing and how to please a woman. He knew all the right spots to touch and kiss her. He knew just the right speed to move his hips, so that she didn't know which way was up.

Elisa feared Brody McDermott had ruined her for any other man.

Did he feel the same way about her? Trying to read him was like trying to read a poker player. Maybe she'd been completely wrong about thinking he loved her. Could she possibly be that way off base?

The front door opened—she'd left it unlocked for Tyler—then shut, followed by the footsteps of his soft-soled sneakers. An ear-to-ear grin broke across his face when he saw Elisa.

"How was your day at school?" she asked him after he wrapped her in a tight hug. What a June Cleaver thing for her to say. Like she was his mother.

Whoa, what? Who said anything about "mother"? Odd, though, but that's the routine they'd slipped into. And too easily as well. Tyler coming home to her house. Her, making him something to eat, helping him with his homework. Seeing Brody every day when he came to pick him up. Sort of like...

*No, don't even think it.* They were *not* a family.

And yet...Was this what it would be like if she were to stay in Trouble? Would it feel this nice, this warm? A small part of her was reminded of the days when she had a family. Of when she'd walk through the door and have the house filled with voices of those she loved most. Sometime, when she hadn't been looking, Brody and Tyler had slipped into those roles. Giving her what she'd missed most in the years following her parents' death. The feeling scared her almost as much as the idea of leaving them.

"Boring, like always," Tyler muttered. "I talked to my mom yesterday, and she's coming home next week." Glee lit up his eyes when he talked about his mother. Elisa hardly ever saw that same look when he talked about Brody.

"You must be excited about that," she said, even though the same excitement didn't fill Elisa. Not because she didn't like Kelly; she had a great respect for the woman. Not having Tyler come over meant not seeing Brody every day.

"Yeah, I miss her a lot." Tyler dropped his backpack and walked to the kitchen table. "Is this sandwich for me?"

Elisa smiled at him. "I figured you'd be hungry. After that, I thought we'd go for a walk and take some more pictures."

"Cool."

Fifteen minutes later, the two of them strolled down the street of their neighborhood. The cloud cover had grown thicker since earlier that morning, along with the breeze. The wind in Wyoming had a habit of blowing nonstop, and today was no different. The limbs of the heavily leafed trees swayed back and forth in the gusts.

Elisa had her camera strapped around her neck and Tyler by her side. He chattered nonstop, asking her about cameras and the developing process. Then she tried to get him to open up by asking him how he'd spend the weekend with his dad.

"Did the two of you do anything fun?"

"He took me to an arcade on Saturday night. I wanted to go to a friend's house instead, but he wouldn't let me."

Elisa's heart ached for Brody. It was obvious he wanted

to right a few wrongs by spending some one-on-one time with his son. Clearly Tyler had been burned by whatever had gone on in the past, and now the boy was hesitant to get close to his father.

"Seems to me the arcade can be just as much fun as a friend's house," Elisa commented, trying to turn the tables in Brody's favor.

Tyler lifted his shoulder in a narrow shrug. "Yeah, it was. The next morning, Dad made bacon and eggs for me like he used to."

They reached a small playground at the end of the street, and the two of them settled on a wooden bench. "Your dad used to make breakfast for you?"

Tyler smiled and kicked at a piece of bark with his shoe. "Yeah, every Sunday he'd make us breakfast and serve it to my mom in bed. Sometimes he would even put a flower on the tray because he liked making my mom smile."

A little stab of jealousy hit her square in the chest, almost knocking the breath out of her. Why she should be jealous, Elisa had no clue. They'd been married, for crying out loud. Things like that between married couples were normal. It's not like they were still together. Brody and Kelly had been divorced for several years, and Kelly had even remarried. What Elisa didn't know was if Brody still held some sort of feelings for his ex-wife. Had Kelly initiated the divorce and Brody still harbored feelings for her?

Elisa cleared her throat and refocused her attention on Tyler. The separation of his parents had been rough on him; that much was obvious. "Did your dad do things like that a lot?"

"Yeah. Then he stopped."

"Because your parents divorced?" Elisa knew she'd had to tread this subject very carefully.

Tyler was silent for a moment. "No, he stopped before that. He started working on weekends, and then he was gone a lot."

She slid her arm around the boy's shoulder. "Did that make you sad?"

He nodded. "It made my mom sad too. Then she got mad because he was gone all the time, and he never ate the dinner that my mom cooked."

This was the most Tyler had told her about his parents' divorce. All the boy needed was someone to talk to. "You miss your dad, don't you?"

He sniffed and shifted on the bench. "Yeah," he whispered. "My dad always told me I was his best buddy, and we did everything together. After he moved out, we stopped doing stuff."

Her heart practically cracked in two at the loss of the relationship between father and son. Both had been terribly hurt and didn't know how to heal past wounds. Tyler was confused, scared, and lonely. Brody was probably just as lonely and didn't have a clue how to repair the damage. She knew he was trying, but Tyler had been through a lot and most likely lost some trust in his father.

Tyler's story tugged at her heartstrings like nothing else had.

Elisa hugged him to her. "Tyler, I know your parents splitting up was hard on you. But I know for a fact that your dad misses the heck out of you. And he would love nothing more than to spend every single second with you." When he didn't respond, she pressed on. "Sometimes two married people can't stay married anymore, but that doesn't mean either one of them loves you any less."

"I know. My mom has told me that a lot."

Elisa giggled at his perceptiveness. "Well, it's true."

He glanced at her and offered a small smile. "I just wish they were still married."

"That's natural for you to feel that way." Did that mean Tyler wouldn't accept any woman in Brody's life? How had the boy handled Brody's previous relationships?

Figuring it was time for a subject change, Elisa held her camera out to Tyler. "You want to take some pictures?"

The boy's eyes grew to the size of saucers, and he took the piece of equipment out of her hands. He stood from the bench and took a few steps forward. Just as he raised the camera to his face, a shaggy mutt with a noticeable limp on his back leg came ambling toward them. The dog was all different shades of brown with black spots on his face and legs. His tail was long with thick matted fur that swung side to side. He ambled over to Tyler and touched his nose to the boy's leg.

"Elisa, look at this dog. I don't think he has an owner." Tyler ran his fingers over the dog's ears.

"I think he's hurt," she said as she stood from her spot and approached the animal. He aimed his doggy brown eyes up at her as if to say "Pet me, love me, I'm lonely." Animals had always been a particular weakness of hers. This dog looked like it had been abandoned and then engaged in a few fights, perhaps in search of food or defending itself from bigger dogs. A small chunk was missing from his ear, like another animal had taken a bite out of him. As he stood in front of Tyler, the mutt held up his back leg. There was no collar or identification.

Elisa dropped to her knees and scratched both the dog's ears. He gazed at her with a sadness that tore her guts up inside.

"Maybe he's hungry," Tyler said. "He looks really skinny."

No doubt about that. The animal's skin was pulled tight over ribs Elisa could easily count. This poor dog had been left to fend for itself. Whoever had done this ought to be ashamed of themselves.

Elisa directed her gaze to Tyler. "We should take him to get him something to eat. What do you think?"

"Like at your house?"

"Yeah, I think he needs some taking care of."

Since there wasn't a leash, or even a collar, Tyler and Elisa had to coax the dog all the way back to her house. Tyler kept snapping his fingers and whistling to keep the animal's attention, which wavered several times by squirrels and foreign scents. They finally got the mutt into her house and in front of a bowl of water.

"Wow, he's really thirsty," Tyler said as the dog lapped water for several minutes, sending splashes all over the floor.

Elisa dug around in her fridge for something to feed the dog. "It's probably been a long time since he's had any fluids. The poor thing has been starved." What in the world could she feed this animal? She didn't have any dog food.

She pulled out a piece of wheat bread, tore it into small sections, and dropped them on the floor. They disappeared within seconds.

"Are you gonna keep him?" Tyler asked after he settled himself on the floor beside the mutt and ran his hand over the dog's back.

Elisa squatted next to the two of them. "I don't know. He's in pretty bad shape and I don't have any dog food here." It would probably take several hundred dollars in vet bills to get this animal in better shape. Her parents never had pets, so she didn't know the first thing about taking care of one. Hell, she didn't even know what sort of dog food to buy.

"But he needs somebody to take care of him," Tyler said.

She refrained from making promises to the boy, for fear of having to break them. All she'd wanted to do was give the animal some nourishment. Maybe she could keep the dog overnight and call the local shelter in the morning.

"Do you have any pets at your mom or dad's house?"

Tyler tore up some more bread for the animal and dropped them to the floor. "No. My grandma had a dog but he died. And my mom says dogs make messes."

"Well, they can if they're not trained properly." Elisa gazed at him for a moment. "Maybe you and your dad could take care of him. It could be something the two of you can do together." When Tyler didn't answer her, she said, "Just ask your dad when he gets here. In the meantime, why don't we give this guy a name?"

The mutt had polished off the last of the bread and lowered himself to the floor. Tyler cradled the dog's head in his lap. The boy had already formed a bond with the animal.

"How about Brinkley?"

"Brinkley?" Elisa asked, testing the name out.

Tyler's face lit up with a grin. "Yeah, that was the name of my grandma's dog, and I always liked it. And this one looks like a Brinkley."

She ran her hand over the dog's coarse, matted fur. "Brinkley it is, then."

First she found this great guy, who had a great kid to go along with him. Now a dog? Maybe next she could throw a white picket fence in front of her house.

Actually it wasn't a bad idea.

• • •

Over the next few hours, after taking Tyler with her to purchase dog food, they took turns feeding the dog and showing it the affection it craved. Brinkley didn't move around very well, due to a slight limp in his back leg. However, he was pleased with the bed she'd made for him out of old blankets. After turning in half a dozen circles, Brinkley settled himself in the blankets and slipped right to sleep. The dog's sleepy whines made Tyler laugh.

"How are you coming on that homework?" Elisa asked Tyler.

The boy didn't lift his head from his task. "I'm almost done."

Just as quickly as Brinkley started snoring, he snapped out of his slumber and whipped his head up off the floor. Damn, the dog may have been sickly, but his senses were sure still intact. His two small, scraggly ears lifted, then he pushed himself up on all fours and limped toward the front door.

"What's he doing?" Tyler asked.

Elisa shook her head and watched as Brinkley stopped at the door and cocked his ears.

"I think he hears something," the boy said.

Then the dog let out a quick *yip*, then another. The two high-pitched barks were followed by enthusiastic tail wagging. The kind that wiggled the entire dog's body.

"See, he's a good guard dog," Tyler said as he ran from the table to the door.

Elisa grinned, even though Brinkley's actions were the opposite of guarding. "I wouldn't really call what he's doing guarding."

"Yeah, but he let you know someone's here. See?" Tyler opened the front door, when Elisa had no clue anyone had been standing there. "It's Dad."

Well, then. Wasn't this just all awkward with them staring at each other, with Tyler in between them, having no clue what was going on. Dammit, she hadn't even had a moment to prepare herself, or even check her hair. She'd tossed it up in haste that morning and it now probably looked like a bad version of an updo.

He, on the other hand...now that was a whole other story. Nothing ever looked sloppy or out of place on Brody McDermott. Even after working ten-plus hours and grease stains on his shirt, the man still managed to pull off *GQ* with little effort.

Immediately Elisa's heartbeat picked up to unnatural speeds, and a wave of goose bumps rippled along her skin. His stormy gray eyes zeroed in on her, as though remembering their rendezvous on the couch. Of course she remembered. How could she have thought about anything else?

She forced her eyes to remain above his waist, out of respect for Tyler, even though she so badly wanted to check out that marvelous muscle he'd masterfully used on her. Brody didn't go to such lengths to hide his appraisal. His attention briefly dropped to her breasts, which tingled in the wake of his scrutiny. Her brain conjured up images of his hands on them, pinching and squeezing, followed by his mouth. Her traitorous nipples grew hard just thinking about it.

"You're blushing," Brody stated when he came to a stop in front of her.

Elisa couldn't hide her reaction, nor did she want to. "You have a strange effect on me." His Old Spice aroma enveloped her in a haze of delicious sexuality. When they'd lain together, the same scent had rubbed off on her, and she'd been reluctant to wash it off in the shower.

The tips of Brody's fingers brushed along her jaw.

Elisa waited with baited breath for him to kiss her, to place those masterful lips on hers and send her to another planet.

But he didn't. He just gazed down at her as if trying to memorize her features. Something dark passed over his eyes. Regret, maybe? Did he regret making love to her three days ago?

"Hey, buddy." Brody directed his attention to Tyler and brushed past Elisa.

The encounter left her feeling much colder than she'd felt a few days ago. Something had changed, and she meant to get to the bottom of it.

"Did you finish your homework?" he asked his son.

Tyler gathered his papers and tucked them away in his backpack. "Yeah, I just finished."

"Great, are you ready to go?"

Tyler nodded, and Elisa stood by idly while Brody all but ignored her. The gesture was like a knife through her heart.

"Uh, what the hell is that?" Brody asked.

Elisa followed his gaze to Brinkley sleeping on the floor. "That's a dog," she answered.

His brow wrinkled with incredulity. "Says who?"

"Dad, we found him." Tyler practically vibrated with excitement.

"Well, what's wrong with him?"

Tyler sat down next to the dog. "What do you mean, what's wrong with him?"

"I think he's been abused or in a really bad fight," Elisa answered. "And he's seriously malnourished."

Brody gazed at the dog and Tyler rubbing his hand in circles over the animal's head. He shot Elisa a glance. "Are you keeping him?"

She tried not to allow herself to fall under the spell of his penetrating stare. "I'm not sure. Tyler's already formed a bond with him." She paused for a second. "I was thinking you and Tyler could take care of him. It could be something the two of you could do together."

Brody's brows pulled together. "You mean like take him home? I can't possibly do that."

"Dad, why not?" Tyler demanded.

"Because no one's home during the day. And we don't know anything about this dog. It could have rabies for all we know."

Tyler rolled his eyes. "He doesn't have rabies."

"How do you know?"

"Because he's not foaming at the mouth." The boy was silent for a moment while he petted the dog with soft strokes. "Mom would let me have him," he muttered.

"Mom's not here," Brody said through gritted teeth.

Tyler didn't respond right away. Then he glanced at his father. "I wish she was."

The muscles in Brody's jaw clenched, and he jammed his hands in his pants pockets. Elisa placed a comforting palm on his shoulder, which was hard and tense. Hearing things like that had to tear his heart up. He hadn't said as much, but Elisa knew how much guilt Brody carried around for spending so much time at work. The rift between him and the boy was a palpable thing he didn't know how to fix.

"I'm sorry," she whispered. "I didn't mean to cause a problem."

He glanced at her, his eyes like a dangerous stormy night, as though accusing her of meddling where it wasn't her business. She dropped her hand from his shoulder and took a step back from him. It was hard to believe this was the same man

who had kissed her and made love to her so tenderly, who'd
looked at her as though the words "I love you" were on the
tip of his tongue. But how could he love her? They'd only
known each other for a few weeks, and there were so many
things, secrets, they'd yet to share with each other.

"I'll tell you what," Elisa said, trying to break the ice.
"Why don't I keep Brinkley here, and you can stop by and
take care of him for me?"

Tyler shot a glance at his father, as if giving him one
more chance to change his mind. Brody didn't relent. He
just stood beside her, utterly and maddeningly still, like
he wanted the floor to open up and swallow him whole.

Then he spoke, and his voice was harder than it had
been a moment ago. "Let's go. It's late."

Tyler expelled a long breath, gave Brinkley one last
stroke, and dragged himself off the floor. He shuffled
slowly to the table where his backpack sat. Brody waited
in silence, his eyes tracking his son's every move. Tyler
headed for the door, and Brody directed his thunderous
eyes at Elisa. She stood her ground, fully expecting him
to reprimand her for causing a problem.

He opened his mouth, then closed it. Elisa's heart
almost punched right through her chest when the palm of
his hand cupped her cheek. The warmth of his skin heated
her entire face. His hand was so large and masculine and
felt like absolute heaven touching her. Her eyes dropped
closed when he pressed a soft kiss on her cheek. Then he
whispered in her ear, "It's not you."

He left the good-bye at that and walked out her front
door.

# THIRTEEN

*I WISH SHE WAS.*

Tyler's softly muttered words tumbled over in Brody's brain like some God-forsaken rerun he couldn't get out of his head. Over and over, the whole way home, then as he stood under the hot spray of the shower. They were there, haunting him along with his son's downcast eyes, as though he couldn't bring himself to look at his father. Brody knew the feeling. There were times when he could barely stand to look at himself in the mirror. Not being able to look at himself he could take. But Tyler not being able to look at him? The thought made Brody feel like a suicidal maniac.

Maybe he ought to have taken the damn dog. The thing had looked like a pathetic drowned rat with his all matted fur and gimpy back leg. His rejection of the idea had less to do with the dog itself and more to do with his shitty attitude. A disastrous day at work, coupled with a phone argument with Kelly, and Brody's mood had been as black as the night sky. Seeing Elisa had helped. It'd been like coming out of a murderous storm and stepping into a ray of warm sunshine. His willpower had barely kept him from grabbing her, burying his face in her neck, and breathing in her scent until the world melted away.

It was edging toward eight p.m. and he was downright exhausted. He pulled on a pair of fresh boxers and went into the kitchen. Luckily for his sanity, there was one bottle of beer left. He snagged it off the shelf, popped the top off and tossed it onto the countertop. His cell phone chirped from where the bottle top landed. Brody seriously thought about letting voicemail pick up, as he knew who the caller was and had no interest in speaking with her. The phone continued to ring, the sound grating on his last remaining nerve. Brody simply took a swig of his drink while staring at the device.

Against his better judgment, he picked up the phone and touched "answer" with a sigh. "What," he barked after bringing the phone to his ear.

"We need to finish our conversation," Kelly said without as much as a hello.

"It's finished," Brody answered while walking into the living room and planting his tired ass on the couch. He sank down low, resting his head on the cushion behind him.

"No, it's not. You hung up on me, remember?"

"You deserved it."

"Stop being such an insensitive asshole and listen to me." The end of the last word came off sharp, in the typical Kelly style when she was seriously pissed. Brody didn't give a shit.

He took another deep swig of the drink before answering her. "No."

There was a long pause, followed by Kelly's heavy sigh. "Brody..."

"You're not taking my son away from me, Kelly."

Brody could actually hear Kelly's teeth grinding together.

"Like I told you a dozen times this afternoon, this is not about you. It's about my mother and her needing someone to take care of her."

"See that's generally what you pay the nursing home big bucks for. The taking-care-of part." Brody allowed his eyes to drop closed and pressed the cool bottle to his forehead in hopes of soothing his pounding head. It didn't work. And this bullshit conversation with his ex-wife wasn't helping either. "I'm sorry; I didn't mean that. I know this is hard for you. I'm just tired and I don't want to have this conversation right now."

"Look, nothing is set in stone," Kelly said as though she didn't even hear. Or maybe she did and just chose to ignore it. "But I wanted to let you know that this is something we're seriously considering. We can't just dump her into a nursing home then leave her there. I'd hoped you'd be more understanding."

"Understanding that you want to move my only child three states away? Not likely."

"Well, what would you suggest?"

"How about not moving? Or better yet, bring her here."

Deafening silence from the other end of the line exacerbated Brody's bitch of a headache. "I already told you, transferring her here isn't that easy." A heavy sigh flowed across the phone lines. "We'll talk about this later. I want to say good night to Tyler before I have to go help my mom in the bath."

Brody was too pissed off to make chitchat as he stood from the couch and went to Tyler's bedroom. Apparently Kelly wasn't in the mood to ask him about the weather either. All that came from the other line was her quiet breathing and the occasional word to her mother. The house was eerily silent as he padded barefoot down the hallway toward his son's room. He knocked once on the closed door, then pushed the thing open. Tyler was kicked back in his gaming chair, flipping through a *Sports Illustrated*. Brody came into the room and held the cell phone out.

"Mom wants to talk to you."

A brilliant grin lit up Tyler's face as he dropped the magazine to the floor and grabbed the phone.

"Hey, Mom. You'll never guess what Elisa and I did this afternoon..."

Brody didn't stay to listen to the conversation. He wasn't in a particular mood to plaster a smile to his face and listen to the rescue story of Brinkley.

The bottle of beer remained on the coffee table where he'd set it a moment ago. The thing was nearly full, so he picked it up and gave a few hard swallows. What he really wanted to do was hurl it against the far wall and watch the golden liquid trickle down the beige paint. Then maybe it could puddle underneath the speckled carpeting because he just didn't give a damn. Instead of giving in to his impulse, Brody stared at the bottle for a few more seconds before taking it into the kitchen. Once there, he dropped it into the garbage can, liquid and all. Technically he was supposed to empty the bottle out. Whatever. What were they going to do, arrest him?

Tyler's voice drifted down the hallway as Brody made his way to his bedroom. It didn't seem like that long ago that Tyler would fit into the crook of Brody's arm. He'd pick the baby up, gaze down into the boy's eyes so much like his mother's, and wonder if he'd ever laid eyes on anything more precious. Brody hadn't known jack shit about kids and had been nothing more than a kid himself when Tyler had come along, a scared-shitless kid who wondered time and time again how he'd gotten himself in that situation. As the provider for his family, it'd been up to Brody to be the strong one, to never let Kelly know how uncertain he'd been through her whole pregnancy.

When most other twenty-year-olds had been getting shit-faced at frat parties and banging as many girls as they could, Brody had been elbow deep in baby shit. When not doing that, he'd exhausted himself working long hours. Despite that, the time following Tyler's birth had been priceless for him. During that time Brody would gaze down at his newborn son and see that unrequited love and hero worship children had for their parents. Tyler would blink up at him as if to say "I trust you to always take care of me." Brody had damn near killed himself living up to that expectation for his son and wife. In the end he'd failed miserably.

Now Tyler was leaving him.

Brody landed face-first on the bed and didn't bother with the sheets. He was too restless and antsy. His brain was pulsing up against his skull and his gut felt like it had a ten-pound bowling ball in it. There had to be a way around this. Some alternative to them packing their bags and moving to freakin' Michigan. Maybe he could talk Kelly to moving her mother to Trouble.

He inhaled a deep breath and flopped over onto his back. That position didn't feel any better. But he stayed there because he simply didn't have the energy to flip back and forth like a fish out of water.

In addition to the confusion in his son's eyes was the wounded look on Elisa's beautiful face. There was no denying he'd behaved like an absolute prick. What he felt for her was completely foreign and scared the piss out of him.

*I think you love me.*

Those were the other words that refused to give him peace. They whispered through his mind day in and day out, taunting him, daring to admit she was right. They were the cause of his sleepless nights and his lack of concentration at work. Bad enough were the memories of being inside Elisa, of feeling her silky softness and her hands caressing his back. All those things had caused him to be a ticking time bomb for the past several days.

Wasn't it just his shitty luck to go and fall for a woman, only to have her leave? Why couldn't he have met her years ago? Why couldn't she have another job? Why did she have to steal his heart so damn fast? Despite the looming end of their relationship, Brody didn't think he could bring himself to stay away from her. The smart thing would be to walk away from her now before either of them got any deeper. The problem was, he couldn't. Not only that, he didn't want to. Her deep eyes and soft voice was the only light in his darkness. He knew they had no future, but he also knew he'd keep going back to her for the short time she'd still be there.

He folded his arms above his head and gazed at the dark ceiling. But instead of the blackness, he saw Elisa's face, the confusion and hurt in her brown eyes. She thought he'd been brushing her off, like she'd been some one-time bang and run. If only she knew what she really was to him.

If only he could tell her.

Charlene practically vibrated with giddiness when she went into Brody's office, holding a piece of paper. He'd been going over the week's numbers and welcomed the distraction. His eyes were crossing from his tedious task.

"Have you seen this?" she asked while waving the paper in the air.

He leaned back in his chair. "No, what is it?"

She dangled the paper between her thumb and index finger. "It's a customer review. I've been monitoring the sites closely since Anthony took over. Want to see what it says?"

"Read it to me." If his eyes focused on one more thing, his head would explode.

A delighted grin lit up her eyes. "I thought you might never ask." She cleared her throat and started reading. " 'The last time we came to the Golden Glove, the experience was downright painful. We swore up and down we'd never return. Then we heard from a friend the place has a new chef, and their meal was very good. So we gave it another chance. What a surprise. Our meals were fresh tasting and delicious. We will definitely be back for more.' " She slapped the paper down on the desk and leaned on her hands. "O ye of little faith," she taunted.

"I had plenty of faith," he replied with a smile.

"Liar." Charlene straightened from the desk. "You were scared."

Rightfully so. He still wasn't ready to count his chickens before they hatched.

"I'm going to quote this for our website," she muttered after snatching the review back up. "By the way, Avery and another lady from the youth center are here. What's this about a catering job?"

Brody swiveled back and forth in his chair. "Avery's organizing a fundraiser for the youth center. She mentioned she was having a hard time finding a caterer with suitable food."

Charlene's eyebrows shot up her forehead in surprise.

"So you volunteered the Golden Glove to feed that many people? You think Anthony can handle that kind of volume?"

"This could be a perfect opportunity to show the town we're better than what we were. And yeah, I think Anthony can handle it. He's got a good support staff in the kitchen."

Charlene stared at him for a moment, then glanced down at the review in her hands. "You're the boss," she said with a shake of her head.

"You don't think it'll work?" It wasn't like Charlene to be doubtful.

She lifted her attention back to him. "Have you told your father yet?" she asked, ignoring his question.

He paused before answering. A cloud of uncertainty hovered over her, as though she didn't agree with his decision. "I'll deal with him when the time comes."

"If anyone can calm your father down, it's you. Oh, when's the photo shoot been rescheduled for?"

"Elisa's coming back next Friday." And the thought of having her here again, of having any sort of excuse to see her, had his heart jackhammering against his ribs.

Charlene nodded and opened the door, then halted before going through. "Are you coming? Avery's waiting."

It was only four in the afternoon and Elisa was already ready for bed. At seven a.m. she'd been bright-eyed and bushy-tailed at a nearby bakery to snap pictures for their brochure. The whole thing had taken about three hours. Then she'd had to make a trip into Cheyenne to replace about half her supplies, which had barely been covered by the check she'd received from her work that morning. Around lunchtime, she'd gone out to take photos for the sheer pleasure of it. Only there hadn't been any pleasure in her trip. Her normal iron-clad focus had gone MIA on her and she'd given up after an hour and a half.

On her way home, she'd picked up more dog food for Brinkley and tried coaxing the dog into eating. After that, she'd taken the time to reread her contract with the crooks who'd been stealing from her. The McDermott family lawyer had yet to get back to her on that issue, and her patience was wearing thin. But the damn bundle of papers didn't make any sense. The clauses had funky language and may as well have been written in Sanskrit. Sometime after three p.m. she'd flung the papers aside in disgust and left her bedroom in a huff. Luckily Tyler hadn't been there to witness her black mood.

To conclude her last bit of business, Elisa had signed the necessary paperwork for the job in Mongolia and faxed them back to Professor Harper. He'd immediately e-mailed her with a big "thank you" and told her to stay tuned for more instructions. The moment was bittersweet, because it had essentially doomed her relationship with Brody. Strangely enough, she felt as though she'd just lost a piece of herself. But if she didn't take this opportunity, she knew she'd regret it for the rest of her life. She owed it to herself to see if this trip would spiral into anything more. She'd worked too damn hard to let another offer pass her by.

If that meant walking away from Brody, however heart-wrenching, then so be it.

His earlier brush-off was like a rusty knife in her gut, then twisting it nice and deep. All day she'd racked her brain, trying to think what she'd done or what had happened that she'd missed. The only thing she kept coming back to was their brief conversation about Kelly after their shower.

Was it such a sensitive subject that it would cause him to shut down like that? Elisa thought after making love, they'd be at a point where they could share things like that with each other. Maybe that was just a woman thing and men viewed intimacy differently.

Or maybe there was no real issue at all. Maybe the sex had taken the excitement away and Brody simply wasn't interested in her like that anymore. The polite "hellos" and chaste kisses on the cheek would certainly point in that direction. Every time she saw him, her pulse went up to unnatural speeds and a funny thing happened in the pit of her stomach, almost like her heart had dropped down to it. Was it possible Brody didn't have the same reaction to her anymore?

Or the more reasonable explanation—Brody knew she was leaving anyway, so why let himself get close? That would be the smart thing to do. So, why did that create an ache in her chest?

He'd called her that morning to tell her he was taking the day off of work, so she wouldn't see him until tomorrow. According to Tyler, Kelly was supposed to come home next week. Then she and Brody would have no reason to see each other. Maybe all they'd had was a fling and she needed to accept it as such.

The idea created a sick feeling in her stomach.

She'd just picked up her phone to make an appointment with the vet to have Brinkley examined when her doorbell rang. Elisa set the phone back on its base and went to answer the door.

Brody stood on her front porch, his hypnotic eyes hidden behind a pair of dark sunglasses. Elisa tried to squash down her reaction to him, which was the same as it always was: her cursed stomach turning over on itself.

Beside Brody, Tyler beamed up at her as though she was the best thing he'd seen all day.

"H-hi," she stammered after finding her tongue.

Tyler launched himself at her and wrapped his skinny arms around her waist. He squeezed so hard, Elisa feared he would crush her ribs. He lifted his head and pinned her with his green eyes. "We came to see Brinkley."

"Oh," Elisa responded, slightly deflated that Brody hadn't come to see *her*. She stepped back from the boy and led the two of them into the house. Brody still hadn't said a word to her. "Well, I'm sure he'll be happy to see you. You really made an impact on him."

"I missed him." Tyler bounded on excited feet to where the mutt had draped himself across her carpet. "Mom says we can't have him but Dad said he'd think about it."

Elisa risked a glance at him. The sunglasses once covering his eyes were hooked in the front pockets of his jeans. "Well, thinking about it is better than a no," she said.

One corner of his mouth kicked up in an almost grin.

Oh Lord, his silence was killing her!

"Can I take him for a walk?" Tyler asked from behind them.

Elisa managed to tear her attention away from Brody's penetrating, borderline-scorching stare and glanced at Tyler. The boy had found the purple leash she'd bought for Brinkley.

"If it's okay with your dad," she replied, and risked another peek at him.

If he stared at her any harder, she would melt into a pathetic puddle of hormones right at his feet.

"Go ahead" were the first words out of Brody's mouth since walking through the door. "Just watch for cars."

"Sweet!" Tyler looped the leash through the dog's collar and managed to coax the animal to his feet. Brinkley hobbled to the front door, eventually following Tyler outside.

Oh, good. Now she and Brody were alone. Just the two of them in her empty house. Near the couch where he'd given her the most exquisite orgasm of the century. Completely and utterly alone.

Hadn't she just been wishing for a moment like this? Now she wanted to crawl out of her skin.

She faced him, took a deep breath, and gave him a piece of her mind. "Look, I don't know what your problem has been, and I can't figure out what the heck I did, but you've been downright frigid with me. Quite frankly, I don't like it—"

Her rant was cut off by his hand curling around her neck and his lips molding to hers.

# FOURTEEN

ELISA WAS TOO STUNNED TO move. At the same time, Brody's mouth felt too divine for her to pull away. She wanted this. She wanted *him*.

His tongue immediately invaded her mouth, swirling around hers in that sensual way of his, as if he'd taken kissing classes and graduated in the top of his class. The kiss was enough to send her comatose, but coupled with his spicy aftershave...what a lethal combination.

He changed the angle without so much as slowing down. His mouth slanted over hers, massaging her lips and threatening to make her black out. Each night her dreams were filled with this, of him kissing her and eventually peeling her clothes off one article at a time. The hand on the back of her neck tightened and his other arm snaked around her waist. The move brought her in full body contact with him, from his thick chest to his feet moving on either side of hers.

Elisa lost her balance and swayed slightly. Brody's arm tightened on her back, keeping her in contact with him. The floor beneath her feet tilted. Was the room spinning? Good grief, she didn't even know where she was.

She threaded her fingers through the downy softness of his hair. The strands were short and neatly combed, and she had every intention of messing them up.

His lips left her mouth and she groaned at the loss of contact. They trailed down her jaw and continued on to her throat. He mixed soft kisses with little love bites, allowing his teeth to just barely nick the skin. When he came to her ear, she gasped. His breath was warm and his tongue wet. He used the latter and ran a trail down the column of her throat to her collarbone. Then he came back up again, nipping the soft skin beneath her ear. Elisa tilted her head to the side, letting him know that he could spend as much time there as he wanted. She didn't want him to leave—ever.

She whispered his name and dug her fingers into his shoulders. His mouth descended on hers again, assaulting her with beautiful sensuality. Would they end up back on the couch? Or would he escort her to the bed this time?

*I think you love me.*

Her own words slammed into her out of nowhere and sucked the sensual haze away. He hadn't answered her. Part of her hadn't been surprised, yet another part had been deeply wounded by his silence.

*What do you expect from someone who obviously has demons he still carries around? And one of them is named Kelly.*

Reluctantly, she disengaged her lips from his and dropped her arms to her side. She took a step back just as Brody's dark brows lowered over his eyes.

"What's wrong?" he asked in a husky voice.

Elisa hugged her arms to herself to ward off the chill that just came over her. "Nothing, I—"

"No, you don't get to say 'nothing' this time. Your whole body went stiff just now. What happened?"

*Just tell him. How's he going to know unless I give him a chance?*

She plunged forward and hoped it didn't send him out the door. "I'm having a hard time understanding you. One minute you're all hot for me, and the next you barely glance at me." He lifted a brow as though questioning her. "With the exception of just now. I mean..." Restless energy coursed through her bones, sending her pacing around the room. She walked to the spot Brinkley had occupied, then back again, this time putting the breakfast table in between them.

"I don't know what you want me to say, Elisa."

"Anything," she replied with exasperation. "Something's happened but you won't tell me what it is. And you're still carrying this weight on your shoulders from your divorce, and you haven't dealt with it. That's why you're pushing me away."

He jammed his hands on his hips and inhaled a deep breath, as though trying to find the strength. "I'm sorry about the other night, when I picked Tyler up. I was a complete jerk, and you didn't deserve that."

Something snapped inside her at his evasiveness. Apologies were nice and everything, but they were not what she wanted from him. She stalked around the table and came to a stop in front of him. "I don't care about sorry, Brody. I just want you to give me all of you and not the parts you want me to see. There's a very big part of you you're holding back from me. Why do you do that?"

The muscles in his jaw flexed and his eyes zeroed in on her. His internal battle was a tangible thing. How long had he been carrying this burden around with him? And why wouldn't he include her? Was she not important enough to him?

"Brody, I can't just be a vessel for satisfying your sexual needs. I have to know I'm more than that to you."

He lowered his forehead to hers. "Elisa, you have no idea what you're asking of me. There are things I've never told anyone before."

The wounds inside him went much deeper than she originally thought. Something other than the pain of a divorce had been consuming him for so long. "But I do know what I'm asking." She cradled his face, and his whiskers bit into her palms. "I wouldn't have asked you if I didn't want to help you."

His hands were big and warm on her cheeks. He cupped her there, then lowered his mouth in a gentle kiss that knocked the breath out of her. Every time he kissed her, there was an urgent desperation she'd barely been able to keep up with. This was a different man kissing her, as though he feared whatever ugliness he kept tightly hidden would surface and scare her away. Elisa didn't care what secrets he had. She loved him, flaws and all. She could take whatever he tossed her way. What she couldn't take was the secrecy.

His tongue ran along her lower lip, just barely slipping inside her mouth. Her body melted, as it always did when he seduced her like this.

"Dad?" The sound of Tyler's voice coming out of nowhere shocked both of them. Elisa jerked away from Brody as if she were some teenager who'd been caught by her parents.

Then another female voice rendered her speechless. "Nice, Brody."

Brody muttered a curse and ran a hand through his hair.

There, in Elisa's doorway, stood Kelly, along with Tyler, who must have opened the front door without Elisa noticing because she'd been too busy sucking on his dad's face. Brinkley's brand-new purple leash was wrapped around one of Tyler's hands. The dog nudged him, and the boy absentmindedly scratched Brinkley's scruffy ears. Both mother and son stared at her and Brody with wide eyes, though both their expressions were different. Tyler's was of confusion and Kelly's was disapproval.

Kelly's gaze lingered on them a moment longer before turning to her son. She placed a palm on Tyler's shoulder. "Honey, why don't you take Brinkley to the backyard so he can go to the bathroom?"

Tyler glanced at his mother as if to say "But I just did that." He didn't argue, probably because he knew better not to. He tugged Brinkley behind him, then went through the sliding glass door.

"So this is what you do with your time, Brody?" Kelly asked him. "Sending our son out to walk a strange dog so you can make out with his babysitter?"

Elisa jumped in to defend Brody, who already had enough to deal with. "I swear that's not what happened—"

"You told me you were coming home next week," Brody butted in as though Elisa hadn't even spoken.

Kelly stared back at her ex-husband, her brows pinching together in disapproval. "Don't you dare try and make me feel bad. I came home a few days early and wanted to surprise Tyler. I figured he'd be here, but then I saw him walking that dog down the street."

"Tyler and I found the dog one day, and I decided to keep him," Elisa said, still feeling the need to defend Brody. "I think he's formed an attachment to the dog."

"We came over here because Tyler said he missed Brinkley," Brody added. "He asked if he could take the dog for a walk. There was no hidden agenda behind anything."

Kelly uncrossed her arms, which she'd been holding tight across her chest. "Whatever, Brody." She stalked passed them and left an icy trail of hostility in her wake. One of Elisa's biggest fears was having a problem with Kelly and confusing Tyler. The look on the boy's face had been one of utter bewilderment, and it pierced her heart. She felt like she'd breached the boy's trust.

"Tyler, time to go," Kelly called through the open back door. The boy came through, wrapped his arms around Elisa's waist, and said good-bye to his father. Kelly opened the front door and slid her sunglasses on. "We still have to talk," she said to Brody.

Seething anger rolled off Brody in waves. Elisa had never seen him so tense before, as if he could break a cinder block with his bare hands. He glanced at Elisa as though he wanted to come to her and kiss her good-bye. But he didn't. Instead, he marched toward his ex-wife. "I'll walk you out," he muttered.

They walked out of the house, leaving Elisa alone and feeling like she wanted to be swallowed up by a black hole.

Several hours later, Elisa felt like she'd been run through the gauntlet. After Brody and Kelly's frigid departure, Elisa had run a hot bath for herself and soaked in the water, along with her own misery, for the better part of an hour. The only reason she got out of the bath was because the water had turned downright tepid. As the water swirled down the drain, she'd wrapped herself in her thickest robe and collapsed on her bed. For the next hour and a half she dozed, although it wasn't a peaceful sleep. No, she'd been tortured by the images of Brody undressing her with those smoldering eyes of his. Then her dreams had slowly shifted into nightmares of Brody and Kelly, yelling at each other, and poor little Tyler caught in the crossfire. Then they turned their hostility toward her, blaming Elisa for everything, saying she ruined their chances at being a happy unit again. What a ridiculous thing, wasn't it? They'd already been torn apart by the time Elisa had come into the picture. But her subconscious didn't know the difference. Her cursed mind was playing out her worst fears and her paranoia.

A fine sheen of sweat coated her forehead and in between her breasts. She rolled out of bed like her limbs were made of lead. It took all her strength to put one foot in front of the other.

*This is what happens when you fall in love.* And this was why she'd tried so hard to protect her heart after her only serious relationship had blown up in her face. Somehow she knew allowing Brody into her heart wouldn't end well. He'd been damaged in more ways than one and didn't have anything left inside him to give.

Hadn't he said so in so many words?

*I don't know what you want me to say.*

She'd wanted to say *How about you love me?* But she'd already given him the opportunity once, and he'd basically slammed the door in her face. Elisa hadn't been too eager to allow him that chance again.

She padded barefoot down her hallway to the kitchen. Brinkley hadn't touched the food she'd given him, and he seemed even skinnier than he'd been when she'd found him. She needed to get him to a vet ASAP.

In the meantime, she opened the fridge door and gave the contents inside half a glance. Why was she looking in here? She wasn't even hungry.

She closed the fridge door with a soft *thump*. What she

needed was a distraction. Something to remind her she actually had some self-worth.

She went back down the hallway and made a detour to her office. A few stock agents had requested to see some of her photos, which she'd already mailed. But she was restless and felt the need to send more queries. In a spiral notebook was a list of all the stock agencies in the country that specifically dealt with landscapes. Elisa retrieved the book and started with the next name on her list. Minutes ticked into an hour, then two as she organized photos into portfolios, and printed query letters. Each one got its own thick manila envelope and was stacked neatly on her desk all ready to be mailed first thing tomorrow morning.

Afterward, Elisa expected to feel better. But now, instead of her mind being occupied by her paying job, it was a jumbled mess of more than a dozen things: Brody, mysterious online crooks stealing from her, and her ability to pay her bills in just a few months. She should have known Brody would have been too hard to shove out of her mind. The man was too dominant of a force.

The moon was nonexistent, and her house was shrouded in a thick blanket of blackness. The darkness surrounded her and made her eyelids grow heavy. For the first time all evening, Elisa felt like she could actually sleep. She had just dragged her weary bones to her bedroom when the phone rang. Briefly she considered not answering, then changed her mind. She went to the phone, hoping it was Brody apologizing and professing his undying love for her.

"Hello?" she answered.

"Hey, *gatinha*."

The Portuguese slang for *good-looking* rolled off her brother's tongue and brought tears to her eyes.

"Marcello?"

"Who else would be calling you this late?" His question was accented by a deep chuckle.

The sound was so familiar and as welcome as a warm fuzzy blanket on a cold day. She sank to the bed and leaned against the headboard.

"Sorry for the phone tag. I've been so swamped with studying, lectures, and logging hours in a clinic that I've barely had time to breathe."

Elisa couldn't respond because tears were streaming down her face like Niagara Falls. She held back a hiccup and tried to gather her composure.

"What's wrong, *irmã*?" he asked when she still hadn't said anything.

Slang word for *sister* made her cry even harder. "I'm sorry, Marcello. I've just missed you so much. I've really needed someone to talk to." The floodgates had opened, and nothing was going to stop her from spilling her guts now.

"Tell me," he demanded in his slightly accented voice.

Elisa pulled in a cleansing breath and emptied everything she had inside her, including Brody. It all came out in such a rush, as if saying the words was a way of detoxing her system. Her brother remained silent, allowing her to say as much as she needed, sometimes crying in between stories. He didn't interrupt her, or tell her to calm down or get over it. Marcello always knew the right thing to say.

"Are you in love with this man?" he asked after she finally stopped whining.

She dropped her head back and stared at the ceiling. "Yes. How do I always manage to fall for the wrong guy?"

"Something tells me this guy isn't going to screw you over the same way Micah did."

"Yeah, Brody definitely isn't gay." Didn't matter. Brody would end up shattering her heart a thousand times more than Micah did.

Marcello sighed. "Do I need to fly up there and kiss this guy's ass?"

Elisa giggled and picked at a thread on her blanket. "You're so sweet. But I can fight my own battles."

"You want my honest opinion?"

She hesitated, then answered with a soft "Yes."

"This guy's running scared. Sounds to me like he's carrying around a lot of guilt, and his first marriage didn't end well. When men get scared, we turn into babies. Our first instinct is to run in the other direction." He paused while speaking softly to someone. Then he continued, "This guy's in love with you, Elisa. I'm sure of it, and I don't even know him."

"How can you be sure of that?" Elisa so badly wanted to believe Brody returned her feelings, but his actions told the complete opposite.

Marcello chuckled. "I know how the male mind works. Our minds are weak. We fall for a woman and we don't have a clue how to handle it. My best advice is to give him space and let him figure it out on his own. If you push the issue, he's likely to shut down completely."

If only. What if he never figured it out? What if she waited her life away for a man who couldn't let go of his demons?

Elisa wiped at her eyes with the cuff of her soft robe. "Enough about me and my poor woes. Tell me what's going on with you."

Marcello went on to tell her about how he spent more time in school than he did at home. Their grandfather had been helping him study for his next round of exams, which were in a few weeks. Then the tone of Marcello's voice changed when he talked about Adriana, a young professional ballet dancer, who was originally from Argentina. He met the woman when she'd come in to the clinic with a sprained ankle, a hazard of her occupation.

"I discharged her and coaxed her into giving me her phone number. I think she pitied my desperate attempt at a date."

Elisa smiled. Her little brother was so grown up. "That's not why she agreed to go out with you. You're charming and good-looking. And you're a med student."

"I feel funny around her, like my heart just dropped to the bottom of my stomach. I've never felt like this before."

Yes, Elisa understood that. Because she felt the same way around Brody.

"Sounds to me like you have your own love problems," she told him.

"I wouldn't say it's a problem." He paused a moment. "I'm sorry, I didn't mean it like that."

"It's okay. I'm really happy for you. You deserve to find a good woman."

Some background noise came through the other end of the line. "Listen, I've got to go. But I wanted to tell you that I'm planning on coming up to see you next year. I could really use the break from studying."

The thought of being with her brother filled her heart with so much joy. "Only if you have time. I don't want to take you away from your work. I know how busy you are."

"I can take a little time away from work to see my sister. And it's not fair that you always have to fly down here."

Elisa smiled at her brother's thoughtfulness. "I've only been down there twice, and once was only because I had happened to already be there."

"Nevertheless, I haven't come to visit since I moved down here."

"Maybe you could bring Adriana with you," she suggested with a grin.

Her brother chuckled, which sounded a bit nervous. "Let's not get ahead of ourselves here. My pager's exploding so I have to go. We'll talk again soon."

They said their good-byes and hung up. Elisa placed the telephone on the nightstand and sank down to the bed. The glowing clock across the room said one a.m. She ought to be fast asleep, but she was afraid. The dreams might return: the one where Kelly and Brody blamed her for causing turmoil, the one where Brody glared at her with accusation and resentment. Or, even worse, the one where his eyes smoldered at her right before he stripped her down to her bare skin. She hated that dream even more, because it reminded her how much in love with him she was.

Thankfully, no dreams came. Just sweet, restful sleep.


"Can I come in?" Elisa practically held her breath while the other woman didn't say anything. Kelly had a suspicious look on her face, as if she wanted to slam the door on Elisa for being so presumptuous. And maybe coming to see Kelly was a bit audacious. But a little voice had been nagging at her, saying *You need to make this right*. Simply dusting things under the rug wasn't the way Elisa operated, and her friend was no different. She'd caught Elisa making out with her ex-husband. Even though the off-limits rule had never been enacted, she felt like she owed the woman . . . well, something. At least an explanation.

Kelly pursed her heart-shaped lips and seemed to consider the situation a moment longer. Then she stepped back and held the door open wider. "Sure."

Elisa resisted the urge to heave a huge sigh of relief. Instead, she followed the other woman inside and tried not to gawk at the interior of the home. Kelly and her husband had completely remodeled their sixties ranch-style home. Everything was contemporary yet homey. At the same time, all the touches, down to the wainscoting in the entry hall screamed top dollar. Kelly and her husband had probably spent more money on the deep-mahogany hand-scraped wood floors than Elisa had for all of her camera equipment combined. Then again, they could probably afford it. Colin was a chiropractor in a neighboring town and worked long hours.

The two women walked down the narrow hallway, which opened up to a great room with a vaulted ceiling. Rich-wooden exposed beams decorated the top of the soaring room, which was twice the size of Elisa's cozy family room. Various photos of Tyler were perched on random shelves of a built-in bookcase. Kelly's home was very comfortable, the type of place where Elisa felt she could curl up on the couch with a roaring fire.

"Would you like something to drink?" Kelly asked.

They entered an eating area, where the centerpiece was a gorgeous antique farmhouse-style kitchen table. On the wall opposite the table was one of Elisa's black-and-white photographs, blown up and adorned in a shabby-chic frame. Elisa was surprised Kelly hadn't taken the picture down and burned it.

"No, I'm fine. Thank you," Elisa finally answered.

"I promise not to poison it," the other woman said with a smile. She gestured toward the kitchen. "And I just made iced tea."

Elisa found herself smiling back, and she relaxed by slow degrees. "In that case, I'd love some tea." She settled in one of the four chairs at the dining table and waited.

The house was so quiet, save for the ticking of the old German-style cuckoo clock. Tyler still didn't get out of school for several hours, and Elisa missed the boy. She missed his inquisitive questions and quiet, thoughtful voice. No doubt, he was back where he belonged: with his mother. Would Kelly object if Elisa were to drop by and visit the boy?

A small smile graced Kelly's pretty face when she walked back into the room. She placed a glass of tea in front of Elisa, then took a seat at the table next to her.

They sipped in silence for a moment, then Kelly spoke. "Tyler was just telling me this morning that he misses you already. And that dog." Kelly took a sip of tea and lowered her glass. "Tyler said you found him while you were out walking. Do you really plan on keeping him?"

"Not at first. I thought maybe—" She almost told Kelly about her suggestion about Brody taking the dog. Then she thought, *Maybe not.* "I thought maybe about taking him to a shelter. But now I'm not sure. He's growing on me."

Kelly shook her head. "Good luck. He looks like he needs some serious TLC."

Elisa ran her finger over the rim of her glass and tried to channel some courage. *Kelly's your friend, remember? She'll forgive you.*

"You have something you want to get off your chest, don't you?" Kelly asked, just as Elisa was about to plead her case.

"Yes, it's about the other day, about…" She paused, trying to find the right words. "What you walked in on." Good Lord, she couldn't even look at Kelly, and her brain was dangerously close to not functioning properly—all because of a man. Finally, she lifted her gaze to Kelly's.

"I just needed to apologize. I felt like maybe you got the wrong impression."

Kelly tilted her head to one side, as though scrutinizing Elisa. "You mean the one where you were making out with my ex-husband?"

It sounded so harsh when Kelly worded it like that, even though that's what Elisa had been doing. And if she and Brody hadn't been interrupted, they likely would have ended up on the couch again.

"Yes, I guess that would be the one," Elisa said with a nervous chuckle.

Kelly shook her head again and offered Elisa a reassuring smile. "It's okay, Elisa. You don't have to say sorry. Brody and I have been divorced for several years now. He's allowed to date whoever he wants."

"I wouldn't really say that's what we're doing," Elisa responded quickly.

Kelly studied her for a moment. "Then what are you doing?"

*Well, so far it's been mad, passionate sex. Don't tell her that, dummy!*

Elisa took a shallow sip of some tea. The drink was cold, smooth, and sweet. Just what she needed. "To be honest, I'm not sure."

"I know what you mean," Kelly said with a laugh. "Brody has a way of making a woman feel unsure about herself. And you have that look about you. Like you're in love with him."

A small, startled gasp escaped Elisa's lips. How in the world had Kelly figured it out? Just from seeing the two of them together?

Kelly pressed on, not giving Elisa a chance to explain herself. "I know, because it's the same look I had when I was nineteen. Trust me, I know how you feel."

And, suddenly, Elisa didn't feel the urgency to ask Kelly's forgiveness, like the words were Kelly's way of forgiving her. Because the woman had once had the same feeling, the same helpless, drowning-in-overwhelming-love that Elisa had. How in the world had she survived that?

"I don't want to pry," Elisa replied softly, even though she really did.

Kelly took a long draw of her tea, then dabbed her mouth with a white napkin. "You're not prying. It's just something I haven't talked about in a long time." The other woman stared at a point over Elisa's shoulder.

"You fell in love with him quickly," Elisa guessed.

Kelly nodded. "Oh, yes. Very much so." She shook her head. "Boy, he could make my head spin. I had never felt anything like that before. Completely blindsided me."

Well, Elisa could certainly relate to that. Apparently Brody had a way of sweeping the rug out from under a woman's feet.

"What went wrong? I mean..." Shit, what did she mean? *Why did you get divorced?*

"A lot happened in a very short amount of time. It wasn't until years later that everything caught up with me, and I realized the life that I'd been waiting to happen was already happening. Does that make sense?" Kelly asked in an uncertain tone.

"Kind of."

Kelly pursed her lips and stared down into her tea. "I found myself pregnant with Tyler two months after I met Brody. I had just turned twenty. By then I was already so much in love with him, I couldn't think straight when he was around." She paused and cleared her throat. "Anyway, we were both living in separate dorms, and because of our situation, we were kind of forced to move in together off campus. Not that I felt forced. The idea of living with Brody sent me over the moon."

"But you think he felt forced?" Elisa asked.

The other woman exhaled a deep breath. "I think if I hadn't ended up pregnant, the idea of living with me wouldn't have occurred to him."

Elisa studied Kelly closely. And for the first time, Elisa saw the signs of old hurts that Kelly had probably been carrying around with her for a long time. She'd fallen in love with Brody, gave him a son, married him, and yet he never truly loved her back. Or so Kelly seemed to think.

"Because we weren't living in college housing," Kelly continued, "we both had to work longer hours to pay bills." She lifted her gaze to Elisa's. "It wasn't easy. Going to school full time, working full time, being pregnant. Hardly ever seeing Brody because our schedules were opposite. He went to school during the day and worked nights, and I took night classes so I could work as a receptionist during the day. But somehow we made it work."

"How did you manage all that after Tyler was born?" Elisa couldn't imagine juggling such a full plate. And Kelly had done it at a young age, when most other twenty-year-old girls were living carefree.

Kelly fingered the pearl earring adorning her ear. "By then we were already living in Trouble. Brody graduated right before my due date, and we moved here so he could go to work for his father."

"You didn't graduate with him?"

"No," Kelly said with a shake of her head. "I still had two years left. But we both knew we couldn't stay where we were. Brody needed to make good money so he could take care of us, and I could stay at home with Tyler. I had never been to Wyoming and I wasn't thrilled at the idea of moving here. But as his wife, it was my job to support Brody in whatever he wanted to do. His father offered him a job with really good starting pay. Plus Brody wanted to be close to his family."

Elisa stared back at the woman. "So you gave up your degree and moved here. And didn't you miss your family?"

Kelly nodded and picked up her glass. "Oh, I missed them terribly. That's why this thing with my mother hit me so hard. I feel guilty that I wasn't there for her when it happened. Anyway, I basically dropped out of school. I was five semesters short of graduating. Then I had planned on getting my graduate's degree." A wistful smile broke across Kelly's face. "I'd always wanted to be a relationship therapist."

"But you never got to be one," Elisa concluded. She'd never realized how much Kelly had given up, how lonely she must have been. "And you never had the opportunity to finish school?"

Kelly shook her head. "Not really, no. After we moved here, Brody worked long hours to support us. I stayed home with Tyler, and I knew there was no way I could go back to school and get my degree. I kept thinking, maybe sometime in the future when Tyler got older, but...things started going downhill in my marriage."

Kelly stopped talking suddenly and took a long sip of her tea. She gulped the drink down and closed her eyes briefly. This was like opening an old wound for her. Elisa sensed the other woman's discomfort and anguish. Then she remembered Brody's words from the other day.

*There are things I've never told anyone before.*

"How long has it been since you've talked to anyone about this?" Something told Elisa that Kelly had been virtually alone during her divorce from Brody. Chances were she didn't have anyone to confide in.

"I've never talked to anyone about it. No one knows what really happened. Not even Colin."

Elisa placed one of her hands on top of Kelly's in an attempt to comfort her. She was still hurting. "Tell me."

The other woman's gaze remained on her tea. "I gave up so much for him," she said, as though she didn't hear Elisa. "I sacrificed everything. I left my home, moved away from my parents, gave up the opportunity to have a career, quit school, and he—" She stopped and licked her lips, then pulled in a shuddering breath. "And he's being so difficult about this situation with my mother."

"What else did he do, Kelly?"

"I loved him more than I had ever loved anyone," she said instead of answering Elisa's question. "Clearly Brody hasn't told you anything about our divorce, and I don't think he'd appreciate me telling you this."

Elisa was curious about the comment regarding her mother. But right now, she felt the need to get to the bottom of Kelly's troubling words. "Whatever you tell me won't affect whatever relationship Brody and I might have. You obviously need to talk to someone about this, and I'm here to listen."

Kelly's distressed green gaze lifted to hers. "I've buried this so deeply, and there were times I told myself it never happened." She tucked a short strand of hair behind one ear. "Toward the end of our marriage, during the last weeks when things were really bad, Brody went to stay in his brother Noah's guest house. I felt like it was a good idea for him to leave because all the fighting was starting to affect Tyler. I also felt like it would be good for us to spend some time apart. He'd been gone for three weeks when I realized I didn't want to be apart from him. I just wanted some things to change." Kelly twisted her wedding ring around her finger. "One night I'd left Tyler with some friends so I could go see Brody and talk some things over." She paused again, twirling that ring around and around. "But when I got there, he wasn't alone."

A sick feeling settled in the bottom of Elisa's stomach. It felt like her heart actually stopped beating for a moment. "Oh God, Kelly."

"We weren't even legally separated and he'd slept with someone else."

# FIFTEEN

ELISA NEVER THOUGHT JUST LISTENING to someone tell a story could leave her so exhausted and mentally drained. Nor had she listened to something so heart-wrenching in her whole life. Because of Kelly's story, Elisa had new understanding for the look of resentment on Kelly's face when she walked in on her with Brody. Seeing that must have stirred old memories Kelly had worked so hard to keep buried.

Heading away from Kelly and Colin's charming home, Elisa felt as though her heart had been carved out with a spoon.

*You wanted to know, didn't you? Well, now you do.*

How heartbreaking that must have been for Kelly, being so in love with a man, giving up everything for him, then finding him in the arms of another woman. How would she feel if she stumbled across Brody locked in a passionate kiss with another woman? Most likely the same way Kelly had felt all those years ago.

*Filing the divorce papers didn't make me stop loving him any less. I just had too much dignity to be with a man who clearly didn't feel the same way about me.*

The same way Kelly couldn't love him less, Elisa couldn't love him less either. Even knowing the unforgiveable thing he'd done, she was still very deeply in love with him. At the same time, she couldn't fathom the Brody she knew doing something like that. Had something driven him to it? Had he done it out of loneliness? Kelly hadn't offered much explanation. Elisa had a feeling telling the story was draining enough, and the other woman hadn't had anything left in her. Or, maybe, Kelly had no idea what had been going through Brody's mind.

*This is none of your business. All this happened well over four years ago. Brody is obviously a different person now.*

Or was he?

Maybe she didn't know him as well as she thought.

*No, the Brody I know would never do that. He's different.*

Elisa drove through town while a dull ache formed in her head. She damn near ran a stop sign and had to slam on her brakes to keep from plowing down some innocent pedestrians.

In her purse next to her, her cell phone rang. She fumbled blindly for it while keeping one eye on the traffic light.

"Hello?" she answered after locating the device.

"I am going to be your best friend until the end of time." The voice on the other end of the line was that of Shelly, the woman who'd originally contacted her about her defrauding issue.

"I know it's taken me a long time," Shelly continued. "But I've done some digging into my old e-mails and I struck gold."

The light turned green and Elisa pressed forward down the street. "I could use a piece of uplifting news."

"Not only do I have the original e-mail, but on the e-mail is the guy's first and last name, the name of their company, address, phone number, and a link to your website. Above the link are several sentences saying they have photos of yours in their possession and they express their intent to sell them. I forwarded the e-mail to you and made a hard copy for our records. I also forwarded you our response to him. The only catch is this e-mail is a follow-up to the original phone conversation I had with him, which I don't have any record of."

Elisa didn't care about the phone call. "They gave you my website address?"

"I know, pretty stupid. But those e-mails should be sitting on your computer, waiting for you. Maybe you can give them to that lawyer who's helping you."

"I really appreciate it, Shelly." Elisa maneuvered her car through her neighborhood. "At this point, I don't even care about being compensated for what they've sold. I just want them to stop."

"Hopefully this will help. If you need anything else, let me know."

"Thanks." They said their good-byes and hung up.

Elisa had never felt so violated before. She'd entered into an agreement with this stock agency, and along with it had given them her trust. Their blatant violation was like a huge slap across the face. What had she ever done to them to deserve this kind of disrespect? Maybe it was her fault for holding humanity to such high standards. But Shelly had offered a glimmer of hope. All Elisa needed now was to hear back from Mr. Frank's office.

She paused at a stop sign and made a left past Tyler's school, then turned onto her street.

What she wanted to do more than anything was go out

and take pictures. She could lose herself for hours and not think about Brody and her confusing situation with him. Unfortunately, the middle of the afternoon wasn't the best time for snapping photos. The light was always best at sunrise or sunset. The shadows during those times of the day were spectacular.

She quickly made mental plans to forward Shelly's e-mail to Mr. Franks's secretary, then go out this evening on a camera outing. As soon as she neared her house, Elisa knew she wouldn't be doing that.

Because Brody was sitting in her driveway.

Brody had just about paced a hole through the solid concrete of Elisa's driveway while waiting for her to return home. He only had a few short hours to spare while Tyler was in school. When not pacing, he'd debated getting into his truck, driving to the market, and purchasing every bottle of liquor they had. His willpower against getting shit-faced had gotten weaker and weaker over the past few days. He'd never been a heavy drinker, but he'd come close to turning into one.

After he'd been waiting for eons and wearing out the soles of his dressier work shoes, the woman who'd driven him to the point of insanity finally arrived. In order to feign nonchalance, even though he didn't feel any, he leaned against his truck and slid his hands in his pockets. The past few days without her had plunged him into a state of madness, the likes of which he'd never known. Add in his dilemma with Kelly, and Brody was about to come out of his skin.

He'd needed Elisa like he never needed anyone. Only her soft voice and sensual touches could offer him comfort and bring his mind back to sanity. Oh, he'd tried to deny it, how much he needed her. Hell, loved her. But what was the point? Denying the reality didn't make it go away. He just needed to be near her. And also make sure she was okay after their encounter with Kelly.

Almost immediately after he and Kelly and Tyler had left Elisa's house, Brody recognized his departure had been cold. There she'd been, practically throwing herself at him, begging him to include her in his troubles, and he'd all but shoved her away. He'd barely glanced at her as he'd stalked out the door. How wrong he'd been. If he could take his behavior back, he would. He would have poured out his entire soul, then dragged her to bed. And afterward he would have told her how much he loved her, how he'd never felt such a profound and life-altering love before, and beg her not to go to Mongolia. His confusion over his own feelings and anger with Kelly had muddled his brain. His mind hadn't been able to churn out one rational thought, only that he hadn't been in any state to have a deep conversation.

Elisa pulled her car next to his in the driveway and stopped without opening the garage door. Brody came around her car just as she opened the driver's door and stepped out. Lord, she was so beautiful and such a breath of fresh air in his lonely life. Her dark hair was pulled back in a sleek ponytail and her eyes were hidden by a pair of sunglasses.

His heart squeezed in his chest and made breathing damn near impossible. She closed the car door and stood in front of him.

"Hi," he said lamely, like some imbecile who couldn't articulate words.

Elisa licked her lips and adjusted her purse strap on her shoulder. "Hi," she said back.

Okay, great. They'd managed to greet each other. Now what?

*You're the one who came over here, moron. Make the next move.*

His eyes strayed down to her ample breasts, which rose and fell gently underneath her cotton shirt.

*You've already made a big enough mess of things. Don't add to it by gawking at her.*

"I, uh..." He paused and glanced down at his feet, like the damn things held all the answers. Then he decided to plunge forward, and damn the world. "You're more to me than just a vessel." The idea that she thought she was nothing more than just some kind of sex buddy had twisted his heart up. From the very first kiss, he'd known that Elisa would be so much more than that. He'd kicked himself repeatedly for leading her to think such a demeaning thing.

"You're more to me than that," he continued. "I just needed to get that out right away."

She exhaled softly. "Do you want to come in?"

Did he want to come in? He was only madly in love with her.

"Yeah," he replied.

She took his hand in her softer one and led him to the front door. Her feminine scent of wildflowers teased him the whole way, and by the time they walked through the front door, he was as hard as a damn iron post. He discreetly adjusted himself while she led him through the house. Brinkley continued to sleep on the floor.

As soon as she set her purse down, he gave in to his desires and grabbed her. He folded her into him by winding one arm around her slim waist. She came to him without any effort or protest. Those glorious breasts came in contact with his chest, pressing up against him and reigniting his hard-on. He cradled the back of her head with his free hand and lowered his mouth to her ear. He breathed in her scent, then whispered, "You're more to me than that."

"Okay," she whispered back, as both of her arms came around his shoulders.

The skin beneath her ear was so soft that he couldn't resist a little swipe of his tongue. He grinned when she shuddered and goose bumps appeared where he'd just tasted her. She was so easy to arouse, so responsive, that Brody had to do it again. He was rewarded with a gasp, then a moan from her. He replaced his tongue with his mouth, dropping kisses down the column of her throat. She tasted so good, like everything soft and feminine. It was a sensation he couldn't get enough of, and he wanted to spend hours tasting her. When they'd made love before, he hadn't taken the proper care with her. He'd been so hot to get himself inside her that any kind of seduction had lost its importance. No way would he take this moment for granted. He'd savor her in a way he should have the first time.

Brody was about to explore the other side of her neck when Elisa suddenly turned her head and fastened her mouth to his. The action took him off guard but was welcome. She had the sweetest mouth and an even sweeter tongue. He didn't even have to coax her lips open. They opened of their own accord and he eagerly swept his tongue inside, swirling it sensually around hers. Her enthusiasm and stamina matched his, which made his dick swell even more than it already was. The muscle strained against his fly and practically had him seeing stars.

He'd missed her so much during the past few days that he couldn't get enough of her, couldn't get close enough.

He wanted to consume her, wanted to imprint himself on her so that every time she moved, every time she breathed, she felt him.

Elisa moaned, driving his need to take her even more hard core. Her fingers tugged on the strands of his hair, until the pain of it mixed with the pleasure of kissing her.

He broke away from her mouth only long enough to give her a warning. "I'm going to make love to you now. I'm going to take you to your bed and bury myself so deeply inside you that you'll be able to feel me every time you move." His words earned him a whimper from her. "If you want to stop me, now's the time to say something. Because once we start, I won't be able to stop."

She glanced up at him, all love and sensuality darkening her brown eyes. "I don't want you to stop. I want you, Brody."

That was all the invitation he needed. Scooping her up in his arms, he carried her down the narrow hallway and figured the one with the giant sleigh bed and the flowery comforter was hers. He didn't bother closing the door and lay her down on the bed with great care. He toed off his shoes, pulled off his socks, and stretched out beside her.

"I'm sorry about my behavior the other day. You didn't deserve that kind of treatment."

She looked up into his eyes, the love she had for him unbelievably apparent. "You don't need to apologize for that."

"But I do—"

"Shut up, Brody," she demanded, then pulled his head down until his mouth was fastened to hers.

Pure fire shot through him at the feel of her mouth against his. She consumed him and devoured him, getting inside his skin and his head. Right then, there was nothing else. No arguments with Kelly, no stress from work.

Only Elisa. Only her intoxicating scent and the way she made him come alive like no other woman had.

Their tongues slid along each other in an erotic and tantalizing dance that had his dick pushing even harder against his pants. Her spectacular breasts smashed against his chest. They were plump and soft and he wanted to get his hands on them ASAP.

Elisa groaned her frustration when he lifted his mouth off hers.

"Don't worry, I'm not going anywhere," he assured her, while finding the hem of her shirt with his hand. His fingers found the creamy flesh beneath the fabric covering her stomach. Elisa was the type of woman who was born to walk around naked. A slim waist, curvy hips, and mouthwatering breasts weren't meant to be covered with clothing. If he could, he'd have her naked all the time.

His fingers trailed up her stomach, dragging the shirt with them until the garment was bunched under her arms.

*Holy shit!*

Her bra was fire-engine red, cradling those sweet plump breasts, the swells of them barely contained. Unable to hold himself back, Brody dipped down and skimmed his tongue just above the edge of her bra. His action was rewarded by a startled gasp, followed by one of her throaty moans. Her back arched off the bed, effectively pressing her breast closer to his mouth. Then he yanked the shirt over her head, tossed it somewhere in the room, and unhooked her bra. He wasted no time returning to his task of torturing her with his mouth. Only now her nipples were free for him to do as he pleased. They were beaded tight from his appraisal, like little strawberries, only a much deeper red, the color of wine.

He savored them with his mouth, dragging his tongue

around one, then the other, in slow circles. Elisa groaned and said his name in a desperate plea, as though she couldn't handle any more and wanted him to show mercy on her. After all the waiting since the last time they'd been together, Brody wasn't about to stop, nor was he going to go easy on her—unless she asked him to.

Her breath was rapid and uneven and her legs thrashed around his on the bed. He lifted his head and pinned her with a look. "Do you want me to stop?"

"Don't you dare stop."

With that demand, she tugged the hem of his shirt out of his pants and whipped it over his head with jerky movements. Her hands skimmed with urgency over his shoulders, then down his chest, stopping at the buckle of his pants. He gazed down at her and watched as her teeth stabbed into that full lower lip, while her fingers quickly undid the silver buckle. A sharp jolt of hunger burst through him when her hand came in contact with his belly, brushing against his skin as she worked the pants over his hips. After a bit of struggling on her part, Elisa finally got his pants down, and Brody assisted by kicking them away. They fell somewhere on the floor.

He wanted to be completely naked with her, so Brody made quick work of Elisa's pants and underwear, easing them down those long legs of hers. He wanted to feel those babies wrapped around his hips.

"I can't get enough of you." He practically growled the words out while drinking in the sight of her. All smooth, olive skin and lean limbs, she oozed sexuality and femininity that made his mouth water and hormones go into hyperdrive.

They were finally both blissfully naked. After days of thinking about her, dreaming about being inside her again, he could once again feel her skin to skin. No barriers, nothing left to his imagination. They had all afternoon, and Brody intended to enjoy her.

He settled down between her legs, allowing the weight of him to press her into the mattress. Plus he wanted her to feel his erection. He needed her to know what she did to him, exactly how she affected him. She sucked in a breath when he pressed himself against her, just a gentle rub to get her juices flowing, which he guessed they already were.

"Oh, Brody," she moaned. "I've really missed you."

"You have no idea how much you consume my thoughts. I've been thinking about doing this for days." And he dropped his mouth to her breast again, giving it more attention than before. He took her whole nipple in his mouth, gently suckling it until the nub was diamond hard. Elisa's fingers threaded through his hair, tugging on the strands while holding his head to her breast.

After giving the mounds ample attention, Brody dropped kisses down her torso. When he came to her belly button, he dipped his tongue into the little crevice. The muscles beneath her stomach contracted and her hands flexed in his hair. Farther south he went, pressing kisses and skimming his hands anywhere he could get them.

Yes, this was it. Being able to get to the very core of Elisa, kissing her and tasting her was what he'd been waiting for. Last time, he hadn't taken the opportunity to explore her this thoroughly. Now she was his. Lying like a goddess on her girly comforter, she was all his.

Brody nudged her thighs wider apart, so his shoulders could fit in between them. He glanced up to find her watching him: those big, deep brown eyes gazing back at him with unadulterated passion. With a grin, he placed a light kiss on her inner thigh. Her gasp pleased him, filled him with male satisfaction. He'd just moved higher, almost to the sweet spot, when his cell phone rang.

Elisa lifted her head off the pillow and glanced to the floor, where his phone was tucked in the pocket of his pants. Brody had no intention of answering the thing. Not when he was moments away from experiencing the most delectable woman on Earth. He placed another kiss on her thigh when she stopped him.

"Brody, wait. Shouldn't you get that?" Her voice was deeper and huskier than usual.

He didn't move from his position in between her thighs. "Are you insane?"

A shadow of uncertainty crossed into her eyes. "What if it's Tyler?"

He forced his brain to function normally, and he glanced at the clock. Tyler would just be getting out of school, so he could be calling.

Shit.

Here he was bare-ass naked, seconds away from losing himself in Elisa's tight body, and he had to take a damn phone call. But he would never ignore his son for anyone or anything. Elisa and her tight body would have to wait.

He reluctantly dragged himself off the bed, fumbled around for the cursed phone, and answered it.

"Hello," he answered with a sharp tone.

"Brody, we really need to talk," his ex-wife announced in a no-nonsense tone, as though she expected him to say "yes, ma'am," like some fucking kid.

He snatched his boxers off the floor and stepped into them. "I really don't need this right now, Kelly."

"Tough shit, Brody. This is not going away just because you don't want to talk about it."

From behind him came the rustling of sheets, as though Elisa didn't want to lie around exposing herself. He glanced back just as she'd pulled a cream-colored sheet over her glorious breasts. Goddamn Kelly.

Elisa's eyes remained fixed to his, a sort of compassion and understanding softening her features. His heart melted a little and he dug for the strength to deal with his ex-wife and her inopportune phone call. He stepped from the room and walked down the hallway.

"I already told you, you're not taking Tyler out of Wyoming. I'll never see him."

Kelly's heavy sigh reverberated through the phone. "And you haven't taken the time to really listen to me. Colin and I don't have a lot of choices or a lot of time. We need to make a decision, and we can't take Tyler out of state without your consent."

The dog Elisa had been nursing trotted over on its gimpy leg and nudged Brody's thigh with his cold nose. He ignored the animal and paced to the sliding glass door. "You don't have my consent. Decision made."

"I understand your concern, Brody—"

"I told you, I can't talk about this right now."

"You keep saying that." Her words had taken on a desperate edge, very similar to how she often spoke to him during the final months of their marriage.

Brody leaned his head against the cool glass of the back door. "I said not now, Kelly. You can't expect me to make this kind of decision over the phone. I need more time."

"You said that the other day. I don't know how much more time I can give you."

"You've only given me a few days to process this. I promise we'll talk about it, but not now. Not over the phone."

Kelly didn't respond for a moment and he heard Tyler's voice in the background, something about a book he needed to check out from the library. Something inside twisted at the sound of his son's voice. Brody could picture him now, his blond hair clipped close to his head, his mother's green eyes lighting up with laughter or looking up at Brody with hero worship.

*Those days are over, dickhead.*

The thing that had twisted inside him grew sharper, more painful, like a living creature had crawled inside his gut.

His eyelids dropped closed and he inhaled a deep breath. He couldn't lose his son. Brody couldn't live in a world that Tyler wasn't a part of. Living a few streets over, he could handle. But three states away? Once-a-year visits and a few phone calls a month? Brody would rather drop dead.

"All right," Kelly finally said. "Come over later and we'll talk." She disconnected the phone call without giving him a chance to respond. Kelly had gotten good at that toward the end of their marriage. Sometime before their divorce, she'd lost her ability to give a shit what he thought. Brody had always known how much in love with him Kelly was. At one point she'd worshipped the ground he walked on. That had changed, and he was one hundred percent to blame.

*So is the situation you're in right now.*

He wrapped his fingers around his cell phone in a death grip, wanting so badly to crush the thing until it was nothing but jagged pieces.

Damn Kelly for doing this to him. Was she still punishing him for what he'd done? If so, he deserved it. He'd been a weak bastard, hell bent on drowning his sorrows and too stupid to think about the consequences. But even if he deserved Kelly's anger, it didn't mean he was going to allow her to take Tyler so far away. And Tyler didn't deserve any of this. He'd been an innocent bystander of his parents' dysfunction. Was Kelly even thinking how moving so far away would affect Tyler?

Brody pushed away from the door and headed back toward the bedroom. The scene was exactly how he'd left it a moment ago: clothes scattered on the floor and Elisa on the bed, covering that sinful body with a sheet.

"Sorry about that," he said as he tossed his phone on the dresser.

"It's okay." She blinked up at him with those big eyes of hers, as though trying to break through his stubborn-assed mind to the thoughts beneath. "Do you want to talk?"

He stood there, staring at her, half naked in his boxers and coming dangerously close to sporting another boner. But his dilemma with Kelly chased away any erotic feelings he'd had.

Elisa sighed. "You won't scare me away, Brody. No matter how hard you're trying to, I won't be scared away."

And for the first time in a long time, Brody found himself wanting to spill his guts.

# SIXTEEN

BRODY'S ANGUISH HAD BECOME SUCH a burden for him, following him around and clouding his everyday thoughts. In the past, he'd become a master at masking over the shell of the man he'd once been, at making his family believe he hadn't changed. He'd once been honorable, marrying Kelly because it had been the right thing, providing for his child, defending Lacy when Chase had thrown out a muddled marriage proposal. There was none of that left in him anymore. The truth was he hated himself. He hated the reality that he was solely responsible for.

So, yeah—without a doubt, he deserved the hell he was going through.

For some insane reason Elisa saw the man he once was. It was evident just by the way she looked at him, very similar to the way Kelly had once looked at him. Elisa believed in him. Hadn't she said that to him once before, at the restaurant? That she believed in him? How had he not managed to scare her off? He didn't deserve her admiration.

"Brody, are you all right?"

He sat next to her on the edge of the bed and tried to ignore the sheet that was barely covering her breasts.

"That was Kelly," he replied.

"I figured as much. What did she say that's got you so upset?"

He pulled in a deep breath and plunged forward. "She and Colin are talking about moving to Michigan to be closer to her mother." Just saying the words out loud was like a rusty knife in his gut.

"And she's talking about taking Tyler with her," she concluded with that observant mind of hers.

Brody nodded while staring down at the floor. "I can't let her take him." He glanced at Elisa. "I won't."

"Of course you don't want him to go. He's your son." Elisa leaned forward and placed a hand on his bare thigh. "Have you talked to Kelly about this? I'm sure if she knew how this was tearing you up, she'd never go through with it."

"Oh, but she would. And she knows exactly how I feel."

"You have to be able to work something out with her. I can't believe she'd just take your son out of state without you agreeing to it."

The sheet had fallen to Elisa's waist, and her breasts hung heavy and free of any restraints. He had to hold himself back from cupping them in his hands. "Kelly is obviously a different person with you than she is with me." He tucked a strand of hair behind her ear. "But I appreciate your optimism."

She leaned forward and kissed him. Not a ravenous, I-want-you-in-bed-now kiss, but a sweet, slow one. One that said *I love you, demons and all. No matter how hard you're trying to, I won't be scared away.*

Yes, he had been trying to scare her away. Because he figured, in the end, he'd screw this relationship as badly as he'd screwed up his marriage. But Elisa proved to be a lot stronger than he'd given her credit for. So far she hadn't given up on him or any potential future they could have together. Didn't he at least owe her a little honesty?

Brody reveled in Elisa's kiss for as long as she let him. Her lips were so tender and pliant, like she'd been born to kiss. He pressed her to the bed and stretched his body along hers, loving the feel of her naked flesh against his. She ran her hands over his shoulders, which were bunched tight with the tension that hummed through his body.

After several minutes of slow, deep kisses, Brody lifted his head and caressed his thumb over her cheek. "You told me you wanted to know everything. Are you sure you're ready for that?"

Little worry lines appeared between her eyebrows, then smoothed out. "Yes."

He rolled off her, even though what he really wanted to do was slide inside her and forget everything. But if there was any chance of them having some kind of meaningful relationship, she needed to know everything. Elisa propped herself onto her side and watched him, waiting for him to speak.

"I wasn't a good husband," Brody started, keeping his gaze fixed to the ceiling. He didn't want to see the disappointment in Elisa's eyes when she heard what he had to say.

She placed a hand on his shoulder. "Brody—"

"Don't try to defend me, Elisa." He cast her a look. "Don't make me out to be better than I am. Right now I need you to listen." She nodded, and he pressed on. "Things weren't always bad between us. In the beginning they were good." When he first met Kelly, he'd been taken with her. She had a way of making him laugh and turning even the most serious moments into something silly. Basically she found a way to take his stress away. For a while he'd relied on that.

"I think part of the problem was that Kelly and I never

had a dating period. We rarely had time alone. Most couples have that time when they can get a feel for each other and figure out how their relationship is going to work. I'd only known Kelly for about six weeks when she told me she was pregnant." He folded one arm behind his head and tried to ignore Elisa's wildflower scent. "To make a complicated story short, we moved in together so I could take care of her the way I needed to."

The pure joy and excitement in Kelly's eyes was still something that haunted him. He'd rushed into the living arrangement, knowing it was what she wanted, but also knowing it wasn't what he wanted. He'd told himself he'd been gallant, basically sacrificing his own happiness for the sake of his child. What a delusion that had been.

"You didn't want to live with her," Elisa guessed.

*Go ahead. It's okay to admit it now.* "No. I think I thought with enough time, I could really love Kelly. And I eventually did start to have loving feelings for her. But I always knew that she loved me a lot more than I loved her." He let out a humorless laugh. "I'm such a bastard."

"No, you're not, Brody."

"Yeah, I am. I led Kelly to believe that I returned her feelings. All along I knew there was a good chance that I never would. Then I talked her into quitting school, telling myself that I was doing the right thing by being able to take better care of them."

"How would her quitting school allow you to do that?"

He ignored the censure in her voice. "There wasn't a whole lot of job opportunity where we went to school, and I couldn't provide for a wife and a baby on minimum wage from the university's bookstore."

"So you came back here and went to work for your father?"

"Eventually. Kelly was about to drop Tyler when we moved here. I knew she didn't want to live in Wyoming. But we desperately needed health insurance, and I needed a good-paying job. My father provided that for us, and I needed to do it in order to provide a good life for Kelly and Tyler."

"But what about the degree you got from school?" Elisa asked. "Couldn't you have taken that and gotten a good job somewhere where the two of you wanted to live together?"

"I could have, yeah. But the job market is so damn competitive. Who knows how long it would have taken. I needed something right away, and it was too good an opportunity to pass up."

Elisa scooted closer to him, her warmth surrounding him with a comfort he hadn't felt in a long time.

"So why are you beating yourself up over that? Sounds like moving here was your only option."

"It was. But I still felt bad making Kelly live somewhere she didn't want to live."

"You did what had to be done. There's nothing wrong with that."

He heaved a sigh. "I told you not to make me out to be a hero."

She touched his cheek lightly and turned his face toward hers. "I never said you were a hero, Brody. Only human."

That was for damn sure. He'd been a weak, stupid human being who'd continually given Kelly false hopes when she'd deserved so much better.

Elisa gazed down at him with so much compassion, so much understanding as though she felt his agony. It was all he could do not to grab her, bury his head in her sweet hair, and never let her go. She gave him hope. She made him feel like he was capable of being the man he once was. And she was going to leave him.

Then, without thinking, he blurted out the words he'd held in for four and a half years. "I slept with someone else. While Kelly and I were living apart."

Elisa's face froze with the exception of her eyebrows, which twitched.

"I was pissed off at the world," he continued like the idiot he was. "Pissed off at Kelly and pissed off at myself. I'd slipped into this weird depression and didn't know what to do with myself. My only thoughts had been for Tyler and how I was losing him." A tight fist closed around his heart and forced a lump into his throat. He hadn't cried over his separation from Tyler in such a long time. He hadn't allowed himself that indulgence, hadn't allowed himself to feel much of anything.

Within a matter of moments, he felt like he'd stepped back in time. Back to those lonely days in Noah's guest house, eating shitty TV dinners and watching useless infomercials in the middle of the night because sleep had abandoned him. In the mornings, he'd be gritty-eyed and brain-dead. Then he'd slump over on the couch and cry like a fucking baby because he'd single-handedly ripped his family apart. Tyler had lost his stable home because his father had been thinking with his dick when a beautiful woman had paid attention to him. Shit, he couldn't even remember the woman's name, or what she looked like for that matter.

*I hope she was worth it.*

That's what Kelly had said to him after seeing the woman emerge from the bedroom wearing Brody's boxers.

*I hope she was worth it.* Then Kelly had turned around

and walked out the door, without saying another word to him. She filed divorce papers the next day.

Brody sucked in a breath and clenched his jaw, trying to erase the memory of that night. Hell, that whole damn year.

His body jerked when Elisa placed a soothing hand on his chest.

"You don't have to say any more," she whispered.

"But I need to explain—"

"No, you don't." She paused, nibbling her lower lip with her teeth. "Besides, I already know this. I don't want you to keep telling something that's too painful for you to talk about."

*She what?*

His heart, which had once been squeezing so damn tight in his chest, felt like it had stopped beating. What did she mean, she already knew?

Then it hit him like a two-by-four. "Kelly told you, didn't she?"

Elisa nodded, and a strand of silky hair slid over her shoulder. "I went to see her today about what happened the other day. She..." Elisa placed a hand on his chest and ran her index finger in circles over his pec. "She told me about your divorce. About what really happened."

Brody hadn't realized the two women were that close. He'd always been pretty sure that Kelly had never told anyone about what he'd done. Yet she'd told Elisa. And Elisa had sat there and let him spout his mouth off like a damn woman. And why hadn't she asked him about it, instead of acting like she didn't have a clue?

"So everything I just told you, you already knew?" Why did that knowledge create a sick feeling in his stomach? "Why'd you let me keep going?"

Her eyebrows pinched together. "You said you needed to tell it. And you told me not to interrupt you. Plus, I only heard Kelly's version." Her voice dropped a notch. "I wanted to hear it coming from you."

He turned on his side to face her. "And now that you've heard it? Are you going to run screaming in the other direction?" If she ran, he wouldn't blame her. In fact, he expected her to. What woman would want to stay with him after the story he just told?

She tilted her head to one side, and a chunk of silky hair slid over her shoulder. "Why would I run? I already told you, you're only human. People make mistakes. What matters is if you learned from them."

"What I did was more than a mistake. It ended my marriage."

Elisa pursed her full lips. "Sounds like your marriage was already over."

"That doesn't make what I did right. I was still unfaithful. And I don't think Kelly ever forgave me." Not that Brody blamed her.

"I think she probably has. I think what you're struggling with is closure. And Kelly probably is too."

How in the world could Elisa be so understanding? Why was she not looking at him with disgust and saying "How could you?" as Kelly had done?

"You think closure is all I need? How do I do that?" If that's all he needed to make that guilt go away, he'd do it, whatever it took.

"It starts with forgiveness. You forgiving yourself and asking Kelly to forgive you."

He skimmed the tip of his index finger over her shoulder. "See, I thought I *had* forgiven myself."

The corners of Elisa's mouth curved up in a smile.

"If you're still struggling with this, then you obviously haven't."

Touching her skin was like touching the softest velvet. He floated his hand from her shoulder to her hair, where he tunneled it beneath the strands. They were cool and practically weightless around his hand. He tilted her head toward his until her mouth was a whisper away from his lips.

"Why are you still here? Haven't you realized by now that I'm a head case?"

Her lips tilted in a small smile. "You're not a head case, Brody. You just have some ghosts you haven't dealt with yet."

"And what, you want to help me? Is that it?"

Her eyes searched his for a moment. "If you'll let me," she whispered. "You've been alone long enough. It's time to let someone in."

"I don't think you'll like what you see," he told her.

"I've seen everything. I've seen the way you look at Tyler and your fear of losing him. I've seen your worry for your employees. You're a lot nobler than you give yourself credit for."

"Or maybe you just think too highly of me."

"You don't think enough of yourself. That's your problem." Her breath was warm and sweet and tickled his lips when she spoke.

What had he been doing, sitting here telling his stupid sob story when the woman he wanted was buck naked, less than a foot from him? During their conversation, she'd inched closer and closer to him, as though she needed that physical closeness—as though she craved it as much as he did.

*Enough of this talking shit.*

He'd spoken so much that he was sick and tired of hearing his own voice. What he wanted to hear about was Elisa. But not now. All he wanted to do was settle her down on the bed, cover her body with his, and grind himself deep.

He massaged the back of her neck with his hand and nudged her head forward. When their lips touched, it was like fireworks ignited in his system. His body came alive and hummed with tension the way it always did when Elisa touched him. She had a way of crawling under his skin and making him feel not like himself. When he was with Elisa, she made him believe he could actually let go of his past mistakes and start over as a new man. She gave him hope to be a better man.

Her tongue snaked out and touched his lips. That was all the invitation Brody needed. He was pretty sure Elisa wouldn't change her mind, but he didn't want to take this slow. They'd do slow later, when they had all night.

In the meantime, Elisa settled back on the bed and pulled him down with her. She stretched beneath him, all long, silky limbs tangling with his. Their lips maintained contact, massaging each other until their tongues took over. Brody slid his tongue inside her mouth, imagining his dick doing the same thing to her body, pumping again and again until he couldn't remember his own name. Elisa made a sweet sound, half moan, half whimper, when he ground the cotton of his boxers against her core. He'd almost forgotten about the damn things. Well, he'd have to fix that.

Brody broke away from her lips and made fast work of his underwear. Elisa helped him, giggling with delight, as their hands fumbled around each other to grab the elastic waistband.

"God damn boxers," Brody cursed when the things became hung up around his ankles. He knew he should have taken them off before getting back into the bed. Being with Elisa made his brain cease to function.

"Let me." Elisa pushed him onto his back and straddled his hips. She braced her hands on his chest, assumed the optimal position of arching her back. "Oh God, Brody," she moaned when his dick rubbed the slick entrance of her body.

"Wait," he said in a strained voice. Shit, he almost allowed himself to go in without double the protection. This woman had him tied up in too many knots.

She gazed down at him out of heavy-lidded eyes. "No condom this time, Brody. Please," she pleaded as though sensing his thoughts.

His back teeth ground together and he shook his head. "No, I can't—"

"Brody." She placed a soft hand on his jaw and forced him to look at her. "I told you I'm on the pill. We don't need a condom. And I would rather feel all of you."

Well, shit, when she put it like that... And how could he refuse when he was *right* there? Ready to take that deep plunge?

She was so hot and moist that his eyes almost rolled back into his head. The tips of his fingers gripped the soft flesh of her thighs, so he could brace himself for her to seat herself. Then she did. Sweet mother in Heaven, she sat down on his penis so he was firmly lodged inside her slippery tunnel. Pleasure like he'd never known before consumed him in a mind-numbing haze. His whole body was on fire and itched like he needed to come out of his skin. He tried to adjust his legs, to cradle Elisa more comfortably. But the fucking boxers were still trapped around his ankles like a pair of handcuffs.

"Elisa, wait." But his demand turned into a groan when

she lifted herself with excruciating slowness, then sank back down.

Her eyelids dropped closed and her head fell back. She looked like a goddess, sitting on top of him and riding his hips like he were some wild horse.

"What's the matter?" she finally asked. Her normally bright brown eyes were glazed over as though she were high on some drug.

"These damn boxers are killing me. I need you to take them off." How in the world he managed to string words together was anybody's guess.

Her movements ceased and she muttered something in Portuguese—probably cursing him. Hell, he was cursing himself. With the skill of an acrobat, Elisa leaned behind her, arching her back and jutting her breasts out. The movement had her inner muscles clenching around his dick even tighter. A single bead of sweat accumulated at his temple. Every single muscle in his body was coiled tight like steel, ready to flip Elisa onto her back and pound out his release.

Finally, she freed his feet of their restraints and Brody was able to spread his legs. Just when he had her in the position he wanted, he grabbed her waist and flipped her onto her back in one swift move. He did it so quickly that he was able to stay wedged inside her.

She narrowed her eyes in accusation. "You did that on purpose."

He offered her a grin and nudged her thighs farther apart with his knees. "Hell, yeah."

# SEVENTEEN

*So this is what it feels like to be thoroughly ravaged by a man.*

She and Brody lay in silence, when just a few moments ago they'd both been groaning and screaming out their release. Elisa hadn't known sex could be like that, so incredibly personal and all-consuming. In the past, she'd never made a habit of having indiscriminate sex. Nevertheless, she'd never been able to feel a partner's presence like he'd imprinted himself on her soul. None had ever stared down at her with such intensity like Brody had. The feeling was so new and foreign that she knew without a doubt she was deeply in love with him. Her love for him was automatic, like breathing. She didn't have any choice in the matter.

His heart beat steady and sure beneath her ear. She hoped it beat for her like hers beat for him. Would now be a good time to bring that up again? Did she really want to risk this glorious postcoital bliss?

No, she didn't. They could have the serious conversation later. Right now, all she wanted to do was continue to feel his naked skin against hers. It was sometime in the late afternoon, and Elisa didn't see any reason to move until nightfall.

Listening to Brody tell his darkest secret had been gut-wrenching to say the least. So much more so than hearing Kelly tell it. Mostly because Elisa wasn't in love with Kelly, and it had been harder for her to feel the woman's pain. Brody had deliberately opened an old wound for her, exposing something he'd been deeply ashamed of. Elisa didn't take that for granted. No, she wholeheartedly recognized the sacrifice he'd made. He'd risked pushing her away by confiding in her. But she'd already known the story, and she'd had no intention of leaving him.

Unfortunately, she was still unclear on where they stood. Was this thing they were doing a relationship? As much as she'd love that, Elisa wasn't sure Brody could handle being in a serious relationship. He was too scarred. In fact, he was the most tortured soul Elisa had ever known. All those years of carrying self-inflicted blame and watching his son drift away had altered him. Granted, Elisa hadn't known him before his divorce, but she'd bet he'd been lighter-hearted and had loved more freely.

But wasn't this the Brody she fell in love with? The man who held her in his arms at this moment? For however scarred he was, this Brody was the one Elisa loved.

The most painful thing, even more painful than hearing him tell his story, was the inevitable end of their relationship. In a short while, she'd be gone. Who knew if she'd come back? But she owed it to herself to explore this possible new career. Plus, she'd already agreed to go, before her feelings for Brody had bloomed out of control. It would hardly be professional to back out now. No, she'd definitely have to go. The question was, did she come back? She wanted that more than anything, but she wasn't sure she'd have anything to come back to.

He stirred slightly, his muscles subtly shifting beneath

her. His thighs were thick with corded muscle and dusted with soft, dark hair. One leg moved, dragging one of hers with it. His body was so much bigger and harder than hers. Being near him made her feel very small and feminine. As if she could surround herself with him and get lost in all that muscle.

Ah, yes. She could definitely stay right here for the rest of the day.

"Tell me what you're thinking," he said. His deep voice rumbled in his chest beneath her ear.

"Nothing much," she said with a sigh. *Nothing much except how desperately in love I am with you.*

Nope, not going to bring that up.

"Tell me what's going on with Kelly's mother," she said.

For a moment he didn't speak. The only sound that came from him was his deep breathing.

"You don't have to talk about it, if you don't want to," she said when he still hadn't responded to her.

"What exactly did Kelly tell you?" he finally asked.

"Just that you were being difficult."

The snort that came out of him told Elisa that he disagreed with his ex-wife.

"You don't see eye to eye on this," she concluded.

"To say the least." He paused for a moment, then spoke again. "We haven't talked extensively about it yet. The one time we did talk, Kelly told me that her mother's health isn't good. She can't walk on her own, she can't bathe herself. Hell, she can't even go to the bathroom. She lives by herself in Michigan, and Kelly's an only child. Kelly and Colin are really all she has."

Elisa propped up on one elbow. The pain in Brody's normally hypnotic gray eyes pierced her heart. "You already said she wants to take Tyler and move. But how easy would it be for Colin to leave his chiropractic practice?"

Brody shook his head. "I'm not really sure about that part. But Kelly's mother can't live on her own. She needs to be in a nursing home, but Kelly doesn't want to dump her mother there and abandon her."

"I'd hardly call it 'abandoning.' Besides, hasn't this woman been alone for several years? Because I remember once Kelly mentioning that her dad had passed on. How would being in a nursing home be any different?"

Brody stared up at the ceiling. "That's a good question. I think Kelly and Colin are trying to absolve their own guilt."

"That's not fair. They can't take Tyler away from you because they feel guilty." She placed a hand on Brody's chest. He was so wonderfully warm—and in pain. There had to be something she could do to ease his troubled mind. "What if they brought her out here? I bet there are a ton of nursing homes in Cheyenne or even Casper."

Brody pulled in a deep breath and wound his arm around Elisa's shoulders. "That would be ideal. But considering the condition Louise is in, I don't think moving her would be the easiest thing. It would probably be pretty difficult for her to travel that far."

"Brody, you can't give up. You need to fight them on this."

"Trust me, I'm going to. I just don't think I'm going to win. If it comes down to it, I'll move out there with them."

Elisa's heart skipped a beat, then dropped down to her stomach, making her physically ill. A frisson of fear snaked through her, and a shudder wracked her body. Of course Brody would go where his son was. Why would she expect him to do otherwise? Just because she was in love with him? Brody had never returned the sentiment. It could very well be easy for him to walk away from her.

*You're going to leave.*

Yes, but what if she came back and he was gone? What if, while she was away in Mongolia, he moved to Michigan? But...

What if he loved her the same way she loved him? What if there was an actual future for them waiting for her? She knew he had some caring feelings for her. But Elisa wasn't willing to potentially alter her entire career for someone who merely cared about her. She needed to know without a doubt that Brody was willing to invest his heart the way she already had hers.

Brody must have felt her body stiffen in his arms. He glanced at her. "I can't be away from him, Elisa. He's my only child. He's my whole reason for living."

His eyes were so very gray that her heart cracked open even more. She couldn't meet his gaze. She just couldn't. "I understand that, Brody."

"But you don't like it," he said in a quiet voice.

She shifted out of his hold and lay down on her back. The ceiling held nothing of real interest for her to look at. But it was better than looking at Brody. If she did, she might allow the tears that were threatening to go ahead and fall. "How I feel about this is irrelevant. It's not like we've declared any kind of serious relationship or even exclusivity."

"But you want to."

Now was not the time to talk about this. Her emotions hung on the precipice and they would break at any moment. The thought of watching Brody walk away was like gutting her heart out with a spoon.

"Elisa—"

She shook her head on the pillow. "I told you, how I feel about this doesn't matter."

He placed his hand under her chin and slowly turned her head so she had to look at him. His expression was guarded, his eyes giving away nothing of how he felt about her. "We're not talking about that anymore. We're talking about us now."

"What about us?" she whispered.

His thumb ran back and forth hypnotically across her jaw line. "I care about you. Probably more than any other woman I've been with."

*Here it comes. The "but."*

"But you're leaving, and right now this is all I can give you. I'm not capable of anything else."

"What if I wasn't leaving? Are you telling me you'd feel differently?"

He paused before answering, and the fact that he couldn't look her in the eye wasn't a comforting sign. "But you are leaving, so there's no sense in asking 'what if.'"

Yep. That hurt just as much as she expected it to. Her heart squeezed in her chest and just about knocked the breath out of her.

"Because you don't think you're capable of a relationship?" she asked.

"I know I'm not."

She wanted to wrap her arms around him and tell him everything would be okay. That he was worthy of being loved and it was okay to love someone back. The man had no faith in love anymore. Sure, he thought it was his fault. In fact, it was. But everyone deserved a second chance. Over the years, he'd started using his infidelity to define him. That wasn't who Brody was. She needed to convince him of that. But, more important, she needed to protect her heart. Walking away from him unscathed was impossible now.

"I told you before, I can't just be a sex buddy to you."

He lowered his head and placed a soft, tender kiss on her mouth. "You're more than that. I'm just not sure what. All I'm saying is that I can't promise you anything. Right now I need to focus my energy on this situation with Kelly and Tyler. Let's enjoy what we have right now."

She threaded her fingers through the short strands of his hair. Now she felt like a selfish twit. The poor guy had so much resting on his shoulders, and all she could do was whine that he hadn't confessed his undying love for her. Perhaps she was being too impatient. Perhaps her expectations were too high. Would it really be so bad to take things day by day? What felt like a lifetime with him had only been a few weeks. In that time, Brody had dealt with so much, and many things had changed in his life. Elisa's mistake had not been taking that into consideration. She'd only been considering her own feelings.

"I know, it's okay. I'm sorry; I didn't mean to add to your stress."

He settled his entire weight on her, and Elisa reveled in his glorious body.

"Hey," he said. "Don't say sorry. You give me solitude in my deteriorating life. Don't ever apologize for that."

Her heart cracked open even more. "You deserve to be happy, Brody."

"*You* make me happy."

They held each other in her bed for a long while after that, talking about nonsense things and enjoying the silence.

Kelly wasn't happy to see him. The thin line of tension pinching her eyebrows together was a dead giveaway. It was the same look he used to come home to after staying at the restaurant for two hours longer than necessary.

"Tyler's still at school," she said instead of saying hello. Brody figured he had that coming. "And he has football practice after that."

"I know." He stepped through the door without waiting for her to invite him in. If he waited for that pleasantry, he might be stuck outside all day. "I came here to talk about him, but I didn't want him to be here."

Kelly shut the door and merely stared at him. It wasn't a friendly look.

"You're the one who keeps saying we need to talk about this," he reminded her. "I can go and we can put this off until later."

She held up a hand and closed her eyes briefly. "No. Let's do this now."

Brody followed her down the hallway and into the great room. Kelly and Colin had a kickass view of the Wyoming foothills and always had front-row seats to impending snowstorms. But, for some reason, he never felt that the house suited Kelly's personality. It was huge and oddly decorated. Like a contemporary log cabin. Almost as though the decorator Kelly had hired had bi-polar disorder and couldn't decide what theme to use. The house was the complete opposite from the one they had shared during their marriage. On the other hand, maybe that had been Kelly's objective.

His ex-wife walked ahead of him and gathered several dishes from the table and carried them to the kitchen. The entire living/kitchen area smelled of the cinnamon candle that was burning on the center of the table. The scent always reminded Brody of his mother. She'd liked to keep cinnamon-scented pinecones scattered all over the house.

Kelly busied herself in the kitchen doing...whatever she always did in there. Brody always swore that Kelly spent more time in the kitchen than she did in their bed.

"Do you want something to drink?" she called from the other room.

"No, I'm fine," he called back. Paperwork and open file folders were scattered without any sort of rhyme or reason all over the table. Next to some bank statements, which Brody tried not to look at, was a book called *What to Expect When You're Expecting*. It was open to chapter five.

Shit, Kelly was pregnant?

A loud sigh came from the kitchen doorway. Brody glanced up to find Kelly scowling at him.

"I was hoping you wouldn't see that," she said.

He set the book back on the table. "You didn't hide it very well. Congratulations," he added.

"Thanks," she muttered, then sat at the table with a glass of water.

Brody sat next to her, which was the only place that didn't have clutter and shit nearby. "You don't sound very happy."

"No, I am." She rubbed a hand across her brow. "I've just got a lot on my mind. Plus I'm really tired and sick to my stomach."

He placed the book back on the table. "Why didn't you want me to see?"

Kelly took a sip of her water. "Because Colin and I haven't told anyone yet. We're waiting for the right time. Then this thing with my mother happened, so right now I need to focus on her."

"How long have you known?"

"About a month."

For the first time Brody noticed the strain on Kelly's face and the lines of fatigue that bracketed her mouth. Her eyelids looked heavy over her green eyes, like she hadn't slept for months. Hell, she looked like she'd aged ten years since the last time he saw her.

He settled a comforting hand on her knee. "I'm sorry, I didn't realize how much you were dealing with. And here I was being an insensitive prick."

"It's nothing I'm not used to," she said with a half smile.

Wasn't that the truth?

During their marriage, he'd never been good at giving Kelly the benefit of the doubt. She'd given up a lot for him, sacrificed everything that made her who she was for the sake of their family. Over the years, Brody had gotten so lost in the shuffle of everyday life that he hadn't appreciated what she'd done until it had been too late. Then, after their marriage had ended, Kelly wouldn't have given a good God damn how appreciative he'd been.

"I'm sorry for everything, Kelly," he found himself saying. "You deserved so much better than the kind of husband I was to you."

Kelly picked at the hem of her shirt. "It's not all your fault, Brody. Lord knows I tried to blame you. I'm just as much to blame. I went into our relationship knowing I loved you a lot more than you loved me. I knew what I was doing."

"Don't say that. I did love you." But not the way he loved Elisa. *Whoa, where had that come from?*

"You were never in love with me, Brody. Not the way I was with you."

When he shook his head, she cut him off. "If I hadn't been pregnant with Tyler, we would have eventually gone our separate ways. We never would have gotten married. You know that."

Even though they both knew it was true, he couldn't bring himself to say the words. He'd already done so many shitty things that he didn't want to place another log on the fire. Hell, he felt like he'd be kicking a puppy.

Kelly moved her delicate shoulders beneath her cotton shirt. "I mean, I basically trapped you."

"You did not trap me, Kelly," he said firmly. He couldn't allow her to think such a despicable thing. Women used pregnancy to trap men all the time, and oftentimes it was downright dirty. That hadn't been what Kelly had done. "Getting married was my idea. I don't regret it."

"I know, but if I'd been honest with myself, I could have saved us both a lot of grief." A humorless laugh popped out of her. "I kept thinking, 'He'll eventually love me. He just needs more time.'" She shook her head. A short strand of blond hair fell across her forehead. "I'm sorry, Brody."

*She* was sorry? "What the hell are you apologizing for? I'm the one who screwed things up."

"I can't allow you to shoulder all the blame. I went into our marriage knowing you didn't love me, then I tried to play the victim all those years." She shook her head again and stabbed her teeth into her lower lip. "That wasn't right of me."

"Kelly, look at me."

She lifted her gaze to his.

"I don't, for one second, regret being married to you. Because of you, I have the best son any man could hope for. You were a great wife and you're a wonderful mother." He paused, trying to find adequate words worthy of her. "I know I wasn't the easiest husband to have. You sacrificed a lot for me, and I'll always be grateful for that. I'm the bastard who repaid you by breaking your heart. I just hope that one day you can . . ." He stopped and cleared his throat. "Forgive me."

She stared back at him, her green gaze boring into his. "All these years I thought you didn't care."

He narrowed his eyes and studied her. "What do you mean?"

"For sleeping with that woman. And then you accepted the divorce papers so readily. I got the impression you were indifferent. Or that you didn't care."

Man, he really was the biggest of assholes. He'd never issued a formal apology to Kelly, which he'd always regretted. But not caring couldn't be further from the truth. All he did was care. In fact, he cared way too much. The feeling had been eating a hole in his gut for the past four years.

Brody took one of Kelly's hands in his. "Kelly . . ." he started, then sighed. "I have no excuse for the way I behaved. I know our marriage was already on the outs, but it was still the dirtiest thing I could have done. I never apologized to you and I'm sorry for that. And I'm sorry for what I did. I completely understand if you don't have it in you to forgive me. I don't deserve it anyway."

She placed a hand on his cheek. "Everyone deserves forgiveness, Brody. The way things ended between us was like a huge weight on my shoulders for a long time. I needed to hear those words from you. Thank you."

Brody guaranteed the weight on her shoulders was nothing compared to the weight on his. Despite that, there'd never been anyone else to blame but him. But even if he hadn't made that poor decision, his and Kelly's marriage most likely would have ended anyway. He just could have spared her a lot of pain if he'd been smarter.

"Don't thank me, Kelly. Knowing I have your forgiveness is enough."

She smiled, one that actually reached her eyes. He hadn't seen one of those from her in a while. "Listen, about this thing with my mother... You know I would never take Tyler away from you if there was another way, right?"

The heaviness was back around his heart. "I know, but I still don't like it."

"I don't like it either, and Colin and I are considering other options. We've been researching nursing homes in the area and trying to figure out a way to transport her this far. Us moving to Michigan is a last resort." She paused, pulled in a breath, and held onto his hand tighter. "But it might be one we'll have to resort to, despite Colin's practice here and however hard it would be for him to close it down and move."

Brody ground his teeth together to keep his emotions in check. The thought of living that far from Tyler made his blood run cold. "I can't be away from him, Kelly. If you go to Michigan, be prepared for me to follow you."

"And I wouldn't stop you. You're a wonderful father, and Tyler worships you."

"I don't know about that," he argued.

Kelly leaned back in her chair and rolled her eyes. "Now you're just being stupid. You don't hear the way Tyler talks about you when he's here. The boy idolizes you."

"Does he really, or are you just saying that to make me feel better?" He would love nothing more than to have the relationship with his son that they used to have. Just another thing Brody was to blame for.

"He really does. The two of you being apart would be

hard on everyone. That's why Colin and I are trying to find an alternative."

He supposed, for now, that would have to do. Moving three states away wasn't something he wanted. However, if he had to, he'd move to Egypt for his son. Tyler was a part of him, and there was no way Brody would survive being that physically distant from him.

Only recently had a small snag developed. Her name was Elisa.

His feelings for her was the closest thing to being in love that he'd ever felt. Could he bring himself to let her leave? Would he be able to find another woman like her again?

# EIGHTEEN

ELISA SET UP HER CAMERA equipment at the Golden Glove with her heart pattering a thousand miles an hour and a pit in the bottom of her stomach. The odd sensation of trepidation and love-sickness made her dizzy. So much so that the breakfast she'd hastily consumed that morning was now dancing at the bottom of her unsettled stomach. While unloading some lights, she'd almost had to drop the things and toss her food in the nearest trashcan. Wouldn't that have been attractive?

*Uh, hi, Brody. Please don't mind my vomit breath.*

Bad enough that she could no longer stand being around him without being smacked with her love for him.

She'd had more than enough time to prepare for the shoot that would finally take place, but nothing ever prepared her for being around Brody. Especially since they'd been intimate multiple times, and he'd have to be an idiot not to know how she felt about him. Hell, she might as well make a neon sign and strap it to her chest.

*Hello everyone. I'm in love with a man who doesn't love me back.*

Whatever. She still had a job to do, and, despite her

unwanted feelings for him, she still enjoyed his company and was willing to spend what time with him she had. She just hoped how she felt wasn't so obvious that it made their work time together awkward.

The setup took about an hour, during which time the dining room was empty except for Charlene and a tall, sandy-haired man behind the bar. He went back and forth between talking on his phone and flirting with Charlene, who'd grin and blush like some teenager who'd been asked to the prom by the high school football star.

"Who is that?" Elisa asked Charlene.

The other woman used one of her hands to fan herself. "That's Brody's brother RJ. He used to work the bar here but now he's only filling in until we can find a replacement for Anthony."

Elisa gestured between Charlene and Brody's handsome and flirtatious brother. "Are you two like . . ."

Charlene's eyes grew wide. "Oh no." She shook her head. "No, no, no. I mean, he's hot but he's just too . . . RJ."

Okay, whatever that meant.

"RJ's just a lot to take in," Charlene said as though reading Elisa's thoughts. "Especially if you don't know him."

"Why, is he obnoxious?"

The other woman lifted one shoulder in a half shrug. "No, not obnoxious. Just . . . consuming." She grinned. "It's hard to explain. But he's a great guy and was a lot of fun to work with. But he's actually not working right now. He just stopped by to talk to Brody."

Elisa nodded, not really sure what else to say. Except to ask where Brody was because she was obsessed and everything. To mask her thoughts, she fiddled with her camera equipment, making sure everything was in place.

Even though it was. Because she'd checked it half a dozen times already this morning.

"Brody's in the kitchen with Anthony if you need him," Charlene announced.

*Oh Lord, she sees right through you.*

Then Elisa remembered why she was there and that she was *supposed* to be working with Brody.

"Thanks," she replied in her most carefree voice, which she wasn't sure was convincing.

This time she'd brought her laptop with her so she could upload the digital images of the dishes and take a gander at them. Before wasting a whole bunch of time snapping photos of the finished dishes, she'd brought her smaller digital camera along with her to make extra sure they could move forward. That way Brody could see them and give his final approval of which plates to use.

Gathering the necessary items, Elisa walked toward the kitchen, while her heart thumped harder with each step.

*You're a professional woman who's done hundreds of shoots. No reason why this one is any different.*

Okay, so she'd told smaller lies than that. But maybe if she repeated the words often enough, she wouldn't come across like a lovesick zombie.

In the kitchen, Anthony was hard at work cooking... whatever Brody had asked him to cook. Elisa actually had no idea which dishes to expect, but she had no doubt they would be spectacular. She may have always preferred to do her shooting outdoors, in nature, but today's assignment still had that familiar excitement coursing through her blood. That was always a nice reminder of why she loved holding a camera.

Brody was nowhere to be seen, and Elisa tried not

to let that little fact dampen her mood. Tried, and was unsuccessful.

Anthony glanced up when she approached and graced her with an ear-to-ear grin.

"Good morning, Elisa," he greeted in that deep rumbling voice of his.

"Looks like you've had a busy morning," she replied with a glance at the food that had already been prepared and plated. Three meals, which consisted of a soup, sliders, and some kind of flatbread, were lined up on a rollaway cart. Elisa studied them, thinking how Anthony had a magic touch with food, a talent he most likely didn't know he possessed. At least from what Brody had told her.

Speaking of Brody, where was he?

"Do you mind if I make some adjustments to these?" she asked the cook in an attempt to take her mind off the man who constantly plagued her thoughts.

Anthony waved his hand toward the food. "Be my guest."

She set her camera down and rearranged the triangular-shaped cut flatbread, then moved a tiny bowl of dipping sauce just a fraction. Most people wouldn't notice the difference, but that small adjustment could be the difference of catching the light perfectly or missing it completely. After that she stacked the two slices of toasted baguette bread, which accompanied the soup, on top of each other instead of leaving them side by side. That would enable her to catch the crisp edges of the bread a lot easier.

When she was satisfied, Elisa picked up her digital camera and captured each dish one by one. While working, she made sure to shoot each piece from different angles, so as to get a better idea of how the food would look most appealing. Of course, the end result was always a different story, but practice shots never hurt anything.

By the time she had finished, Anthony had two more plates done. But Brody still wasn't around. Maybe he didn't know she was there? Then again, he'd asked her to come at this specific time, so he had to know she'd be here by now.

*Now you just sound like a high schooler.*

She and Anthony worked side by side for a little while longer before there wasn't much left for her to do except upload her shots to her laptop. She pushed through the kitchen doors but didn't make it to her equipment because her body instantly picked up on Brody's presence. Dang it, she hadn't even seen him, and her Brody radar had gone haywire.

There, behind the bar, stood the man of her fantasies, talking to his "consuming" brother RJ. The two men seemed to be deep in conversation, but Elisa's eyes barely touched on Brody's blonder brother. No, her eyes were all for the black-haired man with the piercing gray eyes and too-wide shoulders. His arms were crossed over his chest, which only reminded Elisa of how powerfully masculine he was. And yet gentle at the same time. Brody McDermott was a multifaceted man who never failed to surprise her.

What wasn't a surprise, however, was her reaction to him. How painfully predictable she was. Rapid heartbeat: check. Sweaty palms: check. Jittery, overloaded hormones: double check.

*Oh, and let's not forget your deep, unrequited love for him. He can probably feel it from over there.*

Lord, the man had turned her into a head case.

She set her camera down by her laptop, when RJ said something in a low tone. Brody's response was a deep, rumbling laugh, which danced across her sensitive nerve endings like a feather. Then he said something back to his brother, which she missed because her head was too busy spinning like a damn top.

Maybe she could fake some stomach bug, so she could hightail it home. The uneasy feeling in her stomach was close enough to making her want to vomit.

Instead, she pulled in a cleansing breath and forced herself to focus on work. This was, after all, why she was being paid. Not to fall at the man's feet. That was for behind closed doors.

She took the SD card out of her camera and inserted it into the slot of her laptop. The photos took a few moments to transfer from the card to her hard drive, time she used to keep her back to Brody. The conversation behind the bar had stopped. Her willpower around the man was weak, but she somehow managed to keep her attention in front of her and not steal peeks over her shoulder.

But then she felt him. And not because he'd touched her. No, he didn't need to make physical contact in order for Elisa to know Brody was around. Simply being in her personal space was enough for her senses to go on high alert.

And then there was how he smelled. Oh sweet mother, the man knew how to work it. He worked it in such a way that Elisa didn't know which way was up or how to get back down to Earth. Where her sanity was.

"Looks like you've made some progress already," he finally said. Entirely too close to her.

She plastered a smile on her face and hoped the heat flaming her cheeks wasn't all that noticeable. "It's been successful so far. I just have to get these photos uploaded. Then you can take a look at them and we can go from there." Like maybe to a bed?

His gaze ran over her features, and a peculiar look passed in his eyes as though he had something on his mind other than pictures.

Well, she did as well so the man was in good company.

The moment passed when he nodded. "Sounds good."

They spent the next half an hour going over the shots she'd taken in the kitchen, with him making comments and her taking notes of what he liked and what he didn't. The magazine was allowing them only three images, so they had to weed out the photos that weren't strong enough. Anthony thought they all looked good, which was surprising given his hesitancy in the first place.

After they were finished with that, Elisa closed her notebook and worked the kinks from her neck. "Sounds like we're good to go," she said.

"I'd say so," he agreed.

Then the two of them stood there, staring at each other. Elisa was already wound so tightly that her head felt like it was going to explode. She stepped around Brody, grasping her digital camera a little more fiercely than she needed to.

"Well, I'll just get this stuff ready," she said in a lame attempt to pretend to be busy, when what she really wanted to do was grab Brody and yank his mouth to hers.

How could he seem so indifferent when she was ready to come apart?

His had shot out and grabbed her wrist. "Elisa," he said.

She halted in her tracks, mostly because his grasp prevented her from going any farther.

And another thing she didn't understand. How could he come off as being unaffected and then look at her as though he wanted to tear her clothes off?

Before she could say anything, he did something that had her head spinning even more than it already was. He kissed her. And not just your everyday affectionate, nice-to-see-you kiss. Like, a real kiss. A wholehearted, full-tongue-action, melt-your-bones lip action that made Elisa forget she was standing in the middle of his restaurant. With a job to do. A job that she currently didn't give a flying rip about, because Brody was kissing her. Tunneling his hands through her hair and making her forget her own name.

"Get a room already."

The comment from Brody's brother, although too close to the truth, was enough to have her pulling away. For a moment everything had melted away. No restaurant. No photo shoot. No Mongolia.

And in that moment, there was only Brody. And, for the slightest second, it almost felt as though he may have felt the same way that she felt about him. After all, how could a man kiss like that and not feel anything?

Elisa licked her lips, savoring the taste of Brody. "We can't do this here."

One side of his mouth kicked up, like the devilish sneaky man he was. "I know. But I couldn't stop myself. As it was, I had a hard time talking to my brother without stomping over here and dragging you out the door."

Oh my.

Okay, good to know she wasn't the only one on the edge.

Now she felt better. Kind of.

"I'll go talk to Anthony and we can get this show on the road," he said before turning around and stalking into the kitchen.

His retreat gave her ample opportunity to admire his firm rear end.

• • •

Brody had been forced to put all his personal crap on hold when a crisis erupted at the restaurant a few days after the photo shoot. On the same day a critic from the newspaper was scheduled to eat, Anthony had contracted a nasty stomach flu. It was shitty timing, of course, and Anthony had apologized like a man begging for his life. Brody had told him to take care of his health and come back to work when he felt better. Then he'd slammed the phone down on the receiver and gritted out some colorful expletives that would have made a trucker blush.

The only thing that hadn't made Brody go completely postal was the fact that they'd finally gotten the photo shoot done. Hours of cooking, perfecting, and standing around while Elisa snapped one shot after another when she'd been here a few days ago had been as exciting as watching paint dry. The only upside was the time he'd been able to spend with the photographer.

That day Elisa had been there to take pictures had been a long one. After her practice shots, she'd had to snap the real thing all before they opened their doors at twelve o'clock. Then, when she'd finished, they'd cleaned up the staging area, which had been the dining room. And then they'd moved her computer into his office so they could go over every shot and choose the appropriate ones. But at least they'd finally gotten it done.

Man, he loved to watch her work. Talk about passionate. Just the way she held the camera turned him on almost as much as she did in bed. He'd damn near gone apoplectic when he'd slapped eyes on her that day. And in a weak moment, he'd given into his impulse and slanted his mouth over hers. As hot as the kiss had been, it hadn't been nearly enough. That's why, for most of the shoot,

he'd stayed scarce. Because he hadn't trusted himself to
be near her and not embarrass himself with a little tent
action below the belt. Hell, the time it had taken to view
the finished photos on her computer had been torture. It
had been like placing a starving person in front of a buffet
and then shackling their hands and feet together. Yeah,
basically torture.

But he'd plugged through like the professional man
he was.

He should have been relieved. They'd finally completed the task and could move on. Now Brody could
focus on getting Anthony on the road toward head chef.
Isn't that what he'd wanted? Not only wanted but needed
to focus on?

So why couldn't he think of anything else besides
Elisa and not having any real excuse for seeing her
again? Okay, except maybe the fact that he was basically obsessed with her. Thought about her day and night.
Dreamed about her. Was pretty much suicidal at the
thought of her leaving.

Unfortunately, for now he had a much more pressing
issue at hand. "Fuck," Brody muttered, and he paced from
one end of his office to the other, trying to find a solution
that wouldn't backfire in their faces.

The woman who was coming in from *The Trouble Citizen* had slammed them about a year ago, warning Trouble citizens to steer clear of the Golden Glove. Her harsh
words had hurt and had been yet another nail in the restaurant's coffin. Luckily for Brody, Charlene had finessed
her way onto the critic's good side and had even offered
the meal on the house. Charlene had then gone one step
further and had faxed some of their recent good reviews
to Michelle Thompson, the critic. Michelle had obviously

been pleased with what she'd read and the prospect of a free meal, and had agreed to come.

How would it look if they told her not to come after all?

Pretty damn shitty, which was how Brody felt right now.

Just as he was about to make another circle around his desk, Charlene opened his office door and stepped through.

He stopped his pacing and faced his assistant manager. "What did she say?"

Charlene came to a stop on the other side of his desk. Her somber expression didn't give him much encouragement. "It's today or never. She's booked solid for quite a while. If she doesn't come today, she can't guarantee she'll be able to come back at all."

"Fuck," he cursed again. He plowed a hand through his hair and yanked on the strands harder than he needed to.

"Maybe we should call this one off, Brody," Charlene suggested.

"No," he answered immediately. "We need her endorsement. She has a ton of readers." He walked to the side of his desk and perched on the edge. "What did you tell her?"

"Just that we were short-staffed in the kitchen and today wasn't the best day."

Which was technically true.

Charlene nibbled on a fingernail. "Do you think I should call her back and tell her the truth?"

If she did that, Michelle might wash her hands of the restaurant and they could lose a very good opportunity. If she did come in, they ran the risk of the sous-chefs not doing a good enough job, and they could end up shooting themselves in the foot. Yet the sous-chefs had always been good about covering up Travis's mistakes.

"Brody?" Charlene said.

"No, call her back and tell her to come in as planned. I'm going to put Stanley in charge today and have him prepare the dishes for me beforehand to make sure he can execute them properly."

Charlene lifted a skeptical brow. "And you think Stanley can do that? He's good, but he's not Anthony."

No one could replace Anthony. But this was the best Brody could come up with. "He can do it." He'd damn well better. "Besides, he pretty much trained Anthony in the kitchen."

"On procedure, not talent." She held her hands up at the look on Brody's face. Then she nodded, inhaled a deep breath, held it for a moment then blew it back out. "Okay. I'll go call Michelle back."

Brody watched her walk out of his office and sank back into his chair with a weary sigh. Every time they took two steps forward, they'd be forced to take a step back. Although, realistically, today could be the equivalent of going back fifty steps if Stanley screwed up.

That was something he couldn't think about.

"Risky move, Brody."

He glanced up to see his father, who stood in the doorway. Great, just what he didn't need—a nice helpful dose of pessimism and no confidence.

"Stanley can do it," he said to convince himself just as much as his old man.

"The young man is a good cook, yes. But do you think he can prepare a dish worthy of a food critic?"

Brody leaned back in his chair. "He's worked side by side with Anthony for over a month now. He's seen the man prepare the dishes before, even assisted with them. Yes, I think he can do it."

Martin didn't respond. He stared at Brody with those

sharp gray eyes of his, as though considering a way that would be better than Brody's. "If you're sure," he finally said.

"This is our only opportunity, Dad."

"I want to see that mock-up for the magazine now that you're finished with it." He issued the demand instead of acknowledging Brody's statement. Whatever. Martin would always find something to bitch about no matter what Brody did.

Brody glanced at the mock-up that had been sitting on his desk since yesterday. "Sure," he answered.

His father walked back into the hallway, leaving Brody to brood in his own frustration. The mock-up of the article had arrived in the mail yesterday, and he'd yet to take the time to really examine it. Mostly because looking at it made him think of Elisa and remember the way her brows pinched together right before she snapped a picture. Or the look of concentration on her face as she stared at a setup before making a minute adjustment. He'd never seen anyone take a job so seriously before.

He needed to see her again. It had only been a few days since he'd emotionally gutted himself in between bouts of outstanding lovemaking. Being apart from Elisa felt like going through withdrawal from an addictive drug. They'd done a lot of talking, yet he felt like there was so much more that needed to be said between them.

Like, where they stood. Did they have some kind of future? Brody still didn't know. Yes, he loved her. He loved her like he'd never loved any woman before. But he was damaged goods. Since his divorce, Brody had come to learn he existed better on his own. He had the potential to seriously hurt Elisa. In fact, those wheels had probably already been set in motion, especially since she'd already admitted to leaving town in a few months. And possibly not returning...

Yet he couldn't bring himself to stay away from her. He needed to be near her, needed to see those expressive brown eyes.

And even though Brody knew it would be best to walk away from Elisa, he wasn't sure if he could.

Elisa was going to have to break Tyler's heart.

And the knowledge made her sick to her stomach.

After returning from a job shooting photos for a brochure for a woman who'd just started her own catering business, Elisa had come home, gathered Brinkley in her car, and taken the dog to the vet. She'd had to practically carry the animal inside the clinic. His hind legs were in such bad shape, the poor thing couldn't take two steps without slinking to the ground. During the few weeks he'd been with her, his condition had deteriorated. So much so that she'd had to physically feed him because he couldn't get up and walk to his bowl. After a while, she'd known something serious was wrong with him.

When the vet had said the word "tumors," Elisa knew Brinkley's days were numbered. Apparently he had them all over, and he had a bad case of arthritis, which was why his legs were in such bad shape. The vet had done an extensive examination of the dog and determined he was around twelve or thirteen years old. The whole time Brinkley had lain on the table, gazing up at her with those big brown eyes as if to say "Put me out of my misery please." The vet had recommended putting the dog to sleep.

"He's in a lot of pain," the doctor had said. "Given his age, there's not a whole lot we can do. The best thing would be to put him down."

Elisa had only spent a few weeks with the sweet animal, but she'd had to fight back tears as she listened to the vet. The poor dog had wandered around for Lord knows how long, alone, sick, in pain, and probably starving. She'd done the best she could with him. Fed him, walked him when he'd still been able to walk. Then she'd sat on the floor next to him and scratched his ears, which seemed to be his preferred place for attention.

She'd grown attached to him, and now she had to say good-bye. Tyler would mourn, and he'd loved Brinkley more than anyone did.

With a lump in her throat, she'd made an appointment for first thing next week to have Brinkley put to sleep. That meant the dog would be in pain for another three days. The vet, obviously sensing Elisa's despair, had given Brinkley some pain medication so at least he could be comfortable for the remainder of his life—which wasn't long.

The dog whimpered from the backseat when Elisa pulled her car into the garage. He was thin, but still pretty heavy. Elisa lifted him from the backseat as gingerly as she could and struggled to get him into the house. She almost dropped him once and managed to settle him on his favorite spot on the living room floor. He responded with another low whimper.

"I'm sorry, buddy." She stroked his ears as he blinked up at her. "Don't look at me like that." It pierced her heart every time he did.

A single tear rolled down her cheek when she went back to the car and retrieved her purse and pain pills the vet had given her. How was she supposed to get Brinkley to swallow a pill that probably didn't taste very good?

*Just put the pill on his tongue, as far back into his*

*throat as you can get it. If you get it far enough, he'll
swallow it.*

She remembered the vet's instructions but wasn't sure
if she could shove her hand into a dog's mouth. Then her
eyes connected with Brinkley's sad ones, and Elisa knew
she could do it. It wasn't fair to leave the animal suffering
the way he was. Putting her hand in his mouth was little
compared to what he was going through.

She shook a pill onto her hand and walked to the dog.
Should she wash it down with water? Use food to disguise
the pill? Would it have a taste? The directions on the bottle didn't say anything other than the dosage.

Brinkley's eyes were closed, so Elisa assumed he'd
gone to sleep. At least she hoped he was just sleeping. A
nudge to his head had him peeling one eye open. Thank
goodness.

"You're probably going to hate me for this, but it has to
be done." She sat on her knees in front of him and lifted
his head in her hand.

Using her thumb and index finger, she pried Brinkley's
mouth open. It wasn't easy, as though the dog already knew
she was going to shove a tiny pill down his throat. Once
she had his mouth open enough, she placed the pill as far
down his tongue as she could get it. He hacked, much the
way a cat does when it's trying to get a hairball out. The pill
landed on the hardwood floor next to Elisa's knee.

One attempt down. Twenty to go.

"Okay, let's try this again." She picked up the pill and
repeated the process five times before getting the stupid
thing down. Then she dragged his water bowl over so he
could wash the medicine down. The dog wasn't interested
in water. Or maybe he couldn't muster the strength to roll
his tongue out.

Elisa had always had a hard time with the idea of euthanizing animals. But allowing Brinkley to continue to live like this was just cruel. She continued to stroke the dog's ears for several more minutes before she had to get up and wipe away the tears that had leaked out. Her only consolation was that Brinkley hadn't been alone during his last weeks. She'd done the best she could with the dog, and soon he wouldn't be in pain anymore.

In order to give herself a distraction, she went to her office and booted up her computer. The images she'd captured that morning for a job she'd done were still on the camera. She'd have to upload more than two hundred photos to her computer so she could browse through them one by one on her photo software. It was a long and tedious process, but it had to be done. In a few days, her client would expect photos e-mailed to her for approval. Once Elisa had that, she would work on putting a mock-up of the brochure together. Then the rest of the woman's payment would go into Elisa's South America fund. One more good job and she'd have enough to visit Marcello.

For the next several hours she pored over one photo after another. Each shot of the same dish was almost exactly the same. Only her trained eye could pick up slight variations in lighting and angles. Even that minute detail could make the difference between a good brochure and a great one.

Only when her vision blurred from staring at the computer screen so long did Elisa take a break. All that time, and she'd only gone through half the pictures. She still had several more hours of work to do.

Her stomach grumbled because she hadn't eaten anything since that morning. Long ago, she'd trained herself to go long periods of time with nothing more than light snacks in her belly.

She strolled into the kitchen and made herself a ham and cheese sandwich. Not really glamorous or filing, but she didn't feel like making a whole big to-do for dinner. Plus it wasn't worth it for just her. Just as she was about to take a bite of her underwhelming dinner, Brinkley whimpered. He had a habit of whimpering and whining a lot, even in his sleep, because he was in so much pain. Elisa set her sandwich down and went to the animal. Maybe she could soothe him or . . . hell, she didn't know. What could she do for him? She'd already given him his pain pills.

Tears spilled over her eyelids as she stroked a hand over his head. The fur was softest on his head. Elsewhere it was rather coarse, though Elisa had tried to remedy that by brushing him regularly. Brinkley had liked to be brushed. She was afraid to drag a brush along his fur now for fear the slightest touch to his legs would cause more pain.

A knock came from her front door, and Elisa furiously swiped away the wetness on her cheeks. She wasn't particularly in the mood to have a guest, but she changed her mind after looking through the peephole. With equal parts excitement and apprehension, Elisa opened the door.

The small tilt of a smile on Brody's mouth disappeared when he saw Elisa's face.

"What's wrong?" he asked as he stepped through the door.

Oh, his wide shoulders underneath the black T-shirt he had on looked so inviting. What she wouldn't give to lay her head there for a bit of comfort. His arms would feel so good around her: strong and comforting, like he would never leave her.

*He just might.*

*Don't think about that.*

"It's nothing," she replied with a sniff.

Brody set the bag he carried in one hand on the kitchen table. "It's not nothing," he argued. His hands came up to her face and cupped her cheeks. They were so big and warm. "What's the matter?"

Another fat tear rolled down her cheek, which Brody brushed away with his thumb. "Brinkley has tumors," she choked out. "He has to be put down."

"Ah, shit." His arms came around her in a solid and reassuring hug. Elisa went willingly because there wasn't anywhere else she wanted to be. There wasn't anyone else she wanted by her side as she mourned the loss of this dog that had come to mean a lot to her.

"I just keep thinking about Tyler and how much he wants this dog," she mumbled into his chest. Her tears were rapidly soaking his shirt. "I don't know how I'm going to tell him."

One of Brody's hands massaged the back of Elisa's head. "Why don't you let me worry about Tyler? He's dealt with this kind of thing before, so he knows how it goes."

She lifted her head and blinked watery eyes at him. "Won't he be devastated?"

"He'll be upset, yes. But he'll be okay. Kids are resilient."

*Okay, enough of being a basket case. He didn't come over here to watch you sob like a maniac.*

She nodded in the direction of the bag he'd set down. "What did you bring?"

Brody glanced over his shoulder. "Just some dinner. Though I would understand if you're not feeling up to it."

Elisa almost wept—even more—with relief. His arrival could not have come at a more opportune time. "No, that sounds really good. Eating a cold sandwich by myself didn't sound very good." She walked to where he set the bags down and peeked inside. "What is it?"

"A chicken Caesar wrap for you and a bleu cheese burger for me. Accompanied by seasoned fries."

The scent of the hot food wafted up from the bag and had her stomach growling, almost painfully so. She supposed that's what she got for not eating all day.

At the same time, Brody looked just as good as the wrap he'd brought her. The crisp white shirt and navy blue slacks indicated he'd come from the restaurant. His dark hair was neatly combed, and Elisa practically vibrated with the need to thread her fingers through the strands. Every night she crawled into her empty bed, pulled the cold sheets around her, and wished he was there. If he had been, she wouldn't hesitate to curl herself around his hard body and drift into a blissful sleep. Then maybe he could wake her up with some curl-your-toes lovemaking.

*Yeah, you don't have it bad, or anything.*

The two of them unpacked their food and settled on the couch. Elisa sat on the opposite side from him, only because she didn't trust herself around him at the moment. His scent was enough to make her want to abandon her wrap and crawl into his lap. Then she'd bury her head in his neck and go comatose. Her skin already tingled from his unrelenting gaze; it was as if he were undressing her with his eyes.

With the way she was feeling, it wouldn't take a whole lot of persuasion on his part to get her naked. In fact, she might just start undressing for him.

*Girl, show some restraint.*

"I've been meaning to ask you how things are going with your potential lawsuit. Any response from the bastard?"

He said "bastard" like he wanted to knock the guy out.

"Actually, Mr. Frank's secretary e-mailed me a copy of the letter he sent them. Who knows if it'll do any good?"

Brody took a monstrous bite of his burger and swiped a napkin across his mouth. "I don't know, Steven can be pretty intimidating. A few years ago a customer burned the roof of his mouth after biting into a piece of steak. He tried to sue my father, but Steven was able to get the little shit to back off."

Elisa paused before taking a bite. "Someone tried to sue over that? Are you serious?"

Brody nodded and popped a fry into his mouth. "Maybe Steven's letter will be enough to get the guy to back off."

"That's all I ask for at this point."

They ate in silence for a few minutes, and all the while Elisa tried to keep her mouth from watering over Brody. He kept moving around like he wasn't comfortable in his own skin. First he sat with one leg crossed over the other, then he uncrossed the leg and stretched both out in front of him. The position reminded Elisa of how long and power-ful his legs really were. Immediately, erotic images flashed through her mind, like an X-rated movie. Brody's body on top of hers, pushing her down into the mattress. Those same strong legs in between hers, forcing her thighs apart as his pelvis ground into hers with expert movements.

A flush developed, starting at her neck and washing up to her hairline. Why couldn't she think of anything else?

Brody wadded up his napkin and set the thing inside the Styrofoam container as Brinkley let out a low moan. Suddenly, she went from slobbering over Brody to her heart breaking all over again over Brinkley.

"I'll go with you when you take him in," Brody said in a quiet voice.

Elisa glanced at him, but he had his attention focused on the sick dog. "You don't have to do that." The idea of having him to lean on, of feeling his solid presence next to her, eased her heartache a little.

He averted his gaze to her, and his penetrating stare touched something deep inside her. "I know."

They stared at each other for one hot moment, and the images from their last time together continued to torture her. The creak of the bed, the feel of his warm breath in her ear, how his muscles coiled like steel when he came inside her. Elisa cleared her throat and picked at the rest of her dinner, even though her stomach was too unsettled to eat.

"Did you ever get to talk to Kelly?"

He stared at her for a moment longer, like a predator stares at its prey before pouncing on it. "Yeah," he finally answered.

When he didn't elaborate, Elisa prompted him. "And?" she asked.

He set his dinner trash on the end table next to the couch. "She said they don't want to move, and they're looking for a way to transfer Louise here. But moving is a possibility, and I told her to be prepared for me to follow them."

The possibility of Brody leaving had her heart breaking a thousand times worse than it did for Brinkley.

"You don't want me to go," he said into the silence.

She discarded the last of her dinner and picked at the hem of her shirt. "I think that's pretty obvious. So is the way I feel about you."

Something flashed in his eyes, maybe regret or sadness. Sadness because he didn't feel the same way, or sadness at the idea of leaving her? Or maybe it was pity because she'd been stupid and fallen in love with him.

"I'm sorry, Elisa. But I can't sit back and let my son move that far away from me. And you're leaving anyway."

"I know, but..." Dammit, she couldn't finish.

"But what?" he prompted.

She turned on the couch to face him. "I've already committed to this job, so I have to go. But if I come back, will I have anything to come back to?" Again, there was no mention of his feelings for her. "Brody, I need to know how you feel about me. Why did you come here tonight?"

"Because I wanted to see you," he said without hesitation.

She pulled in a steadying breath. "And then what?"

He opened his mouth, then hesitated as though he didn't even know the answer himself. His gaze skittered to a point over her shoulder, then connected with hers again. "Then I don't know. I told you before I care about you. But right now this is all I can give you. Should I go?"

She licked her lips and thought about what he said. His attitude toward their relationship hadn't changed, so she wasn't sure why she expected a declaration of love. At the same time, she was too addicted to him to let him walk away just yet. He said himself that the possibility of him leaving was slight.

But she didn't want to come back to Trouble if he wasn't here.

"No," she said.

He stretched his arm along the back of the couch. His fingertips were just out of reach of her hair. "So, why are you all the way over there, and I'm over here?"

His body had been calling out to her all evening, like a homing beacon. She'd managed to resist him all through their meal, but the memory of him inside of her was too strong. She inched across the couch, her body tingling with anticipation of him touching her. Once next to him, his hand tunneled through her hair and molded to the back of her head. His fingers kneaded lightly, but with enough pressure to have her eyes crossing. His mouth was just centimeters from hers, hovering close enough that she could practically feel the pressure of those wonderful lips on hers.

He moved a little closer, and Elisa thought he was finally going to kiss her. But he didn't. Instead he shifted again and brought his lips to her ear. "What am I going to do with you, Elisa?"

Goose bumps assaulted her skin when the words left his mouth. They held a promise of unending pleasure, one that Elisa intended to hold him to—even if this was to be their last night together.

A soft sigh escaped her when his soft lips touched the sensitive spot below her ear. "Whatever you want to," she whispered.

She felt his grin against her neck. "Are you sure you want to give me that free pass?"

"Oh, yes."

# NINETEEN

T HE MOON HAD LONG SINCE disappeared behind some thick, wayward clouds, leaving the night sky, and Elisa's room, oppressively black. Brody didn't mind the darkness or the quiet. It gave him time to think, time to clear his head and categorize his thoughts. Otherwise they were a jumbled mess he could scarcely make sense of. Yes, the peace was always welcome after a chaotic day in a busy restaurant.

Only Brody didn't have peace now.

What he had was torment and indecision, which was unlike him.

Part of that was due to the situation with his ex-wife. The other part was because of the woman sleeping naked and deeply next to him. Or, rather, on him. Half her body was draped across his, with one of her arms tossed over his mid-section with her hand resting on one of his pecs. He liked her there. She fit perfectly snuggled up against him, like two missing puzzle pieces that were now complete.

She completed him.

Shit, that sounded like it was a line out of a freakin' girly movie.

Earlier she'd asked him why he'd come. He'd given her

as honest an answer as he could. Hell, he owed her that much. Especially since she was obviously in love with him, and Brody couldn't bring himself to admit the same to her. Because he was a fucking coward.

He was also weak. As soon as Elisa had opened her front door, he'd known it wouldn't be a quick in-and-out, no pun intended. No, his body had instantly responded to her, as had his heart. He'd needed to have her again because it had been too damn long since he'd felt those slick muscles clamp around him.

But, man, had the wait been worth it. After dragging her down the hallway and into her bedroom, he'd gotten himself inside of her as fast as humanly possible—which hadn't nearly been fast enough. He'd all but ripped her clothes off her body and had barely given her time to catch her breath.

At first, he'd felt guilty for the lack of finesse. But after seeing the satisfied grin on her face when he'd slid into her, the guilt had dissipated, along with any thought of tomorrow.

Her breathing had been fast and labored after he rolled off her. Their bodies had been coated head to toe with sweat because of their exertion. He'd trailed the tip of his index finger down her slick belly, then pulled her limp body into the shower.

"Brody . . ." she'd protested in a tired voice as he turned the faucet to steaming.

"Hush" was all he'd said.

The next several minutes had been spent with Elisa's back pressed to the tiles, her legs entwined around his waist, and him filling her again and again. Over and over he'd surged up into her until she'd sobbed for him to stop, that she couldn't take anymore. Only after her third orgasm did he show mercy on her. He'd shut the shower off and carried her boneless body back to bed. Within seconds she'd been sound asleep, with her still-damp hair fanning across her pillow.

It had been the most euphoric moment of his life. Sex with Kelly had always been satisfying, but never like that. That had been mindless, frivolous, and fucking phenomenal.

Except now he couldn't sleep.

He didn't want her to leave. Or, more important, he wanted her to come back. But she wanted to know of he'd be here waiting for her. If Tyler ended up leaving...then, plain and simple, no. He wouldn't be here. And he was pretty sure Elisa already knew that. The fear had been tangible in her eyes. However, he couldn't bring himself to confirm her fears. There was a good possibility that whatever they had would come to a quick end. The thought just about ripped his heart in two. He'd finally found a woman who'd captured his heart, and he wouldn't even be able to keep her.

He needed to enjoy what time they had, but he couldn't bring himself to stop thinking about its inevitable demise.

On the upside, things at the restaurant were going well. The sous-chefs had pulled off a damn miracle by cooking, to perfection, for the newspaper's food critic. The woman had had no idea that Anthony hadn't been the one to prepare the dishes. She'd beamed and said, "Outstanding," as her plates had been carted away. Brody had almost kissed the sous-chefs in front of the entire staff. They'd saved his ass, and everyone else's as well. The woman's article was to appear in next Sunday's paper, and Brody would be on pins and needles until then.

They also needed to pull off the catering job for Avery's fundraiser. His sister-in-law kept reassuring him everything would be okay, that she had complete faith in him—and Anthony. So did Brody, but anything could go wrong. There were a thousand variables that could end in disaster for them. Unfortunately Brody still had several weeks to sweat in his own anxiety.

For most of the evening at work, Charlene had glared at him and told him to chill out. She kept saying that he was dragging down her good mood, and that was one thing she would not put up with. He'd told her to get over it, then continued to wander aimlessly around the kitchen, looking for something to do.

For the most part, Brody was waiting for the other shoe to drop, because the other shoe always dropped, no matter what. With everything that was going well with the restaurant, Brody had a hard time believing it wasn't going to explode in his face, as it always did. It seemed things were finally clicking into place, but was it too good to be true?

Nothing had ever been in sync with him. Something had always been off. When things had gone well at work, his marriage had been shit and eventually imploded. Now that things at work were good, his personal life made him want to take a semiautomatic weapon and blow shit up. Just for the hell of it. Then, after it seemed like things were going well with Elisa, Kelly had come along with her big-ass fucking wrench and had overhanded that thing right in the middle of everything.

Never in sync.

For just once he'd love to clear all the thoughts out of his head and not think about anything.

And sleep. He could really use a good night's sleep.

Elisa shifted on him, bringing her leg farther across his and burying her head in his neck. She smelled so damn good. Like everything a woman should smell like—all girly, flowery stuff. It screwed with his head and made his thoughts even more of a mess. But he welcomed it. She gave him enough of a distraction to stop thinking.

Before long, his eyelids were heavy enough to drift

closed. They didn't stay that way for long, though. As soon as he shut everything out, his cell phone rang. His cursed, mother-effing cell phone that he had placed on the nightstand next to him for emergencies and shit.

Brody thought about ignoring it, or maybe throwing the thing across the room. But a call this time of night could never be good, and he had an eleven-year-old to think about. Brody used his arm that wasn't buried underneath Elisa and grabbed the device.

"What?" he demanded after bringing the phone to his ear.

"Hey, man, were you asleep?" his brother Chase asked.

"I'm not anymore. What's up?"

"RJ just called me. Courtney was in a really bad car accident." The strain and concern in Chase's voice had Brody sitting up in the bed.

"Shit," he muttered. "How bad is she?"

"All RJ told me was that she was critical and they'd already rushed her into surgery. I'm on my way to the ER right now. He asked me to give everyone a call."

Brody scrubbed a hand down his face and forced his brain to focus. "Okay. I'll be there as soon as I can."

Chase hung up without saying good-bye, but Brody didn't take offense. He removed himself from the comfort of Elisa's body and went in search of his clothes. His boxers had been flung somewhere on the other side of the room. He snagged them off the floor and yanked them on.

"What's wrong?" Elisa's soft voice penetrated the deafening silence of the room.

He glanced at her before pulling on his pants. "My sister Courtney was in a car accident. She's in surgery, so I need to get to the ER."

"You have a sister? Is she okay?" Elisa's voice was

still husky from sleep, and her hair was a tangled mess. Dammit, he wanted to crawl back in bed with her and shut everything out.

Her first question made him realize Brody hadn't mentioned Courtney before, or much else about his family for that matter. However, now was not the time to talk family dynamics.

"I don't know about her condition," he explained after pulling his shirt on and buttoning it up.

"I'll go with you," Elisa said as she slid out of bed and walked into her closet. Not thirty seconds later, she came back out in a matching sweat suit and running shoes.

"You don't have to do that," he said when she stopped in front of him.

"I know." She grabbed his hand and brushed the top of it with her thumb. "Let me do this for you."

Something inside him shifted at her words, and she managed to steal the last piece of his heart. Why he'd kept that so closely guarded from her, he had no idea. Brody hadn't had good luck when it came to love. He almost always managed to hurt whatever poor woman who'd had the bad judgment to fall in love with him.

"Okay," he found himself saying, because he wanted her by his side. He wanted to spend whatever time he could with her.

A few minutes later they were on the road in his car. Trouble had only a handful of walk-in clinics and doctors' offices. The closest ER was two towns away, give or take fifteen minutes, and Brody was sick with worry by the time he pulled into the parking lot. No one had called him to give him any kind of update since he'd talked to Chase.

Elisa gave his hand a comforting squeeze. "She'll be okay."

Her concern was touching and endearing. Never before had he needed someone to lean on. At first he hadn't wanted Elisa to come with him. Now he was glad to have her by his side.

The bright lights of the hospital interior were shocking compared to the dark night outside. Hospitals had always given him the creeps, knowing that around every corner was either a sick person or someone dying. His mother had spent quite a bit of time in the hospital before she passed away. Thankfully, he'd been so young he had very little memory of her trapped in a hospital bed. Even the time he'd spent in this very hospital when Tyler had been born had made him uncomfortable.

Elisa was a solid, reassuring presence next to him, keeping up with his long and rapid steps. She made him feel safe, as if everything in his life would come together the way it was supposed to. Just her smile alone could chase away the darkest cloud.

He would be a very stupid man to get her go. But he just might have to.

They came to a stop in front of the admitting desk. "I'm here for Courtney Devlin," he said in a gruff voice to the young nurse.

"It's family only," she replied like the good little employee she was.

"I'm her brother." He had to force strenuous amounts of patience in his voice even though he felt none.

The nurse tossed a glance at Elisa, as though she were going to protest the presence of another person. Thankfully she didn't. She typed a few keys on the keyboard in front of her, then swiveled in her chair and pointed to a set of enormous double gray doors. "Go through those doors, and sit tight in the waiting room on your left." The nurse turned back around and pinned him and Elisa with a look. "She's still in surgery."

Brody muttered a "thanks" and tugged Elisa beside him through the doors. They closed behind them and clicked, probably from an automatic lock.

"She's just doing her job," Elisa reminded him as though she sensed his disdain.

He smiled and kissed the back of her hand. "I know."

Before finding the rest of his family, Brody made a detour into a smaller room with some vending machines and a coffeemaker. With the way his brain was functioning and his body feeling like lead, he knew he'd need something strong to make it through the rest of the night. Elisa's presence helped, but nothing could substitute straight-up black sludge.

"Are you all right?" Elisa asked again when he yanked the canister off the base.

"Yeah, I'm just..." He shook his head and sighed. What was he? Hell, at this point he didn't know anymore. "Worried about my sister."

Elisa stood against the counter while he poured the coffee into a paper cup. "Not to mention exhausted," she observed.

Yeah, the bags under his eyes were no doubt a dead giveaway. And possibly the dark circles.

"You probably feel guilty about that, don't you?" she asked in a quiet voice. "Your sister's in there, possibly fighting for her life, and you feel bad for thinking about how tired you are."

He sipped the mediocre but potent coffee, thinking how right she was. And what's more, how easily she'd picked up on his body language. How all it had taken was a couple of glances and she'd known immediately what he was going through.

Damn.

"I remember going through the same thing when my parents died. In the weeks after their passing, my brother and I were grieving. Marcello was young, confused, and devastated and at times all I could think about was how tired I was. And then I'd feel guilty, like I didn't have the right because my parents couldn't feel anything at all. And then I'd feel worse because I'd have to remind myself that I had a little brother to take care of."

She came toward him, and it was all he could do to keep his hands to himself. Instead, he gripped the paper cup so hard, he was surprised he didn't crush the thing.

"I shouldn't be thinking about anything else but her," he said in a low voice.

"But it's okay that you are." Elisa cupped his cheek.

Her soft hand felt like a heavenly caress against his day-old whiskers.

"That's what I'm trying to tell you," she went on. "You're only human, Brody."

Her comment had him grinning, despite the circumstances. How crazy was it of him that he hadn't wanted her to come? Even though it hadn't been that long since Chase had called him, Brody couldn't remember why he'd wanted Elisa to stay home.

"It means a lot to me that you're here," he told her.

One of her brows lifted. "Even though you didn't want me to come," she added.

Ah shit, she'd figured him out. Damn observant woman. Too observant for her own good.

He shook his head, trying to make light of it, even though she was right. "That's not—"

"Brody," she said on a sigh. "Don't insult me by pretending I'm wrong. You're a man, and you feel like you have to be macho and unbreakable all the time. And the last thing you want is the little woman trying to comfort you. I get that." Her gaze softened and she ran her fingers through his hair. "But doesn't this feel better than dealing with it on your own?"

Hell yeah, it did. So why couldn't he admit it?

Before he could say anything, she took the cup of coffee from his hand and placed it on the counter behind him. Then she wrapped her arms around his shoulders and pressed her body close. Close enough to savor her plush breasts and feel the indentation of her waist. Despite his body's instant reaction, it wasn't a sexual hug. She obviously had no intention of seducing him out of his clothes, and the realization created a tingling sensation in the pit of his stomach.

Without really thinking about what he was doing, Brody reciprocated by entwining his arms around her and pulling her even closer.

Yes, he did need this. Despite being bullheaded and "macho," as she'd called him, he needed her. The reassurance her presence offered wasn't something he could find from anyone else. Nor did he want it from anyone else.

Just consider him another man who'd fallen under the spell of a bewitching woman. And he'd damn well fall with a smile on his face.

"Want to go find your family now?" Elisa asked after pulling away from him. Too quickly, if you asked him.

He blew out a long breath. "Yeah, I'd better."

Elisa held out her hand, which he took and linked his fingers with hers.

It turned out the waiting room was just down the hall, with everyone from his family there, except for Avery and Lacy.

Even Rebecca had taken a spot in a chair, with red eyes and a ragged tissue in one hand. Brody had just clapped eyes with his father, whose attention dropped to Brody and Elisa's linked hands, when a man wearing paint-stained jeans and a Denver Broncos T-shirt came strolling into the room. He stopped and ran a hand through his shaggy dark hair. "Rebecca called me. She told me Court-ney was still in surgery."

No one spoke for a moment, most likely because they were all trying to process who this guy was. Then RJ voiced what everyone else was probably thinking. "Who the hell are you?"

The man tossed a glance at RJ and looked like he didn't want to answer. "Her fiancé."

# TWENTY

COURTNEY'S INJURIES HAD BEEN FAR more extensive than any of them had anticipated. Hours had slipped by while the doctors tried to put the young woman's body back together. Elisa had no idea how much time had passed. She'd lost count after hour number four.

Finally, an exhausted-looking doctor with thinning gray hair had appeared in the waiting room. He'd addressed the room as a whole, trying to detail all Courtney's injuries in terms they'd understand. Elisa couldn't comprehend most of it, but she'd managed to pick up a few words here and there. The ones she understood were fractures and broken bones, which apparently were on the lighter side of Brody's sister's injuries. Other, more serious ones were hematomas from severe internal bleeding, a laminectomy, which was something to do with spinal damage, and injuries to several internal organs, including her kidneys and her liver.

Then the doctor saved the worst bit of news for last, essentially dropping a bombshell.

Coma. The result of severe head trauma, including swelling and bleeding of the brain. The word had sent

Carol, Brody's stepmother, into a fit of tears. RJ had turned around and punched the wall. Elisa hadn't known what to do. She'd simply grabbed Brody's hand and listened to the doctor apologize like his life was at stake.

"Wait, I want to see her," Carol pleaded the doctor through a thick rush of tears. "Can I see her please?"

The doctor's eyes softened and he spoke to her in a hushed voice. "I can only allow one of you at a time."

"Go ahead," Brody's father urged.

Carol disappeared around the corner, leaving the room in stunned silence. No one spoke. In fact, it seemed like no one was breathing. Except for Chase, Brody's older brother. He'd been pacing around the waiting room like a caged animal, making Elisa increasingly nervous with the way his long legs moved with agitation. Then he stopped, pulled his cell phone out of his pocket, and glanced at the screen.

A string of soft curses flew out of his mouth. "Mason's awake. Lacy says she can hear him talking in his crib." He glanced up and looked at each person in the room, as though he wasn't sure what to do.

Brody's father, who was just as tall and broad as his sons, stepped forward. He placed a hand on Chase's shoulder. "Go. There will be time for you to come back and see your sister." Chase hesitated as a flash of regret darkened his eyes. "If anything changes before you get back, we'll let you know," Martin reassured his son.

With that, Chase left the waiting room to take care of his bedridden wife and young son.

"Avery's on her way," Noah announced after tucking his own cell phone away in his pocket.

Brody hadn't said anything, or even moved, with the exception of his left knee, which bounced up and down and kept brushing along Elisa's. The sexual awareness that shot through her every time his leg brushed hers felt inappropriate, given the situation. She tried to push the feeling down, but her body wouldn't listen.

The man who'd barged in here, announcing himself as Courtney's fiancé, which Elisa guessed no one knew about, remained by himself in the corner of the room. No one had spoken to him, to demand an explanation, and he didn't bother speaking to anyone else. He probably figured the bombshell he had dropped had been at an inopportune time.

These people were hurting, and Elisa wished there was something she could do to help, or at least to soothe their worry. She couldn't even think of a way to help Brody. She didn't know his sister, and all she could think of was to be there for him and hold his hand.

The redheaded girl next to her, who'd introduced herself as Rebecca, rose from her chair and took slow, hesitant steps toward RJ. Since punching the wall, Courtney's brother had been restless, alternating between pacing and rubbing the knuckles that had put a crack in the wall.

He stopped when Rebecca placed herself in front of him. His face was stone cold and hard, the muscles in his jaw flexing with tension. At first she thought Rebecca was going to tell him to sit down or something, because he was making Elisa nervous as hell. The man was like a predatory animal being held captive.

Instead of speaking words of comfort, Rebecca placed a hand on one of RJ's thick shoulders. She ran her hand back and forth in an awkward attempt to soothe him. RJ didn't move, didn't speak, and his face remained hard. But something else clouded his eyes, something very close to longing, or maybe regret.

Elisa watched the interaction between the two with fascination. Rebecca pulled her hand back and started to move away. At the last second, she changed her mind. She wound her arms around RJ's shoulders and held the man tight. RJ was tall, much taller than Rebecca, and the girl had to stretch to her tiptoes to hold on to him. At first, the embrace looked strained as though the two of them were holding themselves back from something more. After a moment, RJ's arms snaked around Rebecca, one going to her waist and the hand of his other arm threading through the strands of her hair, cupping the back of her head.

The two of them were oddly familiar with each other, and Elisa had the feeling that familiarity had once tiptoed into the intimate category. It was something about the way RJ held her, as if he knew the little nooks and crannies of Rebecca's body. Suddenly Elisa felt like watching them was intruding on something too personal, so she looked away. When she turned her head, her gaze connected with Brody's.

"That's about twelve years too late, if you ask me," he muttered.

"You got that right," Noah added.

Elisa glanced back at the hugging couple. Tears were streaming down Rebecca's face. "What do you mean?" she asked Brody. "Aren't they a couple?"

Noah chuckled and Brody's mouth turned up in a grin. "No. I've never understood them."

"Are you okay?" she asked Brody, and dropped the subject of Rebecca and RJ.

Brody stared at her for a moment and didn't say anything. Just as he opened his mouth to respond, he was interrupted.

"I want to see her." The man, Courtney's supposed

fiancé, emerged from the corner of the room and took a step toward Martin. Brody's father, who'd taken Carol's seat, stood and stared the other man down.

"No, you'll wait your turn," Martin said in a hard voice.

The man, who'd yet to introduce himself by name, stopped directly in front of Martin. "No, I'll see her now."

The muscles in Martin's jaw tensed. "I don't know you, son. Courtney's got a lot of family here to see her." He paused, then repeated his earlier words. "You'll wait your turn."

"I'm her fiancé," the man said through gritted teeth.

RJ pushed away from Rebecca and took a step toward Courtney's supposed fiancé. "Funny, how she's never mentioned you, asshole."

"RJ, don't," Rebecca pleaded with a hand on his arm. She tried to turn Courtney's brother, but he held steadfast in front of the other man. "I could really use some coffee, and I don't know where it is. Can you take me?"

Thank goodness for Rebecca, who seemed to have a level head about her. And RJ at least understood what Rebecca was trying to do, because he shot the other man one last glare, then took Rebecca's hand and led her out of the waiting room.

Elisa let out a breath she hadn't realized she'd been holding. The last thing she wanted to see was people throwing punches at each other while poor Courtney was comatose. She leaned toward Brody so she could whisper in his ear. "Nobody knows who this guy is?"

Brody tossed a glance at the man in question, who'd sunk down onto the nearest chair. "No, I've never seen him before," Brody said. "Court's never mentioned anything about a fiancé or a boyfriend. But apparently Rebecca knows him since she called him. Then again she and Courtney live together, so Rebecca would know any-one that Court dates."

"Do you think they're really engaged?" she asked him.

Brody shook his head. "I don't know." He refocused his attention on her. Exhaustion radiated off of him in waves, and Elisa itched to run her fingers through his hair. Or maybe he could lean his head on her shoulder. "You don't have to stay here with me. Do you want me to take you home?"

The only way she would go home was if he went with her. She wasn't about to abandon him during this difficult and stressful time. He had her love whether he wanted it or not.

"I don't want to go home unless you're ready to come with me," she said.

"We could be here a while. I'm not leaving until I've had a chance to see her."

She squeezed his hand. "I'll leave when you leave."

At that moment, Carol came back in the room with red-rimmed, swollen eyes and a bundle of shredded tis-sues in her hand. Noah stood from his chair and folded his stepmother in a hug. He held her for a long while, while she silently cried into his shoulder. Martin left the room, probably to take his turn to see his stepdaughter.

Rebecca came back into the room, alone, and with a paper cup of coffee in one hand. She blew into the hot liquid as she took her seat next to Elisa.

"How's RJ?" she asked the young woman.

Rebecca glanced at Elisa and smiled. "He got tired of pacing a hole in this room, so he's pacing a hole in the other room. But, honestly? I don't know." Rebecca shook her head. "I've never seen him like this."

"And how do you know Courtney?" Elisa had already

come to the conclusion that the girls knew each other well, just judging by how emotional Rebecca had been throughout the night.

"Well, right now we live together. But I've known Courtney since high school." She took a shallow sip of her coffee. "I'd say about twelve or thirteen years now." She glanced at Elisa, a lock of spiral-curly hair brushed her cheek when she turned her head. "Do you know Courtney well?"

An emergency room was hardly the place to have a private conversation of this nature. Elisa needed to choose her words carefully. After all, she'd just met this girl. "No, I don't know Courtney personally. I just came with Brody. A shoulder-to-lean-on kind of thing." Elisa hoped that was a reasonable explanation, though she knew that showing up with him in the middle of the night could only mean one thing. But, in all honesty, she didn't care if his family knew about their relationship. However, Brody seemed to be pretty guarded about things, so she kept her answers evasive out of respect for him.

Rebecca leaned forward, so she could glance at Brody. "Ah," she said in an I-see kind of tone. "Well, you're lucky. Brody's a great guy. And he seems to have strong feelings for you."

"How do you know that?" she asked the younger woman.

Rebecca looked at her with light dancing in her green eyes. "You're here with him, aren't you?"

Yes, she was, but only because she'd invited herself. If she hadn't offered to come, he probably would have left her at home.

She glanced at his handsome profile and thought, again, where he expected this relationship to go. When they were in bed, he communicated his love with sex. Just the way he gazed down into her eyes when he was inside of her spoke volumes. It spoke of someone who had deep, intense feelings. A person just couldn't fake something like that. She felt it down to her very soul every time he touched her. For some reason he was afraid to say the words. Elisa knew it had to do with his marriage and the way things ended with Kelly. Was that fair for him to deny their relationship because of his past demons?

Elisa didn't think so, and she'd been more than patient with him.

The McDermott family sat in silence for a while longer. Noah's wife, a stunning woman carrying a sleepy toddler, eventually arrived. She passed her daughter over to her husband, then sat down next to Carol to offer the woman her support. RJ still hadn't reentered the room. After his earlier display of taking out his anger on the wall, Elisa worried for him.

She nudged Brody's leg. "Maybe you should go check on your brother. He's been gone a while."

"Nah, he just needs to cool off."

Elisa lifted a brow in doubt.

Brody sighed. "All right, I'll go find him."

Brody's brain felt like a scrambled mush of shit that didn't make sense. It was going on seven a.m. and he'd been awake now for more than twenty-four hours. He needed caffeine like nobody's business. Hell, he needed the stuff injected directly into his veins via IV—that way he could run on pure adrenaline and really feel loopy. The only thing that kept his head from exploding completely was having Elisa by his side. He'd even been willing to overlook the curious glances and snide remarks from his brothers. If they knew about his and Elisa's relationship, Noah and Chase wouldn't hesitate to grill him like seasoned detectives. His relationships were nobody's business, and Brody didn't want or need his brothers' noses all up in his shit. Just the look on Noah's face told Brody he hadn't heard the last of their opinions—jumping back into the dating pool headfirst, and all that crap. He'd heard that before, thank you very much.

Besides, now wasn't the time. They were here for Courtney and needed to focus on her.

Elisa was probably right about RJ not being okay. Years ago he'd taken it upon himself to personally look after Courtney, since the girl was unable to make a responsible decision. At the same time, RJ didn't need Brody checking up on him like he was some helpless kid. RJ had a reputation for being unpredictable and was best left alone when he got in moods like this. But Brody needed coffee like he needed air. He'd grab himself a cup, then make sure RJ wasn't off somewhere ripping doors from their hinges.

Turns out, he didn't have to look for his brother very far. RJ was in the snack room, sipping on some coffee and leaning against the wall. Brody nodded to the other man and grabbed the pot off its holder. RJ didn't say anything, and Brody hadn't expected him to. He simply poured himself some coffee and sipped it straight black. No fluffy creamy stuff for him.

RJ watched him over the rim of his paper cup. When he lowered it, he said, "So, you're with the goddess?"

Brody looked his brother over. The man was in a mood and looking for a fight. He'd already picked one of those with the wall and hadn't gotten a whole lot in return, except for a sore hand. Brody understood RJ's simmering attitude, given the situation. But he'd be damned if he would allow his younger brother to take his shitty mood out on him or Elisa, for that matter.

"Yeah, but it's nothing," he finally responded.

RJ lifted a golden brow. "Really? Do you usually have 'nothing' with you in the middle of the night?" Brody didn't answer because he refused to feed into RJ's anger. "I'm guessing she's the one who's got you so distracted lately. Oh yeah, you've been distracted," RJ continued when Brody opened his mouth to argue. "The restaurant you work at? You know, the one you're never at anymore? Yeah, I'm still tending bar there because you still haven't hired a replacement for Anthony."

Brody jabbed a finger at RJ. "You'd better shut up, while you're ahead."

RJ pushed away from the wall, set his cup down, and took a step toward Brody. Fury simmered just beneath the surface of his blue eyes. "It's none of my business who you fuck. But I care when that woman has you so distracted that you couldn't do the one thing I asked you to do."

RJ's harshly spoken words sent Brody's blood to a low boil. Yeah, RJ was pissed. And, yes, he was worried sick about his sister and was probably just as exhausted as Brody was. But he was inappropriate, and Brody wasn't going to stand for it.

"If I didn't know any better, I'd say you were blaming me for Courtney's accident," he said through gritted teeth.

"If she'd been working tonight, instead of driving around, she wouldn't be in the hospital fighting for her life." RJ tossed out his accusation through tight lips. Brody stared down his younger brother and tried not taking the words personally. "And then you had to bring Miss Victoria's Secret Model here, as if it weren't bad enough that you were at home getting yourself laid while my sister was having her head bashed in."

"You were right before. Who I'm fucking isn't any of your business. And even if it were, I'd tell you that Elisa doesn't have me distracted because she's not important enough to distract me. The only reason why she's here was because she insisted on coming, and I wanted to get here as quickly as possible instead of arguing with her."

Damn his little brother for making him say these things. His own words made his heart twist with brutal pain in his chest. "I don't have to explain myself to you." He slammed the cup of coffee so hard on the counter that some of the black liquid sloshed over the edge and burned his hand. The pain didn't matter to him. His adrenaline was pumping too hard from fatigue, stress, and uncertainty from too many variables in his life.

"Wait," RJ said in a tired voice just as Brody turned to leave the room.

Brody turned around and pinned him with a glare. He was going to tell his brother to fuck off, but something stopped him. RJ had turned to lean against the counter. His head hung down as though defeat and exhaustion had finally taken over. Hell, he was just worried about his sister and had succumbed to a weak moment by taking his fear out on Brody. Too many times in the past had Brody fallen prey to that very thing, so he knew how his brother felt. RJ was coping with this situation the only way he knew how: by looking for someone to blame. It just so happened that Brody had placed himself in the line of fire. He couldn't fault RJ for that.

"I'm sorry," RJ said in a gruff voice. "I can tell you like her a lot and she seems like a great woman. Only someone who was committed to you would accompany you to a hospital to wait for hours in the middle of the night." He lifted his head and looked at Brody. "I shouldn't have said those things. None of this is your fault."

"Hey, don't worry about it. We all say things we don't mean." Except they were partially true. To a certain extent, Elisa *had* been distracting him. But it had been a distraction he'd needed, a way to take his mind off work troubles and worry over his son. And now Courtney.

"This woman is the real thing, isn't she?" RJ asked.

Brody understood what RJ was trying to do: to make up for the things he'd just said. But Brody still didn't want to talk specifics about Elisa. Not until he was able to figure some things out. "Yeah, she is. She's not unimportant. I care about her."

RJ pushed away from the counter. "It's more than that. You're in love with her. You just can't admit it."

"And you would know all about that, wouldn't you?" he countered, because he didn't need RJ reading him that deeply at seven in the morning.

RJ lifted his chin, as though challenging Brody to say more. And then RJ might put his fist in his brother's face. "Don't go there," he said in a low voice.

"Just saying. You're in as much denial as I am, my friend." Then he turned around and left RJ to contemplate those words. Because his little brother, only separated by a year, needed a swift kick in the ass as much as Brody did.

He strolled back into the waiting room to find Elisa, because he'd had enough of this tiptoeing-around-his-feelings bullshit. Time to bring it all out in the open to see if Elisa could really handle it. Martin had finally returned, and Noah had gone to take his turn with Courtney. Avery was reading a book to Lily, and Rebecca had just stood from her chair and was walking toward him.

He stopped her with a hand on her arm. "Where's Elisa?"

Rebecca's brows pulled together in confusion. "Weren't you just with her?"

What the hell? "No, why?"

"She said she was going to get some coffee, then she never came back. I figured she was with you."

Brody released her arm, and the young woman walked away. If ever two people needed to sort their shit out, it was her and RJ. But Brody couldn't worry about that right now. He walked back to the hallway, looked left, then right. All he saw was Rebecca's backside as she walked toward the snack room and a nurse disappearing around a corner.

Where could Elisa have gone?

# TWENTY-ONE

A T SEVEN FORTY-FIVE IN THE morning, nothing looked as inviting or heavenly as her bed. Elisa crawled into the cool sheets without bothering to change, pulled the covers over her head, and willed herself to sleep. A major obstruction in her quest for sweet dreams was Brody and the fact that his scent was all over her sheets and her clothes. Hell, she could still smell him in her hair.

Brody's statement had been like a poisonous knife right through her heart. Since then, the toxins had been working their way through her body, paralyzing her with disbelief, shock, and heartache. She'd been unable to think of anything else, other than getting as far away from him as possible. The nurse at the front desk had looked at Elisa with pity when she, with tears rolling down her cheeks, had all but begged to use the phone. Then she'd called the only cab company within a ten-mile radius.

This was just a temporary solution. Brody would eventually come knocking on her door, wanting to know why she'd bolted. Maybe then she'd have the strength to face him. Right now, all she wanted to do was drift into nothingness and drown herself in senseless dreams.

Instead of going to sleep, a fresh wave of tears hit her, as though her mind was punishing her for stupidly falling in love with him. How could she have been so wrong about him? How could she have allowed her heart to get trampled again?

It's not like she hadn't experienced heartbreak before. But, even then, her breakup with Micah had been like eating cheesecake compared to this. Micah hadn't looked at her the way Brody did. He hadn't stared down into her soul and stolen her heart like Brody had.

She hiccupped and wiped her tears on the sheets. When she pressed her nose to the fabric, she got another whiff of Brody, and an instant image came to mind. Brody's wet, slick body in her shower, towering over her as he backed her against the tiled wall. Brody in her bed, his finely toned, muscled body stretched out across her sheets, with a little smirk on his face while he waited for her to devour him. And, finally, Brody telling her he'd accompany her to Brinkley's appointment, holding her tight and telling her everything would be okay.

She'd never fallen so fast and so hard for someone before, and the aftermath was more than she could take. Her insides felt like they'd been ripped out.

Unable to sleep, she picked up her cell phone and dialed Marcello. Miraculously, he answered.

"*Olá*," he greeted in a rushed voice.

At just the sound of her little brother's deep, accented voice, all Elisa's emotions from the past twenty-four hours rushed out of her like a bad stomach virus.

"Hi," she answered in a wavering voice as tears pooled over her eyes.

"Elisa?" he said in a tone of alarm, which had her angst turning into guilt. "Is everything okay?" he wanted to know when she hadn't said anything else. Mostly because her throat was too tight.

"I'm really sorry to bother you," she started, while swiping moisture off her cheeks with the bed sheet. "You can call me back if you need to." *Though I don't know what I'll do with myself until then.*

"It's okay, I'm in between classes." Shuffling noises came from across the phone, then it got quiet. "Tell me what's going on."

More tears leaked out, which she blotted away with the already damp sheet. "My life is a mess, that's what's going on."

"Are you hurt?" he wanted to know.

She sniffed. "No. Well, at least not physically."

Marcello was silent for a moment. "Ah," he finally replied as though the light bulb had kicked on. "This has to do with a man, doesn't it? This Brody you were telling me about."

Just hearing Brody's name sent her in a new wave of tears, which gathered too fast for her to control. In the past, Elisa had always thought that she knew what a broken heart felt like. After all, she'd been betrayed by the first serious boyfriend she'd ever had. But Micah keeping his true sexuality a secret from her was like a drop in a big-ass bucket compared to the damage Brody had done. She'd rather relive her breakup with the male model a thousand times over than to have this hollowed-out feeling in the pit of her stomach.

"*Merda*," he cursed. "What did the bastard do? Because I'll take the first flight out there and kick his *traseiro*."

Her brother's comments pulled a grin along her mouth, despite hearing him talk about kicking Brody's ass. "I appreciate that, but it's not necessary."

"He made my sister cry," Marcello argued.

"That's my fault because I was stupid enough to fall in love with him," she said on a whine as a new wave of tears blindsided her.

Her sweet younger brother waited her emotion out, giving her time to gather herself before bombarding her with questions. When he didn't say anything, probably because he had no clue how to comfort her, she plugged on. "I'm so done with men. They're all pigs."

"Hey now, not all of us are like that," he argued. "Only the ones who are in love."

Elisa snorted. "Brody's not in love with me." Yes, that was her greatest hope, but there had to come a time when she needed to stop lying to herself. That way she could work on healing.

Her brother cursed again—this time in English. A sure pissed-off sign. "That's it," he said in a tight voice. "I'm flying you down here. I'll get you a one-way ticket and you can return home whenever you want."

Elisa shook her head, even though he couldn't see her. "Marcello, no. Even a one-way ticket is like thirteen hundred dollars. I can't let you spend all that money on me."

Oh Lord, if her brother had to shell out all that money on a plane ticket for her, she'd never be able to sleep at night.

"No arguments, Elisa," Marcello said in a firm voice. "Besides, I bet I could get Avô to pay for it. He racks up a whole bunch of airline miles with how much he travels."

Getting away for a while to clear her head, seeing her little brother do his thing as a doctor, visiting with her grandparents. How could she say no to that?

She burrowed deeper in the bed sheets, already feeling the arms of sleep wrap around her. "You're such a gem, Marcello. I knew talking to you would make me feel better."

"Well, I do what I can. Plus it kills me to hear you cry and not be able to be there with you." The smile in his voice was unmistakable. "Let me know when would be a good time for you to get away, and I'll look into some flights."

"Thanks," she replied with a small grin. "And thanks again for listening to my whining."

"That's what brothers are for, *querida*."

They disconnected the call, and unconsciousness took over.

Elisa couldn't remember the last time she'd slept so deeply. That afternoon, she'd awoken after dozing for about six hours, then dragged herself out of bed and took a quick, hot shower. The whole time, she forced her mind on what was left of the day, and not the time she and Brody had shared this exact space. All naked and wet—

*No!*

Dammit, could she not get through one afternoon without being haunted by the man who'd cracked her heart in two?

She'd scrubbed her scalp harder than necessary, as though it could actually scrub Brody from her mind. All that had done was give her a headache.

After tossing back a couple of painkillers, Elisa forced herself to get something productive done.

By late afternoon, she left the house and drove through town, looking for something to eat. Food hadn't really been on her mind until her stomach let out a low rumble, reminding her that she hadn't eaten since the previous evening. Not that she cared much about food anyway. Really, nothing mattered to her at the moment, but her body would soon start to protest if she didn't give it some fuel.

She spotted a burger joint and pulled her car into the side parking lot. The place was packed with the umbrella-shaded tables full of families and couples. Normally she didn't really do burgers, but her mood wouldn't allow her to put a whole lot of thought process into a meal. The only reason she stopped was because it was the first place she'd laid eyes on. And because making herself something at home would take too much effort.

On the other hand, perhaps going way out of her comfort zone was exactly what she needed. Step one in washing Brody McDermott from her life.

She slung her purse over her shoulder and strolled down the sidewalk, her stride growing stronger with each step. Why should she allow the man to affect her like this? Because she'd fallen in love and had her heart broken?

That had happened to her before, and she'd survived. Hell, if she could survive losing both of her parents, then certainly she could get over one man.

The Greasy Spoon had a guacamole burger on special. Add on a side of fries for only an extra dollar.

What the hell? Why not go for the fries?

At the last minute, she tossed in a chocolate shake because, really, who cared about calories?

*Not this girl.*

It's not like she still had a man to impress.

The freshly grease-dipped fries smelled so good that Elisa couldn't wait to try one. As she pushed through the glass door, she dug a fry out of the bag and popped the thing into her mouth.

Hmmm. Crunchy and not too salty. Just how she liked them. Well worth the calories consumed.

She went for broke and fetched another fry. And ran smack into a broad, unyielding chest. The action had her stumbling back, and the chocolate shake slipped from where she'd had it tucked under her arm. The drink crashed to the ground, sending thick chocolate crap everywhere. All over her, and spattering across the denim-covered legs of the man who...

Ah hell.

"I would be pissed," Brody said, "but at this point I don't give a shit."

The shake oozed down her legs and dripped in between her toes. Would it be totally uncouth of her to ditch the sandals and continue on bare feet?

"Did you ever get to see your sister?" she asked while trying not to cringe at the liquid seeping under her toes.

"Yeah," he muttered through barely moving lips. His jaw was hard set and unforgiving, like granite. And his lips were pressed to a thin line. Not happy to see her. "Where'd you take off to?"

"Home. I was tired." Why did he have to look so damn good, even all wrinkled and unkempt? Hair all uncombed, jaw unshaven. Eyes especially hard, yet even more piercing than ever. And zeroed in on her, although not at all soft as she was used to seeing them, but they still created a patch of heat in her midsection. "And what are you doing here?"

"Getting food," he said without missing a beat. "And yeah, I got that you were probably tired. Why'd you run off without telling me? I looked all over the hospital for you."

Something about his tone, and the irritation lacing it, got her back up. She gripped her bag of food tighter to her chest. "Really? I didn't think I was important enough for you to worry about." She deliberately used his own words against him, because, dammit, she was tired, confused, and just had her heart broken.

A muscle ticked in Brody's jaw. Anger and confusion

was a tangible thing coming off him in waves that it almost knocked the breath out of Elisa. She'd seen him agitated before. But this was something different. This was pure stone-cold ire.

Well, served him right.

"Yes, I heard you," she continued when he didn't respond to her statement. "I heard what you said," she clarified just in case he hadn't gotten the message.

"Then you obviously didn't listen to the conversation long enough. And, anyway, I don't like spilling out my personal relationships for my family. That wasn't the time or place to have an intimate conversation with my brother. Especially with the mood he was in."

Elisa didn't know what to say to that. It wasn't exactly an apology, or any kind of indication that the words weren't true.

"That's not good enough for you, is it?" he asked with narrowed eyes.

"I don't know, Brody. What am I supposed to think after hearing something like that? You've been so evasive about your feelings for me. Quite frankly, I'm tired of waiting."

"What do you mean?"

She inhaled a deep breath and tried to fight the tears that were threatening again. "I told you before, I can't just be a sex buddy to you. There has to be more to this relationship than that."

He took a step toward her, and she backed up into one of the patio tables. Luckily no one was sitting there. "And I told you before that I care about you. But right now this is all I'm capable of."

"That's not good enough. I know you love me, Brody, but for some reason you can't admit it. And I deserve better than that." She deserved better than someone who would lie to her and lie to himself.

"You're right, you do. And I'm sorry you heard what I said to my brother. I didn't mean it, and I shouldn't have said it. But neither my brother nor I were in the right frame of mind to have that kind of discussion. That doesn't mean that I don't have feelings for you, because I do."

She tilted her head and studied him. "But those feelings aren't strong enough for you to stick around, are they?" Elisa accused. "And you might be leaving anyway, so perhaps it's best if we call things off right now." The tightness in her chest returned, the one where she felt on the precipice of having a heart attack. She pulled a deep breath and felt the organ do a little triple beat. Not much better than the tightness.

"You're the one who's leaving," he tossed at her.

"At first it was permanent, yes. But after I met you, I thought about coming back to Trouble and giving this a shot. But you haven't given me any reason to come back, or any indication that you want me to." She stared at him, trying to read his features, but he was poker-faced. "Give me a reason to come back, Brody." She shook her head. The tears were getting harder and harder for her to fight. "I can't keep doing this. I love you, and I'm not afraid to admit it. For some reason, you're terrified."

A woman walked toward the entrance of the burger joint, which had Brody and Elisa stepping out of the way. "You're right, I am terrified," Brody admitted. "Terrified of what I could do to you. That I could end up destroying any faith you might have in me."

*Too late for that.* "Why, because of a poor decision you made when you were still married?" she asked instead, confirming that he'd already destroyed her. "Brody, a moment of bad judgment doesn't define who you are. We all have times of weakness."

He didn't respond to her. Instead he took another step toward her and narrowed his gaze. Those soulful eyes of his cut straight to her heart, like they always did. If she didn't scurry away now, she would find herself succumbing to him again. And she didn't need that. Her heart was too fragile to get any deeper with him. If she had any prayer at all of surviving him, she needed to end things now.

"I can't do this," she muttered again in a whisper. If she forced a normal voice, he might suspect the tears. "I have to go," she murmured with her eyes focused on the ground. She couldn't bring herself to look at him. She took a wide berth that would ensure she could get around him without touching him. Because, really, wasn't being close to him enough torture?

He, however, the persistent, sneaky man, had other ideas. His hand shot out and latched onto her wrist. The touch, his skin in contact with hers, ignited all kinds of buried feelings and sensations she'd spent the better part of the night trying to forget. And all it took was one grasp of his hand to remind her what kind of control he could have over her.

He pinned her with those scorching gray eyes of his. The same gaze that she had drowned in when he'd been buried deep inside her.

In order to mask her reaction, Elisa glanced away and looked at…the ground. What the hell else was she supposed to look at? Certainly not him.

When she thought he would speak, to say anything to reassure her this was nothing more than a misunderstanding, he disappointed her. Nothing but silence and his penetrating presence looming over her.

The only thing she got in return was his thumb grazing back and forth over the inside of her wrist. Like some pendulum clock counting down the seconds until he let her go and she walked away from him. Because, unless he said something really Earth-moving, she'd walk.

Without a word of any kind of hope or confirmation, he turned around and walked into the restaurant. His silence decimated what was left of her heart.

For once in his life, Brody didn't have a damn thing to do. Except brood and kick himself for how things had gone with Elisa when he'd run into her the day before. He'd showed up at the restaurant, ready to drown himself in work, when Charlene all but booted his ass out the door. He supposed the thunderous look on his face and unkempt appearance wasn't really conducive for a professional atmosphere. Whatever. He could use the time off. Charlene knew that and assured him everything was taken care of. Just before escorting him out, she flashed him her pearly whites and slipped a piece of paper in his hand. Brody didn't open it until he got in the car. He wasn't in the mood to read anything, or use his brain in any sort of capacity.

The paper was a photocopy of the review Michelle had written for *The Trouble Citizen*. In the front seat of his car, Brody glanced over the article, just picking up highlights here and there. It was a good review. In fact, it was freakin' glowing. He really should take the time to read the entire thing. There was a small chance it might lift his spirits. But he couldn't bring himself to care. In fact, there wasn't a whole lot he cared about right now—except maybe drowning himself in a big-ass bottle of Jack.

He set the article aside, turned his truck on, and just sat

there, staring out at the parking lot and dwelling on how he'd royally screwed things up.

He'd asked Kelly if he could pick Tyler up from school so he could spend some time with his son. She'd eagerly agreed, saying the fatigue from her pregnancy was overwhelming. Plus he needed to speak with Tyler about Brinkley. And even though he and Elisa were essentially over, a thought that still sent ice-cold water through his veins, he wanted her there with him. Funny how that worked. And funny how he was the asshole who'd put himself in that position.

Tyler didn't get out of school for another three hours. Brody didn't know what the hell to do with himself. He couldn't very well get piss drunk, then pick his son up from school. So Jack and his cure-all would have to wait until later. After several minutes of sitting there, Brody left the restaurant and headed to Chase's house to see Lacy. His sister-in-law was getting dangerously close to her due date, and Brody hadn't gone to see her in a while.

The garage door to his brother's house was open, show-ing both Chase's and Lacy's cars inside. Chase must have been too tired, after their night in the hospital, to make an appearance at work. Brody could sympathize.

He parked his truck in the driveway and got out, then made his way up the front walk. Once at the door, he rapped the back of his knuckles against the solid wood. A moment later a very disheveled and grumpy-looking Chase swung the door open.

Brody gave his older brother a good once-over—he was wearing nothing but boxers.

"Did I interrupt something?" Brody asked.

Chase snorted and stepped aside to let Brody enter. "With the condition my wife is in? These days I'm lucky if I get an 'I love you.'"

Brody followed his brother into the house. The living room was a disorganized mess of toys, a pair of shorts, and a mismatched shirt. Two sippy cups lay side by side on the carpet as though they'd been tossed there in Mason's haste for his next conquest. Some toddler cartoon with bouncing computer graphics children was muted on the television. All in all, it wasn't a pretty sight. When Avery was in charge, the house was much neater and actually smelled good. Chase obviously wasn't as on top of his game, as far as housekeeping went. But one thing Brody did notice was how quiet the house was.

"Where's the little terror?" Brody asked as he just managed to dodge a plastic dinosaur on the floor.

Chase ran a hand through the untidy strands of his hair. "Finally in bed. The kid had me running from one end of the house to the other since six this morning. I don't know how Avery comes here five days a week," he said as he picked up the remote and turned the cartoon off. "I was just trying to catch some sleep myself, but Lacy kept kicking the covers off and complaining about how hot it was."

A smile touched his lips and the mention of his brother's wife. "How is Lacy?"

A curse flew out of Chase's mouth when he tripped over a toy. The thing lit up and launched into some ridiculous ABC song. "All things considered, pretty good. She's worried as hell about Court."

Weren't they all? A report from Martin said things hadn't changed much since that morning. Courtney was still comatose and showed no signs of getting any better. Carol refused to leave her daughter's bedside, not that Brody blamed her. The only reason Martin had left the hospital was to take a shower and pick up food for the two of them. In all the rush of things, his stepmother was forgetting to take care of herself, as she had most of her adult life. And the kicker had been not being allowed to see Court. Because of her condition, the doctors had said no more than two people in her room at a time. Brody and the rest of his family had decided to back out and leave that honor to Courtney's mother and Martin.

"You look like shit," Chase stated rather eloquently, as though he was getting his first good look since Brody had walked through the door.

Brody scrubbed a hand down his face. "Ah, hell, I feel like it." Even if things were to work out between him and Elisa, he didn't deserve her. She deserved someone who wasn't a head case. How he would love for her to come back. The idea of her leaving for good made his stomach turn. But he couldn't bring himself to ask that of her if he couldn't give her what she wanted in return.

"Would this, by any chance, have to do with a woman?" Chase guessed, because Brody figured he was that easy to read. "You forget I went through the same thing with Lacy," he went on when Brody didn't respond. "I know that look, my friend. There ain't no coming back from that."

"Tell me something I don't know," Brody muttered. Maybe he shouldn't have come here. The last thing he wanted to do was talk about how he'd shattered yet another woman's heart. But, on the other hand, he was so damn confused maybe talking about it would help. Maybe that was his problem. He'd spent so many years trying to keep everything hidden.

*Yeah, look how that's worked out for you. You don't know up from down.*

"Come on, tell big brother about it," Chase urged. "Do you remember the whole punching-me-in-the-face-because-I-pissed-off-Lacy incident?"

Hell yeah, he remembered that. It had been the one and only time he'd gotten physical with one of his brothers. And Chase had deserved it because he'd been a stubborn ass. Ah, shit.

"Trust me, sometimes an intervention like that helps," Chase went on.

Brody quirked a brow. "What, are you going to punch me now?"

Chase gathered a handful of crackers off Mason's high chair and carried them to the kitchen. "If you deserve it." He came back in the room, dusting the crumbs off his hands. "Do I need to start throwing some uppercuts?"

Brody heaved a sigh. "At this point, I think that might be what I need."

# TWENTY-TWO

THE SMILE ON TYLER'S FACE was enough to chase all of Brody's dark clouds away. The moment he laid eyes on his son's gangly frame, the weight had been lifted off his shoulders by exponential degrees. Brody smiled for the first time all day and remembered how Tyler used to run to the car when he was little, as though he couldn't get away from school fast enough. Tyler looked happy to see him, and the knowledge lifted his spirits. Too bad he was going to have to break the kid's heart.

Brinkley was supposed to be put down the day after tomorrow. He knew Tyler would want to see the dog again, but Brody wasn't sure that was such a good idea. His son had a knack for being too sensitive about things. And he'd already formed an attachment to the dog, as though he'd already claimed Brinkley as his own.

Tyler threw the car door open, tossed his backpack in the backseat, and climbed in. "Hey, Dad," he said after closing the car door. "Where's Mom?"

Brody fought his way through the school traffic and eventually made it out of the parking lot. "She was feeling a bit tired, so I told her I'd come pick you up." Plus he had something planned for the two of them, something they hadn't done in a long time. Something that was long overdue and would hopefully cushion the news of Brinkley.

"I got a B plus on my history report," Tyler announced with a touch of pride in his voice.

Brody glanced at him. "That's because you're a smarty pants." He held his fist out, which Tyler thumped with his own. "What else is going on at school? Learn anything interesting?"

"Not really," Tyler said with a shrug. "But we're going to the science museum next month and I need either you or Mom to sign a permission slip."

"The science museum? That'll be cool, huh?"

"It's okay. I went there once already in fourth grade."

Brody thought the science museum would be pretty interesting, but what the hell did he know? Obviously eleven-year-olds had a different definition of "cool."

"Dad, you passed our street," Tyler announced a few moments later.

After leaving Chase's house, he'd gone home and tossed in his and Tyler's gloves and a couple of baseballs. It was way past time the two of them spent some one-on-one time together and got back to the basics of their relationship. These days his son would rather text and talk sports stats with his friends. Not too long ago Brody was Tyler's favorite person in the world.

"We're not going home yet. I thought you and I could go have some fun before we get to the homework grind." He glanced at Tyler. "Work for you?"

"Yeah." The smile that spread across the boy's face was a special one the two of them used to share. Back when it seemed like they were the only two people in the world.

• • •

The town of Trouble didn't have a whole lot of money to dump into its Parks & Recreations department. It had only two baseball diamonds, and the "bleachers" to go along with them were laughable and couldn't hold more than two dozen people. Brody had many memories of playing there as a kid, and he remembered them being a lot nicer than they were now. What little grass was able to grow was shin high and wasn't conducive for making a dive catch. That was mostly due to the abundance of weeds that had taken over most of the outfield. Brody had played on nicer fields that had soft red clay on the infield. That stuff was every player's dream and kept scrapes and injuries to a minimum. Trouble's field had sand with patches of cracked dirt that was like running on cement. The ankle he'd twisted on two separate occasions could be credited to that nightmare.

The poor Little League teams had had to resort to meager fundraisers to repair the fields themselves. Unfortunately, they hadn't raised enough money to do anything substantial. But Brody didn't care if it was a bare patch of dirt. All he needed was a place to play catch with his son.

He pulled his car into a parking space, grabbed their gear, and the two of them headed to the field. Brody placed himself on the pitcher's mound, which wasn't much of a mound. And Tyler stood at home plate. This had always been their customary positions, Brody throwing the pitches and Tyler playing catcher. Anything else would feel out of sorts to him.

The glove felt foreign on Brody's hand, almost too tight because it hadn't been used in so long. But it also felt right, and he cursed himself again for letting too much time go by. Tyler tossed the ball in the air a few times, then overhanded it to Brody. The ball landed in his glove with a *smack*. He wrapped his fingers around the ball, tested its weight, then threw it back to Tyler. He purposely threw it a little high just to see if his son would remember what he'd been taught. Tyler didn't disappoint. But Brody had thrown it too high. The ball hit the tip of Tyler's glove, then sailed passed him and bounced off the chain link fence behind home plate.

"Sorry about that," Brody called out. "Bad throw."

"I got it." Tyler ran the short distance and scooped up the ball. He bounced from foot to foot back on home plate and threw the ball back to Brody with a big grin on his face.

"Do you remember when you made Mom be the batter, and you hit her hand?" Tyler asked when he caught the toss Brody had returned to him.

"Thanks for reminding me," Brody said with a smirk.

"The look on Mom's face was hilarious."

Yeah, it had been a real riot. Kelly had insisted on watching the two of them from the bleachers. Only after a lot of cajoling did she agree to hit a few balls. He distinctly remembered being distracted by a pair of shorts his then-wife had been wearing. A pitch had gotten away from him and he'd hit her knuckles, bruising them badly. She'd taken it like a champ, but the daggers her eyes had tossed him had been unmistakable. Brody was surprised Tyler had remembered that day; he'd only been about six at the time.

"She was pretty mad at you," his son added.

Brody clapped his glove around the ball Tyler just threw. "I don't blame her. I damn near broke her hand."

Tyler leapt to the left to make a great catch. "Maybe that's why she never came out with us again." A gust of wind blew Tyler's blond locks across his forehead. He tossed the ball up in the air a few times. "I liked it being just you and me," he muttered.

Brody could only stand there on the pitiful excuse of a pitcher's mound as an ache settled around his heart. He ached for so many things: for the family he used to have, for the way Tyler used to look at him—before Brody had screwed everything up.

"Why don't we take a break?" he suggested, with a nod of his head toward the bleachers.

Tyler dragged his scuffed sneakers along the dirt, kicking up dust behind him as he went. The metal bleachers creaked and groaned when the two of them climbed to the top row. Tyler sat down and set his glove and ball down by his feet. Brody settled beside him and leaned against the back rest. A gust of wind blew some stray leaves across the parking lot as the two of them sat in silence for a moment.

"Something on your mind, son?" he asked after Tyler had been picking at the stitching on his glove.

Tyler pinned him with his expressive green eyes. "Am I going to have to move?"

The question threw Brody completely off balance and had the blood in his veins practically freezing. Kelly had said she hadn't said anything to Tyler, so the boy must have heard something. And he was coming to him for answers, but Brody didn't have many for him, because even he didn't know.

He chose his words carefully. "What makes you say that?"

"I heard Mom and Colin talking the other day. They kept talking about Grandma Louise and how we might have to move to Michigan to take care of her because she's sick."

So Kelly had unknowingly let the cat out of the bag. "Have you asked Mom about it yet?" Brody was dying to know what Kelly's response had been. Last he'd talked to her, they were still trying to figure out a way to get Louise here.

"No," he muttered. "I don't want to go to Michigan, Dad."

Well hell, he didn't want Tyler to move either. But the circumstances were beyond his control. Brody didn't know what to say. This whole situation was killing him, and there wasn't a damn thing he could do. He knew Kelly would never agree to let Tyler stay here. She wouldn't give up her son that easily. But Tyler was probably really confused and scared as hell at the idea of leaving everything and everyone he knew.

He slid his arm around Tyler's small shoulders. When was the last time he'd held his own son? The boy was getting rather old for coddling, even though Kelly still had a habit of doing so. He supposed that was natural for a mother. But as far as he and his own son went… he couldn't remember the last time he'd offered the boy that sort of affection. And why? He hated himself for not being able to answer such a simple question. Even more, he hated himself for falling out of that habit.

He pulled Tyler closer so he could lay his head on Brody's shoulder. The weight of the boy's smaller body against his reminded Brody of the days when Tyler would climb into his lap and sometimes fall asleep. He'd stare down into the boy's face and think about how precious the little life was, a life he'd created. A life he'd always treasure above his own.

"I would never let you be that far away from me," he said in a rough voice. He hadn't been this close to tears in a long time. "Even if you have to go to Michigan, I would be right behind you."

Tyler lifted his head and looked at Brody. The uncertainty in his son's eyes made his insides twist painfully. "You would move too?"

"In a heartbeat."

The muscles in Tyler's throat worked as he swallowed. "But couldn't I just stay here with you?"

Brody offered what he hoped was a reassuring smile. "I don't know if your mom would go for that. Wouldn't you miss her?"

"Yeah," Tyler responded as he lowered his head. He picked up the baseball and turned the thing around in his hands. "But I would miss you too. I miss you all the time."

Ah shit, now he was going to cry. Tyler had been cursed with Brody's inability to express himself. The boy was just as closed off as his father was and rarely said things like that. In the past Brody would have to pry, like pulling teeth, to get his son to admit to anything.

How long had Tyler been carrying this around? Since the divorce?

"Hey," he said to the boy, who kept his attention on the ball. "You're my only son and I love you more than anything in this world. Nothing will ever change that. Not a few miles and not a million miles." He nudged Tyler's shoulder. "Got it?"

This was probably the deepest the two of them had ever gotten with each other. It felt damn good, and Brody promised himself he would always make a concerted effort to be this open with his son.

"Yeah, I got it," Tyler said. "Can we come here again tomorrow?"

"Absolutely," Brody said with a smile. "I'll tell you

what. Why don't I talk to your mom about you spending one more day a week with me, and we can come out here and toss the ball around?"

A glimmer of a smile touched his son's lips. "But don't you have to work?"

"You're right, I do have to work. But I can always cut back." He kissed Tyler's soft hair. "You're worth it."

"Do you think Mom will go for that?" he asked in a tentative voice.

"Let me worry about Mom."

Nothing would come between him and Tyler again.

Never again.

The fluorescent, utilitarian lights of the hospital were like a thousand nails piercing his skull. Nurses and doctors marched from room to room, taking care of one patient and the next like items on a checklist.

RJ didn't pay any attention to them because they didn't pay attention to him. Nor did they pay attention to the grieving and worried families who had loved ones fighting for their lives. The doctors kept their heads bent over their clipboards as though the words were more important than the human lives they were attending to.

They had a job to do, RJ understood that. But once upon a time, when he still believed in happy endings, he'd trusted doctors to save a very important life. And they'd failed.

They were dangerously close to failing again.

He moved down the starkly lit hallway with long, purposeful strides toward Courtney's room. His sister's condition hadn't changed much over the past few days. She was still nonresponsive, still lying peacefully in her bed as though taking a nap. Any minute he expected her to open those big eyes of hers and give him shit about something.

Or maybe make some wiseass remark about the tasteless food. Anything was better than this, than her being so utterly still that she could have been dead.

As he neared her room, he heard a woman's voice. Not the nurses and not the two women standing outside the room next to Courtney's.

No, he would know this voice anywhere. It had haunted him for far too many years. Almost to the point of insanity, and he'd had to take drastic measures to keep his head on straight. Unfortunately, he'd been unable to quarantine himself from Rebecca Underwood indefinitely. They always crossed paths even in the damn hospital, no matter how hard he tried to stay away from her. She always trumped his efforts. The woman was damn crafty.

He came to a stop at Courtney's room but didn't enter. Instead, he leaned against the jamb and watched Rebecca speaking to his sister, as though Courtney could hear and understand every word. Hell, maybe she could. He'd heard people say that it helped to talk to coma patients.

His time at the hospital was limited, but he couldn't bring himself to interrupt. So he stood, unseen, and listened to Rebecca's soft, muted voice. She was telling some kind of story, one he had no recollection of. Not that it mattered. Even if he did have a clue what she was talking about, he wouldn't have paid attention.

Exhaustion had her shoulders slumped in her boxy, completely unsexy dark brown sweater. The thing hung halfway to her knees, which were covered in a pair of black leggings. Now *those* were sexy, because they were like shrink wrap on her amazingly fantastic legs. In that instant an image flashed through his mind, one of her and those legs, only they were bare and cradling his hips with mind-numbing perfection.

*No.*

He shoved the memory away as fast as it had formed.

This was why he needed to stay away from her. Her mere presence muddled his brain.

She continued on with her rambling story. How did he keep running into her? Over the past few months, he'd done well to steer clear of Rebecca, for the simple fact that he didn't trust himself around her. Now, all of a sudden, she was everywhere he turned.

Like the other night, when he'd driven Court home. He'd hoped the late hour would have worked in his favor, and his sister's roommate would have been in bed already. Apparently the stars had not been in alignment for him that night. And not only had she'd been there, but she'd been dressed like some... well, like something he would be having fantasies about for a long time. Her teeny-tiny cotton shorts had left those sexy, creamy legs bare. And her matching tank top had barely been able to hold her breasts from spilling out all over the place. After slapping eyes on her, he thought he would bust a nut in his pants.

He hadn't been able to get out of the house fast enough, because her vanilla lotion, or whatever the hell girly shit she'd slathered on herself, had just about brought him to his knees. No amount of jacking off would have been able to exorcise her from his brain. After leaving his sister's house, he'd gone straight to see Nicole, a woman he'd been seeing off and on for about six months. His and Nicole's relationship was pure sex, and she opened the door for him without question. Not that he would have offered a reason anyway. Their time together had never gotten that deep.

Luckily for him, Nicole liked her sex rough and had stamina that damn near outlasted his. Unluckily for him, the hours of sex and a cold shower still couldn't keep him from thinking of Rebecca. The woman had wormed her way under his skin and created a nice little home for herself.

He was so fucked.

As though sensing his presence, Rebecca stopped her story and turned her head to look at him. She pinned him with those green eyes that always seemed to see right through him. As though she knew he was full of shit and was ready to call him on it.

Her red hair, which had always intrigued him with its wild mass of curls, was loose around her shoulders. He knew from firsthand experience how deceptively soft the corkscrew curls were. That was another thing that had been torturing him for too damn long.

She narrowed her eyes at him. It was a look he was all too familiar with. "How long have you been standing there?"

"Long enough," he said, letting her think he'd listened to every word of her story. Maybe if he was a big enough of a bastard to her, she would stay far away from him. It would be for her own good anyway.

A flicker of doubt flashed in her eyes.

*See? She always knows you're full of shit.*

"It helps to talk," she said with a glance at Courtney. "It stimulates her brain and can lead to a response. Even if it's just a twitch of a finger." She looked back at him. "It could help her recover faster."

How could an unconscious person hear anything? It seemed silly to sit there and have a one-sided conversation with someone. But he would do handstands from the ceiling if it would help his sister recover faster.

"You really believe that?" he asked her.

She turned in her chair so she was facing him. "Of course. There have been studies done on it."

Rebecca and her studies. She was so damn analytical.

"What were you talking to her about?"

She waved a hand in his direction. "You're the one who was standing there listening. Why don't you tell me?"

His only response was a half smile.

She lifted her eyes to the ceiling in a dramatic eye roll. "I was just retelling stories about high school. And asking her about this guy she's supposedly engaged to."

"Supposedly?" he repeated. "You don't think she's really engaged?" That was something he'd been questioning himself.

"I don't doubt the engagement. I doubt the maturity of the relationship."

Maybe he was too much of a caveman, but RJ always had a hard time understanding Rebecca's lingo. She always sounded like she was quoting a textbook—which she probably was.

He pushed away from the door and walked to the foot of Courtney's bed. "Yeah, that would be like her, to jump into something without thinking. And you knew they were dating, didn't you. I mean, you live with her." He looked his sister over and thought how young and vulnerable she looked. Her auburn locks, which a few weeks ago had been jet black, were matted down. Half her head was wrapped in a white bandage. Her left arm was in a sling, and there were angry cuts and stitches all over her face.

"Yeah, I knew about the relationship. But she's also been spending a lot of nights away though. I just never thought anything of it, because she has a habit of disappearing like that."

"Or maybe she's been sneaking him into her bedroom without you noticing."

She shot him a droll look. "To a second-story bedroom?"

He lifted one shoulder. "It can be done." He knew from

experience. It was damn hard, but he'd done it. Funny how she'd seemed to have forgotten. Or maybe she hadn't, if the look on her face was anything to go by. Or the stiffness of her body, as though his words had triggered an unwanted memory.

*Unwanted? Who are you kidding?*

Oh, yes, that trip to the second floor had well been worth it. Even though it had happened six years ago, he remembered it with stunning clarity. It had been the summer she'd turned nineteen. A twenty-three-year-old had no business messing around with someone fresh out of high school. But he'd done it anyway.

That was the year everything had changed between them.

Elisa wasn't prepared for this, even though she knew it had to be done. No way would she survive as a vet. How did those people put animals to sleep on a regular basis? She only had one animal to deal with, and she was a freakin' basket case.

Unable to stand the waiting, she gathered Brinkley in her arms twenty minutes early and barely managed to get the front door open. The dog whimpered when she adjusted him in her arms.

It felt all kinds of wrong for the day to be so sunny and pleasant. The weather was a direct contradiction to her mood, and she didn't like it. The sunshine grated on her nerves. She wanted dark skies. She wanted howling winds and violent claps of thunder so the environment could match the turmoil inside of her.

The cracked sidewalk almost had her landing on her face when her sneaker got caught in the uneven pavement. Damn tree roots. If she had superhuman strength, she'd rip the thing up and put it through someone's front window.

Her car was still in the driveway from where she'd left it yesterday.

So was Brody's.

The sight of him leaning against his truck, as though she should have been expecting him, almost broke up the black clouds swirling around her. Almost.

Had she asked him to come by and forgotten about it? No, she would have remembered—because she would have made an effort not to be home.

She stopped in front of him, barely being able to hold on to Brinkley because he was so damn heavy.

"What are you doing here?" she asked point blank because she was not in the mood for bullshit.

"I told you'd I'd help you with this," he said in that wonderfully deep voice of his, which she still *wasn't* dreaming about.

"Thanks, but I've got it," she replied, and stepped around him to her car.

"Elisa, wait."

Like hell. She kept moving around his truck until she reached her car. Somehow he beat her there and was able to open the back door for her. It was a good thing, because she hadn't thought about how she was going to do it while holding a dog.

"Thanks," she muttered while gently sliding Brinkley into the backseat. She'd just opened the driver's-side door, hoping Brody would get the hint and leave, when he stopped her.

His hands were warm and sure on her shoulders when he turned her to face him. "I know I'm the last person you want to see. But you're barely hanging on right now. And if you can honestly tell me you can handle this by your-self, I'll leave."

The familiar sting of tears puddled beneath her eyes. Only by a miracle was she able to hold them back, because she would *not* cry in front of him. The last thing she needed was Brody knowing how deeply in love with him she still was. And he'd still come here after she'd asked him to leave the other day. Why was he making it so hard for her to stay away from him?

Why couldn't he walk away without looking back like most men did?

"I told you, I don't need your help." She said the words without looking at him.

*Oh, why are you lying to yourself? You know you can't do this without him.*

"Right," he said in a tight voice. "Give me your car keys. I'm driving."

Because it was pointless to argue, and also because a tiny part of her mentally sagged with relief at his pres-ence, she handed the keys over and walked around to the passenger side. As soon as she was in the car, Brody backed out of the driveway and headed toward the vet's office.

They didn't speak, mostly because Elisa wasn't in the mood to shoot the breeze. It seemed Brody wasn't in the mood either if the hard set of his jaw was anything to go by. Maybe he wasn't as happy to be around her as she was with him. Fine. Whatever. They'd get this done and go their separate ways. Her work at the restaurant was fin-ished, and Kelly was back in town. There was really no need to see him again.

The sooner she got away from him, she sooner she could start the healing process. As soon as she got to

Mongolia, she'd put her house on the market and never have to see him again.

They pulled into the vet's office ten excruciating minutes later. Brody offered to carry Brinkley, which Elisa didn't protest. Her arms felt like rubber from carting him around. And also, the look on Brody's face wasn't so thunderous when he made the offer. The way his eyes briefly touched on hers almost reminded her of when they'd first met. And how she'd been blindsided by him.

The technicians inside were overly nice, probably because they knew what Elisa was about to go through. Although she appreciated the effort, she wished they wouldn't bother on her account. Their friendly smiles and sympathetic looks didn't soothe her. The only thing that would ease her suffering was knowing that Brinkley was no longer in pain—and getting away from Brody.

Under normal circumstances, the intoxicating scent of his manly shampoo would have had her toes curling. Now it just made her feel even more on edge.

The young technician in a blue uniform led the two of them to a back room with all sorts of equipment and a metal table. The sight wasn't reassuring. In fact, it only made her feel worse. It was so impersonal, like they trucked animals through here all day long, ending their lives.

*You know that's not true. Stop being so cranky.*

Brinkley whimpered when Brody laid him on the table. The tech told them the vet would be with them in a moment.

"Would you like to stay with him?" she asked Elisa.

For some strange reason, Elisa tossed an unsure glance at Brody. He grabbed her hand. His palm was warm and so much bigger than hers. The feeling of his fingers entwined with hers eased her nerves slightly. As though just being with him could get her through anything. Even the heart-wrenching experience of losing a pet.

"I'll stay with you," he said with a reassuring smile.

The way his lips curved reminded her of the look he'd given her after they'd made love the first time. Her heart had turned over in her chest and had landed at the bottom of her stomach with a resounding *thunk*. Oh man, how could she ever have thought she could erase him from her subconscious? Elisa nodded to mask the need she had for him. "I'd like to stay with him until it's over," she answered. Brinkley deserved to have someone next to him until the end.

She and Brody sat in hard plastic chairs next to the metal table where Brinkley lay on his side. The dog had barely moved. In fact, it looked as though he was barely breathing. Elisa couldn't bear to look at him. She knew she was doing the right thing, yet she felt like the worst possible person in the world.

"You hanging in there?" Brody whispered. His grip on her hand tightened.

He was too close, yet too far away. She wanted to crawl in his lap and bury her face in his neck. Then maybe she could inhale the scent that was so quintessentially Brody and forget everything. Forget about ending Brinkley's life, an animal she'd spent so little time with but loved with all her heart. She could forget that she and Brody didn't have a future together and that, when she left, she'd be leaving her heart with him.

She inhaled an unsteady breath and settled for returning the squeeze he'd given her hand. "I just want to get this over with." Brinkley didn't move when she touched his soft ear and stroked it. One eyelid opened and he gazed at her out of a soulful brown eye. A single tear rolled down her cheek, which Brody swiped with the pad of his thumb.

Shit, why did he have to touch her like that? Like he still cared? "Thanks for staying with me," she said.

He slid an arm around her shoulders and pulled her tight against him. It felt so good to be near him again and feel those solid muscles beneath the fabric of his shirt, muscles that had been pressed intimately to every inch of her body. Now they were reassuring and still so strong but comforting at the same time.

"I told you I would stay," he responded in a low voice.

*I told you I would stay.* Not *I'm here because I want to be with you.*

His presence was just an obligation, merely following through with what he'd told her. The realization should have devastated her. However, she was too numb to feel much of anything.

A moment later in walked the vet, a middle-aged man with thinning black hair and a slight paunch. His white doctor's coat was immaculate and had his name and the acronym *DVM* stitched in blue.

His eyes softened when they landed on Brinkley. He whipped the stethoscope from around his neck and pressed the listening part to the dog's midsection. "How are you doing this morning, Ms. Cardoso?" he asked while moving the device over Brinkley's stomach.

"I'm okay." *But not really.*

"You're going to stay in here with him?" He directed his kind brown eyes at her.

"Yes." She watched the doctor move around Brinkley, examining or looking for something, Elisa wasn't sure. He wound his stethoscope around his neck. "Will it hurt him? I mean—he won't feel any pain, will he?"

The doctor smiled. "It's very fast—it happens in a matter of seconds. The first injection will make him fall asleep. He won't feel a thing."

That was a small reassurance that made her feel slightly better. Over the next few minutes, the vet and his technicians moved in and out of the room, bringing equipment and various supplies with them. They murmured to each other in soft voices, using terms she didn't understand. She sat quietly in her chair with one hand on Brinkley's head and Brody's comforting presence next to her. Touching her. An arm around her, a hand tucked in hers, a thigh pressed along hers. Anything he could do to take away her doubt and pain.

Then the doctor slapped on a pair of examination gloves and held up a needle. "This is going to make him go to sleep. After that, I'll inject him with a solution that will stop his heart."

Elisa could only nod as a sick feeling formed in the bottom of her stomach. Brody leaned in close and pressed a soft kiss to her temple.

Just a few seconds later Brinkley's eyes dropped closed as though drifting into a deep sleep. She didn't want to watch but couldn't tear her eyes away. His stomach still rose and fell with shallow breaths. She wanted to call off the whole thing. Was it too late to whisk her dog away from here and spend just a few more hours with him? It took every ounce of willpower she had to remain seated in her chair, to keep from yelling at the vet to stop the process.

Brody must have felt her whole body go stiff. His arm unwound from around her shoulders, and his hand grabbed hers. "Hang in there," he whispered, then pressed a kiss to the back of her hand.

The vet discarded the first needle and picked up a second one. This time Elisa did turn her head. She couldn't stand to watch him insert that hideous thing into Brinkley's flesh. More tears ran down her cheeks when the doctor set down the last needle and used his stethoscope on Brinkley. He moved the listening device around, probably checking for a heartbeat.

"He's gone," the man said.

Was she supposed to feel relieved? A sense of peace that Brinkley was no longer in pain? Because she didn't feel any of those things. All she felt was a deep sense of loss and mourning for the animal she had come to love.

She was vaguely aware of people moving in and out of the room, picking things up and talking to each other. Were they moving in slow motion? Was that her they were talking to?

Thank goodness for Brody. Elisa couldn't seem to form a coherent thought. He practically lifted her out of the chair and ushered her to her car. She clung to him like the lifeline he was, as though he was the only thing capable of rooting out the despair that latched onto her heart like a leech. Wasn't that why she hadn't put up much of a fight when he'd insisted on coming with her? That she would have known how much she'd need his strong resilience?

He placed her in the car, running a hand over her hair before shutting the door. She leaned her head back and allowed her eyes to drift shut.

Sometime later, they were on their way back to her house with Brody driving silently and the town of Trouble passing by the car windows. Once at home, she could slip into oblivion for days and not think about anything.

Even though she'd protested him accompanying her, she was grateful to have Brody by her side. How could she have driven herself home when she couldn't even keep her eyes open? How would she have sat there in that room by herself, watching Brinkley's life slip away without Brody holding her hand?

She may have been mad as hell at him, but she was thankful—thankful to have met such a wonderful man as Brody.

He finally pulled into her driveway, turned off the car, and came around to open her door for her. She wanted to exert her independence by pulling away from him, but she just didn't have the strength. So she allowed herself to lean on him, to feel all that muscle and rock-solid body holding her up. And it felt so good. *He* felt good. As if he would never let anything bad happen to her. Or so she once believed.

Instead of leaving her at the door, he used her key to unlock it and ushered her inside.

"Can I make you some tea?" he asked, setting her keys on the entryway table.

"Sure," she said without thinking. Tea sounded good; she could get it down without throwing it back up.

"Go have a seat and relax while I make you some."

He didn't have to ask her twice. The couch looked like heaven, so she curled up on the soft cushions and rested her head on the armrest. A second later her eyes drifted shut, taking comfort in the sounds of Brody moving around in her kitchen.

A cabinet opened, then closed.

A gas burner on the stove turned on with a soft *click*.

Brody's shoes made soft thumping noises on the kitchen floor. He moved around with the assurance of someone who knew where everything was and used them on a daily basis. What an odd sort of comfort, knowing he was using those big hands of his to touch the same things she touched every day.

The sounds of his shoes grew louder as he walked closer to her. He placed what sounded like a mug on her coffee table. A second later, his warm hand was on her face, caressing her cheek and brushing his fingers back through her hair. The pressure of his fingers on the back of her head made her body feel even heavier, as if she were sinking into a soft cloud.

"I'm sorry for everything," he whispered.

A moment later she wasn't feeling anything as she drifted off to sleep.

# TWENTY-THREE

W HEN BRODY LEFT ELISA SLEEPING, he'd left a piece of his heart with her. What had he been thinking allowing her to push him away? Hadn't he punched out his own brother for doing the same thing with Lacy? Why was he so blind when it came to his own actions?

A woman like Elisa was a rarity. She wasn't interested in just a romp in the sack. She didn't care about his past mistakes or think he was damaged goods because of it. And she loved Tyler. She'd embraced the boy and interacted with him in a way other women hadn't.

And what had he done?

Screwed things up because he thought himself incapable of being loved by anyone else. He'd allowed the circumstances surrounding his divorce to dictate his life.

The time for that was over.

Time to pull his head out of his ass and live life with his eyes open.

Hell of a time for him to come to that realization. He'd been ready to tell Elisa how wrong he'd been when she'd fallen fast asleep. Not that he blamed her or was surprised. Exhaustion colored dark circles under her eyes and had drawn lines of stress around her mouth. He suspected that was the first time she'd allowed herself to sleep. Revelation or no revelation, he hadn't had the heart to wake her. So, he'd left the tea, along with a note to call him, and he'd left her in peace—reluctantly. What he'd really wanted to do was curl himself around that soft, womanly body and share a deep snooze with her.

Something had held him back. Probably the fact that she'd told him to leave the last time she'd seen him. And she still needed time to process things, so he figured space was the best thing for her right now.

In the meantime, he was supposed to interview a potential replacement for RJ in half an hour.

Even days later, Brody still couldn't get his brother's words out of his head. Over the past few years, RJ had built a very successful business for himself. He'd had to take on employees to handle the workload. Yet he'd stepped up to help out at the restaurant without question. Lord only knew how much work he was missing out on to help Brody out in a jam. Knowing RJ, he was probably working late at his body shop to make up the hours he was tending bar.

By his own fault, Brody had completely taken that for granted. What kind of brother did that? He'd been too busy wrapped up in Elisa and stressing over Tyler to notice that RJ was working almost full days.

His brother had every reason to be pissed at him. So, he'd done something he should have done weeks ago: start interviewing replacements for Anthony. He was so behind that if this guy could string together intelligent sentences, Brody might just hire him on the spot.

• • •

Interviewee number one had a criminal record.

Interviewee number two had been fired for hitting on an employee.

Interviewee number three had no work history and didn't even look old enough to be serving drinks.

Brody had been holding out slight hope for interviewee number four when it turned out the guy didn't speak a word of English.

At this point he was ready to take a number two pencil and jab it through his eye. It would probably be less painful than this. His fifth interview was due to arrive in ten minutes, but Brody was seriously thinking about groveling for RJ to stay full time.

How was it possible that not one person could pull together a decent resume? Anthony must have been the last good bartender within a hundred-mile radius.

"No luck, huh?" Charlene asked when she poked her head in the door of his office.

Brody rubbed a hand down his face. "Not one."

She jabbed a hand on her hip and frowned. "Darn. I was holding out some hope for that second guy. He was kind of cute."

"You wouldn't think so when you're filing a sexual harassment suit against him."

She chuckled and stepped into his office. "So, what's the story with the latest one?"

Brody picked up the resume and glanced it over. "He has eight years of bartending experience, and before he moved here last month he was living in Kentucky." He set the paper back down. "He's got a pretty long list of references."

"So, it looks good on paper?"

"From what I can tell. I just hope that when he comes in here, he can say 'hello' in a language I can understand."

"That's pretty sad when the most qualified guy doesn't even speak English. Are you ready for this shindig to go down next week?" she asked, referring to the catering job for Avery's fundraiser.

He leaned back in his chair. "I'm more than ready. Chase is going to be loaning us his sous-chefs to help out with the preparation."

A sparkle of excitement lit up Charlene's eyes. "Anthony's so giddy about it. It's all he can talk about."

A knock came from his office door. Both Brody and Charlene glanced toward the sound to see a tall man wearing ripped jeans and a leather jacket standing in his doorway. His dark brown hair was a bit too long and curled over the collar of his bomber jacket. He whipped off the pair of dark sunglasses that sat over his eyes and slid them into the front pocket of his jeans.

"I'm here for the interview," he stated.

Brody stared at the guy for a moment, taking in his casual appearance and thinking it didn't match the edginess that radiated off him. There was something about him that Brody couldn't quite put his finger on, something that made Brody unsure about him.

He picked up the resume and glanced at the name. "You're Joel Garrison?"

"Yeah." He jerked his thumb over his shoulder. "The guy behind the bar said I'd find you here."

*Thanks for the warning, RJ.*

Brody set Joel's resume down. "Have a seat, Joel."

Brody could have sworn Charlene actually blushed when Joel looked her up and down. One corner of the man's mouth kicked up in an almost-wicked grin.

*For shit's sake, is this one going to hit on employees too?*

Joel sat down and Brody rolled his eyes when Charlene grinned. She grabbed the door handle and started to pull it closed. "Good luck," she mouthed, and shut the door with a soft *click*.

Good luck, his ass.

Brody wasn't so sure about this guy, who seemed to take in every detail of the office without actually moving. There was a cockiness to him that was reminiscent of RJ, yet not the same. RJ's cockiness was playful to a point where it was a game to him. This guy sitting in front of Brody was anything but fun and games. He'd been in Brody's office for about twenty seconds, and Brody could already tell that Joel Garrison took himself way too seriously.

"So, you just moved here from Kentucky," Brody started. "What brought you to Wyoming?"

Most people just didn't pick up and move to Trouble. Their little town had a growth rate of about ten percent.

Joel moved his shoulders in a restless shrug. "Just needed a change."

"And before that?" Brody asked. He picked up the resume again and read it over. "It says here you lived in Kentucky for three years, and before that you were in South Carolina." He set the paper down. "But you're originally from Mississippi. Do you have a habit of moving around a lot?"

"When it suits" was all Joel said.

"How do I know it won't suit you to pick up and move six months after I hire you?"

"Guess you don't." A hint of a southern twang colored his voice.

Okay, time to try a different tack.

Brody swiveled back and forth in his chair. "Do you enjoy bartending?"

"I'm good at it. And I enjoy being around people."

*Yeah, you're a real people person.*

The two of them stared each other down like they were about to engage in a pissing contest.

*Maybe we ought to just get the dick measuring over with now.*

"Do you ever mix your own drinks?" Brody asked instead of demanding that Joel show a little personality.

When Joel smiled he didn't look like such a hard ass. "Yeah, they'll put some hair on your chest."

"Show me."

Joel stared back at him for a moment, as though he wanted to bolt out the door. Given Brody's luck with interviews so far, he wouldn't be all that surprised. Then the guy unfolded himself from the chair with an almost catlike grace that had Brody wondering what Joel Garrison's story was. Before slapping eyes on him, Brody had no idea it was possible to seem so on edge yet relaxed at the same time.

Must have been a special talent.

They left the office and Brody led Joel to the bar. Behind him, the other man was so silent that Brody had to throw the occasional glance over his shoulder to make sure Joel hadn't disappeared in a puff of smoke.

"This is a nice place you have here," Joel commented. "Nicer than any bar I've worked in."

Brody didn't doubt that. "Thanks," he said. "But we're more of a restaurant than a bar."

Joel didn't respond to that. Instead his eyes were roaming around their surroundings, touching on every surface, every picture, and every person.

Agitated much?

"What happened to the other bartender?" Joel asked as he removed his leather jacket.

"Turns out the guy's a hell of a cook. We moved him to the kitchen."

Joel nodded. "Lucky him. I can't cook for shit."

*What a shock.*

Joel pinned him with dark eyes. "So what do you want me to do first?"

Maybe crack a smile? Brody kept the comment to himself and lifted his hand. "Make me something."

"Anything?" Joel asked with a lifted brow.

"Start with something basic."

Joel was already moving toward the glasses, where he snagged a highball. "Will a gin and tonic do?"

"Yeah," Brody said with a nod.

Then he stood back and watched as Joel Garrison whipped out a bottle of Bombay Sapphire, some tonic water, and a lime wedge. In practically one fluid motion, the guy poured the liquor in the highball glass and stuck the lime wedge on the lip of the glass. He made it look as easy as pouring a soda.

Probably because it was. And Brody realized that any fool could throw together a gin and tonic. He accepted the drink when Joel held it out.

"Not bad," Brody commented after taking a small sip. "Can you do something a little more complex?"

Joel lifted one shoulder. "I can do anything you want."

No kidding?

"Do you serve mojitos here?" Joel wanted to know.

Brody nodded. "Yeah."

Joel grabbed another highball and set it on the bar. Most bartenders took their time with mojitos in order to get just the right amount of mint released into the drink. Not this *Cheers* graduate. And, actually, the speed in which Joel made the drink had Brody a little leery. But he took the finished drink from the guy anyway and sampled it.

"Damn," he said, then took another sip. "That's good. Where'd you learn how to mix like this?"

"Just a lot of practice," Joel answered.

"In the military?" He gestured toward the dog tags hanging around the guy's neck.

"Nope."

Okay, then. "What else can you do?"

Joel grabbed a cocktail shaker, poured a variety of liquors in, some ice cubes, tossed the shaker behind his back, caught the thing midair, and gave it a few vigorous shakes before setting it back down on the bar. He even garnished the drink with a lemon after pouring it in a glass.

"That's called a between the sheets," Joel said with a nod toward the drink. "Also known as a maiden's prayer."

Well, shit. What the hell did Brody know? He wasn't even sure he'd seen Anthony or RJ make that drink before.

"You used apricot brandy," he said as he picked up the cocktail and tested it.

"Peach schnapps is good with it too," the other guy said.

Brody nodded, and tried another sip. Man, if he drank much more, he'd spend the rest of his day with a light buzz. Maybe after this he'd have to go take a nap.

"I've showed you just about everything I've got. Good enough for you?" he asked while running a hand through his hair.

Yeah, Joel could pour drinks better than anyone Brody had ever seen. But how committed would he be? The man had "drifter" written all over him.

On the other hand, he needed to get someone in here so RJ could get back to his own business.

Brody leaned a hip against the bar. "Let me check some references, and I'll get back to you."

Joel opened his mouth, which was surrounded by dark stubble, as though he wanted to argue having to wait. Brody had a feeling that Joel Garrison was a man used to getting his way. I'll-do-what-I-want-and-damn-the-world kind of thing. Well, that wasn't going to fly on Brody's watch. If he was going to work here, that attitude would have to be checked at the door.

To Brody's relief, Joel didn't argue. "All right, then." He walked around the bar, grabbed his jacket, and slung it over one shoulder. "Thanks for your time." With a one-handed salute, Joel sauntered out of the restaurant. A tough exterior like Joel's usually signaled some kind of vulnerability. Something or someone had wounded him in the past, and now he felt the need to give the world the middle finger.

Some men would have felt threatened by someone like Joel. Brody had no reason to be threatened by the other man. Actually, Brody was intrigued by him because he could relate in some small way.

The paperwork on his desk had been mounting for several days, and Brody would rather stick bamboo shoots under his nails than do it. What he would rather do was go to Elisa and make sure everything was okay. Tears had still stained her cheeks when he'd left her that day. Leaving her in peace had been the right thing to do, even if his heart didn't agree.

Just as he turned to head toward his office, RJ pushed through the front doors and walked toward him. "Who was the badass in the leather jacket?" he asked point blank because that was the way RJ functioned. No beating around the bush for his stepbrother.

"Possibly your replacement," Brody answered.

Both RJ's golden brows lifted up his forehead. "No kidding? I didn't know you'd been talking to people."

Brody scrubbed a hand along his already scruffy jaw. "Yeah, listen, you don't have to be here. I know you have your own things to handle, and we can manage without you for the next few days."

RJ waved a hand in the air, dismissing Brody's words. "No, don't worry about it. Danielle is holding the shop down until I get back. This isn't a big deal. I was just giving you a hard time because I was pissed off."

"It is a big deal and I deserved every word you said. You were right about me being distracted." Brody shoved his hands in his pockets because he wanted to pull his brother into a hug. And RJ didn't do hugs or any kind of personal contact, really.

"Hey, a woman will do that to you. I say you get a free pass as long as she's worth it," RJ added with a devious smile.

And RJ would know all about that. The difference between the two of them was that RJ never seemed to allow a woman to muddle his brain. Except for Rebecca, and Brody wasn't even going to go there. RJ always clammed up tighter than a bank vault at the mention of the young woman. The dynamic between the two of them was as mysterious as the creation of Stonehenge.

"So? Is she?" RJ asked.

Elisa was worth selling his soul to the devil for. But he'd been stupid enough not to be honest with her.

"Yeah," he said in a hoarse voice. "Yeah, she's definitely worth it."

# TWENTY-FOUR

THE DAMN PAPERWORK WAS STILL sitting on his desk, as though Brody had expected it to take care of itself. He'd just sat down to get to work when his cell phone rang. Welcoming the distraction, Brody answered on the first ring.

"Yeah?"

"We need to talk about a few things," his ex-wife said. "Can you stop by later?"

This was it. She was going to drop the bomb about them moving. Even though Brody had been expecting this, his stomach still twisted painfully. A dull ache started its usual *thrum* in his head, for which no amount of painkillers could make go away.

"All right," he breathed out. "I have some things to take care of here, so I'll be by in a few hours."

So much for going to see Elisa and not taking *no* for an answer. A possible resolution with her would have to wait. Anything Kelly had to say about Tyler, and Brody had a feeling what it was, came before anything else. Usually he looked forward to discussions about Tyler.

He was sure not looking forward to this.

Only when Brody's eyes started to cross did he force himself to stop the paper pushing. Usually Charlene handled the bookkeeping and technical matters. But she was so bogged down with details of the catering job and other promotions that Brody had offered to take the burden off her hands.

The headache that had crept on him when Kelly called was full blown now. The three pain pills he'd popped hadn't so much as put a dent in the strenuous pounding. He supposed that was too much to ask for. And he hadn't gotten nearly as much done as he had hoped because images of Elisa kept invading his concentration.

He'd made a decision about Elisa, and Murphy's Law was invading his life full force and it was pissing him the hell off.

It was only midafternoon and the bar was surprisingly crowded. Or not surprisingly, considering who was behind the bar. All the women who used to frequent the Golden Glove like a cult following had migrated their way back over. RJ poured drinks with a constant smile on his face like he adored every single one of his female customers, which he probably did.

Whatever. RJ had always been a serial dater, but Brody could never understand how that lifestyle could appeal to anyone. One woman was enough for him.

Brody drove through town as fast as he could without being a menace to the other drivers. Agitation pumped through him, which he tried to exorcise by drumming his fingers on the steering wheel. The sooner he got this painful conversation over with, the sooner he could deal with the aftermath. And wondering how he was going to leave Elisa if he had to move to Michigan.

*She wants your ass gone, anyway.*

Brody couldn't think about that right now. As much as

he didn't want to, he would have to put Elisa on the back burner. For now.

Ten minutes later, he sat in Kelly's living room, taking in the subtle changes in her since the last time he'd seen her. Her blond hair was perfectly styled and her lips were shiny pink. Pearl stud earrings adorned her ears, which matched the long strand hanging around her neck. All in all, she looked like a different woman. Almost like when they'd been married.

"Thanks for stopping by," she told him.

"No problem. Where's Tyler?" He should have been home from school by now.

"He walked to a friend's house."

Kelly strolled to the other side of the room and adjusted some family pictures. When she had them all situated to perfection, which they already were, she went to work on a vase of flowers. They looked pretty good to him, but for some reason Kelly felt the need to move the stems around and turn the buds in different directions. She pushed the vase around in a circle before leaving it in the exact same spot it was before.

Something had her worked up.

"What's going on, Kelly?" *Please just tell me so we can get this over with.*

She smoothed a hand down her lightweight pants. "First of all, I wanted to tell you that Colin and I won't be moving to Michigan."

Brody couldn't move because he felt for sure Kelly was screwing with him before giving him the real bad news. But Kelly had never been one to play practical jokes, so why start now? And why make such a sick joke?

"Brody, did you hear me?" she asked when all he'd done was stare at her.

"Sorry." He blinked himself out of his trance. "Did

you say you're not moving?" Could something finally be going his way?

"Yes, I've been making a lot of phone calls the past few days. We found a company that specializes in long-distance nonemergency medical transportation. Colin's going to help get my mother ready. Then the transport service will pick her up and bring her here. It's a bit expensive, but we figure it will be worth it if we get to stay here. After that we're going to move her into a nursing home in Cheyenne."

A majority of the weight he'd been carrying around on his shoulders lifted by slow degrees. The idea of living far away from his son, or having to leave his home, had been eating a hole inside of him for several weeks. The relief was so welcome that Brody could actually cry.

"Kelly, I—" He stepped around the couch, closer to her. "I don't know what to say. You have no idea how much this has been weighing me down." He shook his head, trying to find the appropriate words. "It's been like my worst nightmare."

She played with one of her pearl earrings, something she always did due to nerves. "I'm sorry, Brody. I know the uncertainty of this was really hard on you. It was hard on me too, knowing that I might have had to take Tyler away from all his friends and family." She paced from one side of the living room to the other with long, slow strides.

"There's something else, isn't there?" Hell, Brody couldn't imagine what else she could possibly shock him with.

Kelly stopped her pacing, thankfully, because she was making him nervous as hell. "Tyler wants to come live with you," she announced. Then she did something that really shocked the hell out of him: She cried.

His ex-wife had always brought new meaning to the phrase *cool, calm, and collected*. Shortly after meeting her, Carol had dubbed Kelly the quintessentially classic lady, a name she always lived up to. The show of emotion was uncharacteristic of her. Despite that, Brody sat on the couch next to her and placed an arm around her shoulders.

"I knew he would eventually want to leave me. I just didn't expect it to be this soon," she said with a sniff. She yanked a tissue out of the box on the table next to the couch.

"He's not leaving you, Kelly. It's only natural for a boy to want to be with his father." The pure, unadulterated joy pulsing inside of him made him want to do cartwheels across the ceiling. But Kelly was hurting, and Brody wouldn't dare say or do anything to rub salt on the wound. He knew full well what it was like to have your child living somewhere else.

"That's what Colin said. But it doesn't make me feel any better."

"And with a baby coming, it might be best to have a quiet house to yourselves."

Kelly sniffed. "Colin said that too." She pulled away from him and pinned him with a look. "Are you and Colin conspiring behind my back, or something?"

The question had him smiling. Cracking jokes was better than crying. "Not even a little, I promise. Most men think alike."

She heaved a weary sigh. "Don't I know it? I'm surrounded by too much logic. Would you be able to handle having him there all the time with your schedule?"

"I'll work it out. I already told Tyler I was going to cut back on my hours."

Kelly's shoulders shook beneath his arm. She leaned forward and buried her face in her hands. A couple of sobs were muffled by her hands and a tattered tissue. "He's my baby boy, Brody," she complained in between sniffles. "And now he's leaving me."

This time Brody couldn't help but chuckle.

Kelly lifted her head and gazed at him out of tear-filled eyes. "It's very dangerous to laugh at a pregnant woman," she warned him. He knew that all too well from when she was pregnant with Tyler.

He took the tissue out of her hands and blotted her eyes for her. "Sorry," he said with a half smile.

"It's okay. I swear I wasn't like this when Tyler and I talked about it. My hormones are all over the place right now."

"I'd say you get a free pass on that one." He set the torn tissue aside and tucked a short strand of hair behind her ear. "Thank you."

She leaned back against the couch cushions. "For what?"

Why had he waited so long to tell her this? "For being a good mom. For forgiving me for everything." Because he certainly didn't deserve it. Kelly had always been a stronger person than he was.

She touched his cheek with her soft hand. "We were too young to know what we were doing. You did the best you could with us. Tyler worships you. It'll be good for him to spend more time with you. But do yourself a favor this time, and don't let Elisa get away from you. I know you love her even if you're too stubborn to admit it."

Did she know him, or what? "You're right, I do love her."

When he didn't elaborate she prompted him. "But?"

He leaned back next to her and stared at the ceiling. "I just really screwed things up. It seems I have a way of doing that."

"You also have a way of making amends. Just use that Brody charm on her. It's probably what sucked her in to begin with."

Only he wasn't sure his charm would be enough.

# TWENTY-FIVE

ONE MINUTE BRODY WAS HOLDING a babbling Mason, enjoying the toddler's giggles, and the next minute he had turkey chunks on his forehead. The boy had distracted him with a slobbery grin, and Brody had fallen for it. Now he had toddler food sliding down his temple.

"Sorry." Lacy tossed him a napkin. "That actually means he likes you."

Brody gratefully accepted the napkin and swiped it across his forehead. "What does he do when he doesn't like you?"

"Trust me, you don't want to know." A few strands of Lacy's hair had slipped out of her already sloppy ponytail. Her face was makeup free, and she had a stained burp pad slung over her shoulder. "Don't say anything" was how she'd greeted him thirty minutes ago. Personally, Brody thought she looked great, considering she'd just given birth to two babies less than two weeks ago. The baby, either Kevin or Jackson, Brody wasn't sure, was swaddled in a blue and yellow striped receiving blanket. Lacy had finished nursing him, changed his diaper, then wrapped him back up. She'd been gently rocking him back and forth for the past several minutes until he'd finally fallen asleep.

Mason had been throwing a fit, as he often did. Lacy had looked around in a panic because she'd been on the couch with one baby and Chase had been bathing the other twin.

"He's probably hungry," she'd said to Brody.

Brody had kind of figured that out for himself when Mason stood in front of the pantry desperately trying to rip the child lock off the doors. "I got it," he said, and grabbed the first package of one of those toddler meals his eyes came in contact with. That was how he ended up with orange vegetable on his face.

"I offer to feed you, and this is the thanks I get?"

One of Mason's little chubby fingers pointed at Brody's forehead. Then he jabbered something incomprehensible as though congratulating himself on a job well done. Brody grinned at his nephew, took him out of the high chair, and set him down on the kitchen floor.

"I don't know how you do this all day long," he muttered, while cleaning up the mess the nineteen-month-old had made. Mason was cute, but damn, he was a handful. The boy ran clumsily, tripping once, into the living room. A red and blue Nerf football lay next to a pile of toys. Mason picked the ball up and overhanded it, presumably trying to make it all the way across the room. He didn't even come close.

"I don't know how she does it either," Chase announced as he came back into the room. He had the other twin cradled in one arm like one would hold a football. The baby's eyes were open and staring unfocused around him. "I made her promise me no more kids for a while."

Lacy adjusted the sleeping baby in her arms and tossed her husband a narrow-eyed look. "You act like I made these babies all by myself."

"Just saying," Chase said with a grin. "He's hungry. Switch with me."

"I swear these kids are going to suck me dry," Brody's sister-in-law complained while she and Chase passed the babies off to each other. "You're dead meat if you wake him up. Will you take Mason outside to play? I think he's bored."

Chase obliged his wife by placing one of the twins—Brody still had no clue which one was which—in a nearby bassinette, then gathering Mason in his arms.

"Why don't we go work on our spiral, dude?" he suggested to the tow-headed boy, who clapped his hands in delight. When the two of them disappeared in the backyard, Brody took a seat on the couch next to Lacy. She had one of those nursing aprons on that allowed her to breastfeed without flashing the world.

"I love my kids," she said. "But I am so exhausted."

"It'll go by fast. Remind me again which baby you're holding?"

She shot him an amused look. "This one is Jackson. And the only reason I know that is because Kevin has a tiny freckle on his left ear. I've been thinking about giving them name tags. Do you think that would make me a horrible parent?"

He tucked a wayward strand of hair behind her ear. "You couldn't be a bad parent if you tried, Lace."

She patted his knee. "You're sweet." Lacy leaned forward on the couch and adjusted Jackson beneath the cloth. "Have you been by to see Courtney? Chase says she's not doing well."

Everyone had been stunned when Courtney had pulled out of her coma a few days ago. Except for Lacy, they'd all rushed to her side to pepper her with questions. Did she remember who hit her? What had she been doing out so late? And, the one thing everyone wanted to know the most, who was the guy she was engaged to?

Unfortunately, Courtney didn't remember anything, at least in regard to the events leading up to her accident.

She remembered her family and her childhood. What she didn't remember was where she worked, where she lived, and her fiancé.

When questioned, the doctor told them that Court suffered from posttraumatic amnesia, caused by the damage to her brain. Carol had gasped when she heard the term. The doctor had tried to reassure them by saying that she could spontaneously recover her memory at any time. He'd also cautioned them against filling in the blanks for her. Simply telling her the missing information wouldn't cure her. She needed to remember it on her own.

The best thing for her at the moment was to be with her. Surrounding her with people she knew was the best way to make her comfortable. To the chagrin of the fiancé, who turned out to be named Grant, Courtney not only didn't remember him, but something about him made her uncomfortable. Just seeing him sent her into a panic, like some dark memory had imprinted itself on her damaged brain. Martin had asked Grant to leave and not come back. He'd left, but Brody had thought he'd heard the man mutter, "Like hell." Brody had a feeling they hadn't seen the last of Grant no-last-name.

All in all, Courtney wasn't in a good situation. She'd need months of extensive physical therapy just to regain use of her left leg again. That wasn't including the fact that she couldn't digest solid foods.

"I guess all things considered, she's not bad," he answered. "She ate some Jell-O and we had a nice conversation."

Lacy's green eyes widened. "About what?"

"Stuff she already knows." He'd been hoping against all hope that even the slightest sliver of memory would come back to her. It had been so hard not to tell her about her house or how she'd finally landed the job of her dreams not long ago. But doctor's orders were doctor's orders.

Lacy shifted on the couch again and moved Jackson to her other breast. "I just wish there was something I could do to help her."

"I'd like to find the guy who did this to her and throw his ass in a dark pit somewhere." White-hot anger coursed through Brody's veins every time he thought about his sister being left for dead in the middle of the street. What kind of person could do that to another human being?

"You and me both," Lacy muttered. "So what did you do to piss off Elisa? Chase said you've been moping around for several weeks now," she said when Brody lifted a brow in an attempt to look confused, even though he wasn't. He knew damn well what she meant.

He sighed because he knew it was pointless to lie to Lacy. She'd always been immune to his bullshit. "I was a stubborn ass and now she's gone." Just saying the words made him sick to his stomach.

"What kind of gone are we talking about here? The fixable kind?"

If only he could answer with confidence. In fact, he was pretty confident there was no mending the damage he'd done. "I don't know about fixing it. As for gone, she's in South America visiting her brother for a short while, then she's flying to South Africa for a photo job that came up at the last minute."

Now, finding *that* information out had been an adventure, and not a fun one. The already open wound in his heart had bled even more when Elisa had been nowhere to be found. For several days, he'd called her and gone to her house. Only after seeing all the drapes pulled closed for a week straight did he realize she'd left town. What he hadn't known was where she'd gone or how long she'd be away.

One person had come to mind to answer his questions. Kelly hadn't wanted to tell him shit—because "Elisa had made me promise not to tell you," Kelly had told him. The groveling he'd resorted to hadn't been one of his finer moments. His ex had probably felt sorry for him after he'd all but begged her to help him out.

"Right now she's in South America visiting her brother, and from there she's flying to South Africa for a last-minute job she was offered. The offer came from a former teacher who needed her to fill in for a sick team member. Or something like that," Kelly had said on a weary sigh. "Before she left, she asked me to water her flowers and bring in her mail. She also asked me not to tell you." She'd crossed her arms over her chest and shot him a disapproving look. "Apparently she had reason to think you'd come asking about her. I can't imagine why," she had said, a little glib.

At that point, he'd been ready to bust through his own skin in frustration. Damn women and their cryptic ways. "When will she be back?" he'd asked through clenched teeth.

"She didn't say," Kelly had replied.

The narrow-eyed look he'd given her finally convinced her to spill the whole story.

"She'll be in Brazil until the end of the week, and she flies to South Africa on Saturday. She'll be home three weeks from tomorrow." She'd stepped back and started to close the door. "And the only reason why I'm telling you this is because I know you love her and will do the right thing."

He swore he'd seen a hint of a smile before closing the door in his face. After hours of deliberating, he'd approached Kelly again and coaxed her into telling him Elisa's itinerary and lodging situation. Kelly *really* hadn't wanted to give up that information, but she'd relented after Brody told her what he had planned.

"Brody?" Lacy pressed when he'd been ignoring her. "Did you hear what I said?"

"No, sorry."

Lacy pulled Jackson out from under the nursing blanket and cradled the baby against her shoulder. The boy was fast asleep. "I said pull your head out of your ass and go after her."

Her blunt statement had him laughing. Then he sobered. "Doesn't matter because when she gets back from South Africa, she's leaving again. This time for good."

"She's moving away?" Lacy asked with surprise.

"She took a job in Mongolia and doesn't plan on coming back." It killed him to just say the words. "Before she left, she asked me to give her a reason to stay. And like an idiot, I didn't say anything."

Lacy placed a hand on his knee. "If you really want to keep this woman, you'll find a way. If you have to follow her to South Africa or even Mongolia, then do it. She needs to know how serious you are about her, and following her halfway around the world might be the only way to do it."

Augrabies Falls was considered one of the natural wonders of South Africa. "The place of Great Noise" was part of the Orange River in the Northern Cape of the country. The falls had a dramatic drop of 184 feet and were surrounded by rocky gorges that no sane person would dare tackle. The only living things brave enough to venture there were the occasional antelope and deadly predators such as leopards.

Luckily for Elisa and other members of the photography team, the falls was a very famous tourist area. They had more than enough places to gather and get the shots they needed for *National Geographic*. They were profiling places in Africa inhabited by endangered species, which in the falls was the black rhino. The animal had yet to show itself, but for the time being, they were shooting the falls. They were expected to find and photograph the rare animal during their last two weeks there.

Helping them was a guide, a local man who knew the indigenous animals and where to find them. The guy was a local, a Nama, who lived in a dome hut called a *matjieshuise,* or mat house. He didn't speak a word of English, but a skilled translator had moved things along nicely.

This part of the world was just as beautiful as Elisa remembered. Today marked their sixth day of nonstop walking, crouching, waiting and shooting. When she'd first arrived, Professor Harper had greeted her with a wide grin and said, "Are you sure you're ready for this?"

Why wouldn't she have been? She'd been waiting for an opportunity like this for years. But after the first day, Elisa had understood what Professor Harper had meant. Shooting wildlife and natural wonders was not for the fainthearted. Nor was it for people who were out of shape or couldn't climb stairs without becoming winded. After several hours of the relentless sun, constant walking, and stopping just long enough to take a drink of water, Elisa had started to wonder what she'd gotten herself into. They didn't stop from sunup to sundown.

And they were supposed to do another eleven days

of this. But in all honesty, no matter how grueling, she needed the activity. The distraction of Professor Harper's last-minute offer couldn't have come at a better time. Her calves may be quivering from the walking and her shoulders burning from carrying the equipment around, but her mind was getting the relief it needed.

Her trip to Mongolia was just around the corner, and the idea of hanging around Trouble, possibly seeing Brody, had been giving her near-panic attacks. Professor Harper hadn't even gotten to the details of this trip before she'd already accepted his offer. Just the idea of getting away, if only for a few weeks, had been too appealing for her to say no.

The hours outside exploring South Africa had taken her mind off Brody and the possibility that he'd all but rejected her—that his demons had been too much for him to overcome. Elisa could no longer compete with his past. How many opportunities had she given him? How many times had she asked him to ask her to stay? A person could only take so much humiliation before enough was enough.

She'd given Brody her whole heart, and she'd walked away with nothing. Just as she'd suspected would happen.

Twilight had descended on the Northern Cape, but the heat hadn't subsided. The Kalahari Gateway Hotel, the accommodations the magazine had set them up in, was a lush retreat with every amenity she could imagine. Her room was huge with a whirlpool tub that she made good use of every night. The jets did wonders on her sore muscles.

They would especially come in handy tonight. After another all-day trek, all she wanted to do was kick off her shoes and soak in the tub. Then figure out what to do after Mongolia.

She walked through the opulent lobby of the hotel, then

down the hallway to the elevators. The air-conditioning was cool and brushed over her heated skin like a sweet caress. It was a heavenly feeling after a full day in the sun.

She pushed the button on the elevator and stepped into it when it arrived.

Although she adored her house, the first major purchase she'd made, Elisa had come to the decision to sell it. She couldn't have the kind of career she wanted from Trouble, although she supposed she could use it as a home base. But what was keeping her there? Certainly not a man. Returning to that house, that street, day after day, would be remembering what she once had with Brody. How she'd caught a glimpse of what deep love was really like, and the kind of life she and Brody could have together.

For the most part, her time here in South Africa was pretty good at helping her deal with the hurt that still lingered in her heart. The hardest time of the day was when she was alone—alone in the elevator, alone in the tub, and alone in her bed. There were no cameras, no colleagues, and no endangered animals to pull her mind in another direction. All she had were bittersweet memories and her own regrets for company. It was a maddening, lonely time for which there was no cure. She hated Brody for not giving them a chance.

But most of all, she hated herself for listening to her heart instead of her head.

The elevator reached her floor, and Elisa stepped out. Her room was around the corner, all the way at the end. This evening the walk seemed so much longer than it actually was, but the thought of climbing into the tub kept her going.

Just as she rounded the corner, all thoughts of soaking the day away abandoned her and turned her good feeling into disbelief.

And bewilderment.

Not to mention shock.

And definitely some desire, because the whole reason she'd left Trouble was standing outside her hotel room. She stopped in the middle of the hall and glanced around, certain someone was playing a joke on her. Or maybe a Brody lookalike had the wrong room. However, a simple lookalike wouldn't affect her the way the real Brody always had.

So, she kept going, mentally trying to prepare herself or come up with something to say to him. He was just leaning against the wall, staring down at his phone as though he belonged there. Or she was supposed to be expecting him.

His hair was a bit longer than the last time she'd seen him, as though he hadn't taken the time to get a haircut. Tan cargo pants fit loosely around his long legs, and the black T-shirt he had on only reminded her how in shape he really was. She'd never seen him look so...unkempt. Yet at the same time, it was the sexiest thing she'd ever seen.

She'd come here to get away from him and the way he'd made her feel. Her heart needed time to mend. How could she accomplish those things if he kept invading her space like this?

He must have sensed her, because he glanced up from his phone and pinned her with those piercing gray eyes of his. Eleven days away hadn't done anything to lessen the impact he always had on her. In fact, the time away had made her want him even more. She just hadn't realized it until laying eyes on him again.

He straightened away from the wall, and the breath she'd been holding left her in a rush. As she came to a stop in front of him, she tried to steady her breathing and act like seeing him was no big deal. Like seeing him was like seeing any other regular Joe. As if her heart hadn't just kicked up when she'd laid eyes on him.

She licked her dry lips. "What are you doing here?" Had she sounded too eager? Because, the hell with it, she was so happy to see him.

"I thought of a reason for you to come back," he responded in that deep voice that she'd been dreaming about.

"And you flew all the way to South Africa to tell me?"

"Yeah," he said with a laugh. "Two tickets to South Africa damn near cleared out my savings."

Her eyes widened. "Two?"

He gestured behind her down the hallway. "I brought Tyler with me, but he got bored waiting so he went back to our room."

So many sensations were hitting her at once, not to mention questions about his sudden appearance. Elisa closed her eyes and shook her head, trying to make sense of everything. "You're staying here in this hotel?"

His grin turned sheepish, and it was the sweetest thing Elisa had ever seen. "We sort of decided to make a vacation out of it. I brought Tyler with me so Kelly could focus on getting her mother settled. Plus I wanted to be close to you."

Those last words created a shiver down her spine and an unsettled feeling in her belly. Had he really come all this way just for her?

"So, do you want to hear my reason or not? I promise you it's good."

More than anything she wanted him to scoop her in his arms and tell her he couldn't live without her. She wanted him to admit the time apart had been just as hellish for him as it had been for her. Just the fact that he was here was hope enough, but Elisa refused to get too wrapped up in her emotions.

"Go ahead," she said after swallowing.

"Well." He rubbed the back of his neck, as though working out the tension. "Tyler and I got this dog, who's with my brother Noah and who we named Brinkley Junior by the way, and we don't really know what we're doing with it. And you seem to know how to nurture an animal..." His words trailed off. "Oh, hell, that's not the reason." He reached into his front pocket and pulled out a box.

A small square box.

Elisa sucked in a breath and told herself that Brody could have anything in there. Anything nonjewelry, though she hoped not.

He gazed down at the box and didn't speak for a moment. "I bought this, thinking I would give it to you when you came back. But then I didn't want to wait." He placed his focus on her. "And then I didn't want to come here without it, so I brought it with me. The only problem is," he said, opening the box to reveal a ring inside, silver with just settings and no diamonds, "it doesn't have a center stone, and I need you to pick one out. That's why you have to come back."

Her heart, which hadn't really slowed down since seeing him, now dropped to the bottom of her stomach. The feeling made her slightly ill because she had no earthly clue how to respond to Brody's gesture. The gorgeous ring, with the empty center setting, was breathtaking and was undoubtedly an engagement ring. Unless Brody had some twisted sense of humor and went way overboard with a friendship ring.

Elisa adjusted the strap of her camera bag and tried to force words out of her mouth. But the lump in her throat prevented any kind of intelligent response.

"Look," he said on a sigh. "You know I'm no good

with words. I've never been a great communicator, and it's something I've tried to work on lately. But the bottom line is I miss you." He shook his head and glanced at the ring. "I know I did a lot of stuff wrong, and, even though it wasn't my intention, I pushed you away. It wasn't until it was too late that I realized what I was doing. And, when I realized you left, I felt . . . Hell, I felt empty."

Elisa held her breath while Brody gazed so deeply into her eyes that her heart felt like it was going to beat through her rib cage.

"Not long after I met you, I knew you'd be different. You'd made me feel things I had never felt before, and it scared me. The only thing I could think was that you deserved better than me. I kept thinking of how I broke Kelly's heart, and I couldn't bear to do the same to you."

"But you did break my heart, Brody," Elisa said softly. "You were trying to protect me when I didn't want to be protected."

"I know." He laughed, but the sound was strained. "Funny how when you reflect on things, they seem so clear." He closed the ring box with a loud *snap*. "I'm not proud of how I acted. And the possibility of you leaving should not have been enough for me to write off our relationship. I used that as my out, and it was wrong.

"The real reason I came was because I didn't feel myself without you. And when I realized I wanted to spend the rest of my life with you, I couldn't sit around and wait. And if that meant bankrupting myself and all but begging you, then that's what I'm willing to do."

Elisa licked her lips again and tried to think of something to say. Her feelings for Brody were so clear, yet the words were a jumbled mess in her mind. The urge to laugh was as strong as it was to cry.

"You came all the way here for me?"

"You and Tyler are the only people I would fly halfway around the world for. And I would do it again too. Even if you tell me to leave you alone, I would still do it again."

She shook her head. "I'm not going to tell you to leave me alone. Just seeing you here is enough."

Something close to relief and joy flashed across Brody's face. His eyes dropped closed and he exhaled a breath as though he'd been through just as much torment as she had. The idea was oddly comforting, even though she didn't like the idea of him in any kind of discomfort. But it was reassuring to know she hadn't been the only one questioning and regretting.

"I know why you did what you did," she said to him. "And I'm not saying it was okay. But I understand it now, even if at the time I didn't." She placed a hand on his cheek, loving the way his whiskers bit into her palm. "We both have some things to work on, and to be honest, I haven't felt right since I left Trouble. I mean, don't get me wrong, I love what I'm doing here and I love South Africa, but ever since I got on the airplane, I've had this sick feeling in the pit of my stomach. And I think I knew in my heart that leaving you wasn't the right thing. I guess I felt like I was protecting myself."

Brody cursed under his breath. "You shouldn't have had to protect yourself. *I* should have done that, and I failed miserably. I'm sorry. Sorry for making you doubt yourself and sorry for breaking your heart."

"Brody, don't you think you've been blaming yourself long enough? Maybe it's time you share that responsibility with someone else." She pressed her lips to his in a soft kiss. "You have my forgiveness, if that's what you need. But you also have my love, so stop beating yourself up."

"As long as you love me, then nothing else matters. Because now that I'm here, you're never getting rid of me."

She smiled and studied his handsome face. "Who said anything about getting rid of you?"

"Just so we're clear," he replied. "In fact, now you really can't get rid of me." Elisa held her breath as he opened the ring box and slipped the ring on her third finger. Even without its center stone, the piece was stunning. She didn't care that the ring was too big. Just having it on her finger felt better than anything had in a long time.

"I love it," she said around the lump in her throat. "I still can't believe you came all the way here just for me."

He cupped her cheek in his warm palm. "You're worth every mile and every dollar."

"Tell me you love me, because I've been waiting a long time to hear it and I can't wait any more."

He dropped a kiss to her lips, and it was the most romantic yet nerve-wracking moment of her life. "I love you, Elisa Cardoso. And if I have to follow you around the world to be with you, then I will."

Heat flamed her up to her cheeks at his words. "I wouldn't make you do that, and I wouldn't make you leave Tyler like that." This was more than a good enough reason to come back to Trouble.

# EPILOGUE

THERE WAS A VERY GOOD reason Elisa never played sports. One was grass stains. Those suckers were damn near impossible to get out and were always in some obvious spot that acted like a freakin' bull's-eye. Like the one on her rear end. On her best pair of yoga pants.

The other was the running. Now, she was no slouch or anything. All things considered, she was in pretty good shape. Ate well, stayed relatively active.

But, shit, did she have to run every single time Tyler hit the ball? Couldn't the kid like strike out or something?

Brody, who stood on the pitcher's mound in a pair of well-worn jeans and a too-tight black T-shirt, glanced back at her. That was her other problem. She kept missing the ball because she spent too much time staring at Brody's ass.

She lifted her baseball glove–covered hand and waved at him. "Don't mind me," she called from the outfield. "I'll just be back here sucking."

He turned to face her. Even with dark sunglasses shielding his eyes, she still felt the scorching heat of his gaze. "Do you want to come pitch?" he asked.

"Oh, no," she replied with a shake of her head. Hadn't

he seen her running around like a headless chicken back here? What would make him think she could pitch the ball? "It's much better for me to be way out here than it would be for me to potentially give your son a concussion. Trust me," she added.

"Dad, come on," Tyler said from home plate. He'd lowered the bat and bounced from foot to foot. So far the kid had rounded the bases countless times. Mostly because Elisa kept chasing the ball around like she was deaf, dumb, and blind. Then she couldn't throw it for shit. One time she'd hit Brody in the shoulder, which he pretended hadn't hurt.

"Just a sec," he said to Tyler. Then he turned back to Elisa. "Come here," he demanded.

Elisa shook her head. Personally she felt like she'd made enough of a fool of herself. Why had she let him talk her into playing baseball with them? Wasn't that more of a father-son thing?

"Elisa," he said in that low tone of his. Almost like the one he used in bed with her.

With a roll of her eyes, she trudged across the field until she came to a stop in front of Brody. His delicious mouth turned up in a grin, as though he sensed exactly how much she disdained sports.

He tossed the ball in the air and caught it with the same hand. "You don't want to be doing this, do you?"

"Because I suck," she said again.

His chuckle danced over her skin. "You don't suck," he reassured her. "You're just . . . not practiced."

One of her brows lifted. "That's a polite way of saying I suck."

With another slow grin, he snagged her hand and tugged her toward him. When he placed himself behind her, Elisa was instantly reminded of that morning, when she'd awoken to feel him placing light kisses down her spine. The memory brought a wave of goose bumps over her flesh.

He tugged the glove off her hand and let it fall to the ground beneath their feet. Sort of how he often tugged the clothes from her body.

"I think I know what your problem is," he said in her ear. "You can't keep your eyes off me."

Well, duh.

But, yeah, she also sucked.

"That's not the problem," she managed to reply as he picked up her right hand and placed the baseball in her palm.

His hand covered hers, so much bigger and harder than her own. Was this supposed to be helping? Because it wasn't. Even though this was so much better than standing in the outfield and pretending that she liked baseball.

"Getting old over here," Tyler called out like the impatient eleven-year-old he was.

"Just a minute," Brody said back to his son. "Now, the key," he murmured in her ear, "is a nice, firm grip."

Oh, Lord.

She cleared her throat. "You're so going to pay for this later."

"Oh, I hope so." He grinned against her neck.

Her eyes dropped closed. Oh, man, she was getting turned on in front of a kid. Bad Elisa. "Not playing fair," she warned.

"This is tame compared to what I really want to do." His lips touched the soft flesh beneath her ear. Not really a full kiss. More of a caress. But it was more than enough to have heat blooming across her belly.

"Dad, seriously," Tyler called out. "I've been standing, like, forever."

Brody straightened almost as quickly as he'd started his seduction. "All right, sorry. I was just...showing Elisa how to hold the ball."

Tyler placed the baseball bat over his shoulder. "No, you weren't. You were, like, kissing and stuff."

Elisa tossed Brody a lifted-brow look over her shoulder.

He cleared his throat. "Okay, here we go," he said in a normal voice as though the past few moments hadn't affected him.

Yeah, right. The bulge beneath the fly of his jeans said otherwise. Maybe that was why he hadn't moved from behind her yet.

"I'm just going to help you pitch the ball. You might like that better than standing in the outfield."

"Doubtful," she replied.

His chest rumbled against her back with a deep chuckle. "Just go with it."

In one fluid motion, he lifted her hand behind her, instructing how to do one of those girly underhand pitches. Probably because he thought she hadn't a normal overhead pitch.

And, yeah, he'd be right.

When he brought her hand forward, she let go of the ball, having really no clue if it was the right time to let the thing go sailing. Felt right to her.

And apparently it was, because Tyler swung the bat and made beautiful contact with the ball, sending it sailing right past Brody and Elisa. The boy dropped the bat and went running toward first base. He rounded the bag and gunned it toward second.

"Uh, shouldn't we get the ball?" Elisa asked just as Tyler touched second and kept pumping his legs.

"Can't move," Brody said from behind her.

Elisa turned and graced him with a grin. Her eyes dropped down to the tenting action in the denim hugging his incredible package.

"Now who's sucking?" she teased as she looped her arms around his neck.

His body was so much bigger than hers yet cradled it in all the right places. Thighs against thighs, her mouth a perfect level to run over the stubble on his cheek. Yes, they were built perfectly for each other. The only cryin' shame was knowing how long she'd lived her life without Brody in it, missing out on the perfection of his body and all the ways he could bring her to another planet with just his hands.

"I already told you, you don't suck," he muttered right before dropping his mouth to hers and teasing her lips open with his tongue.

Oh yes, this was the best part. Having that masterful mouth of his play havoc with her nerve endings until her head spun a thousand miles an hour.

And she kissed him back because…well, she loved him. And she couldn't stand to be near him and not touch him.

"Hey," Tyler said from somewhere behind them. "I just scored again and you guys weren't even watching."

Brody lifted his head but didn't take his eyes off Elisa. "No, we saw you, buddy." Then he lowered his lips to hers again. "But he's not the only one scoring."

And she shut her mind off to everything else except the man who'd given her what she'd been missing for too long.

A family.

## SEE HOW TROUBLE STARTED!

Fleeing her overbearing family, Avery Price flies to a small town in Wyoming—and into the arms of her sexy new boss, Noah McDermott. Is she falling in love...or deeper into trouble?

Please turn this page

for an excerpt from

# LOOKING FOR TROUBLE.

# ONE

THE MAN WITH A DARK-BROWN Stetson pulled low over his eyes appeared in Avery Price's rearview mirror a split second before her back bumper knocked him down. Her Christian Lacroix wedge sandal slammed on the brake pedal before her tires could roll over him and snap his bones like fragile twigs. Her cell phone, which had been pressed to her ear for ten minutes while her brother peppered her with questions, slipped out of her hand and clattered to the wood-grained middle console. Moisture seeped out of the corners of her tightly closed eyes, and she wrapped her hands around the fine Italian leather–stitched steering wheel.

A few seconds stretched into an eternity while she inhaled deep breaths and kept her eyes closed. When she opened them, the dented metal door of her motel room came into view along with the early-morning sunshine.

*Okay, you barely nudged him. Chances are he's just sore and pissed off. Now would be a good time to get out and check on him.*

Her internal lecture was pathetic at best and warranted no action from her hands other than to pick up her discarded cell phone. Her trembling fingers grasped the device and brought it up to her ear.

"Avery, what the hell is going on?" Her brother's unusually demanding voice vibrated through the phone and added to her already jittery nerves. As good as his intentions were, she couldn't deal with his you-need-to-start-making-some-decisions speech.

"Avery, if you don't start talking in two seconds, I'm going to send the Wyoming State Patrol after you."

The man who'd been forced to the ground by her car had yet to pull himself to a vertical position. "I gotta go. I just hit somebody."

"What? See, this is what I'm talking—"

Her thumb hit the end button on her phone, effectively cutting off another one of her brother's annoying but painfully predictable rants.

Her brain fired away commands for her legs to move, to do *anything*, with no success. After several seconds, a thump came from the back end of the car as though the man on the ground was taking his retribution for being plowed over. The sound prompted a squeak from her, and she fumbled for the door handle.

As far as mornings went, this one ranked down in the shitty category. First, she'd slept through the alarm clock's weak *beep-beeping*, and then the fleabag motel couldn't provide her with a decent cup of coffee. Far be it from her to wish for a double-shot latte with no whip. All the shoebox-size lobby offered was the bottom scrapings of hours-old brew and stale English muffins. Not exactly an appealing spread.

Now, in her haste to find something edible and caffeine to rev up her system, she'd bowled over a man who had the bad sense to walk behind a car that had its reverse lights on.

She threw the car in park and exited on shaky legs. The

early-morning sun was still weak enough that the temperature hovered in the tolerable range.

As she rounded the back of the car, trying to swallow her irritation at her own carelessness, the man on the ground pushed himself not-so-gracefully to his feet. He swayed, as some drunk people did when they couldn't walk a straight line, and placed a hand on her car. The fierce protectiveness she had for her German-engineered vehicle almost had her demand he remove his hand from her sunflower-yellow custom paint. The fact that she'd hit this poor man, and would probably have to grovel to keep him from suing the pants off her, stopped the words from flying out of her mouth.

A deep, gravelly groan flowed out of the man, now minus his cowboy hat. Burnt sienna–colored hair, mixed with sun-kissed shades of caramel, was smashed down in untidy disarray to the man's skull. The cowboy hat, which now lay about six feet from where he'd hit the ground, had flattened the edges of his hair to a greasy, slicked-down look. Avery considered herself an expert on personal hygiene and keeping one's appearance as perfect as possible. She'd be willing to bet all the money in her trust fund that this man hadn't seen a shower in at least twenty-four hours or his wrinkled, untucked chambray shirt and faded jeans a washer and dryer. For all she knew, he could be some bum who skulked around motels, looking for a place to rest his head.

Nevertheless, that didn't change the fact that her car had come in contact with a human being, and she needed to make sure he was okay.

With his mile-wide back to her, he bent over and placed both his hands on his knees, dropping his head as though he couldn't catch his breath.

Geez, had she hit him harder than she thought? She certainly hadn't meant to.

"Are...are you okay?" she stammered while taking a tentative step toward him.

He straightened much faster than she expected considering he'd been swaying like a drunk a second ago. When he turned, a gaze grayer than blue—and definitely not pleased—hit her. Thick brown brows slammed down over his eyes, which flashed with anger.

"You hit me, lady. What do you think?" The accusing words came out of a full mouth surrounded by dark growth of beard stubble. It wasn't a full beard; it looked more as if he hadn't made the time to shave, as though he didn't care that his unkempt, wrinkled appearance was less than appealing. Or, maybe, he simply didn't own a razor because he was homeless.

"I know that fancy, expensive car of yours has mirrors, so why the hell weren't you paying attention?"

It's not as if she hadn't looked. She *had*. Her one quick glance had shown a man just standing there, as though he had all the time in the world. She'd lifted her foot off the brake and had already been backing out of the parking space. She'd scarcely rolled two inches before she tagged him and set him on his ass.

Her fingernails bit into the inside of her palm. "I had my reverse lights on because I was backing out of my space. Didn't you see them?"

He snatched his cowboy hat from the uneven gravel and placed it back on his head. "I was walking and not paying any attention to you. You're supposed to look before you back out."

"I did, and it looked as if you were just standing right

behind me. I couldn't stop in time. I'm sorry, but I really didn't mean to hit you."

"Your fault, not mine." His words were short and clipped, evidence that anger, not pain, was his dominant emotion.

Okay, so he had her on that one. Technically it was her fault, regardless of what he'd been doing. She was adult enough to admit when she'd made a boo-boo. As a consolation for hitting—no, *nudging*—him, she tried to be nice even though she felt like a complete imbecile for not paying proper attention. Despite her put-on cheery attitude, she sensed some serious hostility. Maybe she'd messed up his one and only wrinkled shirt.

She stared back at him and tried to dodge the daggers his stony eyes threw her way. "You don't look seriously injured. Again, I'm really sorry." She bounced from one three-inch platform to the next before pivoting and reaching for the car door handle.

"Now wait a minute."

She paused with her hand on the door and tossed him a look over her shoulder. The cowboy hat shielded his hostile gaze and lent only a view of a straight nose and wide mouth.

"You can't just flee the scene of an accident. How do you know I'm not injured?" The words had lost their heat and rolled off the man's tongue with a deliberate slowness.

Other than his disreputable clothing and stubble-covered jaw, there was nothing to suggest he was anything other than normal. No blood sprayed from an open head wound, no bruises or scrapes decorated his masculine face. He had swayed and stumbled at first, giving her the impression of maybe a mild head injury. Since replacing his hat, he'd only leaned one hip against the bumper of her car and regarded her beneath his hooded gaze.

She wrapped her arms around her midsection. "You're

not going to call the cops, are you? I already said I was sorry."

Then a terrifying thought hit her. *He could easily file a report against you.*

He slid one hand under his hat, lifting it crookedly to one side. "I don't know. My head's a bit tingly, and I feel a little light-headed. You might need to take me to a hospital for some medical attention. Or better yet," he continued while rubbing a hand along his rough jawline, "I know the sheriff pretty well. We can get him down here to straighten this whole thing out. I'd call him myself but"— he dug his hand in his back pocket and produced a small black device—"you crushed my cell phone."

Okay, the cell phone was a good indicator that he probably wasn't homeless. Although his attire suggested someone who'd just crawled out of a cardboard box, he was evidently one of those people who just didn't give a damn what he looked like. His nice little speech was also his way of threatening to have her ass thrown in jail if she didn't do...whatever it was he wanted her to do. This was *so* not how she wanted to start her new life.

He nudged his hat lower on his head. "I think the sheriff is on duty today and wouldn't mind coming down here—"

"All right," she said through gritted teeth. "Just tell me what I can do."

He held his hands up in front of him. "I don't want to put you out. I can tell you're in a hurry."

She forced a smile. "It's no put out at all. Is there somewhere I can take you?"

The grin that crept up his face resembled the one the big, bad wolf used to lure the three little piggies. Unfortunately she was at his mercy until he decided to let the whole fake-injury thing drop. "I'm so glad you offered. I need a ride to my car."

She tightened her hands around her keys. "That's it? Just a ride?"

"Oh, I want a lot more than that."

She crossed her arms, then let them drop. Maybe she should have stayed in bed and watched the rabbit-ear-adorned television at the motel. "All you're going to get out of me is a ride to your car."

A lone passing car filled the silence between them. "Okay."

Without giving him a chance to make more threats, she jerked open the car door with all the force her arm would allow and plopped herself in the driver's seat. She had the car started and was rolling backward by the time he yanked the door open and sat himself next to her.

"Are you trying to run me over again?" he asked after folding himself in the seat until his knees bumped against the glove compartment. Her little roadster was not designed to hold men the size of the Jolly Green Giant. His hat remained firmly on his head.

"I can't help it if you don't move fast enough." She jerked the wheel and maneuvered her car around a pothole.

His narrow hips shifted until he'd slid lower, as though he were settling down for a nice Sunday drive. "I think you were trying to ditch me." The leather beneath his backside squeaked when he moved again.

"Can you sit still? You're going to scratch the leather."

"Can you not shout? My head feels as if it's going to crack in two."

Avery eased the car to a red light. "You haven't heard loud yet. Get one scratch on my car and you'll know the meaning of loud."

One corner of his mouth turned up and created shallow lines in his stubble-covered cheek. "Poor princess. Daddy might have to buy you a new one."

She tucked a strand of hair behind her ear and decided to let the "daddy" comment roll off her back.

The light turned green, and she tapped her manicured index finger against the gearshift. "Would you like to tell me where your car is, or should I drop you off wherever I please?" *Like here?*

"Go straight and make a left turn at the fourth light down," he replied without so much as moving a muscle.

She wound her hand tighter around the steering wheel and cursed herself for being so stupid and careless. Avery was the sort of person who treated everyone with respect, regardless of how that person treated her. She'd been caught off guard and lost in her own thoughts about what she was going to do with her life. With practiced patience, she eased off the brake pedal and set off down the street. The inarticulate man next to her didn't so much as utter a grunt. Instead, he remained slouched low in the seat with his hat pulled down so it covered half his face. Only his deep, even breathing indicated he was still alive.

Over the years, she'd worked to develop an ironclad backbone, so she rarely let situations or people intimidate her. The man who sucked all the breathing space out of the car, with his massive shoulders and long legs, sent her nerves tingling in a way they hadn't in a long time. Was it intimidation, or fear that she'd injured another human being? Avery didn't know, nor was she comfortable with the feeling. She couldn't say it was his looks, because so far all she'd seen was half his face and hair that hadn't been combed in days. Perhaps it was just the sheer size of the man. Even though he sat perfectly still, there was an edge to him but also an air of confidence, as though he knew how he looked and damn the world if they didn't like it.

The characteristics defied everything she knew about men. A heavy breath left her lungs.

"You sigh a lot."

Another light turned red, allowing a man hunched over like a question mark to cross the street. "I'm just mad at myself. I'm usually much more observant."

He was silent for a moment. "Don't feel so bad. I'm not that hurt."

The look she threw him went unacknowledged. "But I do feel bad, even if you don't seem that hurt."

"I thought I saw you checking me out." The grin in his voice was unmistakable, although Avery didn't see the humor. Nor did she appreciate it. Whatever. Let him make his wisecracks. In a few blessed minutes, she'd be free of him.

After the old man shuffled his way across the street, the light turned green, and she made her way toward where she was supposed to turn.

Her phone vibrated in the middle console, where she'd dropped it in her haste. She kept her hands on the steering wheel, having no desire to listen to her brother call her incompetent while the stranger who'd kissed the back end of her car listened to her humiliation.

She made the left turn as instructed, then looked to him for the next set of directions. "Go down about half a mile then turn right on Beach Street." The deep timbre of his voice had her mind wandering to unsuitable thoughts as she passed a hay-and-feed store.

"What were you doing at Dick's Motel if your car is way down here?" She'd already come to the conclusion that he wasn't homeless; homeless people didn't have cell phones and wear brand-new Timberland boots. He was just a man who didn't iron his clothes and woke up two miles from his car.

For a moment he sat as still as he'd been since entering the car and didn't answer. Then he said, "What people usually do at motels."

*O-kay.* That could be anything from doing drugs to cheating on a significant other. For whatever reason, the former didn't seem likely. As for the latter, well, what did she know? Maybe the woman he was with had kicked him out and refused to take him anywhere, leaving him stranded without transportation. Then Avery had gone and knocked him down, destroying his cell phone in the process. For all she knew, he could have a wife at home who was pacing herself sick at this very moment. And Avery could be an accomplice to his sordid love triangle. Now she felt even worse than she did before.

Her desire to attempt a conversation with a man who'd strong-armed her into driving him across town was minimal. She kept her gaze on the street in front of her and both hands on the wheel. Under normal circumstances, Avery was a pretty chatty person. She didn't like uncomfortable silences that stretched into eons of nothingness. The silence made her fidgety, and it felt as if worms crawled underneath her skin. Oh, but the cowboy loved it. His answers were clipped and to the point as though he couldn't be bothered with trivial things like speaking to another person.

"It's on the left-hand side of the street at the very end," he muttered after she'd made a right turn onto Beach Street.

A metal sign that read DAVE'S WATERING HOLE sat crooked on top of a masonry building as though someone had just tossed it up there and hadn't bothered to make it sit straight. There were no windows, no landscaping, or anything that was minimally appealing about the place. The building sat away from the street in the middle of a cracked, weed-adorned parking lot. This definitely wasn't an establishment that screamed fine family dining, though Avery was pretty sure anything with the word "hole" in it wasn't suitable for little children. Given the behavior and the dozen words she'd exchanged with the man next to her, she hadn't expected something with gold-plated front doors.

She cringed as the front bumper of her car scraped the pebbly ground when she drove into the parking lot. A handful of early-model trucks and a later SUV sat in the parking lot without any sort of rhyme or reason. Apparently the owners didn't feel designated parking spaces were necessary.

"Just stop right here." The man straightened in the seat and reached for the door handle.

When the car purred to a stop, he opened the door and unfolded his long limbs from the low-slung vehicle.

She grabbed his arm before he had a chance to exit. "Wait a minute. Are you sure you're okay? Can I take you to a doctor?"

His stunning gray eyes lit on hers. "Nothing more than a bruised ego, princess."

She let the "princess" comment slide and withdrew her hand from his arm. "I really am sorry."

"I know."

The car door slammed shut before she had a chance to grovel for more of his forgiveness. What was wrong with her? She didn't just go around hitting innocent people with her car. She was a better person than that.

Executing an abrupt U-turn, she left him in the dust of her Mercedes and hauled ass away from Dave's Watering Hole as fast as she could.

*What a way to start your life over, Avery.*

*Well, son of a bitch.* Noah McDermott withdrew car keys from his pocket and hit the unlock button.

The Mercedes princess was all spitfire and sass.

The curved back end of her car sprayed all sorts of dirt and gravel in the wake of her swift retreat. Maybe Her Highness was late for her manicure.

*Or maybe she just wanted to get away from your grumpy ass.*

It certainly wouldn't be the first time. Mary Ellen hadn't wasted any time kicking him out of the motel room this morning after she'd had her way with him. Not that he'd been heartbroken. He hadn't been expecting to find a hot meal in his lap and a ball game on the television. Instead, Mary Ellen had emerged from the shower and told him he needed to be on his way. She didn't have to tell him twice. He'd quickly thrown on last night's wrinkled, stale-cigarette-smoke-shrouded clothes and let himself out the door. Just before exiting he thought he'd heard Mary Ellen asking him to call her. Yeah, that wouldn't be happening. She was the type of woman who sat around in bars, as she had last night, and waited for a man to pay her any sort of attention.

The argument he'd gotten into with his father had propelled Noah into the dingy and disreputable interior of Dave's. Once there, he'd immediately spotted Mary Ellen, with her too-tight jeans and dark, overly processed hair. Initially he hadn't been looking for a woman, only the comfort of a pool table and a longneck bottle of beer.

By his third game, Mary Ellen had wormed her way into his game and bought him another beer. She'd spent the remainder of the time slipping her hands in his back pockets and rubbing her double Ds against his arm. He'd been just drunk and pissed off enough to allow her to drive the two of them to Dick's Motel and promptly handcuff him to the wooden headboard.

Hours later he'd woken up with a bitch of a headache and blurry memories of new sexual positions he'd been introduced to.

The interior of his car was cool, having not yet been affected by the heat of midday. He tossed his hat on the passenger seat and slid in with deliberate slowness so he didn't make the pounding in his head worse. After dropping his eyelids closed and inhaling several deep breaths, he started the car. A morning meeting with one of his subcontractors prevented him from returning home longer than to take a shower. With the condition his head was in, he'd love nothing more than to wash off the previous night and dump himself into bed.

As he exited the parking lot and headed toward the outside of town where he lived, Noah's thoughts returned to the Mercedes princess.

Someone like her didn't enter the town of Trouble very often. Her sleek dark hair and perfectly pressed clothes screamed wealth. Of course her car was also a dead giveaway. He didn't need to see the little roadster to know she'd grown up with privileges most people in this town only dreamed about.

Having a hundred-thousand-dollar car knock him on the ground had upgraded the pounding in his head to freight-train status. He hadn't noticed anyone sitting in the car when he'd stepped out of the motel room. His mood was already dangerously close to black, and allowing a woman, who hadn't been paying attention, to catch him off guard had pissed him off big-time. Never mind the fact that she was a delectable little thing who smelled like vanilla and peaches.

She had guts and looks that would send most men drooling at her feet. Not him. His mind had been too foggy and his limbs too achy for him to notice anything beyond the fact that she was a knockout with bags of money.

A small smile turned up the corners of his mouth. Sparring with her over who'd been at fault had been enough to erase the previous evening from his mind. For that much he was willing to forgive her affront of hitting him.

Okay, so she'd been genuinely sorry and only his ego had been hurt. The only other thing he'd suffered from was lack of sleep and a broken cell phone. Just to lay it on extra thick, he'd antagonized her into giving him a ride. He'd never had any plans to call law enforcement into the picture. But there hadn't been any harm in making her think he would. The steam coming out of her feminine little ears had been satisfaction enough. And being in the car with her had given him the chance to poke at her some more. So far the morning had been more entertaining than he'd anticipated.

Fifteen minutes later he pulled into his driveway, and as he stepped out of the car he realized his pocket was empty.

His wallet had fallen out in the princess's car.

# THE DISH

*Where Authors Give You the Inside Scoop*

♥ ♥ ♥ ♥ ♥ ♥ ♥ ♥ ♥ ♥ ♥ ♥ ♥ ♥ ♥ ♥ ♥ ♥ ♥ ♥

*From the desk of Jennifer Haymore*

Dear Reader,

When Mrs. Emma Curtis, the heroine of THE ROGUE'S
PROPOSAL, came to see me, I'd just finished writing *The
Duchess Hunt*, the story of the Duke of Trent and his new
wife, Sarah, who'd crossed the deep chasm from maid to
duchess, and I was feeling very satisfied in their happily
ever after.

Mrs. Curtis, however, had no interest in romance.

"I need you to write my story," she told me. "It's
urgent."

I encouraged her to sit down and tell me more.

"I'm on a mission of vengeance," she began. "You see,
I need to find my husband's murderer—"

I lifted my hand right away to stop her. "Mrs. Curtis, I
don't think this is going to work out. You see, I don't write
thrillers or mysteries. I am a romance writer."

"I know, but I think you can help me. I really do."

"How's that?"

"You've met the Duke of Trent, haven't you? And
his brother, Lord Lukas?" She leaned forward, dark eyes
serious and intent. "You see, I'm searching for the same
man they are."

My brows rose. "Really? You're looking for Roger Morton?"

"Yes! Roger Morton is the man who murdered my husband. Please—Lord Lukas is here in Bristol. If you could only arrange an introduction...I know his lordship could help me to find him."

She was right—I did know Lord Lukas. In fact...

I looked over the dark-haired woman sitting in front of me. Mrs. Curtis was a young, beautiful widow. She seemed intelligent and focused.

My mind started working furiously.

Mrs. Curtis and Lord Luke? Could it work?

Maybe...

Luke would require a *lot* of effort. He was a rake of the first order, brash, undisciplined, prone to all manner of excess. But something told me that maybe, just maybe, Mrs. Curtis would be a good influence on him... If I could join them on the mission to find Roger Morton, it just might work out.

(I am a *romance* writer, after all.)

"Are you *sure* you want to meet Lord Lukas?" I asked her. "Have you heard the rumors about him?"

Her lips firmed. "I have heard he is a rake." Her eyes met mine, steady and serious. "I can manage rakes."

There was a steel behind her voice. A steel I approved of. *Yes.* This could work.

My lips curved into a smile. "All right, Mrs. Curtis. I might be able to manage an introduction..."

And that was how I arranged the first meeting between Emma Curtis and Lord Lukas Hawkins, the second brother of the House of Trent. Their relationship proved to be a rocky one—I wasn't joking when I said Luke was a rake, and in fact, "rake" might be too mild a term. But Emma proved to be a worthy adversary for him, and they ended up traveling a dangerous and emotional but ultimately sweetly satisfying path in THE ROGUE'S PROPOSAL.

Come visit me at my website, www.jenniferhaymore .com, where you can share your thoughts about my books, sign up for some fun freebies and contests, and read more about THE ROGUE'S PROPOSAL and the House of Trent Series. I'd also love to see you on Twitter (@ jenniferhaymore) or on Facebook (www.facebook.com/ jenniferhaymore-author).

Sincerely,

*Jennifer Haymore*

♥ ♥ ♥ ♥ ♥ ♥ ♥ ♥ ♥ ♥ ♥ ♥ ♥ ♥ ♥ ♥

## *From the desk of Hope Ramsay*

Dear Reader,

My mother was a prodigious knitter. If she was watching TV or traveling in the car or just relaxing, she would always have a pair of knitting needles in her hand. So, of course, she needed a steady supply of yarn.

We lived in a medium-sized town on Long Island. It had a downtown area not too far from the train station, and tucked in between an interior design place and a quick lunch stand was a yarn shop.

I vividly remember that wonderful place. Floor-to-ceiling shelves occupied the wall space. The cubbies were filled with yarn of amazing hues and cardboard boxes of incredibly beautiful buttons. The place had a few cozy chairs and a table strewn with knitting magazines.

Mom visited that yarn store a lot. She would take her knitting with her sometimes, especially if she was having trouble with a pattern. There was a woman there—I don't remember her name—but I do remember the half-moon glasses that rode her neck on a chain. She was a yarn whiz, and Mom consulted her often. Women gathered there to knit and talk. And little girls tagged along and learned how to knit on big, plastic needles.

I went back in my mind to that old yarn store when I created the Knit & Stitch, and I have to say that writing about it was almost like spending a little time with Mom, even though she's no longer with us. There is something truly wonderful about a circle of women sharing stories while making garments out of luxurious yarn.

I remember some of the yarn Mom bought at that yarn store, too, especially the brown and baby blue tweed alpaca that became a cable knit cardigan. I wore that sweater all through high school until the elbows became threadbare. Wearing it was like being wrapped up in Mom's arms.

There is nothing like the love a knitter puts into a garment. And writing about women who knit proved to be equally joyful for me. I hope you enjoy spending some time with the girls at the Knit & Stitch. They are a great bunch of warm-hearted knitters.

*Hope Ramsay*

♥ ♥ ♥ ♥ ♥ ♥ ♥ ♥ ♥ ♥ ♥ ♥ ♥ ♥ ♥ ♥ ♥

## *From the desk of Erin Kern*

Dear Reader,

So here we are. Back in Trouble, Wyoming, catching up with those crazy McDermotts. In case you didn't know, these men have a way of sending the ladies of Trouble all into a tizzy by just existing. At the same time there was a collective breaking of hearts when the two older McDermotts, Noah and Chase, surreptitiously removed themselves from the dating scene by getting married.

But what about the other McDermott brother, you ask? Brody is special in many ways, but no less harrowing on those predictable female hormones. And, even though Brody has sworn off dating for good, that doesn't mean he doesn't have it coming. The love bug, I mean. And he gets bitten, big time. Sorry, ladies. But this dark-haired heartbreaker with the piercing gray eyes is about to fall hard.

Happy Reading!

*Erin Kern*

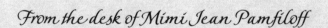

## *From the desk of Mimi Jean Pamfiloff*

Dear Reader,

"If you love her, set her free. If she comes back, she's yours. If she doesn't...Christ! Stubborn woman! Hunt her down, and bring her the hell back; she's still yours according to vampire law."

Niccolo DiConti, General of the<br>
Vampire Queen's Army

I always like to believe that the universe has an all-knowing, all-seeing heart filled with the wisdom to grant us not what we want, but that which we need most. Does that mean the universe will simply pop that special something into a box and leave it on your doorstep? Hell no. And if you're Niccolo DiConti, the universe might be planning a very, very long, excruciating obstacle course before handing out any prizes. That is, if he and his over-bloated, vampire ego survive.

Meet Helena Strauss, the obstacle course. According to the infamous prophet and Goddess of the Underworld, Cimil, Niccolo need only to seduce this mortal into being his willing, eternal bride and Niccolo's every wish will be granted. Thank the gods he's the most legendary warrior known to vampire, with equally legendary looks. Seducing a female is hardly a challenge worthy of such greatness.

Famous last words. Because Helena Strauss has no interest in giving up long, sunny days at the beach or exchanging her happy life to be with this dark, arrogant, deadly male.

Mimi

♥ ♥ ♥ ♥ ♥ ♥ ♥ ♥ ♥ ♥ ♥ ♥ ♥ ♥ ♥ ♥

*From the desk of Jessica Lemmon*

Dear Reader,

Imagine you're heartbroken. Crying. Literally *into* your drink at a noisy nightclub your best friend has dragged you to. Just as you are lamenting your very bad decision to come out tonight, someone approaches. A tall, handsome someone with a tumble of dark hair, expressive amber eyes, and perfectly contoured lips. Oh, *and* he's rich. Not just plain old rich, but rich of the *filthy, stinking* variety. This is exactly the situation Crickitt Day, the heroine of TEMPTING THE BILLIONAIRE, finds herself in one not-so-fine evening. Oh, to be so lucky!

I may have given the characters of TEMPTING THE BILLIONAIRE a fairy-tale/fantasy set-up, but I still wanted them rooted and realistic. Particularly my hero. It's why you'll find Shane August a bit of a departure from your typical literary billionaire. Shane visits clients personally, does his own dishes, makes his own coffee. And—get ready for it—bakes his own cookies.

*Hero tip: Want to win over a woman? Bake her cookies.*

The recipe for these mysterious and amazing bits of heavenly goodness can be traced back to a cookbook by Erin McKenna, creator of the NYC-based bakery Babycakes. What makes the recipes so special, you ask? They use *coconut oil* instead of vegetable oil or butter. The result is an amazingly moist, melt-in-your-mouth, can't-stop-at-just-one chocolate chip cookie you will happily burn your tongue on when the tray comes out of the oven. Bonus: Coconut oil is rumored to help speed up your metabolism. I'm not saying these cookies are healthy...but I'm not *not* saying it, either.

Attempting this recipe required a step outside my comfort zone. I tracked down unique ingredients. I diligently measured. I spent time and energy getting it right. That's when I knew just the hobby for the down-to-earth billionaire who can't keep himself from showing others how much he cares. And if a hero is going to bake you cookies, what better place to be served *said cookies* than by a picturesque waterfall? None, I say. (Well, okay, I can think of another location or two, but admit it, a waterfall is a pretty dang good choice.)

As you can imagine, Crickitt is beyond impressed. And when a rogue smear of chocolate lands on her lips, Shane is every bit the gentleman by—*ahem*—helping her remove the incriminating splotch. Alas, that's a story for another day. (Or, for chapter nineteen...)

I hope you enjoy losing yourself in the very real fantasy world of Shane and Crickitt. It was a world I happily immersed myself in while writing; a world I *still* imagine myself in whenever a certain rich, nutty, warm, homemade chocolate chip cookie is melting on my tongue.

Happy Reading!
www.jessicalemmon.com